DREAM
LOVER

Virginia Henley

Dream Lover

WHEELER
PUBLISHING, INC.
ROCKLAND, MA

★ AN AMERICAN COMPANY ★

Published in Large Print by arrangement with Delacorte Press, an imprint
of Dell Publishing, a division of Random House, Inc. in the United States
and Canada.

Wheeler Large Print Book Series.

Set in 16 pt Plantin.

Library of Congress Cataloging-in-Publication Data

Henley, Virginia.
    Dream lover / Virginia Henley.
        p. (large print) cm.(Wheeler large print book series)
    ISBN 1-56895-824-2 (hardcover)
    1. Kidnapping—Great Britain—Fiction. 2. Large type books. I. Title.
II. Series

[PS3558.E49634 D73   2000]
813'.54—dc21   99-058119
                                                                    CIP

For my granddaughter,
Tara Jasmine Henley

1

As the perfectly formed, timeless shape of the rounded head emerged, still glistening with wetness, Emerald couldn't take her eyes from it. Then came the rest of it, hard, silky, and cylindrical in shape.

He was extremely playful today, sliding up and down with an occasional backward thrust, defying gravity. He moved closer until they almost touched, begging, teasing, taunting, daring her to take him for the ride of her life.

Emerald could not resist the temptation to touch him for another moment. As she reached out and gently slid her fingers down his glistening skin, just under the head, without warning he sprayed her face. The warm, salty taste was so familiar, it delighted her. With one hand still holding tightly, she hoisted up her shift and lifted her body on top, straddling him with her bare legs.

They'd played this game many times before and he knew exactly what to do. He immediately rolled with her, putting her on the bottom, and himself on top, then rolled around again. He waited just long enough for her to catch one great breath, then with a powerful thrust he dived deep into the dark, wet, secret depths.

It was all Emerald could do to stay on the

dolphin's back while he plunged to the bottom of the cave's deep tide pool, playing and sporting as they had done every day since they'd discovered each other.

Sean FitzGerald O'Toole stood mesmerized at the entrance to the cavern. What he saw took his breath away and sent his imagination on a flight of fancy. The exquisite young female riding the dolphin must be an undine from a fairy tale who dwelt in this glittering crystal cave.

At first glimpse he thought her a child with her heart-shaped face surrounded by a cloud of charcoal smoke, which he finally realized was her hair. Then the short white shift she wore turned transparent as the sea drenched her, revealing her breasts, which looked to him like delicious firm fruit. It was then he decided the small-boned female must be close to sixteen because, though she was not yet a woman, she was tempting enough to physically arouse his firm young body.

When her laughter rippled around the high walls of the cavern like a cascade of silver bells, he thought he had never heard a more entrancing sound. The mythic pair obviously had a bond of love and trust and joy such as he had never before witnessed. He was filled with awe that he had chanced upon this place...this scene. Suddenly, the girl and dolphin disappeared beneath the water and he doubted the creatures had been anything but imaginary.

Sean's dark eyes lifted to gaze upward, spellbound by the beauty he had stumbled upon. The high-vaulted cave glittered with iridescence, scattering myriads of rainbows across the surface of the water, turning it into a magic pool. Then his innate intelligence overruled his imagination as he realized he was on the Island of Anglesey, Wales. This mineral must therefore be anglesite, sulphate of lead in white prismatic crystals that were semitransparent, giving off an adamantine luster that resembled the sparkle of diamonds.

His natural curiosity came into play as he moved into the cave to examine its crystal walls more closely. Understanding what gave the cavern its aura of enchantment did not diminish its beauty for him in any way. Rather, his silver eyes gazed upon its iridescent loveliness with the appreciation of a connoisseur.

Suddenly the spell was broken as the young nymph came spluttering to the surface, her long black hair plastered to her head and shoulders. She jumped off the sea creature's back and swam to the edge of the rock pool, clambering onto the ledge, unmindful of scraped knees and her resemblance to a drowned rat. She was naught but a mortal lass. Sean blushed at his own foolishness.

As she impatiently swept her hands up to sleek the hair back from her eyes, her gaze fell upon the intruder. A pair of green eyes widened in the delicate, heart-shaped face as she stared at him with wonder. Her glance slowly moved over each feature of his face, then slid to his neck and wide shoulders. Her gaze moved across his bare chest as if she were tracing every muscle he possessed. Her emerald eyes examined him minutely, as if he were the first man she had ever seen.

Sean O'Toole was used to the sidelong glances of females who obviously liked what they saw when they cast their inviting eyes in his direction. But he was totally unused to being openly examined as if he were a young stallion at Puck horse fair.

"Who are you?" she demanded as if she were a queen on a throne in her crystal kingdom.

She watched his head go up with natural pride as he answered, "Sean O'Toole."

Her face was transformed with delight. "Ooh," she breathed, "you are Irish." She said it with reverence, worshiping his face and form with her jeweled eyes. "My mother is Irish. I adore her! She's a FitzGerald from Kildare and the loveliest lady who ever drew breath."

Sean grinned at her. He knew who she was now. "My own lady mother is a FitzGerald. We are related by marriage." He sketched her a bow.

"Oh, how wonderful for you. That explains your great beauty!"

"My beauty?" he choked. And again, the nymph raked his body with her eyes.

Emerald examined that beauty again. She had never seen an unclothed male before. His torso was heavily muscled, but his sinew was covered with firm, youthful flesh. Her discerning eye appreciated the graceful curve of young cheek, wide shoulder, and lithe back. His skin was naturally olive, then tanned even darker by exposure to the sun. His white canvas breeches, cut off at the knees, were a stark contrast to his swarthy skin. His coal-black hair was a riot of curls and his eyes were a strange pewter color that shone silver in the cave's unusual light. She had never seen anyone more beautiful in her young life and she was completely entranced by him.

"Let's go into the sunshine where I can see you better."

Bemused, Sean agreed, thinking it a fair exchange. He'd be able to see her breasts to much better advantage. As they walked from the cave side by side, he towered over her a good ten inches. When they stepped out onto the beach, bathed in full sunlight, Sean was suddenly ashamed of his impure thoughts. The exquisite young girl was totally unselfconscious about her body. She had no notion that her white shift became transparent when wet. Her natural innocence was that of a child, but by the way she looked up at him with adoring eyes, he sensed that the first flutter of womanhood was upon her.

Like pagans they stretched out on the shell-strewn sand in the hot sun while they conversed. "You've ridden that dolphin before." He said his thoughts aloud, still amazed at the performance.

"It's a porpoise."

"Same thing. Which only goes to show the English don't know everything; they just think they do," he teased.

"I'm only *half* English," she said vehemently.

"And half mermaid. I've never seen dolphins in these waters before. They like warmer places like the waters off France and Spain."

"This one obviously followed the Gulf Stream. Anglesey has extremely mild oceanic climatic conditions, which account for its early, warm spring."

The corner of his mouth lifted. "You talk like a penny-book."

"Encyclopedia," she corrected.

Sean hooted with laughter, exposing white teeth. "You've swallowed that, all right, English."

"My name is Emerald FitzGerald Montague. I'm half *Irish!*" she insisted passionately. The sun had dried her cotton shift and the tendrils of dark hair about her face were beginning to turn back into a cloud of smoke.

Sean laughed with genuine amusement. "Better not let your father hear you say that."

It was as if a dark shadow crossed her face. "You know my father?" She shuddered slightly without even knowing she had done so.

Know him? He's been my father's partner in crime since before I was born. Our sires are inextricably bound together, not only by marriage, but by an unholy alliance of smuggling, theft, piracy, and every other type of chicanery from bribery to treason.

"Are you afraid of him?"

"He terrifies me," she confessed, then added a solemn justification. "It's not just me, he terrifies my brother, Johnny, even more."

The admission touched a soft spot of compassion deep within. How in the name of God the Father, God the Son, and God the Holy Ghost had William Montague ever sired this exquisite elfin creature? Though she was eager to confide in him, Sean was on his guard. This was the daughter of Montague, an English aristocrat, and therefore natural-born enemy of the Irish. Though the O'Tooles and the Montagues had dealt together on a continuous basis for twenty years, it was for profit alone. Sean knew instinctively the two men couldn't stomach each other.

"But my mother's an angel. She protects us from his wrath. He gets so angry, he turns purple in the face. That's when she takes him upstairs to soothe him. She must cast some sort of an Irish spell over him, for when they come down he's always appeased."

Sean could only imagine the acts the beautiful young Amber FitzGerald must perform to protect her children. "You cannot appease a tyrant," he said with disgust.

"He *is* a tyrant. He will never allow her to go back to Ireland for a visit, but she did manage to beguile him into letting us come to Anglesey for the early summer, while he conducts Admiralty business in Liverpool. It's only a couple of hours away. The house is wondrous; it has a lookout tower. My mother spends hours there looking across to her beloved Emerald Isle, watching the ships. How far is it?"

"Dublin is straight across from here, maybe fifty or sixty miles...we sailed it in record time today."

"Are you here on Admiralty business?"

We're here on monkey bloody business, he thought. "Business, yes," he conceded. He wondered if she knew about the smugglers' caves that lay beneath the big house. He hoped not, for her own safety. He glanced toward the house, up on the cliff. Amber must know about the illegal cargoes. From her lookout tower she must see the ships come and go.

His brother, Joseph, had made the last run to Anglesey, while Sean had gone to Liverpool. Today, both their backs had been needed to hump the heavy contraband, and a cooler head than Joseph's was necessary to outwit the customs men. When they were done unloading one cargo and replacing it with another, Joseph had suggested that Sean look about the island. "Take your time. The crew has worked so hard, I think we should let them have an hour's swim before we embark for home. Spring is hot as summer here."

A finger of suspicion stabbed into Sean's solar plexus. What the hellfire was Joseph doing while the lads swam and he explored the island? Sean sat up quickly. "Is your father expected today?"

"No, heaven be praised. If he were I wouldn't

dare be playing at the cave, and Mother wouldn't be singing and adorning herself in her silken robe."

Sean's suspicion hardened into certainty. Joseph must have met Amber on a run to Anglesey when her husband was away. Joseph was his elder by two years, but he hadn't the goddamn brains he was born with. Sean shot to his feet and started to run. Perhaps he'd be in time to prevent damage being done.

"Where are you going?" Emerald cried in dismay.

"To put out a bloody fire," he called back over his shoulder.

Emerald laughed. He said the most amusing things. This really was a magical place where wishes came true. Her prince had appeared and he was Irish. *Exactly as he should be,* she told herself. *One perfect day he will come in his big ship and we will sail off to Ireland where we shall live happily ever after.* Emerald dipped her toes into the sea and shivered deliciously.

Amber FitzGerald, too, shivered deliciously as Joseph O'Toole dipped her toes into his mouth and sucked on them playfully. They lay sprawled in the big bed, resting from their wild gyrations.

"Greedy boy," she purred, "would you eat me, then?"

His Kerry-blue eyes darkened intensely. "I'll eat you," he vowed, moving his dark head between her creamy thighs.

9

Amber moaned. "I dreamed of you last night, Joseph."

"Then you're as greedy as I am."

"Is it any wonder, after eighteen years of a loveless marriage?"

Joseph, with his hot mouth against her pretty cunny, demanded, "Tell me again I'm your first lover!"

" 'Tis true. He's so jealous and suspicious, he guards me like a dragon; watches me like a hawk."

"Old Montague looks more like a vulture than a hawk."

Amber shuddered, and this time not from Joseph's beautiful mouth. Montague *was* a vulture who devoured her, body and soul. But before he devoured her, he punished her. Punished her for being beautiful, punished her for being young, punished her for being *Irish*.

Her intense words, filled with loathing for her aristocratic English husband, made Joseph's cock turn to marble. It delighted him to cuckold the evil old bull. The pair of horns suited him. Montague fucked the English, fucked the Irish, and any other nation that made him money. So this was payback; it was fucking Montague. But Joseph forgot all about the man as he covered Amber's luscious body with his own. She was so lovely, so in need, and so very, very ripe.

As her lover thrust his hard young body into hers, Amber tried to make it last as long as she could. For all she knew, this loving might have to last her a lifetime. But Joseph was too young and virile to draw it out. He was plunging fast and furious, then his neck arched back as he delivered three savage thrusts before he exploded. Amber gave herself up to the commands of his young body. As her woman's center convulsed, erupted, then pulsated, she dug her fingers and toes into his back and cried, "Joe, Joe, Joe!"

Sean, about to burst through the bedchamber door, heard that cry and knew he was too late. The damage had been done. There was nothing he could do except leave them undisturbed while they enjoyed their last throes of passion. He wanted to beat the stuffing out of Joseph for the risky thing he'd done, but the young woman's cries of pleasure were so heart-scalding, he could tell such ecstatic moments were few and far between. What harm? What harm in her seeking a moment's joy in a lifetime of servitude?

He quit the house and walked out onto the long stone jetty where the *Half Moon* was docked. When the crew saw him, they came aboard. They were all related through marriage. All nephews, uncles, or second, third, and fourth cousins. Sean's maternal grandfather was Edward FitzGerald, Earl of Kildare. He had been one of twenty-three offspring. Three generations of FitzGeralds made up an entire clan in their own right. Most of the males crewed the O'Tooles' fleet of merchant ships.

"Danny, Davie, you two lads come below.

We'll just check the cargo." Command came easy to Sean O'Toole. He'd been groomed to take over the family shipping business since he was twelve. His father, Shamus, said Sean's temperament was more suited to handling men than Joseph's, because Sean ruled them with humor. He could almost always defuse a touchy situation with his natural charm and wit. Joseph was being groomed for Irish politics, which called for different skills.

Shamus O'Toole had one of the craftiest minds in Ireland. To avoid the penal laws, he'd registered them all as Protestants, though they were no such thing. Greystones, his magnificent Georgian home, was known as "Castle Lies." The reasons for the name were numerous, not the least of which was the Catholic Mass celebrated in its chapel every morning that God sent. The one piece of advice Shamus always impressed upon his sons was: *Always do what's expedient and ye'll never go far wrong!*

Belowdecks, Sean tested the ropes that secured the brandy casks, then directed the lads to cover them with the barrels of herring they'd used on the voyage over to conceal the casks of smoky Irish whisky. Drink was the foremost vice of the eighteenth century, God be praised. The O'Tooles had made one fortune smuggling out illegal Irish whisky, and another fortune smuggling in illegal French brandy to satisfy the insatiable demands of the wealthy Anglo-Irish who ruled the land, or thought they did.

When Joseph finally came aboard, the crew needed no orders to weigh anchor and hoist sail. Before he reached the cabin, where Sean was falsifying bills of lading, the vessel had slipped from the stone jetty and into the mouth of the strait that opened into the Irish Sea.

"Sorry I didn't get around to the papers, but you're far better at it than I am."

Sean drawled, "You've been dipping your quill, but not in ink."

Joseph bristled instantly. "What the hell's that supposed to mean?"

Sean's pewter eyes looked directly into his brother's and held his defiant gaze. "Exactly what you think it means." Sean's eyes dropped to the neck of Joseph's unlaced shirt. "You've bite marks on your throat."

As his fair skin flushed a telltale pink, Joseph laughed. "A maid up at the house couldn't keep her hands off me."

Sean's eyes locked with his brother's once more. "Lie all you want to yourself, Joseph, but never make the foolish mistake of lying to me. How the hell can I cover your back if I don't know what you're up to?" Sean looked at his brother in amused exasperation.

"If you saw her, you'd understand."

"I don't need to see her. She's a FitzGerald lass, and that says it all." Sean sighed and gathered up the papers. "What's done is done and can't be undone, but next time you're

13

tempted, think what Montague will do if he finds out. At the Admiralty he has a network of spies at his disposal, and servants' tongues never stop wagging."

Joseph swallowed hard, imagining castration. Then, with typical bravado, he laughed. "I'm not afraid of that old swine!"

Then you should be, thought Sean, *for the man has no soul.* He masked the fear he felt for his brother and clapped him on the shoulder. "You thoughtless young devil, my concern isn't for you, it's for Amber FitzGerald."

When the O'Toole merchantman sailed into Dublin harbor, which was supposedly owned lock, stock, and barrel by the English and ruled by the British Admiralty, Sean made short work of getting the cargo through customs. He swung back over the rails with the falsified papers in his hand. "Take that worried look off your face, Joseph. The customs man was in Montague's pocket. For the price of a jar of ale he offered to sell me his musket and throw in his sister, to boot," Sean joked.

As the *Half Moon* headed toward Greystones's own harbor, just north of Dublin, Joseph said, "Father will be pleased with this day's work."

"Aye," said Sean, "but he'll never let on. I'll lay you a gold sovereign the first words out of his mouth will be: *'Where the hellfire have you two young devils been?'* "

14

2

"**W**here the hellfire have you two young devils bin?" Shamus O'Toole demanded. "You should have bin here two hours back."

"Why, what happened?" Sean asked with a straight face.

Joseph laughed and so did Paddy Burke, Shamus O'Toole's steward, who was privy to everything that went on at Greystones.

Shamus gave Paddy a quelling glance. "Don't encourage the young devils."

"Aren't you going to ask how it went, Father?" Joseph grinned.

"No need. Yer both so bloody pleased with yerselves, ye look like bantam cocks." Shamus's twinkling glance roved over the faces of the grinning crew. There were so many FitzGeralds, he didn't attempt to tell them apart. "You lads have done a good job. Mr. Burke will assign another crew to do the unloadin'. Get yerselves up to the kitchen an' tell Mary Malone to feed ye."

Greystones had the best cook in County Dublin, bar none. With a whoop of joy the FitzGeralds jostled each other to see who could race to the kitchen door first.

"Not you two young devils." Their father's voice stopped Sean and Joseph in midstride. "Well, somebody has to supervise the unloadin'.

Need I remind ye what idle sods the FitzGeralds are?"

As their father and Mr. Burke departed,
Joseph said dryly, "He's more pleased with us
than I ever expected!"

Sean grinned. "It's just his way of empha-
sizing we should see our operation through to
its conclusion."

Joseph stretched tired muscles, thinking
they'd had enough exercise for one day. "We'll
not see our beds this side of midnight."

Sean gave him a playful jab in the ribs and
taunted, "What the hell are you complaining
about? Didn't you spend the entire afternoon
in bed?"

The only FitzGerald whom Shamus O'Toole
greatly admired was his wife, Kathleen. To be
honest, he worshiped the ground she walked
upon. When he retired to their bedchamber,
he brought a snifter of the fine French brandy
he'd just acquired.

He was annoyed to see that Kathleen was
not alone. Kate Kennedy, Greystones's housekeeper, who was also his wife's personal maid,
had just picked up Kathleen's hairbrush. She
was a tall, no-nonsense sort of woman, who
could hold her own even with Himself. The
housekeeper wouldn't have lasted five minutes if it had been otherwise.

"Away wi' ye, Kate Kennedy. I can attend
to Kathleen's needs."

"Are ye sure yer up to it? She requires a hundred strokes," Kate said outrageously, as she presented him with the hairbrush.

"Shamus!" Kathleen warned sharply. "None of your off-color remarks, now."

Kate departed, but before she could close the door, Shamus shouted, "The woman has a tongue that could clip tin." He flung down the brush and moved across the bedroom with purpose. Lowering his voice, he threatened lustily, "I'll give you a hundred strokes."

Kathleen chuckled at him as he drew close with the brandy. "A hundred strokes indeed; I wager you can't last longer than fifty."

"Now who's making off-color remarks, my beauty?"

Kathleen sat before her mirror in a pristine nightgown with at least two dozen buttons running up the front from breast to chin. Shamus licked dry lips as he anticipated undoing them, one by one. He set the brandy before her and lifted a long tress of hair to his cheek. "Have a wee sip, my Kathe, it'll put fire in your belly."

"That and other stimulants you have in mind." She picked up the snifter and carried it to the bed. "First we have to converse." At the look of disappointment that crossed his still-handsome face, she promised, "After we talk, we'll share the brandy as we did on our wedding night."

He shook his head, remembering. " 'Tis indacent we're still in love after twenty-two years." The feather bed dipped with his weight.

"Scandalous," she agreed, slipping beneath

the sheet and moving over to his side of the bed. She bent to rub her cheek along the crisp black hair of his arms as he settled them about her. "Now, then, about the birthday celebration," she began.

Shamus gave a mock groan. "Not again. I swear the two young devils dominate yer every waking thought."

"Oh, indeed? And who was it bought two new ships for birthday gifts?"

"They're beauties, Kathe. Schooners that sail faster than the wind itself. It's time they owned their own vessels. Joseph will be twenty-one. Strange their birthdays fall so close together, yet they're different as chalk from cheese."

"That's because they were born under different stars. The constellations decide our personalities. Our sons have different temperaments. Joseph is hotheaded and quick to take offense."

"Aye, he loses his temper at the drop of a hat. His fists are always ready to fly out and plant someone a facer."

"Sean is deeper. He always considers before he acts." She had a soft spot for Sean. He was a beautiful boy with a natural charm. The girls were mad for him and wouldn't leave him alone. He had a repertoire of humor that ran the entire gamut from sophisticated to crude. He could be funny, coarse, bawdy, cruel, witty, charming, or self-deprecating, with the same desired result: He amused others while amusing himself.

"Before Sean fights, he thinks about it, considers his strategy, then goes about the thing deliberately." *Aye, and the results can be devastating,* Shamus thought silently.

"Their birthdays are less than a week away. The celebration requires planning, Shamus. Since Sean's falls on Saturday and Joseph's on Monday, the logical choice for the celebration is Sunday, but that seems blasphemous."

"Not a bit of it. Are we not Protestants?"

Kathleen rolled her eyes. "If you say so, Shamus."

"Well, I do, and now that's settled—" His fingers undid the top button of her nightgown.

She stayed his hand. "We're not done."

He groaned. "We're not bloody started."

"I have to do a head count so I can get the invitations out. The FitzGeralds alone number over fifty."

"Yer never inviting all of 'um?" he asked in horror.

"And what's your objection to the FitzGeralds, pray tell me if you can?" The light of battle was in her eye.

Thinking to soften his words a trifle, Shamus opened his mouth and put his foot in it. "Well, I don't object to yer father, nor of course the lads who make up our crews, but all them females that overrun yer family are worse than a plague of lice!"

"Can I help it if the males die off while the females thrive? You should be thanking heaven for it. Your son, Joseph, will be Earl of Kildare when my father dies, may God forgive me for saying such things aloud."

"I didn't mean to upset ye, my beauty. Of course ye must invite yer sisters."

"And my nieces and cousins and aunts."

Shamus groaned. "But one of 'um thinks she's a Celtic princess and drapes herself in purple veils."

"That's Tiara; she's doolally."

"They're all bloody doolally!"

"You don't even know their names," she accused.

"Course I do," he said defensively. "There's Meggie an' Maggie an' Meagan, and then there's the ones with the fanciful names of gemstones like Opal an' Beryl an' Amber—"

"Amber's the one who married William Montague. I've already sent out the Montague invitation, but he'll attend alone, mark my words. I pity Amber."

"She can blame nobody but herself. She married him fer money and his aristocratic English name."

"She was an innocent lass of fifteen. She saw her chance to get out of Maynooth Castle, which was, and still is, overrun with a tribe of female FitzGeralds that outnumbers the Tribe of Israel." Kathleen saw nothing wrong with doing an about-face in regard to her family and agreeing with her husband.

His arms tightened. "If any could best a Montague, it would be a FitzGerald."

"I doubt that, Shamus, my darling. I believe it would take an O'Toole."

He kissed her then. Thoroughly. He could wait no longer. She was the eldest daughter of the Earl of Kildare and by far the most beautiful and intelligent of all the countless FitzGeralds. She was the first, and she was the best. Shamus would never get over his good fortune.

In Greystones's massive kitchen, Mary Malone was stirring a great pot of porridge for breakfast. As Kate Kennedy entered and began searching for a tray, Paddy Burke opened the outside door and stepped into the warm kitchen. Mary dimpled at the sight of the tall steward. "What's the weather, Mr. Burke?"

"It's raining shoemaker's knives out there, Mrs. Malone."

She ladled him out a bowl of porridge and laced it with whisky. "Throw that across yer chest, Mr. Burke, It'll warm the cockles of yer heart."

"Yer too kind, Mrs. Malone. How's yer toothache this morning?"

"It's a thought better, Mr. Burke. I felt worse many a time when I was only half as bad."

Kate Kennedy spread the tray with a snowy linen cloth and winked at Paddy Burke. "No wonder it's a thought better. You put away enough whisky last night to paralyze a dead man."

"Yes, and it put me to thinking, Kate Kennedy. A wee drap of whisky might be the very thing to sweeten yer tongue, don't ye think so, Mr. Burke?"

"Don't drag me into this, Mrs. Malone, I beg ye. I don't fancy bein' a great ugly thorn between two roses."

"I'd like some of yer special wheat cakes for the mistress, Mary," Kate said.

The cook looked with alarm at the tray Kate was preparing. "Is she poorly?"

"Not a bit of it, Mary Malone. Himself has decided she's to have her breakfast in bed."

Mary was shocked. "It's indacent!"

Kate rolled her eyes. "*Indacent* describes him exactly. I could tell ye things that go on in that bedroom would make your hair curl, Mary Malone."

She'd barely gotten the words out when Shamus burst through the kitchen door, his scowl barely hiding his secret pleasure at the housekeeper's words. He glowered at the women, however, and took the tray from Kate Kennedy's hands. "I'll take it up; Kathleen and I wish to be private a wee spell."

Paddy Burke almost choked on his porridge as he watched the women's jaws drop open. He polished off his food quickly, knowing that stewards from every wealthy Anglo-Irish house in Dublin would soon be arriving to pick up kegs of illegal French brandy. Shamus had raised the price, shrewdly guessing it would double the demand.

"Did ye set aside a couple of casks for the celebration, Paddy?" asked Shamus, descending to the first cellar.

22

"I did that. When's it to be?"

"Sunday."

Paddy rubbed his nose. "I understood Sunday was when the shipment for Captain Moonlight was comin' in."

"It is. The timing's perfect."

Captain Moonlight was a euphemism for all Irish rebels. A secret revolutionary society existed. It had started when England was at war with America. England's necessity had been Ireland's opportunity. While France and Spain allied themselves with the colonies, Ireland was left exposed to invasion. When it had been impossible for the English fleet and armies to protect the entire coast of England, Scotland, and Ireland, fifty thousand volunteer troops were raised. They professed loyalty to the British crown, but when the war was over they did not disband, they just went underground.

Men like Shamus O'Toole's father-in-law, Edward FitzGerald, Earl of Kildare, passionate to win Ireland's freedom from the British yoke of oppression, had achieved legislative freedom of the Irish parliament. But a decade after that achievement Irish Catholics still could not sit in that Parliament, nor vote to elect its members. Edward FitzGerald was one of the founders of the Society for United Irishmen, but under cover of dark, he did far more risky and foolish things for his downtrodden Catholic countrymen. The Kildare wealth, horded for generations, poured forth from his coffers to buy guns and arms for the rebels and food for the starving peasantry who lived on his vast acres.

Shamus O'Toole did not have his father-in-law's bleeding heart. Unlike him, Shamus had not been born with a silver spoon in his mouth. He had been born in stark poverty. His father had deserted his mother and the pair of them had subsisted by cutting peat as soon as he turned five.

In ancient times the O'Tooles had been a powerful clan and Shamus decided early in life *he* would become a power to be reckoned with. Before he had turned ten, Shamus had learned the value of expediency. His innate shrewdness proved more valuable than any silver spoon. At twelve he crewed on a merchant ship; at fifteen he owned it. At twenty he was rich enough and shrewd enough to seduce an earl's daughter.

The unholy alliance he had formed with William Montague a few years after his marriage was absolutely inspired. Montague's brother was the Earl of Sandwich, a commissioner of the British Admiralty who was appointed first lord of the Admiralty during England's war with America. For Shamus O'Toole it was like having a license to print money, and he built Kathleen the Palladian Georgian mansion Greystones. He made sure it was bigger and better than any the wealthy, aristocratic Anglo-Irish were building all over the Pale. When Sandwich became the vice-treasurer and receiver of revenue of Ireland, it was like manna from heaven. O'Toole, with the aid of Montague, had the County of Dublin in his well-lined pocket.

When William Montague opened the invitation to the celebration at Greystones his lips compressed with satisfaction. His high position in the Admiralty allowed him to control people, ships, and cargoes. Thanks to his partnership with O'Toole, he had grown wealthier than his titled brother, but Montague's first love was power, not money. A feeling of omnipotence stirred his loins as he decided he'd wear his best uniform and sail his own Admiralty vessel into Dublin, loaded with arms intended for his country's war with France.

His mouth curved with carnal sensuality as he pictured the effect the invitation would have on Amber. What wouldn't she do to be allowed to attend? His balls tightened pleasurably as he imagined her sexual inducements. He flung open his office door and bellowed, "Jack!"

William had brought his nephew with him to the Liverpool Admiralty Office to act as his secretary, and the lad was proving himself indispensable. "Did you make inquiries about that brothel in Lime Street?"

"I did, my lord." A simple *sir* would have sufficed, for William Montague held no actual title, but Jack knew power was an aphrodisiac to his uncle. "They cater to special tastes, and have girls trained in obedience...Oriental," he added, unable to hide his sudden erection.

"Good lad!" William noticed the youth's

randy condition. "You may accompany me," he said, throwing down his pen.

Venery did not shock Jack Raymond. His father, the Earl of Sandwich, was a notorious profligate, nicknamed "Lord Lecher." He was married to an Irish viscount's daughter who had suffered so many miscarriages, she had become mentally unstable. When that happened, he moved his mistress, Martha Raymond, into his town mansion on Pall Mall and maintained a ménage à trois. Jack was one of five illegitimate children from that union and, fortunately for him, the only male. Though his future was probably secure, Jack suffered from the insecurity of bastardy and he would never be satisfied until he found a way to change his name to Montague.

As the pair left the Admiralty building, William was in an expansive mood. "How would you like to accompany me to a celebration the O'Tooles are throwing next Sunday? I'll be sailing the *Defense* to Dublin; you can act as my lieutenant."

"I would enjoy that, my lord. I've never experienced Ireland. What are they celebrating?"

"Birthdays—O'Toole's sons'." Montague fell silent, his mouth turned down at the corners. He envied O'Toole his sons. He and Shamus had both wedded FitzGeralds, but all Amber had produced was a useless daughter and a sorry excuse for a son, who cowered when his father so much as looked at him. And while cowering was desirable in a female, in a male it was contemptible.

"Will you be taking Emerald and John, sir?"

Montague hadn't considered it, but now that Jack made the suggestion, he realized it had merit. Having his children aboard would allay any suspicion regarding the cargo. "Young John might benefit from the experience," Montague allowed. His son was nowhere near as mature as O'Toole's sons, nor even this young bastard his brother had sired. Time spent in their company might wake him up.

3

Emerald lay on a stretch of sugary sand in the sunlight. A delicious sense of anticipation spiraled about her, dancing on the soft sea breeze that ruffled her dark curls. She felt a sense of joy that went beyond happiness, for she knew that soon, soon he would come to her.

She kept her eyes closed until she felt a flutter, like a butterfly wing, touch the corner of her mouth. She smiled a secret smile and slowly lifted her lashes. He knelt before her, watching her intently, his dark pewter eyes brimming with laughter. Holding his gaze, she came to her knees slowly and knelt before him.

They needed no words, yet the longing to touch was like a hunger in the blood. At the same moment each reached out to the other to trace with their fingertips...a cheek, a throat, a shoulder. Emerald's hand brushed his heart and felt it thud beneath her fingers. He was the perfect male. He was her Irish Prince. He bent to capture her lips with his, but when he was a heartbeat away, Emerald awoke, whispering his name with heart-scalding hunger. "Sean, Sean."

Emerald FitzGerald Montague threw back the covers, ran her fingers through the cloud of glorious dark hair, and stretched her long legs to the rug beside the bed. Without dressing, she climbed the stairs that led to her mother's chamber. As she did most mornings when her father was not in residence, Emerald slipped into her mother's bed to talk over plans for the day.

Amber, who adored her daughter, was acutely attuned to her every mood, every thought. "Darling, you seem different today."

Emerald blushed prettily. It was the first time her mother had seen her cheekbones tinted pink from some hidden thought. "I've been dreaming," she explained.

"Was your prince in the dream?"

Emerald nodded, hugging herself with her arms, seemingly aware of her breasts for the first time.

"How lovely for you. I think you're growing up. What was your Prince Charming like?"

A look of rapture came over her child's face. "He was Irish."

"Then guard your heart well, my darling, for he is sure to be a wicked rogue."

28

Amber dropped a kiss on her daughter's dark head and slipped from the big bed. She opened the French doors and stepped out onto the balcony that led to the lookout tower. As her eyes scanned the horizon she spotted the sails of a ship coming from the direction of Liverpool. The merchantman was no doubt coming to retrieve the shipment of Irish whisky that lay concealed in the caves beneath the house.

A sudden premonition stole over her as she realized the vessel was too small for a merchantman. It was William aboard his favorite ship, the *Swallow*! She stared across the water with dismay, hoping her senses were mistaken, but cold fingers were already squeezing her heart. Amber quickly slipped back into the bedroom. "We'll have to go explore the fairy glen another time, darling. Your father's coming. Go and find Johnny. Tell him not to dare leave, then hurry back. We've only just time to dress appropriately."

Johnny's bedchamber, in the same wing as her own, was empty when Emerald arrived. Without hesitation she ran down two flights, straight through the kitchen, and out the back door, grabbing one of the maids' cloaks to cover her nightgown.

Emerald found Johnny in the stables saddling his Welsh pony. Her brother did not have her dark beauty. Unfortunately he'd inherited his father's florid complexion and lank brown locks.

"You mustn't leave; father's coming," she announced breathlessly. Such a look of alarm crossed Johnny's face, Emerald thought he would mount the pony and bolt. A moment's reflection told her he wouldn't dare do such a thing; rather the news rooted him to the spot.

"What must I do?" he asked desperately as the blood drained from his ruddy face.

"We have almost an hour before his ship arrives. Change your clothes and put on your best wig. I'll help you with your neckcloth. Above all, Johnny, try to hide your fear of him."

"It's all very well for you, Emerald. Mother's sending you to St. Albans Academy for young ladies when we return, but I'm going into the Admiralty division of the navy, where he'll be able to order me about night and day. It'll be a dog's life!"

"I'm sorry, Johnny. I'd change places with you if I could." It wasn't the first time Emerald had thought she should have been born the son, and Johnny the daughter. "Mother will soothe his temper, she always does. Come on, we must hurry."

Less than an hour later William Montague beheld his family, dressed in their formal best. His hard gaze slid over his children, then came to rest on his beautiful young wife, as she came forward eagerly to greet him.

Amber dipped into a low curtsy to give him an unimpeded view of her lush breasts, pushed up by whalebone to swell from the fashionably low-cut gown of cream brocade.

"Well come, my lord, we haven't seen nearly enough of you this spring," she lied prettily.

As he gazed down at her, he saw that she had powdered her own amber-colored curls and piled them high on her head with ribbons and lace. He'd soon have them tumbling about her naked breasts. He took her hand and raised her. He'd have her on her knees again, soon enough.

William's eyes narrowed as he looked down the room to where his children stood, still as statues. His daughter wore a lace cap and starched white pinafore, from beneath which showed lace pantelets and small kid boots. "Have you been a good girl?" he demanded harshly.

"Yes, Father," Emerald answered in a clear, firm voice.

The defiant angle of her chin told him that though he intimidated her, she'd be damned if she'd show it. Finding little sport there, his gaze moved over to settle on his son. "Have you been behaving yourself?" he demanded even more harshly.

"Y-yes, sir," Johnny whispered.

"That's what I was afraid of, you gutless young prig. At sixteen you should be fornicating from one end of Anglesey to the other."

When Johnny flushed bright pink, his father laughed with scorn. "Wait till we get you in the navy; we'll soon initiate you."

William's attention was diverted from their son by Amber's seductive voice. "I hope you'll be able to stay all night, my lord."

Oh, yes, thought William, *it will take me all night to play out my game about Ireland.* He extracted an envelope from his breast pocket and flourished it on high. "I decided to make a quick run from Liverpool to bring this invitation to the O'Tooles' celebration."

"Celebration?" Amber's voice caught on the word.

"Shamus O'Toole throws a birthday celebration each year for his sons. The invitations are much sought after. This year I'm considering taking my family to show them off."

Amber felt a bud of hope blossom in her chest. William had never allowed her to return home to Ireland in eighteen years of marriage. She cautioned herself against letting her hopes rise too high, for disappointment was sure to follow. Yet, in spite of herself, her imagination took wing at the thought of going home, and visiting with all the FitzGeralds again. Then there was Joseph. She closed her eyes for a moment to control her longing.

William smiled when he saw the rapt look on her face. "Come upstairs and we'll make plans for the visit. It's next Sunday. I plan on sailing the *Defense;* it will be no inconvenience to put in here and pick up my family that morning."

Amber smiled back at her husband and placed an obedient hand on his arm. The price he would set for Ireland would be high, but she was prepared to pay it.

Emerald's heart was hammering. She couldn't believe she had heard correctly. The thought of again seeing Sean FitzGerald O'Toole was dizzying enough, but to actually sail to Ireland to be present at his birthday celebration was like an unlooked-for dream come true!

"Oh, Johnny, I can't go to the celebration dressed like a child," Emerald wailed, fingering the edge of her starched pinafore with disgust.

"He'll never take us," John said flatly. "He despises the Irish and considers them sub-human."

"Mother will persuade him. He won't be able to resist her magic," Emerald assured him.

"They'll be upstairs for hours," Johnny said, looking as if he might be sick.

"Don't you see? She keeps him upstairs as long as she can to keep him from savaging us."

Johnny was devoutly thankful Emerald was too innocent to understand their mother's sacrifice. He wished he understood less; knowledge covered him with impotent guilt.

"When Father said you should be fornicating, what did he mean?"

Johnny frowned. "I can't tell you. It will shock you."

"Of course it won't shock me. How am I to learn things, if you won't tell me? Never mind, I'll ask Mother. She tells me everything."

"No—Em, don't ask Mother, I'll tell you. Fornication is getting naked and...sleeping... with girls."

In spite of her protestation Emerald was indeed shocked, as indecent pictures jumped into her head. "I don't believe you," she said faintly.

The invitation also would cause quite a stir at Maynooth, where Sean had gone to deliver it in person. It was a twelve-mile ride from Greystones to Maynooth Castle, where his grandfather, Edward FitzGerald, lived. The earl owned hundreds of acres of beautiful County Kildare, which included the River Rye, all the way up to where it joined the River Liffey at a magnificent spot called Salmon Leap.

A party of young FitzGeralds had gathered to watch the annual attempt of the beautiful fish to return to their spawning grounds. When the girls spied Sean they squealed with delight and surrounded his horse. The lads were just as eager to greet him, for Sean was a favorite with all the FitzGerald clan.

Everyone spoke at once. "Have you arrived, Sean?" "What brings you, Sean?" "Is aught amiss, Sean?"

"Can you not see I've arrived?" He grinned, deciding to dismount since they would let him proceed no farther.

"It's your birthday soon. What would you like for a present, Sean?" asked a saucy female cousin, taking his arm and leaning on it as if his very nearness made her too weak to walk.

"Don't monopolize him, Fiona. Leave some for the rest of us," cried Dierdre.

"Don't fight over me, sure and there's enough to go around," he teased. "We're having a celebration on Sunday; you're all invited."

The girls squealed once more.

"Yer never inviting *all* the females?" asked Rory with disbelief.

"Every last one," Sean confirmed.

The girls were giggling and whispering about what they would give him and what they would *like* to give him.

"I'll settle for a dance with each of you," Sean said, ruffling the pretty tresses of the two who stood closest.

"Do you promise to dance with us?" they chorused.

"Haven't I just said so?"

As they drew closer to the castle, the sounds of workmen's hammers and chisels could be heard. His grandfather was forever renovating and adding on to the ancient building that was begun in medieval times.

Edward FitzGerald left the workmen and came forward to greet his grandson. "Sean, as I live and breathe, ye grow more handsome every time I set eyes on ye."

"I would say the same to you, Grandfather, but it would sound repetitive."

The two men embraced affectionately. "Come inside and we'll drink a toast to your birthday. I can hardly credit you'll be nineteen."

Sean handed his horse over to Rory to take to the stables. As they walked through the vaulted entrance hall, FitzGerald aunts gathered to welcome their favorite nephew.

"Sean, my darlin', 'tis lovely to see you," cried Meagan. "How is Kathleen faring with that devil of a husband to contend with?"

"She never complains," Sean said, tongue in cheek.

"Take no notice of Meagan," said her widowed sister Maggie. "She let her cheese get too hard before she put it in the mousetrap."

Sean realized this was her graphic way of explaining her sister's spinsterhood.

"The sun went off *your* window long ago, Maggie," Meagan replied, giving as good as she got.

Other FitzGerald females touched him, hugged him, and kissed him as Sean tried to navigate his way through the hall.

"Let the lad breathe, will ye?" demanded his grandfather. "Or burying him we'll be before his birthday."

"You're all invited to the celebration," Sean said cheerfully, as his grandfather dragged him to the sanctuary of his library and closed the door.

"Women have always been the curse of Maynooth; nothing but sisters and daughters."

Sean lowered his voice. "The celebration is set for Sunday. The stuff's coming in the same day."

The Earl of Kildare poured his grandson a dram of whisky and then one for himself. "I'm glad yer father didn't let Joseph bring the message. I want his reputation pure as the driven snow. He's the next earl and I don't want him tainted with treason. I never want there to be any connection whatsoever between Joseph and Captain Moonlight."

"My brother knows what he must do. But I'm ready to ride with you, anytime," Sean offered.

Edward FitzGerald felt great pride in the young man before him. His gaze touched his hair, black as the hobs of hell, then fell to his wide shoulders. "Sean, ye've inherited the best of the FitzGeralds and the best of the O'Tooles. Ye have a diabolical brain that can think around corners. The pathways of yer gray matter are like Deviation Road. Ye have it all— the brains, the guts, and the charm—but I cannot let ye ride with me, for Kathleen's sake. It would break yer mother's heart." He drank off the whisky to indicate the subject was closed. "When can we move the stuff to Maynooth?"

"The same night, in the wagons that transport the FitzGeralds to and from the celebration."

The earl nodded, his face grave. " 'Tis a terrible thing to be Irish."

Sean grinned. "Until you consider the alternatives."

Sean ran an appreciative hand across a row of leather-bound volumes.

"This library is yours, when I'm gone. Joseph can have the books on law and politics, but I want ye to have the rest."

"These books are like old friends."

"Ye've read most of them, the histories, the mythologies, the folktales, the ones in Gaelic—you're the only one I know will treasure them."

When they opened the library door, half a dozen female FitzGeralds were lingering about the hallway, lying in wait for the quarry. Now Sean was turning nineteen, he might be in the market for a wife, and wasn't the logical choice a FitzGerald? And if he had no notion to be shackled, but only had dalliance in mind, sure wasn't the logical choice still a FitzGerald?

Sean's mother, Kathleen, along with her sisters, was fiercely chaste as befitted a decent, God-fearing Irishwoman, but the younger generation had no such high moral scruples. During the course of the next hour no fewer than seven females tried to lure him upstairs to Maynooth's parapets and prospect towers.

His humor came to his defense. "There are fifty-five bedchambers upstairs. Sure and 'tis more than my life's worth to set one foot in that direction!"

Though Sean was being circumspect today, his conquests were many and varied. Because his mother forbade congress with the maid-servants at Greystones, Sean occasionally poached the daughters of their tenant farmers. But usually he sought his pleasures in Dublin, where his opportunities were limitless. His grandfather maintained a town house in fashionable Merrion Row that Sean was free to use. In the past month he'd put the town house to good use by sampling the charms of a barmaid from the Brazen Head, a shopgirl from a linen draper's in Grafton Street, one of the actresses from Smock Alley, and the dissatisfied young wife of Sir Richard Heron, an English official at Dublin Castle.

Sean spied his second-aunt Tiara, she of the purple veils, fluttering about within earshot. "Now if it was Princess Tiara here, luring me up to her throne room, I'd be sorely tempted."

"If you don't conduct yourself, I'll pull your ear the length of your arm," Tiara said regally.

Sean slipped his arms about her and gave her an affectionate kiss. "Don't forget to save me a dance on Sunday."

"You may inform Kathleen we shall attend the celebration."

Sean had no idea if she spoke for all the FitzGeralds or was using the royal *we*. He caught a glimpse of another cousin dressed in a white novitiate's robe. The oddities were around every corner when you visited Maynooth.

At the summerhouse on Anglesey, Amber Montague was anticipating the upcoming celebration more than all the rest of the FitzGeralds put together.

She had done everything her husband had demanded of her, sweetly, gracefully, abjectly. Ireland and Joseph were worth the price. Amber felt as if she were floating on a blissful cloud of joy. Already she was breathless with anticipation. She knew exactly what she would wear and was rapidly going over young Emerald's wardrobe in her mind's eye.

How proud she would be to show off her beautiful daughter and her son to the FitzGeralds and the O'Tooles. Amber was dizzy from the thought of going home. Already she could smell the turf smoke, mingled with the scent of sweet green grass. "What time shall we be ready on Sunday, William?" she asked, eagerly searching his face as she pulled her stocking up her long leg.

The soft, dreamy look was banished from her eyes as he said, "You misunderstood me, Amber, my dear. There can be no question of *you* going."

Her heart lurched, then stopped.

"You don't seriously think I'd expose my wife to the vulgar celebrations of a bunch of uncouth bogtrotters, do you?"

"But, William, they are my family. My uncle is the Earl of Kildare."

"Precisely the reason I married you. But an O'Toole celebration will likely degenerate into a drunken debauch. I will not cast my pearl before swine. You are far too tempting a morsel to display before an entire clan of randy Irishmen."

Amber tasted ashes in her mouth. Begging would only swell him with power, while his answer would remain the same. His refusal was absolute.

"I intend to take Emerald and John, along with my nephew Jack. It will be good for the boy. He clings to your skirts too much. I intend to make a man of him. Any youth who can't indulge in drink and women and still retain his wits is a weakling!"

Amber almost cried out, *If it's to be a drunken debauch, why would you take Emerald?* But she stopped herself in time. She would not deprive her beloved daughter of the chance to visit Ireland and her FitzGerald kin. Amber sighed, heartsore. She could see now it had been another cruel game. She felt stabbed to the heart and dared not cry for fear she would shed tears of blood.

To make her humiliation complete, he held out the crop he always used on her and waited implacably with hooded eyes until she kissed it.

4

By the time the first pink blush of dawn touched the sky on the day of the celebration, Greystones was alive with activity. Birthday gifts had arrived under cover of darkness so that the magic element of surprise would not be lost.

FitzGerald grooms from Maynooth had smuggled two Thoroughbreds into Greystones's stables after midnight. The earl bred some of the finest racehorses in Kildare and had chosen a magnificent bay for Joseph and a swift black stallion for Sean.

Two of Shamus's captains, the Murphy brothers, had sailed the new schooners from the shipyards in Birkenhead, near Liverpool. Shamus had warned them not to show a sail before four in the morning, and the Murphys were esconced in Mary Malone's kitchen when Joseph and Sean came down for breakfast.

"Look what the wayward wind blew in," Sean said to his brother. "The pair of water rats can smell a hooley a hundred miles off."

"You two bastards aren't invited!" Joseph said.

Sean took up the taunt. "Just because you married FitzGerald lasses doesn't make you family."

Pat Murphy cursed through his beard. "Arrogant young swines. Neither of youse will ever walk the deck of a ship I'm captain of, ever again!"

At a nod from Sean, Joe gave Pat Murphy a quick shove, while Sean hooked the stool from beneath his brother Tim. With a great howl, all four started throwing punches and ended up in a heap of elbows and shins, rolling about the kitchen floor.

The game ended abruptly as Mary Malone threw a jug of cold water on them. "For very shame, actin' like savages, and this yer birthday celebration. Out of me kitchen this minute, I've to prepare food for a hundred this day!"

For a minute the brothers stared aghast at the very real wrath of their plump cook, before they dissolved into helpless laughter.

Shamus arrived on the scene and said dryly, "They're only larkin' about, Mary Malone. Their spirits are so high, it'll take more than cold water to restore order and decorum. You two devils," Shamus addressed his sons, "on yer feet. There's a couple of ships need unloadin' before breakfast."

Still laughing, all four got to their feet. "Let the Murphys do the unloading, they're the captains of the bloody ships," Sean said, wiping Mary's water from his eyes.

"Now, that's where yer dead wrong, Captain O'Toole," Shamus declared, unable to keep the grin from his face one moment longer.

As Sean and Joseph exchanged puzzled glances, a glimmer of comprehension passed between them. With a sudden whoop of joy they picked up their heels and bolted outside, not stopping until they had torn across the wide lawns and Greystones's own harbor came into view below them.

The schooners, riding at anchor, sparkled like rare jewels in the early-morning sunlight. They were so new, they smelled of tar and fresh paint. Though the ships were similar, they were not identical. The taller vessel was blue and gold; the longer one, black and silver.

"Ye'll find the ownership papers inside yer logbooks and ye might as well pick yer crews today while most of the lads are here," Shamus called, waving them on to claim their new possessions. He let them go alone. They were men full grown and should have the pleasure of walking their own decks while each took command.

Both father and sons hid their deepest emotions for appearance's sake. The Irish did not embrace and kiss in public. But Shamus's proud eyes never left his sons as they strode down to the long stone jetty. Grinning like lunatics, Joseph and Sean took possession of their birthday gifts. No discussion was necessary to decide which ship belonged to whom. Joseph headed for the blue and gold, while Sean boarded the vessel that was black and silver, heaving a great sigh of delightful appreciation, immediately losing his heart to the long, sleek vessel whose clean lines foretold her speed.

Sean spoke to it as if it were a woman. A ship was like a mistress, possessive and jealous, but capable of loyalty and obedience if she was handled firmly and with love. He ran his hand along her polished rail, caressing her with his touch, his eyes, and his low, intimate voice. She was indeed a beauty that set his blood singing and his imagination soaring into the bright future that lay before him, waiting to be grasped in both hands.

By the time the wagons filled with FitzGeralds began to arrive, trestle tables had been set up on the sloping green lawns and the Greystones staff was kept on the trot, carrying out food from the huge kitchen.

Their other guests began to arrive, most of whom belonged to old Irish families, rather than the newer Anglo-Irish. They brought fiddles and soon the air was filled with music and laughter.

Edward FitzGerald smiled at his daughter Kathleen with affection. Though he'd had no sons to carry on his name, his eldest daughter more than made up for it. She'd given him two strapping grandsons any man would envy.

"Now, mind, Father, you can only talk treason half the day, the rest is for laughter."

His blue eyes twinkled. "There's a woman for you, always finding a reason to curtail a man's pleasure."

A crowd of young people surrounded Sean and Joseph as they returned to the house from the jetty and urged the brothers toward the stables, where they knew more birthday surprises were waiting. When they emerged mounted on the Thoroughbreds, their parents and grandfather beamed with happy pride.

"Thank you, sir, he's magnificent. I've decided to call him Lucifer," Sean said, rubbing the black satin neck with appreciation.

"Have you two young devils named your ships yet?" Shamus demanded, trying to take the mickey out of them.

Sean winked at Joseph. "What else would two young devils call their ships but *Sulphur* and *Brimstone?*"

"Irreverence, to say nothing of courting trouble!" their mother scolded, but she adored them both and wouldn't have altered a hair on their dark heads.

Emerald Montague was more excited than she had ever been in her life. Since before she had even learned to talk, her mother had filled her head with tales of Ireland and its people. Her bedtime stories were chosen from the rich folklore of her mother's homeland, the songs Emerald learned were songs of Erin, and the pictures her mother's words painted of her beloved Emerald Isle and the eccentric FitzGeralds had made her long to see them.

If Amber was sad that she was not accompanying them to the celebration, she was doing a marvelous job of hiding her feelings. Emerald suspected that her mother had buried her disappointment and emotions deep within and had focused all her attention upon making sure her children's visit was a success.

John's wardrobe had presented no problem. Since he was seventeen and almost a man full grown, his clothes were made by the finest tailors in London. Though here on Anglesey he preferred to roam about in old riding breeches, he had a dressing room filled with clothes that would make a dandy envious.

It was Emerald's wardrobe over which her mother had fretted from the moment her daughter had brought it to her attention. "These are all little girls' dresses," Emerald vowed, surveying the entire contents of her wardrobe with dismay. "They are very pretty," she amended quickly, hoping she hadn't hurt her mother's feelings, "but I'm almost sixteen and I simply couldn't bear wearing a smock and pantalets.—I don't want Sean—I mean the FitzGeralds—to laugh at me!"

So—it was Sean O'Toole to whom she had lost her heart! He must have sailed with Joseph. God help her little girl if he had a hundredth part of his brother's Irish charm. "You are quite right, darling. There are so many FitzGerald women, and females can be very catty. I want you to outshine them all. You must wear your new velvet cloak; it will be very cold on the ship, but when you remove the cloak we want everyone to stare at you with envy."

"Yes," Emerald breathed, feminine to her fingertips, "that's exactly what we want."

"Come with me now to my chamber, we'll go over everything I own until we find something perfect that can be altered to fit you."

When Sunday morning arrived, Emerald donned silk stockings for the first time in her life instead of the lace pantalets. As her mother helped her into the green velvet gown, Emerald fretted, "I have no corset, whatever shall I do?"

Amber laughed. "Darling, you have no need of a corset."

"But what about these?" Emerald covered her upthrust breasts with her hands.

"*These* will be the envy of every female in Ireland today. Trust me, I know about such things."

From her window Emerald saw the sails of

her father's ship coming down the Menai Strait from the east. "Oh, dear," they muttered in unison, knowing full well William Montague was impossible to please.

"Leave your father to me," Amber said, a hard tone of determination in her voice. "There's just time before he anchors to make sure Johnny passes muster. Tame your hair a bit more. Perhaps tie it back with a ribbon," she called over her shoulder as she picked up her skirts and hastened to John's chambers.

Her son wore a navy-blue superfine coat that had been tailored to fit him to perfection. His fawn knee breeches clung to his thighs without a wrinkle, before disappearing into snowy white stockings. He had chosen a brocade waistcoat in a shade of dull gold to complement the outfit. "Your neckcloth would put the Prince of Wales to shame, Johnny. You look so grown-up today." Her words were intended to imbue him with confidence, but the navy-blue was indeed a good color for him, Amber decided as she tucked an errant lock of hair beneath his tie-wig with loving hands.

"Your father's here. I want him to see you first because I know he can find no fault with you today. Stay beside me while I prepare him for Emerald."

Montague came up to the house alone. He cast a critical eye over his son, and was slightly mollified to see he looked rather mature today. He was also glad to see that his wife was being obedient. When he saw there would be no last-minute pleas to take her with him,

48

a pleasant surge of power shot through him. His eyes frankly assessed her breasts beneath the flowing morning gown.

"When I bring them home, I'll stay the night. No need to wait up for me, Amber, my dear, I shall awaken you."

"William," she began softly, molding him to her seductive will without his knowing it, "I want your daughter to look like a lady today—an *English* lady. I haven't been in Ireland for years, but I imagine the young women still run about in linen smocks, showing their ankles, as I was allowed to do. They don't wear imported silks or brocades from some sort of misplaced pride. They only wear linen and wool, or cloth made in Ireland. But when they see Emerald in her velvet, they'll be grass-green with envy."

Emerald came downstairs on cue, her black silk curls dancing about her shoulders. Because she was small-boned, her father thought of her as a child. Now, however, he saw she was almost a woman. "She looks like a lady from the neck down, but her hair is as wild as a blackberry thicket. Doesn't she have a decent powdered wig?" he demanded.

Amber saw her daughter's eyes fill with the green fire of rebellion and spoke up quickly before there could be a clash of wills. "It's my oversight, William. Emerald, go up and put on a wig. Your father wants you to look like an English *lady.*"

Jack Raymond eagerly held out his hand to assist Emerald aboard. She allowed him to help her, then moved away from him across the deck as quickly as she could. Rebellion no longer showed in her eyes, but it still lurked about inside her. She watched Johnny shake hands with Jack, who was wearing a lieutenant's uniform today. Jack certainly looked like her uncle, with the same thick lips. Though he had a fine athletic carriage, it always seemed to Emerald there was a trace of menace in his eyes.

She would be thankful he would be kept busy giving orders to the crew. He had a way of attaching himself to her like a barnacle whenever he was in her company. She dismissed all thought of her distasteful cousin as her brother joined her. "Johnny, I can't believe we are setting sail for Ireland!" This morning before she awoke, Emerald had once again experienced her beautiful dream. The delicious sense of anticipation had stayed with her, and the joy she felt went beyond happiness, for she knew that soon, soon she would come to him. He was her perfect Irish Prince. She whispered his name with heart-scalding hunger. "Sean, Sean."

"When we leave the strait, I hope it isn't rough. I don't want to disgrace myself in front of Father," Johnny's voice cut into her reverie.

"Take some deep breaths, here he comes."

"Oh, God, Emerald, do something to draw his attention from me."

She squeezed his hand and turned to face her father. "That's a very smart uniform you are wearing, Father."

"A uniform lends a man a great deal of authority. Few challenge that authority. Remember that, John. It won't be long before you're wearing one. We'll make a man of you yet, never fear, boy."

From the tail of her eye Emerald saw Johnny's gorge begin to rise. Deliberately, she leaned out over the rail, knowing just what the result would be. The wind snatched off her wig and sent it careening away across the crests of the waves. "Oooh," she wailed woefully, "that was my very best wig."

Her father's jowls turned the color of turkey wattles. He took her roughly by the arm, marched her to the top of the companionway stairs, and pointed to a cloth bag hanging in the stairwell. "Do you know what is kept in that bag?"

Emerald shook her head, her voice deserting her completely.

"It's a cat-o'-nine-tails. Do one more thing to displease me today and I'll let the cat out of the bag!"

She sagged with relief when he let go of her arm. *It isn't fair! Why does someone always have to draw his sting?* And yet she felt no small measure of satisfaction that she had saved Johnny from a savaging and rid herself of the hideous headpiece into the bargain.

Shamus spotted Montague's sails and went down to the jetty to make sure there was ample space to dock and unload the *Defense.* When he greeted his partner in crime, Shamus hid his amusement at Montague's Admiralty uniform. *He needed it for courage to bring in the guns.* "Ye arrived without let or hindrance, I see."

"As always," Montague replied with his usual touch of English arrogance. He cast an envious eye over the two new ships. "Are these yours, Shamus?"

"They belong to my sons. The taller ship is Joseph's; the black and silver, Sean's," he said with pride.

"Speaking of sons, I'd like you to meet mine. This is John and this is my daughter, Emerald. Jack you already know."

Shamus shook hands with John and bowed gallantly to Emerald. Very little escaped Shamus's shrewd eyes. He had seen the little lass blush at mention of his sons. "A thousand welcomes to our home. The celebration is well under way; the gardens are overrun with young 'uns like yerselves. Go up to the house and enjoy." He turned back to Montague. "Yer crew can unload the cargo onto the dock. There's plenty lads about if they need a hand."

As usual Montague showed no curiosity regarding the cargo's final destination, which was likely the reason the two men had been able to deal together so long. William seemed only interested in the gold the shipment would bring him, and that was the way O'Toole wanted it. Montague left Jack to oversee the unloading and accompanied Shamus to the house.

"I didn't bring much ammunition for the guns, but I can supply you with a shipload next week."

"Good enough." Shamus nodded. "Get it as far as Anglesey, and we'll do the rest." When William looked relieved, Shamus chuckled inwardly; he'd bet a penny to a pinch of shit the ammunition was already on Anglesey. Montague was too big a coward to transport a cargo of explosives that could blow him to kingdom come. Wicked Willie had too many sins on his soul to meet his Maker with equanimity.

As Kathleen saw them approach she gave her father's arm a warning squeeze and stepped forward to greet Montague. "Welcome to the celebration, William." When she offered him her hand, he took it to his lips, openly assessing the beauty of her face and form. She knew the Englishman found the FitzGerald women highly attractive. It was no wonder he'd lost his head entirely when fifteen-year-old Amber had cast her lure his way.

"I didn't come alone. I've brought my son and daughter to acquaint them with their mother's side of the family."

"And about time, too, but where is Amber?" Kathleen asked pointedly.

"She sends her regrets; her delicate constitution makes a sea voyage a penance," William said smoothly.

If she can stomach you, she has a constitution of iron, and as to penance, I suspect she pays that every day of her life. "I'll go and find them and make sure they are enjoying themselves. Father, pour William a double; by the sober look of him, he's a deal of catching up to do."

Edward FitzGerald and William Montague hadn't had dealings together in years, at least none that Montague was aware of, the earl thought wryly. He had given Montague one of his brother's daughters in marriage, knowing full well the little minx wouldn't take no for an answer. Amber had seduced the English aristocrat, all right, but only by being clever enough to refuse him sexual liberties until he'd proposed marriage.

Edward poured him a glass of smoky Irish whisky. "Yer a fortunate man, Montague. Ye have something I was denied, a son." His first-born, Kathleen, had been a twin, but her brother had been stillborn. "The daughter was inevitable, every FitzGerald dead or alive has produced one, but the odds were against a son."

"I understood you were one of twenty-three children. Your father obviously produced sons."

"Not many, and none save me who survived. One died in infancy, another three lived long enough to produce daughters before their early demise."

"So all the male FitzGeralds who crew the

merchant ships are third generation," Montague concluded thoughtfully.

"They are indeed," said Edward, raising his glass. "A toast to grandsons! Where would we be without them?"

William Montague cursed himself for a fool. The FitzGeralds were so numerous, he'd never given the succession a thought. Why had it never dawned on him before that Shamus O'Toole's eldest son was Edward FitzGerald's heir and the next Earl of Kildare? A plan almost full blown came to him. Why not betroth his daughter, Emerald, to Joseph FitzGerald O'Toole? Perhaps a daughter could be of some use after all.

5

Emerald caught her breath at the magnificence of the Georgian mansion in its perfect setting. *So this is Castle Lies,* she thought with a shiver of anticipation as she scanned the throng, looking for a certain face. When she did not find it, she took her courage in both hands and approached a group of young FitzGeralds. "How do you do? I am delighted to make your acquaintance."

There was a moment's dead silence as the girls' eyes fixed upon the intruder and swept over her velvet-covered high breasts.

"Well, now, if it isn't the queen of England," said Fiona. The other girls laughed maliciously.

Emerald bravely swallowed the taunt and tried again. "I'm a FitzGerald on my mother's side...I'm half Irish."

"Which half would that be? The top half?" Fiona drawled as two young men ogled Emerald's breasts.

"Sure, if she's Irish, she must be one of the little people," Dierdre suggested.

The warm blood drained from Emerald's cheeks. Never had she been more painfully aware of her small dark appearance.

"What's your name, then?" one of the girls asked.

"The lady's name is Emerald," a deep voice said from behind her.

Emerald turned and looked up into Sean O'Toole's dark laughing eyes and suddenly it didn't matter that the girls had been cruel to her. Nothing mattered except *he* was there, laughing down at her, close enough to touch. She tossed her dark curls over her shoulder and gave him a radiant smile. "Happy birthday, Sean."

He grinned, remembering their last encounter. Her admiration for him was plain for all to see. His heart skipped a beat. A dose of hero worship on his birthday was no unpleasant thing. His gaze traveled over the green velvet gown that showed off her feminine curves, then he bent and whispered, "This fashionable lady is never Emerald Montague? How did you become a woman in one short week?"

She laughed up into his face, clearly delighted that he thought her grown-up.

Sean took hold of both her hands and heard her swift intake of breath as he gallantly lifted her fingers to his lips. He saw her eyes on his mouth and guessed she was wondering for the first time in her life what a man's kiss would be like. "I know what you want to do," he teased.

"What?" Emerald gasped, her cheeks rosy.

"Dance, of course. Shall we?" He offered his arm and when she took it, Sean twirled her across the lawn. He bent again to whisper, "We'll have to wait until we're alone to do the other."

With Sean's strong arms about her, Emerald felt as if she were floating on air. Her heart sang with the nearness of him and excitement spiraled all about her. When the dance ended she was thrilled that Sean kept his arm about her, then swept her into the next dance as the music changed. She wanted to stay in his arms dancing and flirting forever.

His cousin, Fiona, tapped him on the shoulder. "Sean, you promised to dance with all of us."

"So I did," he said gallantly, but before he let Emerald go, he winked at her and whispered, "Meet me later at the stables."

The females, both old and young, now clustered about Sean, and as promised, he danced with every last one. When the fiddles struck up a familiar tune, the cry went up, "Give us a jig, Sean!" Always ready to oblige an audience, Sean jumped onto a keg of ale and danced the jig without missing a step, on a stage that measured less than a foot across.

Though he laughed and talked with everyone around him, Sean was acutely aware of Emerald. He knew the moment she headed in the direction of the stables. It took him less than a minute to get away from the FitzGerald cousins, but before he could follow Emerald, Shamus joined him for a quiet word.

"Did ye check on the guns from the *Defense*?"

"Yes. The count was exact, but the ammunition's short."

Shamus nodded. "I'm aware. We'll have to get it ourselves from Anglesey." They joined Montague, who stood talking with Edward FitzGerald and Joseph.

Disappointment had swept over Joseph like a cold wave when he saw that Amber had not accompanied William Montague. He was drawn to the Englishman's side despite his aversion to the man, in hope of hearing him speak her name. Joseph was beginning to suspect he was badly infected with the disease known as love.

Montague said, "I appreciate the invitation, Shamus, and I'd like to extend one of my own. Since Joseph here is being groomed for politics, I offer the hospitality of my home in London for the season. It would give him the opportunity to sit in Parliament and the Commons and observe things from the other side. I could introduce him to some influential people. Don't forget my brother Sandwich has the entrée to every great house in London, political and otherwise, and he's a crony of the Prince of Wales himself."

Shamus looked at his father-in-law to gauge his reaction. FitzGerald hated the British Parliament with a vengeance.

Edward smiled at Shamus and said with noble tolerance, "London would be an invaluable learning experience for Joseph. Though I hope it will never happen, I am cynic enough to realize that one day the parliaments of Ireland and England could be united."

Suddenly the idea of London appealed to Joseph immensely because Amber would be returning there soon. He held out his hand to Montague. "Thank you for the invitation. I have sailed into the Pool of London with cargoes, but I've never had an opportunity to enjoy London's social life."

"I'm returning to London earlier than usual this year. The Admiralty has its hands full with this French business. Another fortnight in Liverpool is all they will allow me."

Sean bit down on his lips to stop himself from laughing in their faces. Joseph's brains were all in his cock at the moment. Still, he wouldn't say no himself to a visit to London. It was the world's center for merchant shipping and with the war in France the opportunities for profit would be rife. Sean caught Joseph's eye and the brothers excused themselves and strolled off in the direction of the stables.

"Are you insane, Joseph? The lust on your

face was written plain for everyone to read. When he offered his hospitality, it didn't include tupping his wife. Christ, Joseph, stop lusting after forbidden fruit. Get yourself laid this afternoon. We are crotch-deep in willing wenches today. Open your eyes and see what's beneath your nose."

Joseph stared after his brother as Sean went into the stables. By God, why *hadn't* he seen what was under his very nose? Montague would be here the rest of the day, while Amber was alone on Anglesey. Joseph smiled. *I will get myself laid this afternoon!* He headed for the house to retrieve the present he had for his love. As soon as he had seen the precious amber in a cargo from the Baltic Sea, he knew she would love a pair of earrings with their sun-spangled inclusions.

When Sean entered the stables, he found Emerald admiring his new Thoroughbred. "Hello again, Beauty. This fellow is Lucifer."

"I guessed he was yours—he suits you. He looks dangerous."

Sean laughed. "Meaning I look dangerous too?"

She gave him a provocative sideways glance. "Perhaps."

"We're both gentle as lambs," he teased, "let me show you." Sean rubbed the stallion's long black nose, then, resting his hand against the sleek neck, mounted onto its bare back. "Would you like to come up?" he invited.

When Emerald hesitated, he urged, "Don't be afraid."

She tossed her curls at him. "I'm not afraid." The moment she stepped close, he swooped down and lifted her before him with powerful hands. "Ooh!" she cried breathlessly, clinging to the black mane.

He set her between his thighs. "I won't let you fall." As he slipped an arm about her tiny waist, the scent of her hair stole to him. He lifted it, then set his lips to the nape of her neck and felt her shiver. "You're the prettiest girl here today."

Sean's head shot up as someone came into the stables. "Damn!"

A formally dressed youth stared up at them. "Emerald, I've been looking for you."

"Johnny! This is Sean O'Toole." She slipped down from the horse guiltily.

"You must be Emerald's brother. Welcome to Greystones."

The youth flushed to his eyebrows. "Hallo, I—I hope you don't mind my looking through the stables, I'm mad about horses."

"Of course I don't mind," Sean said, trying to put the timid boy at ease. *So this is Montague's son. He looks afraid of his own shadow, no wonder his father terrifies the shit out of him.*

"He's a beauty," Johnny said, reaching out a hand to stroke Lucifer's neck. "Do you plan to race him?"

"Possibly," Sean said, dismounting. "Are you interested in racing?"

"Oh, yes," Johnny said eagerly. "My mother

has told me Kildare is the center of Irish horse racing. What I wouldn't give to see the Curragh. Is it still the same as it was when she lived there?"

Sean nodded. "Yes, it's a plain of luxuriously thick grass that stretches for five thousand acres without a fence or a tree."

"Johnny is good with horses," Emerald said proudly.

Opening up to Sean's warm personality, Johnny confided, "I'd like to breed them, but my father has very different ideas. He's shoving me into the Admiralty, even though the sea terrifies me and I suffer dreadfully from mal de mer."

"That's too bad, I was going to invite you to have a look at my new schooner, later." Sean glanced at Emerald, silently inviting her to his ship.

"Thanks, but I'd rather stay here with the horses, if you don't mind," Johnny replied.

"Be my guest. Sometime you'll have to visit Greystones without your father and we'll go to the Curragh and watch the races."

"God, I'd like that!" Johnny impulsively shook Sean's hand. Not many young men befriended him and he could hardly believe O'Toole, who captained his own ship, had treated him as an equal.

"I'd better get back to the celebration," Sean said, excusing himself.

When he'd gone, Johnny said to Emerald, "This place is fabulous, are you enjoying yourself?"

Emerald wrinkled her nose. "I was, until you interrupted us."

"You shouldn't have been alone with him."

"You didn't give us a chance to be alone!"

"I'm sorry," he relented. "Go and find him, you don't have to stay here with me."

As Emerald walked past the stone balustrade, Kathleen O'Toole's graceful skirts swept down the steps of the terrace. "Why, there you are, I've been looking everywhere for you, darling." She took Emerald's small hand in hers. "Come with me so we can have a private word."

Emerald was led into a magnificent receiving room. Kathleen sat her on a cushioned window seat overlooking a walled garden and placed a glass of wine in her hand. "I'm Kathleen O'Toole; now, then, tell me how my dearest cousin Amber fares."

Emerald realized the lady was Sean's mother and an older cousin to her mother. With great daring she swallowed a mouthful of wine and then another. Her words came in a rush. "My mother is well, but she longs to come home for a visit. My father will never let her...I think he's afraid she would never come back to him."

Kathleen's heart turned over at Emerald's innocent confidence. "Well, now, she's a beautiful young woman and we cannot fault your father for being possessive of her."

"She misses the FitzGerald clan fiercely. I

tried to make friends with the cousins, but because I'm from England they think me an enemy."

As Kathleen looked at the exquisite elfin creature, gowned in fine velvet, she could easily believe the FitzGerald females had behaved like jealous cats. "Darling child, you've got hold of the mucky end of the stick. The FitzGeralds saw no farther than your velvet gown and lovely high breasts. One look was enough to tell them you'd steal the lion's share of attention. Go back to the dancing and enjoy yourself. Isn't this my sons' birthday celebration?"

Emerald finished the delicious wine and confided, "I met your son on Anglesey when he came on Admiralty business."

Kathleen watched her black lashes flutter to her cheeks and saw the pretty blush transform her face. They both glanced up as a tall figure descended the staircase in the entrance hall. For a moment Emerald mistook the dark head for Sean's and Kathleen heard her swift intake of breath.

"Joseph," his mother called, "here's an acquaintance of yours would like to join the dancing."

Joseph stuck his head into the parlor and looked blankly at the female sitting in the window. "I thought I'd take the schooner for a run," he said smoothly, not wishing to be rude, but extremely impatient to round up his crew and be on his way.

"Splendid! Here's a wee lass would just love to go for a sail."

With the light behind her, Joseph had no notion which FitzGerald cousin it was, but he'd soon palm her off on another when he got her outside. He gallantly held out his arm, and Emerald, both tongue-tied and embarrassed, allowed Joseph to escort her outdoors. "Do I know you, sweetheart?" he asked, looking down at the unfamiliar face.

"No, it's your brother Sean I met before."

"I might have known," Joseph said with a relieved laugh. "All the prettiest girls lose their hearts to him. If it's Sean you want, you'll likely find him aboard his new schooner."

Emerald's eyes followed Joseph's hand. Her heart fluttered wildly in her breast at the thought of Sean O'Toole being captain of his own ship.

"Just keep your heart under lock and key," Joseph warned as he left her so he could seek out his crew.

When William Montague saw his daughter stroll by on the arm of Joseph O'Toole, he nudged Shamus's elbow. "There's a match made in heaven. An English wife would be an asset to Joseph, especially the niece of the vice-treasurer of Ireland."

Yer a wily sod, Willie. Ye know Joseph is heir to an earldom, Shamus thought. "The idea bears thinking on, William. I'll mention it to Kathleen, but ye must understand the final decision rests with Joseph. My sons are men who make their own choices in life."

Emerald wasn't the only female to search out Sean O'Toole. Bridget FitzGerald decided the time was ripe to give Sean the ultimate birthday present. Suspecting his new ship would draw him like a lodestone, she watched until she saw him walk down toward the jetty, waited a few minutes, then followed him aboard.

Sean's pewter eyes lifted expectantly from the logbook where he was making his first entry, hoping it was Emerald. But when the young woman in white stepped into the captain's cabin they filled with amusement as he took in the novitiate's robe. He could think of no one less suited to a convent than this saucy baggage.

"Happy birthday, Sean," she said, holding out a small package. "I made you a shirt."

"That was a lovely thing to do, Biddy," he said, unwrapping the fine linen garment.

"Put it on; see if it fits across your wide shoulders."

With a flash of white teeth Sean removed his shirt.

Bridget immediately launched herself against his naked chest. "I've decided not to save myself for Christ!"

"That is blasphemous, you young baggage," he said, laughing.

Emerald Montague boarded the sleek schooner and made her way belowdecks, her pulses racing with excitement. "Sean?" she called. "Are you down here?"

Not wanting Emerald to find him half-naked with Bridget, he gave his cousin a stern look of warning and ordered, "Not a word!" He grabbed his shirt, departed the cabin, and firmly closed the door behind him. Slipping his arms into the shirt, he walked forward to meet Emerald and lead her in the opposite direction.

"I know you'd prefer to show your ship to my brother, but will I do?" Her green eyes teased him.

"I knew you'd come," he said boldly.

"I couldn't resist"—the corners of her mouth lifted—"seeing the ship."

" 'Twas me you couldn't resist, Emerald."

"No, really," she denied, "I've never seen a new vessel before." Her glance swept over his open shirt and lingered. As in her dream, a delicious sense of anticipation spiraled about her.

"I'll warrant there's lots of things you've never seen before." His fingers burned to touch her. He reached out and traced the soft fur that edged the neckline of her gown. Then with his fingertips, he caressed her cheek, her throat, her shoulder.

The longing to touch him back was like a hunger in her blood. Emerald traced her finger over the embroidered initial on his open shirt, imagining what his warm olive skin beneath it would feel like. With great daring her hand brushed his heart and felt it thud beneath her fingers. Breathlessly, she saw him bend to capture her lips and knew that this time she wasn't dreaming.

His mouth was firm and quite insistent, parting her lips so that he could taste all her sweetness. The kiss went on forever and when he finally let her go she was dizzy from his closeness.

"You taste like wine, and woman," he murmured huskily, touching her lips with his fingertips, wanting more.

Emerald was shocked to realize that what she felt racing through her body was desire. She stepped back, disconcerted, then, to cover the turmoil she felt inside, whirled about and moved down the companionway. "This really is a beautiful ship. Is this the captain's cabin?" Before he could stop her, Emerald opened the door and stood transfixed.

Bridget FitzGerald had thrown off her novitiate's robe and lay naked on the captain's berth. "I thought you were going to get rid of her," Bridget said pointedly.

Emerald's hand flew to her mouth as comprehension dawned. Sean O'Toole had been dressing as he came out of this cabin. "You were f-fornicating!"

Sean, though fairly caught in what appeared to be a compromising situation, could see its element of humor. "You've been reading the encyclopedia again, English," he drawled wickedly.

"Ooh," she cried, whirling about, almost stumbling in her haste to escape from the scandalous scene.

"Emerald!" he called after her, but the plea fell on deaf ears. His humor deserted him. "Now see what you've done." He was suddenly beyond all patience with Bridget's overt concupiscence. "Why can't you act like a lady?" he demanded. He sighed with resignation, knowing he might as well ask pears of an elm tree, and sprinted after Emerald Montague.

Tears flooded Emerald's eyes and threatened to spill over as she ran along the deck of the *Sulphur* trying to find her way off the ship. In her agitation she ran all the way to the prow and stopped running only when she ran out of ship. She whirled about and came face to face with the author of her misery.

Sean planted his feet on the deck, effectively blocking her path. "Emerald, don't run off. Don't be silly about this; it was nothing."

"By 'nothing,' I suppose you mean it happens every day," she cried angrily. The wind snatched her black curls, playing havoc with them. Her upthrust breasts rose and fell with her great agitation. Her green eyes blazed at him in outrage. Visions of him had crowded her thoughts daily and dreams of him had filled her nights. Since she had first laid eyes on him in the cave, she had become totally infatuated with the beautiful Irish youth, casting him in the role of prince.

Sean could clearly see her innocence had been outraged and he was thankful that it was so. It delighted him that she was so refreshingly innocent in mind and body. "What a proud little beauty you are," he murmured, half to himself.

His words fanned her anger to blazing point. "I hate Ireland and everyone in it. But most of all, I hate you, Sean O'Toole!" She flung the words at him so passionately, he could not resist her fiery beauty. He snatched her into his arms and set his mouth to hers, tasting the heady combination of hot fury, freezing disdain, and sweet innocence all at once.

Emerald offered little resistance, but the moment he released her, she drew back her hand and slapped him full in the face with all her might.

Sean stared at her in disbelief, unable to credit the wallop her small hand had delivered. He captured her wrists to prevent further violence and grinned down at her. How could one small female infuriate and delight him at one and the same time? He pulled her against his powerful young body, then bent his head so he could capture her gaze with his own dark eyes. "Someday, my proud beauty, I'm going to do something to you to earn that slap!"

Sean's attention was diverted from Emerald as the *Brimstone* weighed anchor and glided away from the jetty. He strode over to the rails and called across to his brother, "Where the devil are you going?"

Joseph cupped his hands about his mouth and shouted, "Three guesses!"

Sean knew immediately he was on his way to Anglesey. "Are you daft? Come back!" Sean cursed and contemplated sailing after him, but he knew if he caught him he'd beat the living tar out of him. He shrugged. *To hell with you, Joseph. If you call the tune, you'll have to pay the bloody piper.* By the time he remembered Emerald, she had departed the ship.

6

Kathleen sought out her husband. She had just inspected the lambs that were spitted and slowly roasting in the kitchen and wanted to be certain the roasted pigs in their outdoor pits would be ready for carving at approximately the same time.

"Where's Joseph?" Shamus asked his wife.

"He's taken young Emerald for a sail. I must say the pair of them seemed quite taken with each other."

"What did I tell you?" William asked with a wink.

"I thought the lads would be racing their ships; where's Sean?"

"He's with the FitzGeralds and John Montague at the stables, organizing a horse race at the moment," Kathleen informed him. "Check on the roast pigs, Shamus. I want everything cooked and ready to serve at the same time."

"Right ye are, love. Paddy Burke just added more turf to the cooking fires." He watched his wife as she joined her sisters and felt his heart swell with pride. There wasn't a woman in six counties could hold a candle to her. He turned back to his father-in-law and William Montague. "Come on, the Murphy brothers have arranged a boxing match for this afternoon. I know yer both bettin' men, so let's be seein' the color of yer money!"

Jack Raymond seethed with envy. He had always been led to believe the Irish were a downtrodden people in an oppressed land. This he considered entirely justified because the Irish were inferior. But the FitzGeralds, and especially the O'Tooles, gave the lie to this theory.

His own father was a titled English aristocrat while Shamus O'Toole was nothing but Bog Irish, yet Fate so favored the sons of this household, it had bestowed upon them everything in life that was worthwhile. Not only did they live in a mansion with servants at their beck and call, they owned a thriving shipping business that made them filthy rich. To boot, they were surrounded by a loving family that heaped affection and admiration upon them, and they had been endowed with devilishly handsome looks and strong physiques. The injustice of this stuck in Jack Raymond's craw, but the thing they had that rankled the most was happiness.

It made Jack's blood boil to see how much these people enjoyed life. They did everything with a passion, whether it was eating, drinking, or dancing, and they never seemed to stop laughing. The fact that they were considered inferior by their betters; such as himself, on the same level as animals, didn't seem to bother them one whit.

Jack would not lower himself to join their vulgar entertainment. He stood apart as an observer, aloof and alone. He wished that he had not come today to witness such an excess of enjoyment, but most of all he wished that Emerald Montague had not witnessed it. Jack secretly coveted her, and thought of her as his. More than anything in the world he wanted her for his wife and he wanted her for her name. Today, he realized he had two formidable rivals in Sean and Joseph O'Toole.

He must make himself indispensable to his uncle. He would keep his eyes and ears open and relay any information that might be of use to William. If it was information that hurt the O'Tooles, so much the better. Jack Raymond couldn't remember having had a more miserable day.

Johnny Montague couldn't remember when he'd had a better time in his life. Though he found it hard to believe, Irish girls seemed to find him irresistible. He vaguely realized his clothes, his speech, and his nationality made him different from the other young men present, but the females seemed to relish that difference. They attached themselves to him in pairs, quizzing him about London, listening with rapt attention to his answers, then offering to wait on him hand and foot. No sooner did Dierdre run to fetch him a drink, than another FitzGerald sidled up and offered him cake. It was clear he could have his pick of the flowers that danced about him today, and his fancy settled on a fair-haired lass named Nan.

Sean O'Toole generously offered him a mount so Johnny could compete in the horse race and when he came in second, flushed with victory, Nan rewarded him with a kiss. Johnny Montague believed Ireland was the closest place to heaven he would ever know.

Heavenly bliss described exactly what Amber was feeling at this moment. Adorned in nothing but the amber teardrops Joseph had brought her, she tumbled about the bed in playful abandon.

"I've another surprise for you, my beauty," he murmured intensely against her throat. "I'm coming to England."

Amber lay still, wanting it to be true, hoping he wasn't teasing.

"Here's the hilarious part—William invited me."

"William?" A haunted look shadowed her lovely eyes.

His fingers reached out to thread through her glorious hair. "I've been going mad, knowing you'd soon be leaving, but your husband has solved the dilemma. He has invited me to London for the season so I can observe English politics firsthand."

"Oh, Joseph, promise me you'll be careful. If he suspects anything at all, he'll destroy you!"

"If he suspected something, would he invite me to be a guest in his house?"

"You mustn't stay with us, you must have a house of your own so I can come to you."

He knelt before her in naked splendor. "Come to me now," he ordered softly.

"God help me, I love you so much, Joseph. Love me once more, then promise me you'll leave while I've no strength left to stop you."

Back at Greystones the roasted lambs and pigs were done to a turn and the guests lined up with platters as Mary Malone, Paddy Burke, and Shamus O'Toole carved up the succulent, juicy meat.

Under his breath Sean cursed his brother's absence. Joseph should have had the decency to be present for his own birthday feast. To make up for Joe's absence he made a point of talking with each and every guest, sharing a joke or a drink and thanking them for attending the celebration. As he made one excuse after another for his brother's thoughtlessness, his anger grew steadily.

Shamus refilled the platters of Montague and his nephew Jack. "What about yer crew, William?"

"The *Defense* has a galley; the sailors get their own meals."

"Not today they don't. Jack, be a good man and fetch the lads up for some roast pig and a jar of ale."

"And while you're down at the jetty, see if Joseph O'Toole has returned with my daughter."

Jack stiffened, appalled that Emerald had been allowed to go sailing off with his Irish rival.

"She'll be safe with our Joseph, never fear," reassured Shamus.

"She'd better be safe or we'll be having a wedding before the day is over," William promised, only half in jest. "Jack, would you go fetch the men off *Defense* to participate in the O'Tooles' generous hospitality?"

When Jack went down to the ship to send the men up to the big house, he was surprised to see the small, dark figure of Emerald curled up on the companionway stairs.

"What are you doing here all alone, Emerald?"

She raised defiant eyes. "I wanted to be alone. I prefer my own company to the company of rabble!"

He moved down the stairs and sat beside her. "Everyone thinks you're off sailing with Joseph O'Toole."

"I wouldn't go sailing with an O'Toole if he were the last man on earth," Emerald said with a disdainful toss of curls. "They've neither manners nor morals!"

"They're not fit to polish your boots. The Irish are uneducated, unwashed savages."

"Who asked for your opinion? My mother

is Irish and I won't hear a word spoken against her!" Emerald was ready to vent her spleen on any victim to ease the pain in her heart.

Little bitch, Jack cursed silently. His father and his uncle had the right attitude when it came to women—total subjugation. They had to be kept in their place and ruled with an iron hand. He curbed an overwhelming desire to take hold of her and master her. He kept his hands to himself, knowing he'd have to bide his time, but someday if his careful plans came to fruition, he'd have the pleasure of bringing her to heel.

"It's getting late, I can't leave you here alone in the dark."

"Keep your pity to yourself. I don't need you to feel sorry for me," she bristled. "Go and tell my father I'm ready to leave."

They both fell silent as the unmistakable sounds of a large vessel approaching echoed across the shadowed water. They heard sails being furled and the sound of the anchor chain dropping through the hawsehole. Suddenly, they heard the deep, angry voice of Sean O'Toole.

"About bloody time! What the hellfire game are you playing at, Joseph? While you're off bedding your whore, I'm left to explain your absence."

"You'd better watch your mouth, dear brother. Amber is not my whore. I happen to be in love with the lady."

"Stop kidding yourself, Joseph. If you loved her, you wouldn't put her neck in a noose. Montague would kill her if he found out about your little game of love."

Emerald tried to breathe and found it impossible. She groped out before her until her hands came into contact with the gold buttons on Jack's uniform. Jack gathered her hands in his and drew her against him. "Hush," he warned in a muted murmur.

Lies! Lies! Lies! Emerald screamed over and over in her brain. She opened her mouth and drew in a ragged breath before Jack's hand clamped over her lips. Their silence allowed them to hear Joseph O'Toole's next words.

"Montague won't find out. He's too busy exchanging guns for gold. Christ, why haven't these guns been loaded onto the wagons for Maynooth?"

"Why don't you shout it to the bloody world, Joseph? As you can see for yourself, the *Defense* is still here. We can't load the wagons until Montague leaves."

As the angry voices trailed away from the jetty, Jack Raymond felt almost dizzy at the knowledge he had just acquired. Knowledge was power. The heady feeling engulfed him. One piece of information he would share with William immediately; the other he would savor until the moment was ripe. Raymond slowly became aware of the girl who was desperately clutching the front of his uniform in her fists. Suddenly he wanted to laugh out loud. Someone who wouldn't hear a word spoken against her mother had just received a very nasty shock.

Emerald thought she might die from the pain that smote her heart. Was it only this morning she had been happy? It seemed a lifetime ago. In the space of one afternoon her world had been destroyed. Destroyed by the bloody Irish! God curse every last one.

"Emerald, you must come up to the house and say your good-byes."

"I cannot," she whispered, distraught.

"Come, take my arm. I'll remain at your side. Simply hold your head high and walk with me." Jack gathered up her cloak and wrapped it about her shoulders.

Emerald's thoughts were in such shocking disorder, she allowed Jack Raymond to help her from the ship, leaning on his arm as they climbed the steep path that led up to Greystones. The laughter and music of the revelers assaulted her ears as Jack led her across the lush lawns where darkness had descended. How she wished she had never come to *Castle Lies*!

William Montague looked at his daughter with new eyes. "I'm very proud of you. You flew your colors well today, my girl."

"Father, I'd like to leave," she murmured.

"What, no dancing? Mmm, maybe you're right. A lady doesn't cavort about and make a spectacle of herself." Montague turned to Jack. "If you'll round up John, we'll be on our way."

Somehow, Emerald got through the leave-taking. She held her head high, fixed a polite little smile upon her lips, then withdrew inside herself to a very private place. She did not hear Shamus O'Toole's teasing good-bye, nor feel Kathleen's kiss upon her cheek.

On the voyage back to Anglesey, Johnny couldn't stop talking. Greystones had made such an impact on him, he seemed like a totally different person. He recounted story after story as Emerald stood beside him at the rails, mute with misery. She took in little of what he said, but it was obvious he had become enamored of Ireland and everyone in it. Emerald mentally detached herself from Johnny and clung desperately to the ship's rail, wondering how long it would be before her legs buckled beneath her.

Up on the quarterdeck Jack Raymond apprised William Montague of some of the things he'd learned that day. "Sir, Greystones has its own chapel where they celebrate the Catholic Mass, and I overheard that the guns are going to Maynooth in the wagons tonight."

"There is precious little about the O'Tooles and the FitzGeralds I don't know, Jack," William said quietly. *But that piece of information is one of them,* he said to himself. *By Christ, the bloody Earl of Kildare is up to his neck in treason!*

Jack didn't divulge everything he knew. He savored the secret of Amber and Joseph O'Toole, almost gloating over it. There were so many people he could blackmail over the information, including Emerald, he didn't know where he would begin. For now, he decided to tuck it away up his sleeve. It was far too valuable a card to throw away without giving it careful thought.

The moment Amber saw her daughter's face, she knew there was something terribly wrong. Emerald was pale unto death and swaying on her feet.

William had a self-satisfied look on his face, as if he'd done something damnably clever, and Johnny couldn't stop talking about the O'Tooles' horses. She realized immediately the men had been drinking and wondered if that's what ailed her daughter.

"Emerald?" she said softly.

Black lashes lifted slowly to reveal the intense green fire burning in her daughter's eyes. "Mother."

Her daughter's voice dripped with accusation and contempt. Amber's hand fluttered to her breast in apprehension. The bond between mother and daughter had always been absolute. Had something happened today to sever it? That was impossible; her imagination was running away with her.

Amber turned to her son, afraid to probe Emerald's strange mood. "John, I'm so happy you enjoyed yourself, dear. You can tell me all about it in the morning." Amber licked her lips nervously as she again glanced at Emerald. *Someone has hurt her terribly today. My God, whatever did they do to her?* She looked at her husband again. He seemed fairly bursting with news. "Is there something you wish to tell me, William?"

"As a matter of fact there is. I believe I have talked Shamus O'Toole into a betrothal between Emerald and his son Joseph. Our daughter will be the next Countess of Kildare!"

Amber stared with disbelief into green eyes, which suddenly widened in shock. "Joseph? That cannot be," Amber cried.

"No!" Emerald swayed toward her father, then sank to the floor, unconsciousness sweeping over her.

Amber knelt, cradling her daughter's head. "She's ill," she said in an accusing voice.

"Nonsense," William said, picking Emerald up and ascending the stairs rather unsteadily. "Too much excitement, that's all."

Moments after her father deposited her on the bed in her own chamber, Emerald's eyes flickered open. She flinched away from her mother's hands, which were trying to remove her gown.

"Darling...you fainted," Amber murmured distractedly.

"I'm all right now. Leave me alone," Emerald whispered. The pain she witnessed in her mother's eyes matched the pain in her own heart, and she could bear neither one nor the other.

"We'll talk tomorrow after your father has gone. Try to get some rest."

Emerald turned her face to the wall, wishing

with all her heart that she would awaken and find the whole day had been nothing but a nightmare.

With great trepidation Amber joined William in their chamber. It took a good deal of courage to challenge him, but she knew she must protest against the plans he was concocting. "Emerald is too young for marriage, William."

His greedy eyes traveled down her lush body. "You were less than her age when you trapped me."

"That—that was different. I was much more mature than Emerald."

"Not to worry, my dear, I've only just planted the seed. But it is a seed I intend to nurture. I want you to pack up here; we'll be returning to London the moment my business is finished. We shall be entertaining the future Earl of Kildare very shortly."

So that is the maggot he's got in his brain. He wants Joseph only because he's the heir to Kildare!

William closed the distance between them and reached out a possessive hand to squeeze her breast. "It occurs to me you will be a great asset in these plans. If sweet little Emerald's charms fail to attract the young devil, I doubt if he could ignore your fatal allure."

7

Emerald closed her eyes, too emotionally exhausted to do anything but deny the things she had heard. None of it could possibly be true; not the lies about her mother and Joseph O'Toole, nor this lie about a betrothal.

She slipped into a merciful slumber and began to dream that she was lying upon a stretch of sugary sand in the sunlight. A delicious sense of anticipation spiraled about her, dancing on the soft sea breeze that ruffled her dark curls. She felt a sense of joy that went beyond happiness for she knew that soon, soon he would come.

She kept her eyes closed until she felt a flutter, like a butterfly wing, touch the corner of her mouth. She smiled a secret smile and slowly lifted her lashes. He knelt before her watching her intently, his dark pewter eyes brimming with laughter. Holding his gaze, she came to her knees slowly and knelt before him.

They needed no words, yet the longing to touch was like a hunger in the blood. At the same moment each reached out to the other to trace with their fingertips...a cheek, a throat, a shoulder. Emerald's hand brushed his heart and felt it thud beneath her fingers. He was the perfect male. He was her Irish Prince. He bent to capture her lips with his, but when he was a heartbeat away he whispered, "I am giving you to Joseph."

"I don't want your whore, I want my own, I want Amber!" Joseph demanded.

"No, no, we are not whores!" Emerald cried. She opened her eyes and stared wildly into the darkness. The dream! She had had the dream again, but it, too, had turned ugly. Even her beautiful dream had been destroyed!

In the morning Emerald left the house the moment the sun climbed above the horizon. She did not want a confrontation with her mother; she did not even want to be under the same roof today. She wanted to be alone, and sought the sanctuary of her crystal cave.

William Montague sat in his Liverpool office checking the tally of the revenue due from Ireland. Quite apart from the account books William allowed Jack to work on, Montague had his own. He was not fool enough to share all his ill-gotten gains with his brother. The Earl of Sandwich might have the coveted title, but William had the brains and cunning.

He would not be sorry to leave Liverpool. It was the grimiest port in England; even its brothels were second class. He noted the amount at the bottom of the page and closed the ledger. Only one piece of business remained before he could leave for London. He had to collect the revenue owing from Ireland. A quick voyage across to Dublin Castle, then he could collect his family from Anglesey.

His pouched eyes narrowed as he thought of Joseph O'Toole's fine new schooner. He and Joseph might deal very well together. Shamus had refused to pledge one of his vessels in a slaving venture, but young Joseph might be easier to persuade. William decided he would test the water when Joseph came to London. One thing was sure, when old FitzGerald was dead and Joseph in possession of the title, no more gold would be frittered away on Ireland's pathetic cause, not if he had any say in the matter.

The germ of an idea began to foment in William Montague's brain. He poured himself a glass of smoky Irish whisky while he examined its consequences from every angle. As he sipped, the glimmer of a smile exposed his yellowed teeth. Perhaps he had the means to shorten the time it would take for Joseph to acquire his title!

A whole week had slipped by since Joseph had seen Amber, and his abstinence was playing havoc with his temper. At breakfast, Shamus finally gave in to his frustration with his son. "Ye've had a mouth like a torn pocket all week," Shamus accused. "How about pickin' up a cargo today?"

"I was going into Dublin for new clothes. I can't go to London in rags and tatters."

Sean said, "If it's the ammunition from Anglesey, I'll go."

"Anglesey?" Joseph asked eagerly. "I'll go."

"It's better if *I* go," Sean said pointedly.

Shamus hid a grin. "Let Joseph go. He wants to see Montague's lass."

The blood drained from Joseph's face as his Kerry-blue eyes turned on Sean with disbelief. *Surely to Christ you haven't betrayed me?*

Sean warned quickly, "He means Emerald."

"Emerald who?" Joseph asked blankly.

His father said, "The lass ye took sailin'— Montague's daughter, the one he suggests we betroth ye to."

"Daughter?" Joseph said, puzzled.

"Betroth?" Sean demanded.

"Were ye so drunk at the celebration ye remember nothin'?" Shamus asked, getting to his feet. He suspected his sons were trying to take the mickey out of him, as usual. "Sort it out between yerselves who sails to Anglesey, I've work to do."

The brothers stared at each other, aghast. "Montague wants to betroth me to his daughter?" Joseph asked with disbelief.

"Over my dead body!" Sean declared emphatically.

"That settles it," Joseph decided. *"I'm* going to Anglesey. I have to tell Amber what the old swine is trying to do."

Sean couldn't argue with his logic. He knew Montague would be returning to London by week's end and the sooner Amber was out of Joseph's reach the better. Sean was beginning to doubt the wisdom of the proposed visit to London. He examined his own feelings about Emerald. Strange that he had entertained no proprietary feelings toward the innocent young girl until the suggestion of a betrothal with his brother raised its disturbing head.

He asked himself what exactly he did feel for her. He recalled their first meeting when the mere sight of her entranced him. When she spoke she exposed a quick imagination and a wide-ranging association of thought. Her tongue revealed every nuance of a rich fancy. Sean was shocked by the possessiveness he felt toward her. Then he remembered the slap she had delivered on his birthday. His eyes lit with amusement. He rubbed his cheek, still feeling the sting of her hand. A man probably never forgot the first woman who slapped him.

While Joseph O'Toole was sailing to Anglesey to warn Amber of her husband's plans, William Montague was received with all pomp and ceremony at Dublin Castle by Sir Richard Heron, the official from England who had been appointed to assist Lord Castlereagh, Ireland's chief secretary.

When the business of the revenue was concluded, Montague asked for a private word with Lord Castlereagh, whose job it was to govern Ireland and keep the peace. At the moment he was a man beset by trouble. Insurrection had broken out in four different counties and Castlereagh had sent in English soldiers to quell the trouble before England had a full-scale Irish revolution on its hands.

After being ushered into Lord Castlereagh's presence, William wasted no time with small talk. "I have information that could prove invaluable to you," William confided.

"And how much will this information cost, Montague?" the beleaguered chief secretary inquired cynically.

William looked offended. "Not a penny piece, my lord secretary. My loyalty and my duty to England compel me to come forward with this information."

"Then speak on, Montague. The troubles escalate by the minute. Insurrection is spreading from Belfast, at the top, to the tip of Ireland in Cork."

"I have information about the identity of a Captain Moonlight."

"Captain Moonlight!" Castlereagh exploded. "There are a dozen such renegades arming the peasantry and inciting them to treason!"

"I have no doubt of it, my lord. But surely if you apprehended just one of them, it would be a simple matter to extract the other names from him?"

"You'd be surprised just how closemouthed and clannish the Irish can be, Montague. They are a breed unto themselves, God rot them! But tell me, who is this particular Captain Moonlight?"

"Since the name I am about to divulge is a noble and powerful one, I will need complete anonymity."

"You have my word on it," Castlereagh pledged.

Two armed guards from Dublin Castle carried the strongbox aboard the *Swallow*. As the small ship left Dublin's harbor, William felt quite patriotic. After all the petty disservice he had committed, today he was making amends by helping his country. The fact that he was helping himself at the same time filled him with satisfaction. There was no feeling on earth to compare with the knowledge that he was at the helm controlling events that shaped Destiny, so that she smiled upon him.

Amber held Joseph at arm's length. "You shouldn't have come today. This is wrong, Joseph. We must stop seeing each other."

"Stop it, Amber." He loosed her hands to take her by the shoulders. "I've never felt this way before; I can't just turn it on and off like a tap!"

The shadow of Emerald stood between them. "I'm old enough to be your mother, Joseph," she said miserably.

"You're little more than thirty, for God's sake, young and alive and married to an old man!"

"Emerald must have found out about us when she went to Greystones. She looks at me with loathing. She won't even stay under the same roof with me; she leaves the house at dawn and doesn't return until dusk."

"I don't even know what the child looks like, Amber. It's ridiculous to entertain the notion we could ever be betrothed."

"I've told William she's too young. She is going away to school when we return to London. All our boxes are packed; we're leaving tomorrow, Joseph."

"I'm coming to London." His voice was implacable.

Amber gazed deeply into his blue eyes with sorrow. It could never be. She would have to take him to bed and use the persuasion of her body to try to bend him to her decision.

Amber reckoned without Joseph's powers of persuasion. Their tryst had such urgency, touched with the painful poignancy that it might be their last time together. They clung, they whispered, they promised, they pledged their undying love; they parted.

Amber, filled with delicious lassitude from too much loving, drifted into slumber in the warm afternoon. Joseph remained awake, watching as Amber lay peacefully beside him. He dared not sleep. He knew his crew had the ammunition loaded and were anxious to get it past customs inspection and into Greystones's own harbor.

As Joseph's blue-and-gold *Brimstone* slipped from the mouth of the Menai Strait, William Montague walked the deck of the *Swallow*, humming a tune. He was almost past Anglesey when a most pleasant idea came to him. Why wait until tomorrow to pick up his family? He could spend the night with Amber and close the summerhouse in the morning. The farther away from Ireland they were when the warrant was issued, the less suspicious Shamus would be.

Montague called out an order to head south. The *Swallow* rounded Penmon Point, sailed past craggy Beaumaris Castle, and entered the Menai Strait from the east. He spotted Joseph FitzGerald's schooner under sail and assumed he'd been to pick up the rest of the ammunition. As he departed the ship and climbed the steps that had been cut into the rock leading to his home, silence met his ears. He discerned no activity about the house; it almost seemed deserted. Perhaps Amber had already dismissed the servants in anticipation of tomorrow's departure.

The downstairs rooms were indeed empty; boxes and packing cases stood piled in the entrance hall. The chambers echoed with his footsteps. William's eye fell upon a violet silk robe discarded on the stairs. It inexorably drew him up those stairs.

As William came into the chamber the unmistakable musk of sex assailed his nostrils. His steps drew him close to the bed in fascinated horror. Amber's naked body was lush, still soft with surfeit, still warm with passion, still damp with exertion.

Amber stirred in her dreamless sleep. She half awoke and stretched her naked limbs across the rumpled sheet. When her ears caught the sound of his step, her mouth curved softly. "Joseph?" she murmured.

As he stared at her, hearing the name she called, it all fell into place. William's face contorted with rage at the destruction of all the plans he had so carefully laid down. This filthy Irish whore had ruined his life! Not only had she been putting horns on him, but she had rutted with the man he had chosen to marry his daughter; the man he had just plotted to make the Earl of Kildare! It was as if the Irish were in a conspiracy against him. From the moment he had laid eyes on Amber FitzGerald, he had been cursed!

A bloodred tide of passionate hatred engulfed him until insanity took possession of his brain. He gripped Amber by the scruff of her neck and rubbed her face in the semen her lover had left upon the sheet. "You filthy Irish whore," he ground out, "fucking with another Irish pig in *my* bed! I'll kill you," he vowed.

Montague snatched his riding crop from the bedchamber cupboard where it always lay ready. The fear he saw in her eyes fueled his need to punish her for the sins she had committed against him. He lashed out at her violently, savagely, taking perverse pleasure in her screams. When she tried to protect her breasts with her hands, he lashed out at her face. Her arms came up to shield her face and head, so Montague slashed at her body, over and over again.

Amber managed to roll from the bed to the floor, but there was no escaping his insane fury as he suddenly began to kick her. Amber's screams subsided into moans; her silence did not come until she lost consciousness.

"Get back to Ireland where you belong; you'll never see your children again." Montague gave her one last vicious kick before he spat upon her, and left the chamber. Then he took out his keys and locked the door.

The full spate of his fury had by no means been spent. "John!" he roared at the top of his lungs. "Emerald!" he shouted, cursing aloud because he did not know their whereabouts. It incensed him that he had not been able to control his wife. In fact, the entire household was out of his control. Montague vowed he would immediately remedy that situation and went outside to search for them, calling their names in a voice that brooked no disobedience.

Down at the crystal cave Emerald heard the summons. A sense of foreboding came to her when she heard her father's voice. It was filled with fury and she knew someone would have to bear the brunt of his anger. Suddenly, she was afraid. Earlier, she had seen Joseph O'Toole's ship on the horizon and had put as much distance between herself and the house as she could. Anger at her mother's shockingly wanton behavior almost consumed her. Now, however, that anger paled beside the fear she felt.

Her father wasn't supposed to come until

tomorrow. What if he had caught her mother in the arms of Joseph O'Toole? Emerald picked up her towel and started toward the house with lagging steps, her heart beating so furiously, it almost deafened her. When she came in sight of the jetty, she was relieved to see that O'Toole's schooner had departed and that her father's ship was the only one in evidence.

William Montague saw his daughter before she saw him. He couldn't believe his eyes at her appearance. She wore only a damp shift that shamelessly exposed her body for the entire world to see. Her long dark hair hung down her back in wet strands and her limbs were entirely bare. She looked like a tinker's brat...she looked Irish!

Emerald saw him striding toward her, brandishing his riding crop, his face purple with wrath. When he raised the whip, her feet became rooted to the path.

"Get in the house! Get some clothes on! Have you no shame! Is this how you've been allowed to run about the island?"

Further incensed at Emerald's failure to move, he screamed, "Now! Do you hear me, girl?"

His words galvanized her into motion. As she ran past him toward the house, he lashed out at her bare legs. She swallowed a scream and flew toward the house, panic beating wild wings inside her breast. She ran upstairs to her chamber, but she knew there was no escape from him and his terrible wrath. She heard his inexorable step upon the stairs and suddenly the terror she felt for her mother drowned the fear she felt for herself. She dragged on a dry petticoat and gown with hands that shook as if she were palsied. When his menacing presence filled her doorway, she swallowed another scream and whispered, "Where's Mother?"

She watched in horror as he was gripped by a spasm of uncontrolled rage. "Never dare to utter her name again! The Whore of Babylon has gone! Run off with her filthy Irish lover! She is dead to me! Get aboard the ship, we are leaving immediately."

"Wh-where's Johnny?" she dared.

"I'll find him!"

When Montague lurched from the doorway and she heard his footsteps thudding down the stairs, she sagged to the bed. He had found out about her mother and Joseph O'Toole! What had happened in this house while she'd been hiding at the crystal cave? Surely her mother would never leave her and Johnny, she loved them far too much, didn't she?

Emerald began to cry softly. *It's my fault she's gone. I wouldn't come near her, I looked at her with such loathing, she thought I didn't love her anymore.* How could her mother have run off with O'Toole? How could she choose him over her children?

With great trepidation in her heart she crept from her room and climbed the stairs to the next floor, up to the wing where her mother's chamber was located. She turned the knob and found the door locked. "Mother?" she cried softly, her mouth against the door.

There was no reply save silence. Had he killed her? She knelt down to the keyhole, saw only the rumpled, unmade bed, and got slowly to her feet. No. There was no one there. Emerald could barely believe it, but her father, in his rage, must have been telling the truth.

Emerald heard activity below and silently fled back to her own chamber. She gathered her belongings and placed them in a small wicker trunk. She pulled up her gown to examine the red welts on her legs left behind by her father's whip. They were puffy and swollen. Her mother would know exactly which herb would take away the pain, except of course her mother wasn't there.

Emerald covered her legs with stockings, slipped on her shoes, and stole a glance at the mirror. Her hair was half dry now, its natural curl springing into hundreds of tiny spirals. She took a final look about her chamber. She had been happy here where she had enjoyed the freedom of sand and sea and sunshine. Happy, that is, until that fateful day she had gone to Ireland. That was the day her world turned to ashes. *Damn you, Mother, damn you for being Irish!*

Emerald carried her trunk downstairs and saw the crew of the *Swallow* carrying the boxes from the entrance hall down to the ship. A cold hand seemed to clutch at her throat as she heard her father's voice, ranting and raving at Johnny as they came from the direction of the stables. When she saw her brother she was appalled; her father had used his riding crop on Johnny's face, splitting the skin across his cheekbone. He was so pale, she thought he might faint.

"Emerald," he croaked when he saw her.

"You will never call your sister by that ridiculous name again! Vulgar Irish fancy! I'll have none of it, do you hear me? From now on she will be plain Emma, a decent *English* name!" He looked at his daughter with loathing. "Get that ugly Irish hair covered, while you're at it!"

"Oh, Johnny, you're bleeding," she whispered.

"His name is *John;* I'll make a man of him if it kills him." His eyes narrowed dangerously. "If I find out the two of you conspired with your Irish whore of a mother so she could deceive me, I'll kill you both!"

Emma's stomach knotted painfully to hear her beloved mother vilified in this way. *My God, Mother, why did you do it? Why did you betray us? How could you just run off with a boy young enough to be your son!*

"Get aboard the *Swallow!* I can't bear the sight of either one of you. From this day forward I'll stamp out every last trace of Irish in you. I'll crush it out if I have to!"

8

Rory FitzGerald's horse was white with lather as he rode into Greystones's yard. "Where's your father?"

Sean was about to upbraid his cousin for the way he'd used the horse, but he suddenly smelled trouble. "He's on a run to Belfast, what's amiss?"

"Jaysus!" Rory muttered as panic wedged in his throat.

"Come inside, Rory. Is it my grandfather?"

Rory nodded, almost afraid to tell anyone except the capable, down-to-earth Shamus O'Toole.

"Whatever's the matter?" Kathleen demanded the moment she saw Rory green about the gills.

"They've a warrant out for his arrest," Rory blurted.

"How many came to Maynooth?" Sean asked.

"Four soldiers in uniform. They searched the castle and the outbuildings and found the guns in the secret vaults."

Sean wished Rory had kept his mouth shut in front of his mother.

"If my father lets anything happen to himself, I'll kill him!"

"Hush, now. I'll find him. I'll get him out of the country," Sean pledged.

"Your father will have a rare fit if you get yourself involved, and no mistake!"

"Are the soldiers still at Maynooth?" Sean demanded.

"Two of them stayed to wait for him, the other two left with evidence."

Sean immediately sought out Paddy Burke and apprised him of the alarming news.

"Damnation, yer father has ostensibly gone for linen, but he's carrying messages between the earl and Wolfe Tone."

"If you know where my grandfather is, or how I can get a message to him, for God's sake tell me, Mr. Burke."

Paddy Burke hesitated; Shamus would have his balls if his sons became involved in the Troubles.

"Mr. Burke, I have to get him out of Ireland. They're waiting to take him if he returns to Maynooth!"

"The Dublin connection is Bill Murphy in Thomas Street."

Sean was amazed that the father of the Murphy brothers was involved, yet he shouldn't have been, for both brothers were wed to Fitz-Geralds. "My mother's upset. I'm for Dublin, but I'll be back with news as soon as I may."

Sean was shocked to see Edward FitzGerald sitting large as life in Murphy's front parlor. "Grandfather, there's a warrant out for your arrest. The militia is waiting for you at Maynooth."

"Jaysus! I don't want ye involved in this; I'm surprised yer father sent ye, Sean."

"He didn't. He's on a run to Belfast. Young Rory came hotfoot to Greystones and my mother is beside herself with worry. I must get you out of Ireland while the ports are still open to you."

"If there's a warrant, the ports won't be open to me, and if the bastards arrested me aboard your ship, it would kill yer mother."

"The *Sulphur* has a secret hold," Sean pressed, but he could see the stubborn set of the FitzGerald chin. "Then let one of the Murphy brothers take you across to France."

"I'm the Earl of Kildare, do ye think for one minute I'd let the *English* run me out of my own country? Not bloody likely!"

"That's just stubborn Irish pride! You know my father's motto: *Always do what's expedient.*"

"Sean, lad, if our people are to survive, we must break England's stranglehold. It's up to men like me. If an earl of the realm of Ireland doesn't take a stand, who will?"

"Then I'll stand with you," Sean declared.

"Ye'll not! You and Joseph are the next generation. If we fail, you are Ireland's only hope. If my generation fails at insurrection, your generation must try to achieve independence through diplomacy. Promise me ye'll keep Joseph out of this; ye know what a hothead he is."

Though Sean O'Toole was thoroughly frustrated by his grandfather's attitude, he had to accept it. The Earl of Kildare was his own man, who made his own decisions, and Sean believed that was the way it should be. He went straight home to Greystones, hoping his father would return today. At least he was able to assure his mother that he had warned her father, and that Grandfather was safe for the moment. He did not tell Kathleen of her father's stubbornness, but he did share the information with Paddy Burke.

The light was fading from the sky when Joseph arrived home from Dublin, where he had gone to buy new clothes for his trip to London. He burst into the house as if the devil were on his tail. One look at his ashen face was enough to tell them he had nasty news.

"It's all over Dublin that Grandfather has been taken!"

"But I just spoke with him this afternoon at the Murphys' house," Sean protested.

"That's where they say he was taken, in Thomas Street...rumor says there was shooting!"

"Mother of God, if he's been arrested, they'll have him fast in the bowels of Dublin Castle. I must go to him," Kathleen insisted.

Paddy Burke tried to caution her. "I think ye should wait for Shamus."

"I should, but I won't," she said bluntly.

"We'll come with you," Joseph decided.

"That you won't, and no mistake!"

"I'll go with Kathleen," Paddy Burke said. "We have to keep you out of this if we possibly can."

Sean fixed Mr. Burke with a piercing dark

look. "*I'll* take my mother to Dublin Castle. You prevent Joseph here from following us. I promised Grandfather I'd keep my brother out of this."

They took the carriage into the city. Small groups of Dubliners stood about on the streets with grim faces. At the castle Sean's mother insisted he let her do the talking. She announced herself regally. "I'm Kathleen FitzGerald, eldest daughter of the Earl of Kildare. I demand to see my father."

They had to wait ages while one official brought another. To each one she repeated her demands, which were met by excuses, delaying tactics, and outright refusals, but Kathleen would not take *no* for her answer. Sean's admiration for her was boundless; she epitomized the traditional Irish take-charge woman, and he watched the English officials back down, one by one.

Finally, they were escorted to a cell beneath Dublin Castle where Edward FitzGerald had been incarcerated. When Kathleen saw that her father had been wounded, her Irish temper flared. She berated the guard who accompanied them for not tending to him properly.

The Earl of Kildare, however, was furious with his daughter and grandson for coming to his prison and involving themselves.

Sean bribed the guard to step outside the cell and give them a few moments of privacy.

Kathleen's anger was now mixed with a liberal dose of fear. "If you die, I'll never speak to you again!"

"Ye might think ye have a duty to me, but your first duty is to your sons. They should be out of Ireland by now!"

"You had no right to sacrifice yourself for Ireland, Father!"

Sean knew what his mother did not: His grandfather was in great pain and weakened from loss of blood. When their eyes met, Sean realized his grandfather knew he was dying.

"I've been struggling for our nation's soul. The English practice degradation, persecution, and exploitation on us. Sean, pledge to me that you'll take care of Joseph."

They clasped hands. "I will," Sean vowed.

With most of his strength gone, Edward allowed Kathleen to tend the wound in his belly. Bravely, she cleansed it and rebound him tightly with linen strips torn from her petticoat.

The guard opened the cell door. "Your time's up."

"Your bloody time in Ireland is up, you English pig!"

The guard raised the butt of his rifle, but Sean stepped in front of his mother and fixed him with a malevolent stare from dangerous pewter eyes. The guard took an involuntary step backward.

"If aught happens to the earl, we'll be bringing charges of murder." Sean's low tone held such threat, the guard backed off completely.

By the time they arrived home, Shamus

had returned. He listened in silence until Kathleen had exhausted her outrage, then he slipped his powerful arm about her to lend her his strength. Turning to his sons, he said, "You two young devils are on your way to London. Tonight!"

Sean and Joseph, with a crew of three FitzGeralds, boarded the *Sulphur* just after midnight. It was decided the crew would drop them off in London and return for them in a month's time, provided they were not wanted men.

The O'Toole brothers were almost torn in half, wanting to stay with their family in the face of grave trouble, yet knowing they must get away before they became embroiled in Ireland's Troubles. It was what their family wanted, it was the intelligent thing to do, but it wasn't easy. Both were covered with guilt and felt akin to rats deserting a sinking ship.

Safe on the *Sulphur,* headed for England, Sean took first turn at the ship's wheel while Joseph rested. He gazed up at the stars thinking they looked like diamonds scattered across black velvet. As the *Sulphur* cut cleanly through the sea, Sean's thought processes cut through the emotion, down to where suspicion had taken root.

Someone had betrayed Edward FitzGerald. Why did his mind come back again and again to William Montague? On the surface there was no logic to it. Montague was deeply involved in the treasonous business. He was the one who had stolen the guns from his own country. The O'Tooles and the Montagues had been partners for eighteen years and neither had ever betrayed the other.

Sean probed deeper, searching for motive. How could Wily Willie profit from such treachery? And then it came to him. Why was he interested in betrothing his daughter? The answer came back: *to make her Countess of Kildare!* Sean sighed and admitted the real reason he suspected Montague was because he was an Englishman. That was reason enough.

Later, in his bunk, when sleep finally claimed him, his dreams were vivid. *A woman sat with her back to him. She was completely naked. Her back was beautiful, curved delicately, skin like pale velvet. Dark hair covered her shoulders like a cloud of smoke. He lifted the silken mass to expose the nape of her neck. He touched it with his lips, lost in the taste and smell of her. His mouth trailed a possessive path down her spine to the small of her back. That secret place was so sensual, he was in a frenzy of passion to make love to her. He knew full well who she was, without glimpsing her face. But she was not his to take. Why was it forbidden fruit always tasted sweeter? She belonged to William Montague; she belonged to Joseph O'Toole; she did not belong to him; not yet.*

His mouth moved lower. The tip of his tongue traced the cleft that separated her beautiful bottom cheeks. His need was so great, he began to quiver with longing. He gently turned her to face him, then drew back his hands in horror. Blood poured from a belly wound; the eyes were those of Edward FitzGerald. "Sean, pledge to me that you will take care of Joseph."

Sean awoke with a start and slowly became aware of where he was. Damn William Montague, damn Amber Montague, damn Emerald Montague!

And indeed, Emerald Montague thought she *had* been damned. The ugly redbrick house in Portman Square, filled with ornate antiques, was like a mausoleum without the laughter of her mother. Emerald was bereft, mourning her mother's loss as if she had died. She longed to be off to school as a blessed escape, but her father quashed that hope immediately. School would take her out of his control and that was unacceptable to Montague.

Instead, he employed Mrs. Irma Bludget as governess. Bludget was no such thing; she was disciplinarian, jailer, spy, and informer. She was a big-boned woman who dwarfed Emerald, or Emma, as she was now called.

After her mother's radiant beauty, it was difficult for Emma to even look at Mrs. Bludget. Her eyes bulged from her face in the most unattractive way, and they missed no detail; her mouth was virtually lipless, her teeth small and pointy.

Montague had not been reticent when he explained her duties. "I want you to obliterate any and all traces of Irish tendencies you find in my daughter. The Irish are abhorrent to me! She is no longer to be known as Emerald. From now on, she is only Emma. I want her appearance changed also, starting with her hair. I want everything changed: her clothes, her speech, her books, her music, her attitude, and most of all her defiance. Her mother was a wanton, so you must see that she is never tainted. I want her obedient, I want her chaste, and I want her *meek*."

From the day Bludget arrived she made Emma's life a study in misery. All mirrors were removed, food was rationed, and Emma was chastised over every word, every action. Her hair was clipped off and she was forced to repeat droning prayers to keep her from sin and cleanse her of the devil.

Mrs. Bludget agreed wholeheartedly with William Montague that to spare the rod was to spoil the child. When Emma complained bitterly to her father that Mrs. Bludget had beaten her, he informed her with grim determination that if she ever again gave that good woman cause to beat her, she could expect another beating when he arrived home.

In her silent misery Emma railed at her mother for having abandoned her to a life that was so joyless, it was no longer worth living. In her mind she divided her life into two periods, before the O'Toole celebration, and after it. That was the day her nightmare began.

Because her days were so bleak, Emma

dreamed almost every night. She dreamed of her mother, but never with pleasure. The dreams were filled with accusations, recriminations, and tears. Her recurring dream of Sean came again and again, always starting the same, but now ending differently.

Emerald lay on a stretch of sugary sand in the sunlight. A delicious sense of anticipation spiraled about her, dancing on the soft sea breeze that ruffled her dark curls. She felt a sense of joy that went beyond happiness, for she knew that soon, soon he would come to her. She kept her eyes closed until she felt a flutter, like a butterfly wing, touch the corner of her mouth. She smiled a secret smile and slowly lifted her lashes.

He knelt before her, watching her intently, his dark pewter eyes brimming with laughter. Holding his gaze, she came to her knees slowly and knelt before him. They needed no words, yet the longing to touch was like a hunger in the blood. At the same moment each reached out to the other to trace with their fingertips...a cheek, a throat, a shoulder. Emerald's hand brushed his heart and felt it thud beneath her fingers. He was the perfect male. He was her Irish Prince. He bent to capture her lips with his, but when he was a heartbeat away, Sean turned into Joseph O'Toole. "I've decided to take you. I have Amber, but I want you too!"

Emma awoke covered with guilt, for in the dream she had been willing to go with him so that she could join her mother. "I hate Ireland and I hate the Irish," she whispered. Emma had never hated before, but now she became intimately acquainted with that dark emotion. She hated Irma Bludget, she hated her father, she hated the O'Tooles, and secretly she even hated her mother.

When Amber regained consciousness, Montague and her children had been gone a day and a night. Though she did not know it, she had a dislocated shoulder, three broken ribs, and a bruised kidney. When she tried to move she found it so painful that she simply lay there hoping someone would come to her aid.

When night fell once more, she had such a raging thirst upon her that she crawled across the floor to the door. When she found it locked, she did not have the strength to break it open. Amber drifted in and out of consciousness until day dawned once more.

Using her left arm, she pulled herself across the room to a copper jug that held blue delphiniums; flowers she had placed there in longing anticipation of Joseph's visit. Had that only been yesterday? It now seemed like a lifetime ago. She pulled out the dead flowers and tipped the jug to her mouth. It tasted so foul, she spat out the first mouthful, but realizing she had no alternative she took three gulps and swallowed them in rapid succession. The brackish water not only stank, but it had a horrid metallic taste.

Then she remembered the brandy decanter Montague kept in the cupboard along with his riding crop. She got to her knees and reached up onto the shelf. Her pain almost made her drop the decanter. With a shaking hand she lifted it to her lips and swallowed some of the fiery liquid. A bloodred rose bloomed in her breast, and as she drank down more of the amber liquor, it seemed that her pain lessened.

Amber used the copper jug to smash the lock on the bedchamber door. It took a long time and all of her energy. When she regained her breath, she slowly donned the only clothes she had—the clothes Joseph had removed when they unknowingly made love for the last time. With bravado she fastened the amber drops Joseph had given her onto her ears.

The two flights of stairs were such an ordeal that she literally snaked down them on her belly, an inch at a time. The boxes with all her belongings that had been stacked in the entrance hall were gone, and she realized all she had in the world were the clothes on her back. Using her left arm, she pulled herself up to look in the entrance-hall mirror. She recoiled with shock when she saw her reflection. Her face was bruised black from brow to chin. When she let go of the hall table, she fell back onto her right shoulder. The pain of the impact nearly made her faint, but she held on and when the pain subsided, she realized the fall had pushed her shoulder back into its socket and all she felt now was an aching soreness.

The larder was empty; the servants had done a thorough job of cleaning before they departed. In the herb garden she found chives and parsley growing and devoured all that was edible. Amber's fractured ribs prevented her from getting fresh water from the well, but the bucket had a couple of inches still in the bottom that she thirstily drank down.

She knew she must get to Ireland and Joseph; he was her only hope. When darkness fell she crawled almost two miles to the village and waited for one of the fishing boats that departed at dawn. They stared at her as if she were a specter, then finally one of the Anglesey fishermen recognized her. They took her across, back to the homeland she hadn't set foot on for seventeen years. Amber took off her gold wedding ring and pressed it into the man's hand after he had helped her ashore. "My thanks; I have no further use for this," she whispered.

9

The *Sulphur* sailed into the Thames estuary in the late afternoon and navigated the wide river past Tower Wharf and the brooding Tower of London. At the old Customs House the ship was inspected and allowed to carry on to the Pool of London.

"I've been thinking we should get a place of our own, rather than accept Montague's hospitality," Joseph declared.

Although Sean had been anticipating another

encounter with Emerald, he agreed whole-heartedly that it was best not to put Joseph under the same roof with Amber Montague. "That's a good idea. Until we've had a chance to look about, we needn't let Wily Willie know we're even here for a couple of days."

Wily Willie, however, knew of their arrival within the hour. He received a note from the Customs House and another from the Navy Office near Tower Wharf that the O'Tooles had arrived aboard their schooner the *Sulphur*.

Sean and Joseph carried their trunks up on deck just in time to see the Admiralty vessel, the *Defense,* slide into the berth beside them. Aboard was William Montague, his son, John, and his nephew Jack.

"Well, that was good timing," William called heartily.

Too bloody good, thought Sean.

"I'd no idea you'd be in London this month, but you are more than welcome. Is all well at Greystones?"

"Couldn't be better," Sean replied before Joseph could open his mouth. If the swine had had a hand in their trouble, he'd learn of it soon enough.

"Jack, John, bring their trunks aboard," Montague ordered, and immediately the two young men disembarked from the *Defense* to do his bidding.

Sean summoned the crew. "Meet us in one month, right here, lads. If we've had enough before then we'll swim home," he said with a wink.

"Bring the *Brimstone* when you return, I'm tired of Sean giving the orders," Joseph joked. Then the brothers turned serious for a moment. "Help Granddad if you can," Joseph urged.

"Go with God," Sean blessed, "may He hold you in the palm of His hand and not squeeze."

As they boarded the *Defense*, Sean could feel in his bones the only one genuinely glad to see them was young Johnny, who attached himself to Sean's side like a Siamese twin; the boy's admiration was manifest.

"This calls for a celebration," William Montague boomed with a hearty handshake to each, "and I have just the place in mind for red-blooded young rakehells like yourselves. When my brother, Sandwich, returned from the fleshpots of the East, he founded the Divan Club. I guarantee you've never seen anything to compare."

Jack looked eager, while Johnny looked alarmed, Sean thought silently. He didn't imagine Joseph was in the mood for a brothel either; the only woman his brother lusted after was Amber. Sean admitted a degree of curiosity. He hadn't been exposed to the customs of the East, and wasn't averse to broadening his mind even at the expense of his morals.

The five men went below to the captain's cabin, where Montague poured fine French brandy and proposed a toast. "Here's to the sins of the flesh!"

Sean saw Montague's glance flick to Joseph,

114

and the seeds of suspicion again found a fertile place in his mind. He wondered if Joseph's thoughts mirrored his own, but if they did, he was doing a damn fine job of disguising them. Sean decided to share his suspicions with his brother. He would warn him about Montague playing cat and mouse with him regarding Amber, he would suggest that Montague could have informed on their grandfather, and he would hint that the earl was dying.

Jack Raymond said something off-color and Sean watched Joseph throw back his head in laughter. Tomorrow would be soon enough, Sean decided. He'd let Joseph enjoy his first night in London.

On the carriage ride to the Divan Club, Montague entertained them with the story of the Earl of Sandwich's grand tour. "To be different my brother chartered a ship in Italy that took him to Greece, Cyprus, and Egypt. He became fascinated with the sultan of the Ottoman Empire, a despot who ruled with pomp, splendor, and cruelty, especially over his harem. My brother became influenced by the Moslem religion with its acceptance of polygamy and subjugation of women. It has much to recommend it. When women know their place, life is much more pleasurable."

Sean watched Joseph's mouth tighten and his eyes narrow and knew his brother couldn't stop thinking of Amber. It would be a miracle if they got through the evening without coming to blows!

Stepping through the portals of the Divan Club was like entering another world. The air smelled of incense; Eastern music made by flutes, sitars, cymbals, and other strange instruments floated through the rooms.

In the first chamber they were greeted by eunuchs who offered a colorful array of garments, turbans, and daggers. The choice was theirs, they could keep on their own clothes or change into Eastern garb. William Montague led the way, choosing a flowing robe belted with a sash and a gold turban and dagger to match. His nephew Jack followed suit, choosing a peacock robe and silver dagger.

The O'Toole brothers were bemused. Joseph declined the ridiculous attire when he saw how ludicrous Montague looked. Johnny, torn by the choice of following his father's example or risking the insecurity of removing his own clothes, asked Sean, "What about you?"

Sean hid his amusement, not only at Johnny, but at the whole masquerade. The fancy robes didn't challenge his masculinity, but he knew his sense of humor would get the better of him if he decked himself out in full regalia. Sean compromised by removing his shirt and jacket, then donned a cream djellaba over his own breeches. Johnny smiled with relief and did the same.

The five men were ushered into an inner room that was lavishly decorated to give the impression of splendor. The walls were mirrored, the floor covered by Oriental carpets strewn with brocaded hassocks and cushions. In the center was a fountain with a naked nymph spouting water from her nipples. Potted palms completed the suggestion of a desert oasis. Sean bit his lip. *All it lacks is a bloody camel,* he thought irreverently.

A door opened to admit five females carrying small trays. They wore diaphanous pantaloons, and though their faces were veiled, their breasts were completely bared. Each female knelt, abasing herself while offering up a demitasse of Turkish coffee. As Sean rolled it about his tongue, he knew it was laced with something he could not put a name to.

Laid across each tray was a flagellum. Montague and Jack Raymond picked up theirs immediately and brandished them with a flourish. Montague, seeing the O'Tooles' lack of response, explained, "These are slave girls to do your bidding and obey your commands. If they do not please their masters, they expect to be whipped."

"Do I not get to choose my whore?" Joseph asked with sarcasm.

Montague laughed. "These five are merely drink slaves to quench our thirst. Beyond that door are myriads of maidens to choose from who will slake our other needs, no matter what they are. Do not think to choose just one, polygamy is encouraged here."

The wide doors were thrown open by two enormous black eunuchs to reveal a harem filled with scantily clad beauties lying upon divans. The room was warm and slaves stood around the chamber's perimeter, wafting huge ostrich-feathered fans. Beaded curtains led to private alcoves, or the gentlemen were free to indulge in the midst of the harem in true orgy fashion.

Montague prodded a female with his flagellum. When she fell on her knees before him, he lay down upon the divan she had vacated and proceeded to point at the other women he wanted.

Joseph threw himself down on a cushion next to three houris smoking a hubble-bubble water pipe. He wasn't in the mood for whoring, but he was willing to try an intoxicant or two. Johnny was glued to Sean's side, so O'Toole did his best to encourage the youth to lose his apprehension and relax a little. Sean's glance rested upon the youngest-looking girl in the room. He nudged Johnny's arm. "Why don't you talk with that one, she has a very sweet face." When Johnny took his suggestion, Sean selected the female with the cheekiest face.

He held out his hand. "Would you like to come with me?"

She placed her hand in his and with downcast eyes allowed him to lead her through a beaded curtain. Sean's glance traveled around the alcove, taking in the low divan, wide enough for two. The half-clad female fell to her knees, kept her lashes on her cheeks, and murmured, "What do you desire, master?"

"You'll do anything I ask?"

"Yes, master," she whispered.

"Then I want you to drop the act and talk with me."

The girl's startled glance met his as she raised her lashes and looked into silver eyes brimming with laughter. She began to giggle. "Coo, what a larf this place is!"

Sean stretched out on the divan and indicated that she join him. "Come and tell me about it." He grinned with delight as she jumped onto the low bed, her breasts bouncing impertinently.

"You look like a sportin' gent to me, not like the usual customers we get. Gor blind me, the old bleeders can't get it up unless they play master and slave girl. We 'ave to lick their bleedin' feet and other disgustin' parts, and even then it usually takes a whipping before they can stand at attention."

"Why do you work here?"

"The money's good. I earn a hundred bleedin' piasters a night."

"That's only one pound," Sean said, showing his knowledge of foreign currency.

"Well, none of the other knocking shops pay their girls that well, and there's always the chance that one of the nobs will take you for 'is mistress."

"What's your name?"

"Turkish Delight," she said, almost choking with laughter. "My real name's Nellie Carter. You don't really want to just talk, do you?" She slid her hand beneath his djellaba and up his powerful thigh. As he hardened in her hand she said, "Christ, the only thing that would make the old farts who come here that hard, would be embalming fluid!"

Sean laughed. "You *are* a Delight; the name thoroughly suits you. Why don't we enjoy a good old-fashioned fuck, then indulge in something exotic to smoke?"

"Ooo, yes please. We have Turkish tobacco, hashish, hemp, or opium; name your poison."

By the time they were ready to leave the Divan Club, all save Johnny were showing the effects of their debauch. Jack and William Montague had a skinful; the former was unsteady on his feet, and the latter's temper was considerably the worse for wear.

Sean could feel the effects of the hash he had smoked, which were not altogether unpleasant, but Joseph needed his aid to remain upright. Sean wondered what the hell had been in the pipe besides water to make his brother so rubber legged.

By the time they arrived back on the deck of the *Defense*, the walk seemed to have restored Joseph somewhat, so Sean withdrew his support and stepped over to the rails, gazing out at what was reputed to be the greatest city in the world. Lights from ships' lanterns blinked in the darkness, and beyond, the city seemed bathed in a halo that glowed in the dark sky.

Behind him Sean heard someone mutter "Irish scum," followed by words that sounded like "I'll teach you a lesson for taking another man's wife."

A scuffle broke out between Jack Raymond

and Joseph, while William Montague stood to one side shouting to his crew. Without a moment's hesitation Sean reached for a heavy wooden belaying pin and joined the fray. "English bastards," he swore as he smashed three or four crew members' skulls in an effort to reach Joseph's side.

Montague roared, "String them up by the thumbs!" Sean was grabbed by four sailors from the *Defense,* who rendered him totally immobile. Snarling with fury, trying to kick every groin in sight, he watched helplessly as Joseph, too, was held fast. He saw a look of horror cross Johnny Montague's face just before everything went black.

When Sean slowly regained consciousness, his first thought was that the hash he had smoked was producing a nightmarish reaction. It was as if he had no hands at all, but his shoulders were in agony. He shook his head to clear it and felt his whole body swing slowly through the air. The pain in his arms and shoulders increased steadily, but still he had no hands. He came fully awake and stared into the darkness. He relived the minutes before he lost consciousness and realized he had been strung up like a bloody flitch of bacon!

The pain in his arms and shoulders was unbearable. He tried to separate himself from it as he stretched his neck backward to look up at his shackles. No wonder he could not feel his hands, he had been tethered by the thumbs and the circulation was gone, rendering them numb. A filthy epithet fell from his lips as he lowered his head and gazed about trying to penetrate the darkness. *Christ, no!* his mind cried out, for across the deck he could make out another slowly swinging body. Joseph, it could only be Joseph!

"Joe, Joe," he called out, but when there was no reply, he decided his brother was better off unconscious than suffering agonizing pain. Sean's mind groped about for answers. He no longer had any doubt that Montague knew Joseph had cuckolded him. The son of a whore must have planned this revenge. He had invited them to the brothel with a purpose, knowing the evening would incapacitate them, and like lambs to the slaughter, they had accepted and indulged. *Christ, no wonder the fucking English call the Irish thick!* he thought, disgusted with himself.

The pain racking his body was excruciating. When he could no longer keep it at bay he lapsed into merciful unconsciousness. When Sean came to again, gray daylight had just dawned. Joseph's head hung on his chest, and to Sean's horror he saw blood dripping onto the deck from a wound in his belly.

Sean's arms as well as his hands were now numb, but he still had his voice. He began to bellow and shout loud enough to make the mainmast tremble. A handful of uniformed sailors drew about in a wide circle, but none dared to release him without Montague's order. Finally, Jack Raymond approached the brothers. He examined Joseph, gave Sean a grim glance, and went off to rouse his uncle.

When Jack opened the captain's door, Montague was struggling into his Admiralty uniform. "Who's making that caterwaul?" he demanded.

"Sean O'Toole...Joseph's dead," he blurted, white faced.

Triumph flared in Montague's eyes for one brief moment, before the consequences of their assault occurred to him. "Christ, what will we do?"

Jack saw his vulnerability and took immediate advantage. "Sean O'Toole killed his brother, of course, in cold-blooded murder."

"That's brilliant, Jack," Montague said with relief. He did not need to add that he was in Jack's debt; his nephew was quite aware of it.

Montague strode out on deck. "Cut them down," he ordered.

Jack cut Joseph down first and lowered his stiffening body to the deck of the *Defense*.

Sean stared in horror as he realized the fate of his brother.

Jack gave as wide a berth as possible as he cut through the leather thongs that bound Sean by the thumbs, but he needn't have worried. Sean had no feeling in his hands or arms and fell to the deck like a rag doll the minute he was cut down.

Using his elbows and knees, Sean crawled to his brother's side, then knelt helplessly beside Joseph's corpse. It was the worst moment of his life; on his knees before the English who had stuck his brother like a pig. "Joseph's dead!" he accused, not wanting to believe what his eyes told him was the truth.

"Yes, and you murdered him," Montague charged.

"A curse upon your black soul, you depraved English degenerate!"

"Men, put him in chains!" Montague shouted. It took four of them to carry out his orders.

"Either you or your bootlicker, Jack, stabbed him—you both wore fucking daggers from the brothel—all because he gave Amber the only pleasure she ever had!"

"Hold him tight," Montague directed, then he kicked the chained man in the groin. Montague looked about him at the faces of the gathered crew. "I have plenty of witnesses for what happened on the *Defense* last night." William saw his son. "John, speak up, you saw them fighting."

Johnny opened his mouth three times before he could get out the words "I was drunk, Father."

Sean's pewter gaze stabbed into him. "Tell the truth, Johnny!" When all he saw in the boy's face was a haunted look of fear, his hopes plummeted. As the men dragged him belowdecks, Sean's eyes fastened on Joseph's body and a heart-scalding grief engulfed him.

When the circulation returned to his arms, the pain was sharp. He welcomed it, hoping it would blot out the torment inside him. As he lay chained in the hold, his body became fevered. He began to shiver with chills as guilt washed over him. "Joseph, Joseph, I swore an oath to Granddad I would keep ye safe!" Sean sank into devastation, then began to ramble as his thumbs turned black and swelled out of all recognition.

During the next twenty-four hours he went in and out of consciousness. Someone was with him, urging him to sip water, cooling his fever with a cold sponge, massaging his hands, murmuring his name. "It will be all right, Sean, it will be all right." Sean was greatly comforted and settled his restless thrashing whenever Joseph spoke to him, but when he finally opened his eyes, he saw that it was Johnny Montague.

"I'm sorry, Sean, I'm sorry. Your thumb is gangrenous; the ship's surgeon says it has to come off."

Sean stared at the tears running down the lad's face. "I just lost a brother, what the hell does a thumb matter?"

Johnny unfastened his chains and helped him to the surgeon's cabin. It was none too clean, but then neither was the doctor. He poured Sean a jig of rum, but O'Toole refused it with contempt. The surgeon downed the rum, which was obviously not his first of the day. He placed Sean's left hand on a heavy wooden block and picked up a meat cleaver. "This will hurt you more than me, mate."

One quick chop severed the blackened thumb at the second joint. Sean almost severed his own tongue as he clamped his mouth shut to stop the scream in his throat from escaping. When the surgeon cauterized it with a red-hot poker, Sean fainted.

The Admiralty trial was swift; the evidence concocted. Sean O'Toole was accused of murdering his brother the same day they had signed on as crew for the *Defense*. His signature was produced, William Montague gave evidence, and Jack Raymond was the chief witness against him. All Sean's protestations, struggles, and Irish curses were ignored by the Admiralty Board.

He was found guilty as charged. Within forty-eight hours of arriving in London, Sean FitzGerald O'Toole was condemned to a ten-year sentence aboard one of the prison ships known as the Woolwich hulks.

10

Amber FitzGerald, for she no longer thought of herself as Montague, made her way on foot to Castle Lies. The purple bruises on her face were now fading to yellow around the edges. She could not simply walk up to the front door and ask for Joseph; there were too many servants who would ask too many questions.

She concealed herself until dusk, then saw a man go into the gatehouse. Memories of Paddy Burke flooded back to her. She would know him anywhere, even after all these years.

When he opened the door to her timid knock, his heavy eyebrows drew together in a frown. "Jaysus and his Apostles, who did this to ye, lass?"

"Mr. Burke, I'm Amber FitzGerald. I must see Joseph!"

"Come in, ye look half dead. I didn't recognize ye till ye spoke yer name." He moved to pour her a restorative.

"Do you have milk, Mr. Burke? My stomach is empty as a drum."

He sat her down before the turf fire and poured her a cup of milk. He looked at her keenly. "Did Montague do this?"

She nodded.

Her next word told him why.

"Joseph—"

"Mother of God, Joseph and Sean are away to London...guests of yer husband." He saw the look of defeat on her face change to fear for Joseph. "I'd better get Himself," Paddy decided.

"Is my cousin Kathleen at home?"

Paddy hesitated. It had been a tragic day for Kathleen. Her father had died of his wounds in the bowels of Dublin Castle and she had brought his body to Greystones. Tomorrow they would bury the late Earl of Kildare at Maynooth. Then he remembered that Edward FitzGerald was Amber's uncle. "We are in mourning here. Kathleen's father, your uncle Edward, was captured by the English and died of his wounds."

"Ah, no..." she wailed softly.

He put his great hand on her shoulder and though she gasped with the pain of it, there was comfort in the touch. "I'll fetch Shamus," Paddy said quietly.

In the big kitchen both Mary Malone and Kate Kennedy were dressed in black. "He died in the best of health," Mary said, shaking her head and crossing herself at the same time.

"I knew he'd gone last night when I heard the banshee," Kate murmured.

"Where's Himself?" Paddy Burke inquired.

"He's carried her up to bed in a state of exhaustion," Kate replied. "An Irishwoman can face anything with strength and upright propriety, but all melts into helpless anguish when Death takes away a member of the family."

Paddy went upstairs, tapped on the bed-chamber door, and murmured, "Shamus."

After a minute Himself opened the door and stepped into the hall.

"We've an unexpected visitor at the gate-house. I wouldn't disturb ye, if it wasn't needful." On the way over Paddy told Shamus that it was Amber and described the state she was in.

But even that didn't prepare him for the sight

of her. "Montague did this to ye?" Shamus demanded. "Why?"

The question hung in the air while Amber tried to think of a polite way to tell Shamus that she and Joseph had committed adultery. There was no way. She ran her tongue about her lips. "Joseph and I were lovers. I had nowhere else to go."

Shamus stepped back from her as if she had stabbed him to the heart. "Joseph's gone to Montague!"

"I know, Paddy's told me," she said, tears flooding over at last.

Shamus glared at her with icy blue eyes. "Troubles come in threes," he said bitterly. He motioned Paddy upstairs to the watchtower.

"I'll have to go to London, but it can't be tomorrow. Kathleen will need me at the funeral. Not a word of this to her, man; she's enough to bear." He circled the tower room like a caged beast. "Provide for her, give her money, whatever she needs, but get the wee whore away from Greystones."

F our days later Shamus O'Toole sailed up the River Thames into the Pool of London.

William Montague was expecting him. He waited for Shamus O'Toole to come to him at the Admiralty, which lent him power and authority.

"Montague, I've news for my sons, where are they?" O'Toole said without preamble.

"Sit down, Shamus. My news is all bad. Your accursed son Sean fought with and killed his brother, Joseph, the first night they arrived in London."

"Liar!" thundered O'Toole, smashing his fist onto the oak desktop.

"It happened aboard my own Admiralty ship, the *Defense*. I saw it with my own eyes, as did my nephew Jack, and my son, John."

"A fucking Holy Trinity of liars! Where is Sean?"

"Condemned for murder and serving a ten-year sentence. Our English courts showed great leniency in not hanging him for fratricide."

"Where is Joseph's body?" Shamus O'Toole was shaking with the effort of keeping his hands from Montague's throat. Killing him on his own midden would not be expedient, and life had taught Shamus to always do what was expedient.

"It happened five days ago. The Admiralty buried him close by in All Hallows Churchyard; I'm deeply sorry about this tragedy, Shamus."

"Yer not," O'Toole said flatly.

"Why would you say such a shameful thing to me?"

"Because I've seen Amber FitzGerald."

Montague recoiled.

Shamus O'Toole stood up to leave. He couldn't stomach this piece of English offal another minute. "I'll tell ye this, Montague: If ye ever again set foot on my bailiwick, yer a dead man," Shamus vowed.

O'Toole went straight to the magistrates in the Old Bailey Court to find out about Sean's trial and imprisonment. They found no record whatsoever and when Shamus explained where it happened and who was involved, he was told anything that happened upon an Admiralty vessel would be tried by the Admiralty Court.

Since the head of the Admiralty was the Earl of Sandwich, William Montague's brother, Shamus O'Toole knew defeat stared him in the face. But only for the present. He'd be back with a plan, with bribes, with whatever it took to gain Sean's freedom.

It took him two more days to obtain a court order to have Joseph's body exhumed, and then Shamus carried his son's coffin aboard Joseph's own schooner, the *Brimstone*. As they weighed anchor and sailed from the Thames, Shamus wondered how long his beloved son Joseph had been Earl of Kildare. *A day, mayhap.* His heart was heavy as a stone. He had ordered his sons to London; now he was leaving one behind and taking the other home. *How am I to face Kathleen?*

Amber FitzGerald wondered where she would go. Dublin was out of the question; she did not want the FitzGeralds to learn of her fate. She finally decided upon the port of Wicklow in the next county.

She knew Shamus O'Toole had been more than generous, instructing Paddy Burke to give her an ample amount of gold that would keep her for at least a year. But the thought of what she would do when the gold ran out haunted her. Never again did she want to ask for charity, not from any man breathing.

If she took a chance and spent all the money on a business, Amber knew she would be forced to make a success of it. With a flint-hard resolution she decided to gamble it all. She bought a house in Wicklow, devoting eighteen hours a day making her business a success, and she vowed that someday she would seek her revenge.

Sean FitzGerald O'Toole had his head shorn. It was the last haircut of his imprisonment. He was issued a pair of canvas breeches, canvas shoes, and a cotton shirt. The day he entered the hulks was the last day he would ever be clean. As a new prisoner, he was assigned to the lowest deck, the third down, on an old Indiaman, the *Justicia,* which housed five hundred convicts.

An act of Parliament stated that convicts aboard the hulks were to be kept at hard labor, so they were put to work loading and unloading vessels, moving timber, cleaning ships at the dockyard, and, the worst job of all, raising sand, soil, and gravel to keep the Thames navigable.

The convicts were infested with vermin

and begrimed with filth. The food was inadequate and beds nonexistent. At night they were secured in pairs; one man was chained to the wall, the next manacled to the man beside him. Then the hatches were screwed down, burying all five hundred in suffocating, fetid blackness.

As a direct result of these unspeakable conditions, sickness, disease, and death were rife. When a prisoner died, he was buried in the nearby marsh, where the grasses soon erased all trace of disturbed ground.

During Sean's first months of imprisonment he made seven escape attempts. Each time he was caught and beaten within an inch of his life. He stopped being rash and realized that patience and perseverance were likely the only way out. Sean O'Toole did not fear death. He wished a thousand times over that he had died in Joseph's stead. But gradually it was borne home to him that *death* was the easy way out. It was *life* that was hell on earth. Life without freedom was worse than any death.

The deprivations, the hunger, the vermin, and the cravings affected him harder than the brutality, the filth, and the bone-breaking labor. He was so filled with rage, so consumed by hatred, that faith in a merciful God did not sustain him for long. After only a short time he began to realize that only faith in himself would see him through this ordeal.

Survival was paramount; he must survive in order to take vengeance. The elements necessary for survival were at hand. He needed only three things: food, sleep, and work. To survive he knew he must let go of everything else. There was no room in his head for thoughts other than survival. Longings for freedom, food, or love were utterly useless. All thought, all effort, must be directed toward survival.

The guards aboard the *Justicia* exercised complete physical control over him, while Sean O'Toole exercised total mental control over himself. But, oh, his dreams were another thing entirely! At first he was too exhausted to dream, but as he became toughened to the heavy physical labor, his sleep took wing. He sailed the seven salty seas, he dined upon ambrosia, and when he made love, it was usually to a woman with hair like smoke. The sex of his dreams was so highly erotic, it was like riding wild horses on a magic carpet!

The first year was the hardest. After that he was inured to everything. O'Toole grew an iron carapace about himself that protected him from all emotion save one: the need for revenge. His hatred was a burning, living thing inside him.

He controlled pain, hunger, fatigue, sorrow, and most of his thoughts, but thoughts of his family were so guilt ridden, he vowed never to think of them again until he gained his freedom. Thoughts of his enemy's family, however, were another thing entirely. His hatred for Montague extended to every member of his family: his brother, the Earl of Sandwich; his nephew Jack; his wife Amber; his son John; and his daughter Emerald; he would take his revenge against each and every one. Like a litany, the last thing he said every night was *"I'll get them if I have to go all the way to hell!"*

Sean O'Toole ate every scrap of food he could lay his hands on. He cared not if the biscuit was weevil infested, the gruel rancid, the bread moldy, or the water fetid; it was all grist to his mill. Because of his youth and strength he intimidated many of the older, weaker prisoners, and as a result he was able to steal rations from them. He did this without one pang of guilt because he no longer had a conscience.

Gradually the round, firm flesh of youth fell away with hard labor. He was the hardest-working convict aboard the *Justicia*. He relished the toil because it made him lean, hard, and strong. After the second year he stopped being chained to the ship's wall and chose to be chained to the man beside him. That way, at least, one side was unfettered.

By the third year he had even learned to control his anger, at least to the point where it never showed. He often made sardonic comments and witticisms so that even the guards sometimes laughed with him. The Irish traits for survival were bred into his bones; a mixture of fatalism and hope that was a curious paradox. For over six centuries Irish oppression in the form of famine, murder, enslavement, and persecution had given him the control he needed to survive. The only thing he could not control, *would* not control, was his thirst for vengeance!

It gave him the only pleasure he knew. He carried a talisman with him always to remind him: the stub of his thumb. Death was too easy for his enemies. Death was a sweet, gentle reward. It was life, made a living misery, that was a hell. Life that was a living hell on earth! He wanted them all to live long so they could endure all the suffering, all the pain, all the humiliation, he had planned for them.

His fourth year of incarceration came and went. He had now been there long enough to be housed only one deck down. His favorite job was the hardest: dredging the silt from the bottom of the Thames. He was a superb swimmer and diver who excelled at what he did. He was totally oblivious to the cold water and seasoned to the wet clothes that dried on his back.

Just as his body had become all lithe sinew and muscle, his brain was razor sharp, always looking for that one opportunity to escape. As his fifth year aboard the hulks began, escape attempts were no longer anticipated. An attempt simply was not good enough. The next escape must be successful.

*   *   *

Sean O'Toole floated up through the depths of sleep reluctantly. The ever-pervading stench assaulted his nostrils and then his tongue; the smell was so rank, he could taste it. Nothing stank so foully as men incarcerated together for years. Piss, shit, vomit, sweat, running sores, rot, and human misery formed a miasma that clung to every dripping timber of the prison ship.

The familiar sounds of dawn greeted his ears: coughing, spitting and moaning, mingled with the relentless rattle of chains and the constant plash of the Thames against the hulk. He shifted slightly against the hard planks, stretching muscles that continually ached. As he stirred, cockroaches scurried away from his toenails, their nightly feast over until he slept again.

He became aware of the relentless gnawing of hunger deep inside his gut, but the flesh-chilling cold and bone-softening dampness no longer touched him. He opened his eyes to darkness, yet he saw everything; the dark was no longer a barrier to his sight. His nostrils flared wide, welcoming the familiar stench. The grating, raucous noises were music to his ears. The ache in his muscles and the hunger in his belly told him he was still alive. He had survived another day. He was one more day closer to achieving his goal.

Glorious revenge!

When the guard unmanacled him from the wretch beside him, he stood and stretched the musculature of his arms, shoulders, and legs.

"There's a smell of spring in the air this morning," the heavyset guard remarked.

Sean quirked a black eyebrow and breathed appreciatively. "An' here's me thinking that queer stink was you."

The guard was used to O'Toole's cutting disparagement and took it in good part. He tucked the phrase away in his memory so he could use it later in the day.

Sean wolfed down the gruel, then without hesitation wolfed down the gruel of the man he had been chained to. The older convict seemed lethargic today and not much interested in food. As they were herded up onto the deck of the *Justicia* and assigned their work for the day, O'Toole smiled with sardonic appreciation that he would again be diving and dredging. "I'm the luckiest bastard alive; what other job would allow me to perform my ablutions while I work?"

An hour into his diving, the words he had spoken in jest proved true. Today he was the luckiest bastard alive! There on the bottom of the Thames lay a knife, begging to fit into his palm. Sean did not pick it up immediately. He surfaced first to see where the guards were. When he saw their attention was not riveted upon him, he dived to the bottom and slipped his fingers about it with an almost caressing motion.

He had been lucky enough to find the knife, but now came the gargantuan problem of holding on to it all day while he dived and dredged. He could not simply stick it in the

138

waist of his canvas pants, because the haft would be visible. He knew he could grip it between his legs for a short time, but not all day while he labored. He thought of concealing it somewhere and retrieving it at day's end, but because of shifting tides and because he could not bear to let it out of his possession for one moment, he dismissed that idea.

There was only one possible place he could conceal it and that was down the back of his canvas pants, with the sharp blade resting in the valley between his bottom cheeks. It would be almost impossible to hide it there all day, but Sean O'Toole was up to the challenge.

During the long hours of his labor the blade cut into his flesh more than once, but each time he felt the sharp stab he wanted to shout with exultation. After five hours dragged by he was seized by a cramp from continually clenching his arse cheeks, but not by word or action did he reveal that he was in pain. Rather, he embraced the agony, relishing the acute spasms that told him he was alive and that this was the last day of his imprisonment.

A thought skittered through his brain: *How many will I have to kill to gain my freedom?* He banished the thought instantly; it did not matter how many. This time he could not fail.

He did not sit down for the noon food break. He stood while he wolfed down the stale bread and the tin cupful of odiferous cabbage soup. In that instant Sean O'Toole vowed never to eat cabbage again.

"Take a load off yer feet," one of the guards offered casually.

"No, thanks," Sean replied with a twisted grin. "If I squatted after your cabbage soup, I'd shit myself to death!"

The guard guffawed, deciding to forgo the soup today.

The interminable workday finally came to an end. Before they were chained for the night, the inmates were served gruel and ship's biscuit à la weevil. The man O'Toole had been chained to for the last month again showed no interest in food, so Sean consumed the double rations eagerly.

At last the men lay down; the guards shackled them in pairs, then screwed down the hatches, leaving them in blackness. Sean O'Toole curbed his impatience. He had waited almost five years for this night; he could wait another five hours. The top level of prisoners only one deck down fared better than those lower in the ship because of two portholes, which were protected by iron bars. It wasn't long before Sean's eyes adjusted to the darkness so that he was able to see everything.

He counted his breaths to pass the time and control his impatience. He breathed fifteen times a minute, nine hundred times an hour. When his count reached four thousand breaths, most of his fellow inmates had been asleep for three hours.

Holding on to the chain so it wouldn't

rattle, he stirred and quietly shook the man whose wrist was manacled to his own.

Nothing.

Again he shook him and, for good measure, jabbed him in the ribs. When there was still no response, Sean peered into the man's face. His pallor was clearly ashen, even in the dim light. On further examination Sean O'Toole was stunned to realize he was shackled to a corpse. It took him a minute to get over his shock, then he tried prying the wrist manacle off with the knife. The iron would not give. He did not want to risk breaking the blade, so he ceased what he was doing and gave his total attention to ways he might free himself.

Nothing brilliantly clever came to mind, so he simply took the knife and cut off the dead man's arm at the wrist, which at least gave him freedom, though the shackles now hung loosely from his arm. He lifted the dismembered hand, carefully carved off the thumb, and took it with him.

As he made his way to the nearest porthole, he gave each prisoner he passed a quelling look that effectively silenced him. Before he had loosened the bars across the porthole, the convicts watching began to pull for him. Though they themselves could not get free, they knew that his escape would somehow be a great victory over oppression.

It was an extremely tight fit through the small hole and at one point Sean panicked that his shoulders would prove too wide, but his determination was so set that he knew he would manage even if he suffered a broken shoulder to accomplish it. When he silently slid through the opening and dived down into the black water, a great cheer went up.

11

Emma Montague sat passively before her mirror. Today was her twenty-first birthday, yet she felt little excitement. Her life was narrow, monotonous, and downright dull and she had no expectations that her birthday would be different from any other day.

For over five years she had suffered the rigid guidance of Irma Bludget, and as a result everything about her had changed. Emma's personality had been subdued, turning her into a passive, almost puppetlike creature. In the beginning she had rebelled, but a combination of Bludget's and her father's corporal punishment had brought forcibly home that life was infinitely more bearable if she conformed.

Her dark, vivid looks had been declared *too Irish* and had been covered by powdered wigs and pale face powder. The clothes selected for her were always in pastel shades of pink or blue so that she resembled a Dresden shepherdess. She knew it delighted her father that she looked like a young English lady, all milk and water.

Emma tried never to think of her mother because it upset her too much. How could a woman abandon children who worshiped her? The thought that her mother had never loved her was unendurable, so she stopped thinking of her. Emma was not allowed to attend Almacks' or other assemblies, since her father and Mrs. Bludget considered the young ladies who frequented such places forward and vulgar. Her social life was restricted to taking tea with respectable pillars of society and an occasional dinner party with her father, when he considered it politic to his career.

Her hatred for the ugly brick mansion in Portman Square had been tempered to mere dislike; hate was too strong an emotion for a well-bred young lady to display. Sometimes she daydreamed of marriage, which was her one hope of escape. Her night dreams were another matter entirely. Often she awoke covered with blushes and guilt after dreaming of Sean FitzGerald O'Toole. He was wicked, and she felt shameful that she sometimes dreamt of him. What a naive little girl she had been when she first met him and thought of him as her Irish Prince. She told herself that she was not like her mother. She could never be a wanton, tainted by depraved Irish blood.

As Emma stared in the mirror, to her horror she saw a tear slip down her cheek. She brushed it away impatiently, determined not to cry on her birthday. How wicked she was to indulge in self-pity when she lived in a mansion, furnished with priceless antiques, with servants to do all the work.

She heaved a tremulous sigh and rang for her maid. When Jane arrived, Mrs. Bludget was on her heels and Emma hid her annoyance. No matter what she chose to wear for her birthday dinner, Mrs. Bludget would disapprove and make her wear something else. Emma's shoulders drooped; what did it matter? One pastel satin gown was much like another.

The dinner party was attended by her uncle John, Earl of Sandwich, and his son Jack. All throughout the evening Emma had the impression that her father, brother, uncle, and cousin shared a secret to which she was not privy. Later on, when Jack Raymond escorted her to the conservatory, she learned what that secret was. Jack asked for her hand in marriage.

She was so surprised, she was speechless; and yet she knew she should not have been the least surprised. None was closer to her father than Jack; their mutual admiration was apparent. Emma did not wish to marry Jack; she knew she could never love him. Yet what was her alternative? She had no other suitors, nor prospect of any. The thought of remaining a spinster all her life in this ugly mausoleum of a house made her blood run cold.

If she accepted Jack's proposal, she would at least be able to get out from beneath her father's dominant thumb and Irma Bludget would leave to ruin some other unfortunate's life. The alternative was to refuse Jack outright, and she blanched at the thought of defying her father. When she compared Jack with her father, she thought him the lesser of two evils.

She desperately needed someone to love her, whom she could love in return, and Emma believed children would fill this need in her life. She would adore her children and be the best mother who ever existed. *No force on earth could ever make me abandon* my *child,* she vowed.

The decision before her proved so difficult, she sought counsel from her only ally in the world, her brother, John. Jack Raymond was forced to cool his heels in the conservatory until Emma returned with an answer for him.

"Jack asked me to marry him," Emma said quickly, knowing they could be interrupted at any moment.

"Ah, I've seen it coming for ages," John said.

"Then why didn't you warn me?" she asked.

"Em, I thought you knew. He's dangled after you for years, it can't be a complete surprise."

"I suppose I did know, I just didn't want to think about it."

John understood exactly what she meant. It was so much better to leave some thoughts alone so that they settled to the bottom of your mind undisturbed. The trouble was, every once in a while you poked a stick into the murky depths, making all your thoughts turbid. "Did you accept his proposal?"

"Not yet; he's waiting in the conservatory," she said lamely.

"It's something you should decide for yourself, Em."

"Well, if I do accept him, it will get me out from under Father's dominance, but on the other hand I don't love Jack and fear I never shall."

"It's your decision, Em," he repeated.

"Is it?" she asked wistfully. "I think it's Father's decision, and I haven't the courage to refute it."

John was silently appalled. Where had that spirited girl gone who tossed her wig to the wind and the sea? She'd always had twice his courage when they were children, even though she was three years his junior. He had wished a million times he'd had the guts to defy his father the night Joseph O'Toole had been murdered. He thought that if he had it to do over, he would stand beside Sean O'Toole and deny the lies that his family concocted.

He had admired Sean so much and wanted to emulate him, but when put to the test, he had failed miserably. John despised his own cowardice. He had never been sure whether his father had killed Joseph or whether Jack had done the deed for him, but it was assuredly one or the other. From the accusations hurled by Sean O'Toole that night, John realized his mother's faithlessness was at the root of the murder. He wondered briefly if she, too, was dead. His mind shied away from the thought; he preferred to think her free and living in Ireland. He was glad she had escaped from his depraved father.

The first years after she'd gone, his father

had tried to make an officer of him aboard one Admiralty vessel after another. He'd suffered from seasickness every miserable day. Then miraculously his father had done an about-face and put him behind a desk in the office, while at the same time promoting their cousin Jack from his position as secretary to that of naval lieutenant.

John now excelled at what he did, though he still had to lick his father's boots because his sire was in charge of the Admiralty Office. Lord God, how he hated him! John scanned Emma's pale face, hoping against hope she would decide to defy their father and tell Jack Raymond to go to hell.

"Well, I suppose I can't put this off any longer," Emma said with quiet resignation. Then she brightened. "As a wedding present I shall ask for Irma Bludget's dismissal."

Sean O'Toole swam from Woolwich to Greenwich, then waded from the Thames. From there he walked the five miles to the City of London. He had never felt so euphoric in his life. Thoughts of having real food, a bath, and a woman speeded him on his journey. They were the first thoughts he'd had apart from revenge for a long, long time. The pleasure would be in the pace. He would eat slowly, savoring every morsel. He would bathe at leisure, soaping, sponging, and soaking; and he would never again take a woman in haste as long as he lived.

He cut through the back streets of a section of the city where gaming hells vied for space with expensive brothels. The first cloak he saw, he snatched from the owner's back in a flash. When the man turned to protest, one look at the thief was all he needed to silence him.

Sean shrouded himself in the black cloak that covered a multitude of sins and proceeded to St. James's Street. With a discerning eye he chose his marks. All that his victims had to be was wealthy and drunk, which at this time of the morning in Mayfair was just about everyone on the street.

He lifted three bags of gold coins with little difficulty. One glance at the black-cloaked figure with beard and wild black mane unmanned his victims.

As he made his way to a less fashionable part of town, Sean smiled to himself. He had managed to escape and line his pockets with gold without actually having to kill anyone at all. His luck had turned. Satan helps his enemies.

Sean O'Toole went into the George and Vulture by the Blackfriars water-stairs and sat at a table with his back to the wall, facing the door. The smell of food and ale affected his taste buds so acutely, his mouth began to water with anticipation. He ordered a steak, kidney-and-oyster pie, and a pint of brown ale to wash it down.

When the serving wench set the steaming dish before him, he gazed at it for long minutes admiring the golden crust, the juice oozing through the slits on top, and the way the smoke curled into the air from its piping-hot depths. Then he bent over it appreciatively to inhale its aroma. His eyes narrowed with expectation of what it would taste like, then he lifted the first mouthful to his lips, his eyes closing in blissful satisfaction.

He savored each and every mouthful of the food and drink he ordered, then paid with a silver sixpence. When the serving girl brought his change, she saw immediately that her customer had placed a golden sovereign on the table. It gleamed in the candlelight in a most inviting manner. At last she forced her eyes from it and lifted them to his.

"Is there summat I can do for you, m'lord?" He did not look like a milord, but anyone with that kind of blunt to spend deserved respect.

"What will you do for a sovereign?"

"Anything," she replied, glancing at the gold coin.

"Anything?" he asked softly.

She licked her lips apprehensively and thought it over for a moment. He looked a dangerous customer, but how often in this lifetime would she get the chance to earn a gold sovereign in one night? She nodded her assent.

"I'll need a private room for the night and a bath. As well as soap and a razor I'll need a rasp file from the stables."

He paid the landlord for the room and followed the wench upstairs. With the help of a potboy she dragged a tub into the room, and while the lad filled it with steaming water, she went in search of the file.

When she returned, Sean O'Toole was standing in the center of the chamber, still wrapped in his cloak. "What's your name, lass?"

"It's Lizzy, m'lord."

"Well, Lizzy, I need a shave, a haircut, and a good delousing."

Lizzy giggled; he was so unsavory looking, he hadn't needed to tell her he was lousy. "If you get in the water, 'alf of 'em will float off you."

"Before I get in the water, you're going to have to file a set of manacles off me," he said quietly.

"Is that what you've been 'iding under your cloak!"

"Don't be afraid, Lizzy; I won't hurt you."

She saw his mouth curve in a half smile that did not reach his eyes. She straightened her spine. "Go on, then, I believe you—thousands wouldn't!"

They took turns working on the manacle, which was on his right wrist. If it had been on his left, Sean would have had it off in no time. Lizzy watched with fascination as he grasped the file in his left hand, gripping it tightly with the stub of his thumb, then dragging the points of the rasp back and forth with little concern for the skin beneath that was by now bleeding from a dozen gouges.

Finally, the stubborn iron gave way. It separated suddenly and she jumped back in surprise as it fell to the floor. Sean picked up the manacle, set it on the table, and covered it with the cloak. Then he undressed quickly and stepped into what was now tepid water.

"Your bath's gone cold...let me call for more hot water."

"Let me befoul this water first.... I'll likely need a second bath to remove my gamy stink."

Lizzy had been amazed when he undressed; beneath the rags was a strong, lithe body that rippled with hard muscle.

"Would you take the razor and rid me of most of this wild hair?"

Lizzy opened the razor and moved behind him. As she lifted the matted black locks, exposing his neck, it occurred to her that he was at her mercy. With growing confidence she hacked away his hair, lice and all. "I bet you could tell some tale," she ventured.

"You don't want to know, Lizzy." His voice was quiet, but it held an unmistakable note of finality.

When she had his hair cut so it just curled on his neck, she began on the matted beard. She went about it gingerly, afraid of cutting too close.

"I don't bite," he said softly.

She looked into pewter eyes. "I'll bet you do," she contradicted.

"You're a brave lass, Lizzy, to tackle the likes of me."

She winked at him. "I've a strong stomach!"

He laughed then, throwing back his head so the cords in his neck stood out like ship's cables.

When she had the beard down to about half an inch he lathered his face, then took the razor from her and shaved. Lizzy's eyes widened in appreciation. The transformation was stunning. His face was so lean, his cheekbones stood out like the sharp edges of a saber. His dark eyes burned with zeal. He was so palpably male, her heart began to hammer. He was the image of Satan.

Sean O'Toole stepped from the befouled water and wrapped the towel about his loins. "Would you call for the potboy and another bath?"

When the steaming water was brought, he tipped the boy and watched him leave. Then he took Lizzy's hand and pressed the gold sovereign into it. "Thank you."

He removed the towel, stepped into the clean water, and slid down. The feel of it as it closed over his hips was so pleasurable, it made him quiver. When he glanced at Lizzy, she was watching him with yearning eyes.

"Would you care to join me?"

"Gor blind me, I thought you'd never ask, m'lord!"

By the time he slept, the sun was climbing up the sky. Lizzy reluctantly slipped from the bed and dressed. She threw a wistful glance at the sleeping figure. "Coo, the Irish sure could teach the English a thing or two," she murmured.

Sean O'Toole slept the sleep of the just. When he awoke it was early evening and he saw that his filthy old clothes had been washed and laid beside the bed. "Lizzy, you are too kind. It will get you nowhere in this bloody world!"

He dressed, then put on the black cloak to cover his shabby attire. He carefully wrapped the dismembered thumb in a towel and tucked it beneath his arm. He went down to the tap-room to break his fast with a bowl of barley and mutton stew, followed by crusty bread and Lancashire cheese. Nothing he could remember had ever tasted so heavenly.

Lizzy was all smiles, and to Sean's amusement she even produced a blush or two.

"Are you on your way, then?" she asked, wishing he would stay awhile.

"I am, Lizzy. But I'll never forget you."

Before he left, he gave Lizzy another generous tip and bade her good-bye.

"Godspeed," she said earnestly.

Sean stared at her. Did she really believe there was a God?

He made his way to Meyer, Shweitzer & Davidson, a gentlemen's tailors in Cork Street. When he first entered the shop and they looked at him askance, he immediately produced gold. The staff became instantly obsequious and could not do enough for him. He purchased a complete outfit of ready-made clothes, including stockings and shoes. He kept the new clothes on and told them to dispose of his old garments. Then he ordered two more sets of clothes, one for daytime wear, the other for evening. He paid for them and told the tailor they must be ready by tomorrow evening.

It was full dark when he left the shop, and London by night was an experience he couldn't resist. He walked the streets, familiarizing himself with the ancient city and enjoying his newfound freedom. When he reached the Strand, he entered the Savoy Hotel and took a room. He looked the clerk directly in the eye and said, "My luggage won't be arriving until tomorrow. I want the bed linen and towels changed twice a day. Be good enough to give me the name and address of London's finest glovers, and send up a bottle of your finest Irish whisky."

Sean FitzGerald O'Toole stood before the mirror in his chamber. He had not seen his image in almost five years. He stared dispassionately at the man in the looking glass. His youth had gone. Gone, too, was all the firm rounded flesh from his body. He was all bone, sinew, and muscle. The face that looked back at him was pure Celt—dark, stark, and dangerous. They had turned him into the Prince of Hell!

When the clock struck midnight, he locked his room door, walked down to the Strand, and made his way to Portman Square.

12

As John Montague came up through the layers of sleep, he sensed something was wrong. When he felt the cold blade of a knife between his legs, he was certain of it.

He did not dare move or even breathe, for the knifepoint pricked his sac.

"Johnny, lad, do you remember me?"

He remembered the deep voice with the Irish lilt as if he had heard it yesterday. "Sean...Sean O'Toole. Christ, is this another nightmare?" John Montague whispered.

"Let's call it a living nightmare, Johnny."

"Wh-what do you want?"

"Think about it for a minute; I'm sure the answer will come to you."

All that broke the silence was John's labored breathing. Finally, John's voice broke the silence. "You want revenge."

"You're a clever lad, Johnny."

"Sean, I'm sorry—I acted like a sniveling coward that night. I was terrified of my father and didn't dare defy him. I swear to you I don't know which one knifed Joseph, but it was either my father or Jack Raymond."

Silence met his words in the darkness, so he babbled on to fill the void. "I've regretted not speaking up every day since!"

"You betrayed me with silence, but it will

be the last time you ever betray me without retribution."

"I swear if I had it all to do over, I'd stand beside you and tell the truth!"

"I thank the devil we don't have it all to do over, Johnny, for Joseph wouldn't enjoy dying a second time and I assuredly wouldn't enjoy serving another five years on the hulks."

"Forgive me, Sean, forgive me. You have no idea how I admired you, idolized you, and how much I despise myself for what I did to you!"

"If you ever cross me again, not only will you end up without thumbs, you'll have no cock and balls when I'm done with you."

John Montague was now trembling so violently, he was in danger of doing himself an injury.

"Don't piss yourself, Johnny," Sean said, removing the knife from between his legs. "I'll not do it tonight."

Johnny drew a ragged breath, not reassured in any way.

Sean O'Toole struck a sulphur match and lit the candles at John Montague's bedside.

Johnny stared at the intruder with wide eyes. O'Toole had changed drastically; only the voice and the pewter eyes that burned with a silver flame were the same. "You've not come to kill me?" Johnny asked.

"I don't want to kill you; I want to own you, body and soul, Johnny Montague."

"What do you want me to do? Just tell me and I'll do it." He sat up on the edge of the bed and his visitor took a chair facing him.

"You work in the Admiralty Office. I want you to remove my records and destroy them. The name of Sean FitzGerald O'Toole must appear never to have been there. Every trace of my arrest and conviction must be wiped out. If it is not done, Johnny, my knife and I shall return."

"It will be done, exactly as you say. They won't be able to arrest you again, because there will be no record of your trumped-up crime or sentence."

Sean's mouth curved in a half smile. He propped his feet up on Johnny's bed and stretched his arms behind his head. "I've been out of touch with the world. What has happened in the last five years, Johnny?"

"My mother ran away a few days after your birthday celebration. My sister and I have never seen her since. She was in love with your brother, but I don't even know if she's aware of his death...for that matter I don't even know if she's alive."

"Amber was a whore."

"An Irish whore!" Johnny retaliated.

"Touché, Johnny, you're not quite as gutless as you look."

"I suppose you knew that your grandfather, Edward FitzGerald, died of his wounds when he was arrested for treason?"

"I knew he could not recover," Sean said quietly. "That's another gravestone I shall lay at your father's door. I believe Montague was the informant."

Johnny's eyes widened in shock, but when

he thought it over he saw it was a probability. "I wouldn't put anything past him. I hate and despise him!"

"Good, it will make you a better ally, and if you are not my ally, you are my enemy."

"I am your *willing* ally, Sean, never your enemy," Johnny swore.

"I suppose your family's fortune has flourished as the green bay tree?" Sean asked, his voice tinged with irony.

John replied guiltily, "Yes, we have a fleet of merchant ships now, known as the Montague Line."

"Mmm, I believe you are going to prove invaluable to me, Johnny. I'll see you on Saturday. That should give you time to see to the records."

"My sister is getting married on Saturday," Johnny blurted out.

"To whom?"

"To our cousin Jack."

Sean's face was a dark mask. Then he smiled, although the smile did not reach his eyes. "Perhaps the Earl of Kildare will attend." He bowed to Johnny and melted into the darkness.

It took John Montague a moment to realize that Sean FitzGerald O'Toole was now the Earl of Kildare.

Sean spent most of the day at the glovers recommended by the Savoy, who reassured him that the Prince of Wales and his great friend,

George Bryan Brummell, would have their gloves made nowhere else.

He displayed his left hand and explained that when he put a glove upon it, he wanted it to look completely normal.

Two craftsmen were called in from the workroom and presented with the problem. They made sketches of his hand in every conceivable position. They measured it precisely from every angle. They compared it with his other hand and then they brainstormed ideas, encouraging the earl to make his own suggestions.

Finally, they made a trial pair that fit perfectly. Inside the thumb of the left glove a thumb carved from wood was glued into place. It came halfway down, and when O'Toole inserted his hand and stretched the leather taut, it was impossible to detect that the top portion of his thumb had been amputated. Sean O'Toole was so pleased with the glovers' product that he ordered two dozen pairs. Two pairs were to be made from gray kidskin, the rest from supple black leather.

He spent the rest of the day shopping. He bought Hobey boots, riding boots, breeches, and hacking jackets. He ordered shirts of silk and linen, vests and waistcoats, cravats, muslin neckcloths and top hats, and a many-caped greatcoat. He even took a fancy to a Malacca cane with an ebony top. He ordered all delivered in the name of Kildare to the Savoy Hotel.

As he strolled down Bond Street on his

way back to the Savoy, he stopped to admire the pieces displayed in a jeweler's window. His eye was held by a silver dolphin brooch and he entered the shop to take a closer look. When the jeweler placed it in his gloved hand, Sean saw that it was made of sterling silver and that the eye of the dolphin was an emerald. It was the perfect gift for a woman named Emerald. He had the jeweler wrap it for him, then asked if he could have an extra box about the same size as the one that held the brooch.

When he surveyed his purchases at the end of the day, he saw that everything he had selected was either black or white. His mouth quirked with self-derision as he realized he could no longer bear aught but immaculate, snow-white linen next to his person. The black he had chosen for authority. From this day forward he would be in charge of himself and in charge of anyone who came into his venue.

That night, Sean FitzGerald O'Toole took the severed thumb from the top of the wardrobe where he had concealed it, and placed it in the empty box from the jeweler's. He scrubbed his hands, then wrote out two small cards imprinted with the Savoy emblem. On one he wrote *Bride,* on the other, *Groom;* then he signed both: Earl of Kildare.

When Emma Montague awoke on her wedding day she experienced many emotions, but the predominant one was resignation.

160

She had no objection to the fact that Jack and her father had agreed that the groom would change his name to Montague. She knew he had coveted the family name since he was a boy. It was his way of wiping out his illegitimacy.

What really upset her was that as a married couple they would be living in her father's house in Portman Square! She used every inducement to persuade Jack to live elsewhere. She explained that if he could not afford to buy a house, they could rent one. It need not be large; she would be happy in a small house, just so long as it was theirs. But of course Jack would never be content with a small house when he could live in the Montague mansion in Portman Square.

Emma gathered her courage and approached her father, but he was adamant that the newlyweds must live in the family home; as a great concession he suggested they turn the third floor into their private living quarters.

As Emma was being dressed for her wedding, it began to dawn on her that instead of removing her from her father's authority, marriage would impose two masters she must answer to. In the white gown with the white wreath and veil atop the powdered wig, she looked pale unto death. Even the ceremony was being performed at Portman Square, giving her the uneasy impression that her home was her prison.

The words said over her were a blur to Emma. Jack's loud response of *"I will"* made her jump, bringing her out of her introspective reverie. The minister was soberly addressing her now, but the only phrase that stood out in her mind was *"Wilt thou obey him?"* Her subdued *"I will"* was heard by very few.

Later, at the wedding reception, there was such a crush of people, Emma recognized only some of the faces. The wedding gifts were piled onto a long refectory table in the ballroom and when it came time for the couple to open them, they sat upon matching carved chairs on the dais, where all could see from the crowded floor.

The Earl of Kildare slipped his small gifts onto the table and retreated to the back of the room. His height gave him an unimpeded view of the newlyweds. His pewter eyes first sought out William Montague. The man had aged slightly and was somewhat uglier, if that were possible, but he looked much the same as he had five years earlier.

Vengeance rose up so strongly in him, Sean could smell and taste it. He almost felt sorry for Wily Willie. Then his eyes traveled to the dais and rested upon Jack Raymond Montague, as he now called himself. The pupils of Sean's eyes dilated with pleasure as he contemplated his plans for the groom.

Almost as an afterthought his glance rested on the bride. Surely this small, pale, uninteresting girl could not be the wild, vivid creature he had met in the crystal cave! Perhaps his memory had played tricks on him, so that the female his erotic dreams conjured bore no resemblance to the actual Emerald. He felt no regret that she was unremarkable, in fact he felt nothing for her whatsoever.

None save Johnny Montague recognized the tall, dark man with the pewter eyes. The moment John saw him at the back of the room he joined him. "As far as Admiralty records are concerned, you never existed."

Sean's saturnine mouth curved in a half smile, then his glance traveled to Johnny's uncle. "I want to know the names of the Earl of Sandwich's enemies," he said softly. *All Montague enemies are my allies.*

"I understand," Johnny murmured, before he melted into the crowd.

Sean's patience was limitless as he watched the newlyweds unwrap their wedding presents. When his gifts were in the hands of the bride and groom, he saw a look of pleasure cross Emerald's face as she opened the small box. His full attention, however, was focused upon Jack as he unwrapped his present.

Sean waited only long enough to see him recoil, then blanch, as the blood drained from his face.

By the time the groom sought out his new father-in-law to share the contents of the grisly gift box, the Earl of Kildare had quit the premises.

Emma Raymond Montague sat nervously in bed awaiting her bridegroom. Something had gone wrong in the late afternoon at her wedding reception that made her husband and her father shut themselves behind the library door for over two hours. She did not expect her father to discuss the trouble with her; she had learned long ago that women did not interfere in men's business. Perhaps when Jack came he would tell her what had happened to throw them into turmoil.

She slipped from the bed and took the small box from the night-table drawer. When she lifted the lid her eyes lit up with delight. Her mind flew back over the years to the days she had ridden the porpoise in the crystal cave and that fateful day when her Irish Prince had discovered her.

She got back into bed still holding the small treasure. She touched the silver dolphin's eye with a fingertip. "Emerald," she whispered, delighting in the jewel, delighting in her real name. The card read *Earl of Kildare,* but Sean O'Toole must have chosen the brooch and given it to Edward FitzGerald to deliver. She could not remember having seen the earl this afternoon, but then most of the faces had blurred together in the overcrowded ballroom.

As she held the dolphin, her heart beat a little faster. She had not shown it to Jack, nor would she. He had been so preoccupied, he hadn't even asked her what was in the small box. She wondered again why her husband had not joined her, and was beginning to suspect he would not come at all. Emma yawned and slid down in the bed. She infinitely preferred to sleep alone anyway. She closed her hand about the brooch, tucked it beneath the pillow, and drifted into sleep.

She lay upon a stretch of sugary sand in the sunlight. A delicious sense of anticipation spiraled about her, dancing on the soft sea breeze that ruffled her dark curls. She felt a sense of joy that went beyond happiness, for she knew that soon, soon he would come to her. She kept her eyes closed until she felt a flutter, like a butterfly wing, touch the corner of her mouth. She smiled a secret smile and slowly lifted her lashes. He knelt before her watching her intently, his dark pewter eyes brimming with laughter. Holding his gaze, she came to her knees slowly and knelt before him. They needed no words, yet the longing to touch was like a hunger in the blood. At the same moment each reached out to the other to trace with their fingertips...a cheek, a throat, a shoulder. Emerald's hand brushed his heart and felt it thud beneath her fingers. He was the perfect male. He was her Irish Prince! He bent to capture her lips with his, but when he was a heartbeat away, Emerald awakened.

She recoiled from the man who held her close and was about to kiss her.

"Emma, what's wrong?"

"N-nothing, I was asleep...you startled me."

He pulled her to him again and covered her mouth with his. At the same time his hands began to remove her nightgown.

Emma stiffened at the bold assault. She was shocked to feel that Jack was completely naked and any second would have her in the same condition. "Jack, don't! Stop, please!"

"What the devil is the matter with you?" he demanded.

"This is wrong...it's wicked," she panted.

"Emma, you're my wife! I waited until we were married before I touched you, but I'll wait no longer." His hands were rough as he tore the nightgown from her body and covered her breasts with his hot hands.

A small sob escaped her and he let go of her in disgust. "My God, don't you even know what goes on between men and women?" he demanded.

"Well...yes...but it's so wanton. I'm not like my mother. I've been taught to be chaste...to be a good girl," she said softly.

Drawing on a patience he did not feel, Jack said, "That is the way you should be until you are married. But with your husband it is different. I have the right to use your body whenever I wish. If you will stop acting like a child, you will enjoy what I'm about to do to you."

Emma doubted that with every fiber of her being.

"Lie still and stop pushing me away."

Emma wasn't completely ignorant. She knew that a man and a woman must join their bodies together in order to make a child. She simply hadn't realized how unpleasant it would be. Resolutely she closed her eyes and lay rigid.

Jack's assault was as distasteful as it was painful. When he was finished and he lay panting from his exertions, Emma felt violated, yet she also experienced overwhelming relief that it was over.

Jack leaned over her. "You're a cold little creature, but I'll change all that, never fear."

As her new husband lay snoring beside her, silent tears crept down her cheeks. *I hate and detest all men.* She wished she could escape into sleep, but blessed sleep seemed a thousand miles away. Emma had felt trapped for a long time, but now the walls of her cage seemed to be closing in on her. A wave of nausea swept over her as she realized that tomorrow night could be a repetition of tonight. In her innocence she had thought marriage would be some sort of escape; instead it was a lifetime sentence.

13

Sean O'Toole went down to the Pool of London to secure a passage to Ireland. While he was there he made it his business to learn all he could about the Montague Line. They owned eight private merchantmen, and though none of them was in port at the moment, Sean learned the names of the vessels, their size, and on which trade routes they sailed.

He waited at the end of Whitehall's tiltyard, close by the Admiralty Office, until Johnny

Montague had finished his work that day. John handed O'Toole a list of names that cataloged the enemies of the Montague brothers. As Sean scanned the list he did not recognize all of them, but some were so politically powerful, they were familiar to everyone.

"How can I contact you?" Johnny asked O'Toole.

"You can't," Sean said quietly. "When I want you, I'll find you."

John Montague did not doubt his word for one moment.

The Earl of Kildare, along with a considerable pile of luggage, sailed the next morning on the mail packet to Dublin. As Ireland's misty coastline came into view, Sean O'Toole thought he'd never before seen anything so heart-stoppingly beautiful. His eyes shone silver as he sailed into the horseshoe-shaped harbor. Then he lifted his gaze to the fields and hills beyond, which were lushly green after the winter rains.

He hired a horse from the stables of the Brazen Head and paid to have his luggage taken by wagon to Greystones. He was filled with both anticipation and dread to be going home. He felt like the prodigal son. Would his father kill the fatted calf when he arrived? Without Joseph at his side, he gravely doubted it.

The first one to see him at Greystones as he rode over the short causeway, then beneath the arch of the gatehouse tower, was Paddy

Burke. The steward knew him immediately, though he was vastly changed.

"Glory be to God!" Paddy said, crossing himself, then he took hold of the horse's bridle to hold him steady. "Welcome home, my lord."

"Mr. Burke, God had nothing to do with it. 'Twas the devil allowed me to escape so I could wreak vengeance."

"Amen to that."

"How did you know me?" Sean asked, amused.

"I felt your presence. I did not recognize you with my eyes. You are older, taller, leaner, harder, and your back is straight as a ramrod."

Sean's mouth curved in a half smile. "The more they heaped humiliation upon me, the straighter I walked. Where is my father?"

Paddy Burke hesitated only a moment. "He's in the gatehouse tower, my lord."

Sean took the steps two at a time. Shamus O'Toole was sitting at a window with a gun resting across his knees.

"It's Sean, Father. I'm home."

Shamus stared at him for long minutes before he spoke. "Forgive me. I tried everything to get you released, but the Montagues held the whip hand."

"They hold it no longer." Sean lifted his head high as he spoke. "Father, I did not kill Joseph, you must believe that."

Shamus held up a forbidding hand. His eyes burned like the coals in the hobs of hell. "You think you need tell me that? I know who murdered Joseph and also deprived me of you for five years. English vermin!" He spat. "Now that you are free, we shall even the score."

"Never doubt it," Sean pledged. "Where's Mother?"

"She's out in the garden. You know how she loves it."

Again Sean O'Toole took the tower stairs two at a time, then strode purposefully to his mother's lovely walled garden. His gaze traveled over the beds of spring flowers, looking for the woman he loved most in life. He didn't see her for a minute or two, but as his eyes looked beneath the weeping willow, he found her.

His heart stood still as he went down on his knees before the small gravestone.

Kathleen FitzGerald O'Toole
Loved Forever

Sean O'Toole thought he had plumbed the depths of hatred, but as he knelt at his mother's grave, he learned otherwise. For five years he had plotted revenge for the two lives the Montagues had stolen, never dreaming they had taken a third life. Kathleen was the heart and soul of Greystones; the precious female they all cherished. He would not know a moment's peace until he had avenged her. On his knees he pledged a sacred vow to his beloved mother.

Paddy Burke placed a hand on Sean's shoulder in a vain attempt to comfort him.

" 'Tis heartbreaking entirely. She's been gone two years now. Shamus lives in the gatehouse with me. He cannot abide the big house without her. Himself nearly went mad when he lost her. He suffered a stroke an' his legs are very weak. He sits up there with the gun, waiting to put a bullet through William Montague when he comes—an' he swears he will come, one day."

"Death is too kind for William Montague, Mr. Burke. First he must drain the cup of life to its bitter dregs."

Sean spent the next day in solitude aboard his ship, the *Sulphur*. When he again joined his father in the gatehouse tower, he listened with amazement as Shamus, too, revealed he had a plan for revenge.

"I've not wasted my time while you were indisposed, Sean, my lad. I've worked for five years against the day ye'll avenge us. There's a FitzGerald sails on every private Montague vessel afloat, as well as on most of the English Admiralty ships."

Sean's mouth curved with wry amusement. "That certainly saves me a lot of time. You are the shrewdest man who ever lived, Father."

The servants at Greystones could not get over the change in Sean O'Toole. He was now the Earl of Kildare, of course, and they treated him with great deference, but their tongues wagged endlessly, cataloging the changes in the man.

Kate Kennedy, sharing a dish of tea in the big kitchen with Mary Malone, said, "He's not the same fun-loving boy who left here. Castle Lies used to be filled with mirth and merriment, clatter and clamor, disputin' and gnashin' of teeth."

"Don't I know it? He's that quiet, he comes into the house like a drop of soot. My heart's scalded for him, so it is," Mary replied.

"He's that fastidious, he changes his linen three times a day. I've had to hire a special woman just to wash and double-starch his shirts. An' he never removes his gloves—it's as if he cannot bear to dirty his hands."

"That's not the half of it, Kate Kennedy. When he comes to the table it's like a ritual. The cloth must be white as driven snow an' he'll dine off only the finest porcelain an' lead crystal. An' if yer thinkin' he's particular about what the table looks like, 'tis nothing compared to his food. He's a fanatic about the food."

When Sean went over the books, he saw that between his father and Paddy Burke, their shipping business was flourishing. He heaved a sigh of relief that he need expend little time or effort in that direction and could use their fleet to ruin the Montagues.

He joined Shamus and Paddy in the gatehouse one evening after he'd been home about a week. They told him of the terrible uprisings after his grandfather was killed, and the brutal British troops who had been sent to beat the Irish into submission.

"That bastard William Pitt keeps proposing an Act of Union, to transfer legislative control of Ireland from Dublin to Westminster. He'll buy the bloody votes with bribes!" Shamus said with disgust for his fellow Irishmen.

Sean said quietly, "I'm sorry to be leaving again so soon, but I've pressing business in England."

"Now that yer the Earl of Kildare, I suppose ye'll be takin' up the cause where yer grandfather left off," Paddy mused.

Sean's jaw hardened. "Ireland can wait, Mr. Burke, I've my own agenda to accomplish."

"Quite right," Shamus agreed. "May the strength of three be on your journey with you."

With a stout crew of FitzGeralds, Sean O'Toole sailed his own ship, the *Sulphur*, back to London. On the voyage he perused the list of enemies Johnny Montague had supplied and singled out a few names. Sir Horace Walpole and his son were both clever politicians who opposed everything that John Montague, Fourth Earl of Sandwich, stood for in the House of Lords. Sandwich had received his Admiralty commissions through his great friend the Duke of Bedford, and when the two joined forces, their influence in the House was hard to beat.

Sean O'Toole smiled at a notation Johnny

had made against the name of the Duke of Newcastle. Johnny Montague was far shrewder than he appeared. He had made special note of the fact that the Duke of Newcastle was the archenemy of the Duke of Bedford.

The Earl of Kildare decided to invite the people on the list to dinner at the Savoy Hotel. When he was finished revealing the acts of treason the Montagues had perpetrated against their king and country, he doubted they would keep their stranglehold on the Admiralty for much longer.

After her wedding Emma Raymond Montague drifted from day to day in a sort of vacuum. She had had years of practice at hiding her feelings and emotions so that her existence might be bearable in the ugly brick mansion in Portland Square.

A disturbing pattern had formed in her life. Each day at precisely four-thirty in the afternoon she was swept with a wave of nausea and a feeling of dread. At first she did not understand the source of her feelings, but then one day she realized that four-thirty was the time he left the Admiralty each day, and at that dreaded hour her safety and security were stripped away. To combat the stifling feeling of suffocation Emma fell into the habit of grabbing her cloak and going for a quick walk. She shunned the company of a maid in her desire to escape from the Portman Square mausoleum into the fresh air.

Today, Emma felt particularly trapped. Last night, after Jack had tried to make love for two hours before he accomplished his goal, he became so frustrated he told her bluntly how unsatisfactory a wife she was.

"You're not just cold, you are frigid! There is something wrong with you, Emma—you're not normal!"

"You should never have married me," Emma said miserably, wishing with all her heart that he had not.

"It cannot go on like this. Starting tomorrow night things are going to be different around here. I want no more of your tears. You will respond to me, Emma, show me some warmth! I might as well be making love to a corpse!"

At precisely four-thirty P.M., swept with the usual wave of nausea and dread, Emma grabbed her cloak and flung from the house. Instead of walking around the square, Emma's steps carried her into Baker Street, where occasional horse-drawn cabs and pedestrians lent the thoroughfare a less confined air than Portman Square.

Suddenly, Emma became aware of a carriage that drew up to the pavement and stopped beside her. It momentarily distracted her from her troubled thoughts as she stopped to see who had followed her. The carriage door opened and a man stepped out into her path. A pair of green eyes widened in the delicate, heart-shaped face as she stared at him with wonder.

"Emerald."

Her glance slowly moved over each feature of his Celtic face. Sharp cheekbones slanted against his dark visage and she saw that his pewter eyes missed no finest detail. He was in black and white. Black thigh-high boots topped tight black breeches and a black cloak sat upon impossibly wide shoulders. Immaculate linen and black kid gloves completed the picture.

"Sean," she said, knowing it could be no one else.

He held out a black-gloved hand. "Come. Ride with me, Emerald."

She hesitated. She knew she should not. She was a married woman; this was simply not done. She had not seen Sean O'Toole in over five years. He was Irish; everything she had been taught to hate and despise. She felt so timorous standing there before him. Did he not realize they were different people now? He was different, she was different, circumstances were different; things could never again be the same.

She looked at his outstretched hand and placed hers in it.

Without a word he helped her into the carriage and tapped the roof with an ebony stick to signal the driver.

Questions crowded her mind. He had undergone a complete metamorphosis. His youth was gone. He had a man's face now, boldly masculine and dangerous. Everything about it was sculpted and hard, even his mouth that had kissed her so many times in her dreams.

His body, too, was lean and hard, exuding strength and power.

"Come with me to visit the *Sulphur,* Emerald."

"I'm called Emma now."

With his silver eyes on hers he said, "No, you are called Emerald now. You will be Emerald forever. It is a beautiful name."

She, too, thought her name beautiful, especially when he said it. She suddenly realized how much she had resented being called Emma; it was so plain and ugly-sounding. "I shouldn't go down to the Thames.... I have to go home."

"Why?" he asked softly. "Is there someone there waiting for you?"

Emerald thought about Portman Square and inwardly shuddered. She was in no hurry to go home, yet she knew if she stayed out, she would be in trouble.

As if he read her thoughts, he said, "You may as well be hung for a sheep as a lamb."

She wondered if she dared visit the *Sulphur* and realized miraculously that she did dare with Sean O'Toole beside her. When the carriage stopped she glimpsed ships' masts through the window and heard the raucous cry of gulls as they wheeled above the herring boats.

Again he held out a black-gloved hand. "Will you come, Emerald?"

She allowed him to assist her from the carriage to the dock. He did not let go of her hand until she was safely aboard his ship. He watched her head lift and her nostrils quiver at the salt tang of the sea. She breathed it in as if it were the elixir of life; as if she had just been given her freedom. Sean did exactly the same these days, and he recognized the gesture in Emerald.

He watched her intently, never taking his gaze from her. He saw the dullness in her eyes vanish at the simple pleasure of watching the traffic on the river. He saw her hand caress the mahogany rail as she descended belowdecks and watched her cheeks flush as she remembered catching him with a very naked Bridget FitzGerald.

"I remember everything as if it were yesterday."

"It wasn't yesterday, Emerald. It was five years ago."

She turned to look up at him. "I thought I'd never see you again. After my mother... died...my father moved us back to London and we've lived a very different kind of life. I don't know anything of your family. Where were you for five years? What have you been doing?"

He looked at her through narrowed eyes, then turned to her and said, "I'll tell you all about it on our voyage to Ireland."

"What! You can't mean—" She became aware that the ship was moving and ran up on deck to see that the *Sulphur* was taking on sail. "What are you doing? I cannot let you take me to Ireland!"

His eyes filled with amusement. "I'm stealing

you, Emerald. You have absolutely no choice in the matter."

"Are you mad, Sean O'Toole? I'm married!"

His amusement increased. "Yes. You are married to my enemy, Jack Raymond. My other enemy is William Montague, your father. They have something in common, something they prize highly that I intend to deprive them of."

"What?"

"You, Emerald."

"You are mad! You cannot do this!" she cried.

"I have done it, Emerald."

She ran to the rail in time to see the *Sulphur* slip from the mouth of the Thames.

Without taking his dark eyes from her, Sean walked a direct path to her side. Her green eyes widened in alarm as he reached out a black-gloved hand to her head. He plucked off her powdered wig and let the wind snatch it from him. Her black curls were wildly disheveled as she stared after the wig with disbelieving eyes. Then suddenly she laughed.

I'll wager that's the first time she's laughed in five years. He wanted to see Emerald unfold her feelings and begin to enjoy her freedom. He recognized every detail of her emotions, because he had felt them when he was released from prison. Textures were so rich, you had to touch them, colors were so vibrant, they made everything seem opulent, fertile, lavish. The beauty of simply looking brought tears to the eyes. He knew.

"The Montagues turned you into a pallid and pathetic English lady. I intend to strip away every layer until you are transformed back into a vibrant Irish beauty."

"But the Montagues hate and despise the Irish."

Sean's grin was wide. "I know. Such sweet revenge."

Full realization came to her that he meant exactly what he said. He *was* stealing her; taking her with him to Ireland. And as he said, he was giving her no choice in the matter. Thoughts from the past came crowding in on her. The first time she met him she remembered thinking that one perfect day he would come in his big ship and they would sail off to Ireland, where they would live happily ever after. That had all been make-believe, and yet the day had arrived, and it was today!

Sean O'Toole was a devil! He was actually doing this maddening, impossible, outrageous thing. And yet, at her heart's core, she was relieved that she did not have to return to Portman Square tonight and face the Montagues who inhabited the mausoleum.

14

"Emerald?"

She jumped as he spoke her name. She had been aboard two nights, yet she had hardly seen him. "What do you want?"

"I want you to stop jumping at shadows. I want you to let go of your fear. It is a demon that sinks its sickening claws into you and chokes your breath." He made no effort to touch her, so she had no excuse to back away from him. His arm swept over the vista of sea and sky. "I want you to appreciate Ireland and what it is to be Irish."

She could see the island clearly now, rising from the mist.

"This is where the storms of the sky and the wild seas beat without ceasing from generation to generation. It is a romantic, mystical isle; a unique place out of time. It is Paradise and Hell. Drink in its beauty. It will live forever in your blood. Inhale deeply, Emerald. Do you smell it?"

Emerald's nostrils quivered as she filled her lungs. It smelled green, lush, piquant, mysterious. "Yes...what is it I smell?"

"Freedom. The most glorious smell in the world."

She took another lungful as the sky above her constantly changed. *Freedom, yes. I do feel free, like I've been let out of jail.* Emerald turned her eyes upon Sean O'Toole. "Have you been in prison?" she asked incredulously.

"I have." His dark eyes never left her face.

"Did my father and Jack have anything to do with it?"

"They put me there."

She was shocked, yet not. Her father was capable of anything and Jack his fawning slave. So that was the reason he had stolen her, to punish them! A bubble of laughter escaped her lips. Ironically, it *would* punish them; not because they loved her, but because he had stolen their property.

As he watched her, Sean realized she was so vulnerable, he would be able to seduce her in a heartbeat. But for his own dark pleasure he would draw it out and savor it. He had no interest in seducing Emma, the little English mouse. He wanted the challenge of a full-blown Irish beauty. He wanted her contentious and delightful, imperious and playful. He wanted her carefree and reckless, bold and beautiful. And then he would seduce her. Gloriously!

Emerald sat patiently upon a coil of cable as the *Sulphur* docked at the stone jetty and the ship's anchor was lowered through the hawsehole. Sean approached Emerald and again held out a black-gloved hand.

"Come. Castle Lies awaits you."

She placed her hand in his and allowed him to escort her from the ship. He led her up the causeway, beneath the gatehouse tower, and across the wide green lawns to the entrance of the magnificent Georgian mansion known as Greystones.

In the entrance hall Kate Kennedy, Greystones's housekeeper, sketched the master a curtsy. "Welcome home, my lord."

Without taking his eyes from the female at his side, Sean said, "This is Emerald FitzGerald, Kate." His mouth curved. "She has come to live with us."

Emerald tried to withdraw her hand in embarrassment, but Sean would not allow it. Instead he threaded his fingers through hers possessively and squeezed to give her courage. He was gratified when Emerald curled her hand in his and lifted her head with an inner pride.

"She shall have the bedchamber that adjoins mine." He took his eyes from Emerald only long enough to wink at Kate. "Purely for the view, you understand." His mouth curved even deeper. He moved toward the grand staircase and Emerald had no choice but to ascend with him.

The room was primrose-yellow, giving the illusion of continual sunshine. Leaded casement windows from floor to ceiling overlooked the fragrant garden and the woods behind. Rising beyond all were verdant, rolling hills that led to towering purple mountains.

With Kate trotting behind, Sean led Emerald through the connecting door into his own bedchamber. "And if you get tired of your view, you must come in here." He swept her over to his own windows, which overlooked the wild sea with all its differing moods. He watched her face, seeing her in diminutive detail.

He never seemed to take his eyes from her, and it made Emerald aware of herself. She stood taller and had the urge to toss her disheveled curls about. With pink-tinted cheeks she extricated her hand from Sean's and walked back into the primrose chamber. For the first time she noticed there were mirrors everywhere—along the walls, beside the bed, above the dressing table. Her reflection showed her plainly how colorless and unremarkable she looked in the prim English dress. She lowered her eyes as she was accustomed to do.

Sean was again towering at her side. She looked up at him and blurted, "I've no other clothes!" Her face went scarlet as she realized how that must sound to Kate.

Sean laughed aloud. "And no doubt you are offering up thanks that you have no others like the ones you're wearing. At Castle Lies we have cloth smuggled in from all over the world. Tomorrow you can take your pick. We have silks, velvets, laces in every hue and shade; some you've never yet dreamed of."

"I can't let you clothe me," she announced primly.

He shrugged. "Then you'll have to run about naked, for I intend to burn those—unless, of course, you'd like the pleasure of burning them yourself?"

"Oh, I would!" Emerald spoke spontaneously.

Sean smiled at her with total approval. "Then naked it is."

"For shame, my lord! Keeping the lass in perpetual blush for yer own wicked amusement," Kate scolded.

Sean rolled his eyes and winked at Emerald. "I am beset by women. I must be out of my mind to go out and steal one."

"You stole her?" Kate gasped.

Sean's eyes lingered on Emerald's lips, dipped to her breasts, then lifted to her green eyes. "I simply couldn't resist," he said, disappearing into his own chamber and shutting the door.

To cover her confusion Emerald moved to the long casement windows, saw the wisps of opal vapor rolling through, and gently closed them. "Where's the mistress?" she asked timidly. Kathleen O'Toole was most conspicuous by her absence.

"In her grave, God rest her soul. I'll be back in a whisker to plenish yer chamber, ma'am." Kate disappeared through the other door.

When she was alone, Emerald felt her legs tremble and knew she must sit down before she collapsed. She sank down on the soft, wide bed, her thoughts in total disarray. Her emotions warred against each other as if she were two completely different people: one Emma, the other Emerald.

Whatever are his intentions? Emma asked.

You know very well what his intentions are! Emerald answered.

I know no such thing, Emma said primly.

He wants you to run about naked! Emerald

declared. She got no further with her argument. The thought made her go weak all over.

Her mind took wing, flying back to the halcyon days on the Island of Anglesey, where they had lain on the sun-drenched sand together. She had been completely infatuated with the beautiful Irish youth. He had stolen her heart and never given it back. She realized with a jolt that she found him twice as attractive now with his lithe hard body, his dark sculpted face, and pewter gaze that pierced her to the core, melting her very bones.

You are as wickedly wanton as your mother! Emma accused.

Perhaps I am, Emerald said dreamily.

She ran her hand over the brocade bedcover, richly embroidered with a green vine. Tiny flowers grew along its stems, cunning insects sat on its leaves, and songbirds perched in its branches. She thought of all the time and all the love it had taken someone to embroider it.

She moved to the tall windows to watch the deep shadows gather in the trees. In her childhood she had been enraptured by tales of enchanted forests. Her heart jolted against her ribs as she heard a noise at the door and saw it slowly open. *He's come!*

But it was only Kate Kennedy, her arms filled with sheets and towels.

"The bed is already made up," Emerald ventured.

"Stab me, child! It's not made up to the master's exacting standards. He's a fanatic about bed linen. It must be spotless, fresh, ironed smooth as silk, and scented with lavender."

"I see," Emerald said slowly. The implication was that the *master* would be using the bed.

"Ye'll get used to the earl's ways in time. Nothing short of perfection satisfies him."

"The earl?" Emerald puzzled.

"He's the Earl of Kildare, did ye not know it, ma'am?"

Emerald shook her head, confused once more.

"I'll get Mary Malone to make you up a tray. Sure an' ye must be starvin' by now."

Once more alone, Emerald sat down in an elegant wing chair and relived the painful night she had returned from the O'Toole birthday celebration. Her father had announced, *"I have talked Shamus O'Toole into a betrothal between Emerald and his son Joseph. Our daughter will be the next Countess of Kildare."*

If Sean was the Earl of Kildare, then Joseph must be dead. Somewhere in the hidden recesses of her mind she had always assumed her mother had run off with Joseph. Emerald had so many questions Sean hadn't answered. Was his entire family dead and gone? Emerald moved across the room to the adjoining door. After a moment's hesitation she knocked. There was no answer. With great trepidation she opened the door a crack and looked about. His chamber was empty.

In the gatehouse tower three men sat drinking smoky Irish whisky.

"Ye've been gone a whole month. I was starting to worry."

"Never worry about me, Father. I laugh at Fate and tell it to kiss my arse! I have pledged to destroy them and nothing shall ever stop me."

"But the Montagues are so cunning—"

"When it comes to cunning, the bloody-fool English are rank amateurs."

Paddy Burke frowned. "Ye've brought their lass back with ye."

"I have, Mr. Burke," Sean said quietly.

"Too bad ye didn't bring her father," Shamus stated. "The minute his shadow falls on my land, he's a dead man!"

"I don't want him dead yet, Father. I had a long session with Sir Horace Walpole and other ambitious politicians. I told them the Montagues had the whole of the Pale in their pockets and could smuggle anything in or out of Ireland with impunity. They knew bribery was rife, but they did not suspect the Montagues themselves. I then informed them William Montague had used his high position in the Admiralty to sell guns to the previous Earl of Kildare; guns that were meant to fight the war in France. I pointed out he was only able to do it with the complicity of his brother, Sandwich, who is conveniently first lord of the Admiralty."

"Did they believe you?" Shamus demanded.

"Oh, yes, their reaction was as explosive as if I'd thrown gunpowder into the fire."

Shamus downed his whisky and licked his lips with glee. "The Montagues are so busy hating and despising the Irish, they have woefully underestimated us."

"I took time to cultivate the friendship of the Duke of Newcastle. We hit it off quite well; he has a charming and receptive duchess," Sean reflected, sipping his liquor.

"I hope ye're not planning on making a career of collecting other men's wives. I think stealing Montague's daughter is enough."

Sean's mouth curved in the familiar half smile. "They're so susceptible to a little Irish charm."

"How can Newcastle help us?"

"He has the king's ear. At this very moment he could be telling His Majesty that the Montagues are running two slave ships. They are too cunning to have them registered in their own name; they are registered to Jack Raymond."

"Has the law abolishing slavers finally passed?" Paddy asked.

"A bill prohibiting English vessels from the slave trade is before Parliament, Mr. Burke, but that has not stopped the filthy practice. The king and Prime Minister Pitt are incensed that English vessels are still actively involved. When they learn their first lord of the Admiralty owns slavers, he will be instantly condemned."

"Won't the fact that the Montagues are friends of the Prince of Wales keep them from being thrown out of office?" Shamus worried.

"Make no mistake, Father, King George rules England. His fat son is a laughingstock."

"That's good. If those filthy bastards lose their positions at the Admiralty, it will cause such a scandal, we'll have our revenge!"

"Part of it," Sean said softly. "They'll lose stature in the eyes of society, but they'll still be wealthy. I intend to ruin them financially as well. I've given new orders to the captains of over half our fleet."

Paddy Burke saw the determination in the set jaw. Sean often smiled, but Paddy noticed his dark eyes rarely matched the smile.

Sean set his empty glass on the mantel and stretched his arms above his head. "I'll bid you both good-night."

Paddy Burke followed him to the door. "Does the lass know that her mother lives just down the coast in Wicklow?"

"No. She knows nothing of Amber, and that's the way I want it."

"Do you intend to ravish the lass?" Paddy asked baldly.

"Ravish her? I don't just want her body, Mr. Burke, I intend to own her soul."

The veneer of civilization was very thin over the savage man who stood before him. Mr. Burke knew that beneath the humor and charm, Sean O'Toole was the Prince of Hell.

Emerald ate her dinner in solitude. The food was perfection itself, far superior in quality and taste to anything prepared in Portman Square. Each time her chamber door opened, Emerald's heart lurched against her ribs, but each time it was Kate Kennedy.

"I've drawn ye a bath, ma'am, if ye would be so good as to follow me."

Emerald, in the habit of being amenable, did as she was bid. She was surprised at the size of the bathing room. It was all pristine white marble with mirrors everywhere. A silver basket held a generous assortment of soaps, lotions, sponges, and loofahs, and beside the basket sat a mountain of snowy Turkish towels.

It took her a while to get up enough courage to remove her dress. Her fingers went to the silver brooch, which she had fastened to her shift where it couldn't be seen by prying eyes. Suddenly she knew that Sean had been at her wedding. He had brought the gift himself! Why, oh, why hadn't he spirited her away before they had legally wedded her to Jack Raymond? Now everything was in such a terrible coil! She sighed heavily and, keeping her eyes downcast, managed to bathe without looking at herself.

Back in the primrose bedroom she realized she would have to sleep in her shift, since she had no nightclothes. She climbed into bed and nervously fingered the little dolphin.

She sat rigid, waiting for him to come. He was a devil! Why didn't he come and get it over with? She would fight him, when he came. She shivered with distaste as she thought about the physical intimacies Jack forced upon her.

As her candles burned low, Emerald began to yawn. Her mind flitted about over the unbelievable things that had happened to her today. Briefly she wondered what Jack and her father would do when they discovered that she was missing. Her mind shied away from thoughts of them. Her eyes closed as sleep beckoned. They would never in a million years know where she was.

At Portman Square, Jack Raymond and William Montague knew exactly where she was. They ground their teeth in impotent rage as they stared at the note that had been delivered to them. Though it was unsigned, both knew instantly who it was from.

When Emerald has an Irish bastard in her belly, I shall return her to the bosom of her loving family.

"You should have killed the Irish swine, the night you stabbed Joseph!" Montague charged.

"We both had a stab at Joseph O'Toole. Don't think you can wash your hands of murder!" Jack Raymond's tone held a threat.

"For Christ's sake, we're in this together, let's not savage each other's throats."

Both men had enough to worry about without the added humiliation of Emerald's bringing dishonor to them. It seemed when troubles came, they came in multitudes. The Earl of Sandwich was not only being accused of incompetence and corruption, he was being investigated for treason. The Montagues were all running about in circles trying to control the gossip, but the scandal was on every tongue in London.

"We'll go together and fetch her back!" Jack declared.

"We can't do that. The minute we set foot on their land, we'd be dead men. Shamus O'Toole has been waiting years for me to make that fatal mistake."

"Then send John, let him talk terms...see how much O'Toole will take to let her go," Jack suggested desperately.

"Sean O'Toole is the powerful Earl of Kildare. Do you think John capable of dealing with him?"

"He's the only hope we've got," Jack said flatly.

With no thought for John's safety, Montague agreed, then directed, "Burn that note before it falls into the servants' hands. We've scandal enough in the family."

15

The early sun seeped through the casement windows of the primrose room. At the same moment Emerald realized she was alone, Sean came through the adjoining chamber door. She clutched the sheets to her chin and lowered her lashes.

"I won't allow you to waste one precious moment of this glorious day." His face brimming with mischief, he took hold of the covers at the bottom of her bed and with one quick snap of the wrists removed them entirely.

Emerald huddled in her shift, trying to make a small ball of herself.

Some of the mischief left his face. "Devil take it, where's the fun in teasing a lass who won't play?"

"What do you want?" she murmured guardedly.

"I want you to raise your lashes and reveal those beautiful emerald eyes. I want you to smile and laugh and play the coquette. I want you to use every emotion that should come naturally to a gorgeous woman. You've been kept in a box. I've just opened the lid! When you are vastly amused at something, I want you to laugh so hard, you have to hold your belly while the tears run down your face. When you get angry, I want to see the sparks fly from the fire in your eyes. I want to see you give as

194

good as you get. When I pull off your covers I want you to kick me and spit in my eye. I want to see you shake your curls and admire yourself in every mirror in the house. I want you to be so extravagant with your dress bills, you try to make a pauper of me. I want to see you in a full-blown passion over something...anything!"

His words were so unexpected, her body uncurled from its tight ball as she listened.

His eyes fell on the silver brooch. "I want you to wear jewels on your shimmy because you are unconventional, not because you have to hide them. Devil take it, Emerald, you are an Irishwoman; flaunt it!"

His words gave her the courage to raise her eyes to his. She saw he was wearing tall black boots and tight black riding breeches. His white linen shirt was open at the neck, and again he wore black leather gloves. He sat down on the bed beside her. "What would you like to do today?"

Before Emerald had a chance to answer, Kate Kennedy came in with a breakfast tray in her hands. At sight of the couple on the bed, she stopped dead in her tracks.

Sean winked at a blushing Emerald. "Kate, I'm a man, not a bloody monk. She attracts me like a lodestone." His mouth curved. "Better get used to it."

Though he spoke to Kate, Emerald knew the words were for her.

He arose from the bed, took the tray from Kate, and set it across Emerald's knees. "I've sent to Dublin for a dressmaker, but she won't be here for hours. If I find you something to wear, will you ride with me, Emerald?"

The moment she nodded her assent, he took himself off in search of suitable attire, and Emerald found it much easier to eat without his amused eyes on her.

"He slept in his own chamber," she told Kate timidly.

"Sure an' 'tis none of my *affair* which chamber the earl chooses. I'll make myself scarce," Kate said, shutting the door firmly behind her.

Emerald chewed slowly, digesting Sean's words along with the food. Though she hadn't had much experience of suitors, she was almost certain that Sean was wooing her. Confidence in her attraction rose a notch.

Sean returned and flung one of his shirts and a pair of boy's riding breeches on the bed. "I'll give you exactly five minutes. When you're ready, knock on my door."

For four of those minutes she sat looking at the male attire he expected her to wear. She suddenly realized the time of his ultimatum had almost run out and she scrambled into the shirt and pants in less than a minute.

When she tapped on his door, he flung it open and grinned down at her. "Hello, Irish, will you never learn? When a man gives you five minutes, you push him out the door and let him cool his heels for an hour."

"Please be serious for a minute. I can't go out like this...look at me!"

"You'll make the stableboys randy as hell. You've the sauciest round bottom I've seen in many a year, and the outline of your upthrust breasts shows through the cambric shirt with impudence. What's your problem?"

She groaned. "You, sir, are my problem!"

He put a black-gloved finger beneath her chin and raised it until her green eyes met his. "Irish, I've only just begun."

She slapped his finger away, dug her fists into her hips, and planted her legs firmly apart. Just as she opened her mouth to berate him, he swooped down behind her, thrust his head between her legs, and lifted her onto his shoulders.

"Hang on, Irish," he warned as he galloped from the room.

Just as she was about to scream, he did something worse. He cocked his leg over the polished banister and the two of them went careening down its graceful curve and shot clean off the end of the newel post in a heap on the carpet.

"Ouch!" she cried, lying full on top of him.

"I cushioned your fall," he protested with laughter.

"Cushioned? You're harder than the floor!"

Sean rolled his eyes wickedly. "Irish, you have no idea."

Mr. Burke came into the hallway with two dogs at his heels. When they saw the couple sprawling on the floor, the animals joined in the fun. Sean's wolfhound rolled on his back in ecstasy and pawed the air. The greyhound

197

sat in Emerald's lap and licked her ear with a delicate sweep of pink tongue.

Emerald squealed and dissolved into laughter. "Ooh, I always wanted a dog, but they wouldn't let me," she gasped breathlessly.

Sean took her hand, pulled her to her feet, and they began to run with the dogs at their heels. "Have two!" he offered. When they reached the stables, Sean said, "Here, have a cat. How about a chicken?" He pretended to chase one.

"Stop, Sean, stop." She was laughing and trying to catch her breath at the same time.

"I like to play with you." The intensity of his words stopped the breath in her throat.

Then he broke their gaze and said casually, "The tack room's through there. Find a pair of riding boots that fit, while I saddle the horses."

As he lifted her into the saddle, she wished his hands would linger. To cover her confusion when they did not, she said, "It's not lady-like to ride astride."

"I don't want you to be ladylike," he murmured low, imagining her riding astride him. "I'll teach you to ride neck or nothing." His mouth went dry at the thought.

"Is that Lucifer, the stallion you got for your birthday that year?"

He nodded and rubbed the glossy black neck. "He was just a colt then."

"So were you."

Their eyes met briefly and Emerald grasped

the moment to put some questions to him. "Are you the Earl of Kildare?"

"I don't want to be the earl of anything to you; I just want to be Sean."

"If you are the earl, that means your brother Joseph must be dead."

"May he rest in peace," Sean murmured. Then he moved his mount closer to hers. "Emerald, the Irish temperament follows the weather. Today we have sunshine, so our mood must be light and happy. The sky here changes so rapidly, we'll have lots of time for gloomy, melancholy thoughts that plunge us into black despair."

She sensed he would tell her nothing, no matter how she probed. Emerald looked up at the sky and let her worries drop away from her. This was her beloved Ireland, she would seize the moment and enjoy it. As she rode along, the sky above her changed constantly. One minute it was a clear, bright blue, then a mass of gray clouds sailed in to threaten. Then suddenly, long golden beams of sunlight slanted down between the clouds and the menace was gone. It did it over and over, one minute sullen, threatening to close in; the next minute the sky sparkled with a joyous brightness that gladdened the heart.

He pointed a finger up the rolling green meadows. "The colors change like magic."

She saw a golden field turn light green, then dark green, then on through blue and purple to black.

"The feel of the air changes with the hour

of day. In the morning it can be soft, in the afternoon, heavy; then miraculously light and clear in the evening."

"Ireland is quite unique," she said with appreciation, seeing and feeling it as he spoke.

"And no matter how gloomy the day has been, when the sun sets in summer, the sky is streaked red, pink, or yellow."

"The words drip off your tongue like cream."

Her words conjured such an erotic picture, he instantly turned hard as marble.

The sudden barking of the dogs told them they'd have company on their ride. Sean broke into a gallop and the greyhound streaked past him. Emerald hadn't ridden like this since her summer on Anglesey. She gripped the mare with her knees and spurred her onward to catch up with the devil who was leading her a merry chase.

They followed the banks of the River Liffey for miles, admiring the waterfowl and wildflowers. Sean slowed so that Emerald could keep up with him. "Would you like to see a spot called Salmon Leap?"

She nodded, ready for a rest from the saddle.

At the junction of the rivers Rye and Liffey, he lifted her down from her mare and tethered their horses to a hawthorn in full bloom. It was a magical spot where one river waterfalled into the other twenty feet below. Sean took Emerald's hand as they made their way to the lower water. He lay on his stomach in the lush green grass and pulled her down beside him.

She watched in fascination as large, beautiful fish made unsuccessful attempts to gain the top of the waterfall, then fell back with a great splash, some on their tails, some on their backs. "Oh, poor things," she murmured.

"No, watch carefully. The next time they swim to the foot of the falls, the salmon leap just above the water to observe the height and the distance. Their second attempt comes so close, they almost make it."

"It's the falling water that drives them back," Emerald said breathlessly.

"On their third and fourth attempts they rise far above the water, then drop into the curvature of the waterfall."

"There! One made it!" Emerald cried joyously.

"The only successful method is to dart their heads into the water just where it goes over the rocks and lodge there for a moment, then scud upstream."

"Why do they do it?"

"The instinct to survive and procreate drives them." The lesson the salmon taught him had served him well.

"You've lain here many times." Their hands were so close, Emerald reached out and curled her hand into his. The black leather glove was a stark contrast against her creamy skin. His silver eyes searched her heart-shaped face for long minutes, then slowly he drew her hand to his mouth and kissed the tip of each finger.

At the intimate gesture Emerald's insides curled over and a frisson of pleasure spiraled deep in her belly and high in her breasts. She had never been more aware that she was female in her life; and Sean O'Toole was definitely male, all male, dizzyingly male, dangerously male.

The way she felt was nothing new, he had always affected her this way. She couldn't help it. When she hadn't seen him for years, she had managed to submerge her thoughts of him, but that only made her dreams of him the more vivid. When she was with him like this, she had no control over her feelings or emotions whatsoever. He overwhelmed her with his powerful presence.

"Come on, Irish," he said, tugging her to her feet. "It's time to see to your wardrobe."

The greyhound was ready for another run, but the wolfhound preferred to stay until he caught a salmon.

Kate Kennedy put Mrs. McBride and her assistant in one of the receiving rooms. The dressmaker was thrilled to have been asked to Greystones by the Earl of Kildare, but curious as a cat to know the identity of the female upon whom he was lavishing gowns. When Mrs. McBride put some pointed questions to Kate Kennedy, she was thoroughly rebuffed. Kate wasn't averse to telling tales, but never to outsiders.

When the master strode into the hall with

a bedraggled Emerald in his wake, Kate communicated without speaking. She jerked her thumb in the direction of the receiving room and Sean said, "Have Mary prepare them a nice lunch. We won't be ready to see them for at least an hour."

With his foot on the bottom stair he held out his black-gloved hand to Emerald. "Come."

As they ascended the staircase together, her heart thudded against her ribs. Sean had a way of keeping her off-balance. She did not know what next to expect from him.

It certainly wasn't the large chamber on the third floor. Whole bolts of cloth stood at the center of the room, while shelves from floor to ceiling were built in around the perimeter. Material of every shade and texture imported from around the world was stored on the shelves.

"Take a few minutes to see what you like," he invited. "Use the ladder if you can't reach. I'll be back shortly."

The ladder was one that slid around the room on rails, as in a library. To a woman the storeroom was like Ali Baba's cave. Emerald's delighted gaze swept around, then up and down, taking in everything at once. Then gradually she began to single out the colors that appealed to her most. She used the ladder so that she could reach the various bolts of cloth, but all she did was touch the material in wonder.

When Sean returned he was immaculate and she realized he had changed into a fresh shirt.

"Have you not chosen anything yet? I expected to find a pile as high as a mountain."

"Everything is so lovely." Her eyes sparkled with pleasure, but still, she did not reach for any one bolt of material.

"How about a serviceable brown superfine for a riding dress? Here's a dark wine bombazine for afternoon, and I suggest this baby-blue satin for an evening gown."

He watched the sparkle leave her eyes.

"I suppose a riding dress should be serviceable," she murmured, trying to sound enthusiastic, but failing miserably.

"Serviceable and drab and dowdy, and don't forget downright ugly!"

She looked at him uncertainly. "Why are you taunting me?" she whispered.

"I'm trying to goad you into speaking your bloody mind and choosing exactly what pleases you; not what might please others, not what might please me, but what would please *Emerald*! Be extravagant, lavish, indulge yourself. Or do you not know how to indulge?"

Inside, in all her secret places, Emerald knew she had been born to indulge. She lifted her chin and pointed to a bolt of peacock silk, then to one of emerald green. Sean lifted them down. When she came to the muslins it was difficult to choose among primrose, apricot, lavender, and pale seafoam-green. She glanced at Sean, saw his mocking silver eyes, and said grandly, "All of them."

She saw his smile and realized he was

enjoying himself. "Would it be impractical to have a cream-colored riding habit?"

"Wickedly impractical," he said, adding it to the pile.

Her fingers ran possessively over a bolt of burnt-orange linen. "I don't want to be greedy."

"Why not? Borrow a page from my book and take what you want in life."

His encouragement spurred her on to choose a bolt of filmy white fabric with silver threads running through it. The wools were so fine-spun and soft, she sighed over their beauty. With great daring she chose scarlet, imagining how vivid it would be with her black hair.

When she thought she had indulged herself more than he ever expected, she thanked him prettily and he carried all the bolts of cloth to her chamber and piled them on the bed.

"Mrs. McBride can have the chamber next to yours. By the look of things she'll be here for a month of Sundays. Shall we have some lunch?"

"Oh, I'm too excited to eat. Can't we get started?"

"You may do exactly as you please. Impatience can be an exciting quality in a beautiful woman."

Emerald caught her breath. Sean O'Toole had a few exciting qualities of his own. The looks he gave her, to say nothing of his innuendos, made her heart race.

She spent the next two hours being measured and listening to Mrs. McBride describe the latest styles. Most of the wealthy Anglo-Irish ladies came to her establishment for their wardrobes and she kept apace of the fashions in London and Paris. Emerald made some of her own suggestions, some quite bold, and Mrs. McBride realized the young woman knew exactly what colors would enhance her dark looks to make them vivid.

The earl stuck his head in the door. "Mrs. McBride, could I have a word?"

His dark looks made her all fluttery. He was a most charming man who made all his requests in a polite manner, rather than issuing orders as most wealthy men did.

He handed her a bolt of rich cloth. "Do you think you could design the lady an evening gown in this crimson velvet and perhaps a matching cape, lined in white satin?"

"Indeed, your lordship."

"I've asked Kate Kennedy to gather half a dozen of our maids who are talented with a needle, and, of course, you'll need some worktables. Whatever rooms you need to use, just inform my housekeeper."

"Thank you, my lord. How very thoughtful you are."

Almost as an afterthought he said, "Oh, and Mrs. McBride, could you make her one of those cunning little masks of red velvet to hide her identity? I'd like to take her to the theater tomorrow night and don't want all Dublin to know that she is William Montague's daughter. Especially when she is so recent a bride."

The woman blinked rapidly, not believing her good fortune at the juicy piece of scandal she had just learned. Everyone in the Pale knew William Montague, brother of the vice-treasurer of Ireland. She anticipated how her patrons' mouths would fall open when she informed them that the Earl of Kildare had taken Montague's daughter as his mistress and that they were living openly together!

16

By afternoon of the next day, two chambers upstairs and one down had been turned into sewing rooms. When Sean strode in, Emerald noticed that every female in the room stopped whatever she was doing to gaze at him. His dark looks were so arresting, she could not blame them; he had the same effect on her.

She smiled a secret smile. She hadn't given him the chance to pull the covers from her this morning; she had been up and dressed when he came through the adjoining door. His mouth showed his amusement that she was one step ahead of him. Her smile deepened; if he wanted her saucy, then saucy she'd be.

"I've a fancy for some tight black riding breeches and some black leather gloves, just like his," she told Mrs. McBride. Then she cast Sean a sideways look from beneath her lashes that was so tempting, it made her feel feminine down to her fingertips. Then she forgot the seductive act and asked earnestly, "Are you really taking me to the theater tonight?"

"If that would please you." He lifted her hand to his lips and Emerald could not hide the excitement she was feeling. "Wait until you see my gown; you simply won't believe it's me!"

"It's time to get ready if we are going into Dublin. Kate is waiting for you upstairs."

An hour later Emerald had to admit that Kate Kennedy made an excellent ladies' maid; one who could work miracles with a hairbrush. Emerald knew she had never looked this elegant in her life. The crimson velvet left her shoulders bare as well as a shocking expanse of creamy breast. The velvet mask didn't really hide her identity, but it certainly made her look provocative.

She turned from the mirror as she heard his deep voice. "Are you ready, Beauty?" The sight of him stopped her breath in her throat. His black evening clothes contrasted with his immaculately starched shirt and neckcloth. In formal clothes he looked every inch an earl of the realm. His attraction was magnetic. Desire raced through her blood like wildfire.

She wanted him to pick her up, carry her into his bedchamber, and kiss her all night long. A sigh escaped her lips as he moved forward, lifted her satin-lined cape to her shoulders, took her hand in his, and said, "Come."

In the carriage he sat her on the seat opposite him. "I want to look my fill and drink in your beauty."

Being enclosed in such an intimate space with him made her heart hammer and her pulse points throb. She watched his pewter eyes smolder as his gaze licked over her, moving slowly, sensually, from eyes to mouth to upthrust breasts. Emerald found herself doing the same thing. Her eyes lingered hungrily on his mouth, then dropped to his powerful black-gloved hands. She longed for both his mouth and hands to take possession of her. The sexual tension between them built until Emerald was ready to scream from excitement, then his deep voice broke the tension.

"What would you like to see tonight? A play, an opera, or perhaps the music hall?"

She explained how vastly ignorant she was about the theater. "I'm sure I will enjoy whatever gives you pleasure."

Her words made him smile. "I promise you *shall* enjoy it," he murmured intimately. Emerald suspected he wasn't speaking of the theater. He made love to her with his eyes, he teased her with his words, yet the only physical thing he'd done was kiss her fingers.

Emerald longed for him to do more. She closed her eyes and imagined his mouth on hers. Surely he knew she wanted to be kissed? When she opened her eyes, twilight had fallen and the interior of the carriage was very dim, but she imagined he had withdrawn from her. Was he tempering his desire for her because she was forbidden fruit?

Sean had seen Emerald's eyes close, hiding her desire beneath lowered lashes. And he knew that slight curve of her lips betrayed her anticipation of his kiss. His hunger for her grew hourly, along with her growing sense of freedom and her willingness to turn her back on all the things her father and husband represented. But he wanted Emerald's need for him to turn to craving. When her desire turned to hunger and her ache became insatiable, then he would take her, body and soul, and make her his.

At the theater Sean paid for box seats, the best in the house. Before the lights went down they were on display for the entire audience. The men openly admired the beautiful woman and envied the earl, while the women trained their opera glasses upon her, envying both her gown and her lover.

Sean could see that Emerald reveled in the attention. It gave her confidence in herself and the confidence made her more beautiful, if that were possible. As the lights dimmed, the orchestra played the overture, and the curtain lifted. Sean watched Emerald lean forward and focus all her attention on the stage. He couldn't take his eyes from her. She was so lovely—how her husband must be longing for her. Imagining the pain Jack Raymond was suffering over his loss gave Sean deep satisfaction. Rumors would fly back to London about this night at the theater, and Sean hoped it would be like twisting a knife in Raymond's gut.

Emerald was enjoying her night out so much, Sean couldn't resist taking her to a restaurant close by the theater for a late champagne supper. He guided her into one of the private alcoves curtained off from the main room and gave her his undivided attention while she raptly told him how much she had enjoyed the performance.

This time he did not sit across from her, but took the seat beside her, which was far more intimate. As he watched her talk, he saw that her eyes sparkled and she had a glow about her that was new, tempting him as never before. The candlelight in the alcove cast flickering shadows all about them, turning the supper into a romantic tryst.

Their fingers entwined and he fed her champagne. "Have you any idea how beautiful you are tonight? Look at yourself." He nodded toward the mirrored wall. When Emerald raised her eyes to see their reflection, he dropped a kiss upon her bare shoulder. "What is making you so radiant, my own beauty?" he murmured.

"It's because I'm so happy."

When they were ready to leave he slipped her cloak about her, then captured her shoulders in possessive hands to pull her back against him. He dipped his head to whisper against her ear, "We won't go all the way to Greystones tonight; we'll sleep at the town house in Merrion Row."

Emerald felt as if the bubbles from the wine were flowing through her veins. As the carriage rolled through the streets of Dublin on the short ride, she experienced a giddy excitement and a feeling of expectancy. He had stopped calling her "Irish" and started calling her "Beauty." She adored the things he said to her. Tonight, would he tell her that he loved her? She hoped with all her heart that it would be tonight. What could be more perfect?

Sean opened the street door with his own key and waved back the manservant who had been in charge of the town house for a decade. Then he swept Emerald into his arms and carried her upstairs to one of the bedchambers.

Her arms slipped about his neck and she clung to him, weak with desire. When he set her feet to the deep-piled carpet she swayed slightly. It wasn't the champagne that affected her, she was dizzy from the feel of his hard body. Emerald did not see the elegant Sheraton bedroom suite made from rosewood as he lit the lamps; she had eyes only for Sean.

He took her hand in his and drew her toward the cheval glass. "I want you to see yourself, Beauty."

In Emerald's eyes the couple reflected in the mirror were deeply in love. He towered behind her, a dark figure in powerful contrast to her vivid crimson velvet. He took the cloak from her shoulders and let it slither to the carpet. Next he removed her mask, then his hands lifted to take the pins from her hair. The heavy mass fell to her bare shoulders.

"You are a true Irish Beauty," he declared, and for the first time in her life Emerald realized how vividly attractive she was.

Sean led her to a dressing table and sat her down before its mirror. "I want to get you ready for bed," he said huskily. His dark eyes held her mesmerized in the looking glass. Finally, her eyelashes fluttered shyly. "I have nothing to wear to bed." It was the merest whisper.

He pushed a flacon of perfume toward her. "This should suffice."

Emerald's breasts rose and fell with her efforts to breathe. She watched him take up a silver brush, watched his hand poise above her head.

"When I first saw you I thought your hair was a cloud of smoke. It lures me to touch it. May I brush it, Emerald?"

She nodded wordlessly, all ashiver with anticipation. The long slow strokes made it crackle beneath the brush. "Take off your gloves?"

Her plea scalded his heart. Slowly, he peeled the right glove from his hand, then buried his naked fingers in the silken mass, touching, caressing, toying, and teasing until the black curls wrapped possessively about them. He lifted a handful to his cheek and nose, nuzzling and inhaling the scent of her. Then he scooped it away from the nape of her neck and set his lips to the exposed place that was usually hidden from the world.

Emerald drew in a quick breath as she felt his fingers undo the fastenings of her gown. She wore nothing beneath it and wondered if he had guessed her secret. Then she felt his hot mouth trail down the curve of her back and knew this was the way a man should make love to a woman. She felt a tingling thrill run down the entire length of her spine and closed her eyes to savor it.

Emerald's lashes flew up as his hands moved from behind, inside her gown, to cup her naked breasts. Seeing him do these things to her in the mirror added to her excitement. His eyes held hers with an intensity she'd never seen before. They were black with passion as he watched her face reveal the sensual cravings of her body. His fingertips stroked her nipples until they ruched into tiny jewels.

The feel of his hands on each breast was different and she realized with a little shock that one breast was being caressed by his naked palm, while the other was being fondled by fingers encased in black leather. The gown concealed from her view what his hands did beneath it, but her imagination painted such an erotic picture of black leather and creamy flesh, she felt a wetness start between her legs. When she moaned deep in her throat, Sean's powerful hands, still beneath her gown, dropped to her waist and lifted her.

She watched, panting, as the crimson velvet fell away and she saw herself completely naked in the mirror. He swept her up against his heart and she buried her face against his wide black shoulder as he carried her to the bed.

He laid her back, spread her hair across the pillow like a black cloud of smoke, then lowered his mouth to hers.

She had waited so long for this kiss, her mouth softened in welcome while her body arched from the bed in wanton, raw lust. The taste of him made her ravenous!

Sean's hot mouth moved down to her throat. His words vibrated against her skin. "Good night, Emerald."

She felt a scream building in her breast as he quietly moved across the room and disappeared through the adjoining door. The scream turned into a low sob and ended on a whisper. "Love me, Sean, love me."

Emerald tossed and turned in the wide bed; sleep a million miles away. All her senses were heightened to such a degree that even the feel of the sheets against her skin was arousing. It seemed to take hours for her blood to cool and her heart to stop racing.

Gradually she realized that her feelings and her longings were totally out of character for her. Wasn't she the one who hated the physical things men expected of women? How could she abhor being a wife, yet long to be a mistress? Her conscience lightly pricked at her. She had been frigidly cold to Jack.

The accusations he'd thrown at her were all true. Yet here she was panting after Sean O'Toole.

She was profoundly grateful to him. Not only had he given her freedom, he had given her back *herself*. She could no more stop loving him than she could stop breathing. Emerald's mouth curved into a soft smile. She trusted him completely. Should she allow him to set the pace or should she do her very best to heat matters up between them? When the time was right for him to make love to her, he would know. Sean would make everything perfect!

When Emerald awoke she was heavy eyed and felt she hadn't slept at all. Before she could leave her bed, Sean came in with a tray.

She eyed his riding breeches and linen, open-necked shirt.

"I'm sorry you don't have a change of clothes, Emerald."

She waved a dismissive hand. "Flaunting convention seems to come quite naturally to me these days."

"Am I creating a monster?" he teased.

"Perhaps, but I'm a very sleepy monster this morning." She pushed back a mass of disheveled black hair, brilliant against the creamy white pillow, and cast him a languid look from beneath her lashes.

He sat down beside her on the bed. "You have *Irish eyes* this morning. The dark smudges look as if you've been rubbing them with sooty fingers." He bent toward her and she wedged the breakfast tray between them.

"Don't you dare to kiss me," she murmured provocatively. "Don't start something unless you're willing to finish it," she said lightly.

Sean threw back his head and laughed. "So, Beauty, you've suddenly developed a mind of your own!"

She shrugged prettily and let the sheet fall a fraction. "I've simply decided to make a few rules of my own for this delicious game we are playing."

Later, in the carriage, when Sean was about to take the seat opposite her, Emerald said imperiously, "No, no, you must sit beside me."

He cast her an amused look, deciding to humor her.

She pulled her cloak more snugly about her and leaned into his shoulder. "I didn't get nearly enough sleep; you may awaken me when we arrive back at Castle Lies." She yawned prettily, covered her mouth with her hand, then let it drop to rest on his chest. She imagined his mocking look and the words that ran through his head. *You are learning to play the game well.*

Before long, however, the swaying of the coach and the warmth of his body lulled her into more than pretend sleep. When he felt her completely relax against him and saw her shallow breathing, he was amazed that she felt secure enough to fall asleep in his arms. What a foolish little female she was to trust the prince of hell.

With gentle hands he moved her into a more comfortable position, cradling her in his lap. Almost immediately he realized his mistake. The feel of her soft body against his sent desire flooding through him. Though he tried to control his response he could not. His erection was instantaneous and marked. Sean shifted imperceptibly on the seat to ease the pressure of his tight riding breeches, but that only made his situation worse. Pressed against the cheeks of her bottom, his shaft now grew longer and harder with every heartbeat.

Her cape had fallen open and her breasts swelled against his arm as it lay draped over her body. He couldn't take his eyes from her; she filled up his senses. The scent from her warm body stole to his nostrils, making his desire rampant. What a fool he had been last night. He'd had her naked in the bed, her body so willing and responsive, it had arched against his when he kissed her good-night.

He spread his legs and she slipped down between his thighs, pressing against his testes until the sweet ache became almost unendurable. The heat from her body mingled with his, flooding his whole groin, then began to seep into his blood until he pulsed and throbbed in an agony of need. He knew he wouldn't be able to hold out much longer before he claimed her body.

As he cradled her in his lap he saw how

small she was and a protective feeling rose up in him and threatened to engulf him. He ruthlessly crushed it down. He would not allow his heart to become entangled in this seduction. Perhaps he had made a tactical mistake. By holding off until Emerald craved him, he'd let his own craving become that of a ravenous beast. If he wasn't careful she would become an obsession, and he could not afford that.

Should he undress her now and take her right here in the carriage? He glanced out the window and realized there would not be enough time. He cursed beneath his breath. How would he be able to deny himself until afternoon?

17

When the coach jolted to a stop in the court-yard of Greystones, Emerald opened her eyes, stretched sensuously, then quickly extracted herself from Sean's lap. Miraculously refreshed, she sprang from the carriage and ran up the steps into the hall.

Kate Kennedy, hands on hips, said, "And about time!" She took in the evening gown. "Has the devil of a man kept ye up all night?"

"We stayed at the town house in Merrion Row."

Kate rolled her eyes. "Then my question still stands. Has the devil of a man kept ye up all night?"

Emerald was beginning to appreciate Kate's ribald humor. "Kate, I'm starving. Go and raid Mary Malone's kitchen for me while I see how Mrs. McBride is coming along. Then you can come upstairs and help me change while I tell you what a grand time I had."

It took a few minutes before Sean was in any condition to climb from the coach. When he entered the house he went directly upstairs, his senses still saturated with the feel and the scent of her. Now he needed to taste her, to enjoy her to the full, and he intended to spend the entire afternoon indulging in carnal knowledge.

He moved swiftly across his room and opened the adjoining door between their bedchambers. He knew the first thing she would do was remove the crimson velvet gown, and he wanted nothing to impede his view.

He waited what seemed an interminable length of time, yet still Emerald did not come. *What the hellfire is keeping her?* he wondered impatiently. He paced for another ten minutes, then decided to make good use of his time by undressing. He stripped to the buff, then adjusted the door so it was slightly more ajar; he didn't want anything to impede Emerald's view either.

Suddenly, to his great consternation, her chamber filled with chattering women. He heard Mrs. McBride along with her gaggle of

220

sewing assistants and wished them all at the back of beyond. He took a deep breath, held on to his temper and schooled himself to cool his ardor for a short time. He was filled with dismay when he glimpsed armfuls of garments being brought in and piled on the bed for Emerald's approval.

Then Kate Kennedy came to the adjoining door that stood ajar. Her eyes ran up and down the length of the earl's lithe body, frankly admiring such rampant male splendor. "Ye might as well put yer clothes back on. She has a dozen outfits to try before she puts you on for size." Then she firmly shut the door.

"*Bloody women!*" They were in a conspiracy against him. Slowly, reluctantly, Sean put his breeches back on and went to his wardrobe for a fresh shirt. He knew he must be patient a little while longer, and hadn't he attended the finest school in the world for honing patience? The trick was to focus on what you wanted, know with absolute certainty you were going to get it, and be ready for any opportunity presenting itself that would allow you to achieve your goal.

He laughed at his own folly. Surely fucking one small female wasn't a matter of life or death. He pulled on a pair of black leather gloves and went down to Mary Malone's kitchen. He had forgotten he had another appetite to slake.

Two FitzGerald captains were holding court with the kitchen staff, telling tall tales about the peculiar items that were considered edible in the Canary Islands.

"An' if ye think that strange, wait till ye hear of their mating customs."

Mary Malone lifted her apron to wipe the tears of mirth from her cheeks.

The men sobered as Sean joined them. They had been on a mission and were eager to tell him all his plans had been carried out with amazing success.

"Both ships?" Sean asked sharply.

"Aye, the information you gave us was dead on," David confirmed. "The poor buggers might never find their way back to the Ivory Coast, but free them we did."

"Any trouble selling the ships?"

"Nay, we flogged both in Gibraltar an' divided the money amongst the crew as ye ordered, but I think ye were too generous. We should have kept the ships."

"No, David. You can never get the stink off a slave ship." Sean's nostrils filled with the remembered stench of men imprisoned together aboard a ship, and suddenly he wasn't hungry after all. "Any worthwhile cargo?" he inquired.

David FitzGerald grinned like a Cheshire cat. "Forty-two-inch brown Bess infantry muskets—a thousand of 'um."

"Good work, Davie. We'll distribute them to our crews. Paddy Burke knows which ships need extra arms."

"He already gave us a list an' took one of the muskets to show Shamus."

"I'll have a few kegs sent down for your men.

Tomorrow will be soon enough to give them their new orders."

"The more diabolical the plot, the more they enjoy themselves!"

"Then they should be jubilant," Sean said dryly. He left through the kitchen door and headed toward the stables. All at once he stopped and lifted his head like a stag scenting the wind. The opportunity he needed was at hand. He ran back into the house, taking the stairs two at a time. Without knocking, Sean strode into her bed-chamber.

"Emerald, it's raining!"

A dozen pairs of female eyes gazed at him, but he spoke as if he and Emerald were alone. "You've never experienced anything as soft as an Irish summer rain." He held out his hand. "Come, walk with me."

The Greystones servants exchanged glances that implied the earl was mad, but Emerald, wearing a new pale green muslin, smiled with delight. "That will be all for now, ladies. I'm going out to play in the rain."

Handclasped, they opened the kitchen door and went outside.

"Sit on the step," he invited. When she obliged, he pulled off his boots, then knelt down before her to remove her slippers. "You must go barefoot in Irish rain, it's one of the rules." He lifted her toes to his lips before he released her foot, and she was thrilled at the pretty gesture.

He pulled her to her feet. "We must run like hell and dodge the raindrops until we get to the stables. Are you ready?"

"Ready, milord!"

They dashed across the courtyard, ran laughing through the stables, and came to a halt at the rear exit that opened onto the meadow. He examined the green muslin covering her shoulders and breasts. "Are you sure you avoided every last one?"

"I did! Dry as a bone," she declared.

"Good. Now we stroll."

Hand in hand they sauntered into the meadow. Before they had gone a yard the lush green grass soaked them to their knees. "Feel how soft and warm." They turned up their faces in worship. "Catch it on your lashes; let it drip off your nose."

"It's magic—I can smell it," she cried, then put out her tongue to taste it.

"Is it good?"

"Delicious," she declared.

He lifted her arm and sniffed her wet skin with appreciation, then he ran his tongue from her wrist, up the inside of her arm, to her elbow, licking the raindrops as they ran in tiny rivulets. "Mmm, rain-drenched skin is intoxicating. Try it," he invited.

She cast him a provocative look from beneath lashes spiky with wetness, then set her tongue to his throat where his soaking shirt fell away. His hands closed over her buttocks and he pressed her against his body as his cock lengthened and hardened. "The rain makes everything grow," he whispered.

"I told you it was magic." She eluded his embrace and went dancing across the meadow, shoulder deep in wildflowers. He watched her go, then followed in hot pursuit. When he caught her, he pulled her beneath him in the long grass and lay full on top of her.

She laughed up into his dark face, falling more in love with him every minute.

"Wriggle your shoulders. You have to get wet all the way through to your skin."

Emerald wriggled more than her shoulders, and Sean rolled his eyes in mock bliss. "Now you," she said imperiously, and he rolled with her in the wet grass until she lay atop him.

Outrageously he rubbed all his hard body parts into her soft ones and left the both of them breathless with desire.

Emerald didn't want their play to end. Sean could tease unmercifully, then suddenly stop, leaving her devastated. This time she wanted to take him beyond the limits of his control. She sensed a pattern in his play. When she advanced, he retreated; if she withdrew, would he become ravenous?

"Sean, will you take me into the garden?"

His eyes, silver as the rain that drenched them, looked up into hers with unconcealed lust. He watched her luscious breasts rise and fall. She was panting with need, in a fever to have him plunge inside her. Only a moment ago she was writhing all over him. Why in hell was she asking to go into the garden?

With a sweet and charming patience he did not feel, he replied, "When you ask so prettily, how can I refuse you anything? It would be my greatest pleasure to take you into the garden."

He followed her from the meadow, across Greystones's wide lawns, and into the magnificent garden. The drenched roses temporarily hung their heads; when the sun came out again they would lift their faces and shamelessly flaunt their beauty.

Emerald walked beneath the spreading branches of a young copper beech that sheltered her from the rain.

"Don't move," Sean ordered. Framed beneath the leaves, she looked like a beautiful water sprite. He reached up to a branch and gave it a vigorous shake. A million water droplets cascaded down upon her, making her laughter ring out like a silvery bell. As they strolled past the resplendent flower beds, the fragrance was heady enough to make them drunk.

Sean reached out to pluck a foxglove blossom, then held the tiny chalice to her lips so she could drink from it. Seized with playful mischief, Emerald waded into the pond and bent to pluck a water lily. Its curved petals, shaped like a bowl, were brimful of rain. With a provocative laugh she tossed the water all over him.

Without hesitation he waded in after her and, with a great whoop of victory, lifted her high in his arms. With his mouth against her ear, he whispered, "Now comes the best part, where we rub each other dry."

He carried her through the grand front

entrance to the foot of the staircase. With his lips still against her ear he coaxed, "Put your wet legs around me."

Emerald complied, her wet arms about his neck, her legs about his hips. In this intimate position he climbed the stairs, then paused at his bedchamber door to open it.

She lifted her face so that they could look deeply into each other's eyes. "Isn't this where I kick you in the groin, spit in your eye, and let you cool your heels for the next two hours?"

His humor had deserted him. He brought his face close to hers without breaking eye contact. "No! This is where you yield up to me everything I desire." He slammed the door shut behind them with a bare foot, then set her down in the middle of the chamber. "Don't move an eyelash!"

He pushed back the drapes from the tall windows. The sky was clearing now and the late-afternoon light flooded in. He brought a pile of towels and dropped them at their feet. First he dried her hair, rubbing it furiously until it fell about her shoulders in a thousand tiny black ringlets.

Emerald was mesmerized by the deliberation of his actions. He was in no hurry, but seemed to have a definite plan in mind for this loving. He was meticulous about which parts he wanted uncovered first and which he wanted concealed. He undid the top of her muslin dress, which was completely drenched and clinging to her body. He slowly peeled it away from her breasts, then did the same with her now transparent shift. He pushed the garments down until they were below her waist, then stared at her breasts hungrily.

Freed of their constraint, they sprang forward impudently, all shiny and wet from the warm rain. She watched him peel off one black leather glove, then thought he was reaching down for a towel, but he was not. Instead, both hands went beneath her skirts and slowly slid up her wet legs and thighs. When he reached her bare buttocks he pressed her forward, then dipped his head so that he could tongue the wetness from her breasts.

As his mouth moved ever closer to her nipples, so, too, did his hands slide round to her mons. At the same moment his tongue snaked out to lick the taut tip of her breast, his thumbs pressed open the tiny wet folds between her legs. He felt her body begin to quiver from the sensations he was arousing. He gently blew warm breath on the hard little buds and watched them ruche even tighter.

"It excites a woman when a man puts his hands up her gown. It makes her think he is doing something wicked and makes her feel very naughty."

Emerald gasped as he drew one fingertip along her cleft. What he said was absolutely true. He was wicked and she was naughty. Already she wanted to scream from excitement, yet knew with a knowledge as old as Eve's he had only just begun.

He licked and tasted her from throat to

navel in a very delicate manner. Then his mouth devoured her breasts. At the same time his thumbs, one bare, one sheathed in black leather, alternately drew circles about the rosebud that nestled in the damp black curls at the tip of her cleft.

Emerald uttered incoherent love sounds as he played with her body and aroused sensations she'd never dreamed a woman could feel. "Ooh, ahhh, ummm, oooh." As she surrendered her body to his hands and mouth, expressing her joy with such surprise, he could tell she had never been pleasured before. A wild thrill ran through him. Her husband had taken her virginity, but he had never been her lover.

"Now it's time for you to watch what I do to you," he murmured intensely, "and for me to watch you receive your pleasure." He pushed the pale green muslin down over her hips, all the way to her ankles, then helped her step daintily from the rain-soaked garments. As she stood before him in naked splendor, Sean's dark pewter eyes made love to her.

He made her feel utterly beautiful. Then he picked up a towel, rolled it into a tight rope, and slipped it between her legs. He drew it back and forth, slowly, sensually. He watched her eyes become sultry as he initiated her into foreplay, watched the scream build in her throat as the stimulation became almost too much for her to bear. Then he enfolded her in his arms so the kissing could begin.

He took possession of her mouth just as her

scream erupted. He kissed her until her scream turned to sighs. Sean was certain her woman's center had never built and erupted in climax. He wanted to teach her body to be so sexually responsive, she would come at his touch.

He slid down on his knees so that her lower body lay across his hard thighs. Then he slipped one long finger up inside her and held it still. Her eyelids were heavy with sensuality as his mouth covered hers. By kisses alone he intended to bring her to orgasm; feel her sheath tighten, throb, and pulsate as it gripped and squeezed his finger.

Emerald's thighs sprawled open wantonly, inviting him to thrust, to plunge, to slide, to surge, but his finger remained motionless. His tongue, however, did all the things to her mouth that her body craved. At last he was rewarded as he became aware of a pulse point deep within. It fluttered erratically and the walls of her sheath tightened as her tension built. Her mouth opened fully so she would not impede the hot, sliding friction of his tongue.

Sean felt the exquisite pulsations upon his finger, feather light at first, then becoming stronger with a rhythm that matched her heartbeat. Sean began to ravish her mouth with savage abandon, mastering her with his tongue until he felt her yield, above and below.

Emerald spasmed, squeezing the entire length of his finger. Her climax was so hard and fast, he thought her walls might crush him. She cried out into his mouth and thought she might faint from pleasure.

He was so pleased with her generous response, he wanted to reward her. He slipped his finger from her and covered her entire mons with his cupped palm. Then he caressed, squeezed, and stroked until her hot shudders melted into liquid tremors.

Suddenly the air was rent with a sharp crack. Emerald's eyes flew open and a jolt went through her body. "What was that?" she cried.

"It was a gunshot." Sean was already on his feet, heading toward the door. "My father."

"Your father?" Emerald asked incredulously.

Sean quit the chamber without further explanation.

Emerald sat back on her heels, stunned by the revelation. She had seen no evidence of Shamus O'Toole at Greystones and assumed Sean's father dead along with the rest of his family. Her hands tried to disentangle her damp dress from her shift. She pulled the muslin over her nakedness, then followed in Sean's wake.

She ran outside and the sound of men's voices drew her across the lawns in the direction of the sea. A small group of men had gathered on the causeway that led to the harbor below. She stopped, hesitating to go farther, until suddenly she recognized the figure of her brother, Johnny. Fear gripped her throat as the men helped him to his feet and the realization dawned that Johnny was the one who had been shot at.

18

Emerald picked up the hem of her wet skirt and her bare feet fairly flew across the distance that separated her from her brother. "Johnny, Johnny, are you all right?"

Though he was white and looked shaken, his voice was calm enough. "Emerald, I'm fine."

She threw her arms about him, almost sobbing with relief.

The English crew who had accompanied John on the *Swallow* stood glaring at the Irish crewmen commanded by the FitzGeralds. Tempers were so explosive, a brawl threatened.

Sean gave terse orders. "There will be no trouble; get back to your vessels." The men cast wary glances in the direction of the gatehouse tower, but obeyed the voice of command.

"Someone tried to kill you!" Emerald shook her brother to make him understand.

"Em, if Shamus O'Toole had aimed to kill, I'd be a dead man now."

Sean grinned at John and thumped him on the back. "You have the right of it. Let's go and get a drink into you."

They walked off like the best of friends, leaving her with her mouth open. She had disappeared from home over a week before, yet John wasn't surprised to find her at Greystones. Sean and her brother seemed thick as thieves. Did he come here often? If so, why the hell had someone been shooting at him? *Bloody men! If they think they are going to keep me barefoot and ignorant, they can think again!*

Emerald's Irish was up. She was never going to suppress her anger again. She intended to vent it on someone. She headed for the gatehouse in search of a victim. She gave a perfunctory knock and walked straight in. She was met by Paddy Burke, who was on his way out.

"Who's doing all the shooting?" she demanded.

"One shot," he corrected.

Her eyes blazed her anger. "Who?" she demanded, hands on hips.

Paddy Burke jerked his thumb toward the tower. "Himself."

She watched him make a hasty departure before she headed up the stone stairs.

Shamus O'Toole sat by a tower window, gripping a spyglass. Beside him, four guns stood against the stone wall.

"You almost killed my brother!" She flung the accusation with angry passion, not caring about the consequences.

Shamus chuckled with glee. "I wasn't trying to kill him or he'd be dead. I only wanted to scare the shit out of him."

"Well, you didn't! You scared it out of me! Why did you shoot at him?"

"He's a Montague," Shamus explained.

"So am I."

"Never boast about that, lass." His bright blue eyes examined her from head to foot. "Yer a FitzGerald by the looks of ye; now, *there's* something to brag about. Come over here to the window and let me have a gander at ye."

She moved forward, not because she wanted to, but because she didn't want him to think she feared him.

"Ye have a definite look of my Kathleen; no wonder Sean is enamored of ye. Have ye been walking in the rain, lass? She loved to do that too." His eyes took on a faraway look and Emerald had the uncanny feeling he had gone back to the past. She decided Shamus O'Toole was a bit unstable. He probably wasn't responsible for his actions. Whyever would he live up here like a recluse when the magnificent Greystones was so spacious? Someone must lock up the firearms. She would speak to Sean about it tonight.

"Go an' get those wet clothes off, Beauty; ye'll be late fer dinner."

Emerald had the distinct impression that Shamus thought he was speaking to his wife. "I—I will.... I'll go and do it right away."

Back in her chamber the mirrors showed her she looked like a ragtag Gypsy girl. She chose a lavender-blue silk to boost her confidence and her courage. She had a lot of questions she intended to pose. She whirled about as the connecting door opened.

"My love, I'm sorry we were so rudely interrupted before, but I had no idea your brother would drop in on us today."

She refused to blush. "Where is he?" she demanded.

"Why, in a guest bedchamber, of course, two doors from your own. Shall we collect him for dinner?"

Emerald bit her lip; she wanted to talk to Johnny alone. Sean held out a gallant arm and it would have seemed childish to rebuff him. When they stepped into the hall, John was there before them and they went down to the dining room together.

Sean pulled out her chair. "Will you sit between us, my love?"

Johnny smiled at her. "I've never seen you look so radiant, Em."

Then the two men engaged in conversation, totally excluding her. They spoke of merchant vessels, cargoes, and shipping routes. They spoke of the Admiralty, politics, the House of Commons, the House of Lords. They spoke of Prime Minister Pitt, of Newcastle, Bedford, and King George. They spoke a sort of code, which they understood perfectly, but she did not. John said things like: *that information you asked me to get* and *that private matter,* while Sean referred to *that confidential bit of business* and *I have another agenda for you.*

After the main course they made small talk, they joked, they laughed. The subject changed to horses. Sean promised to take him riding on the Curragh, and John asked about visiting Maynooth and someone called Nan FitzGerald.

Emerald listened to them in amazement. How dare they act as if she weren't present? She had expected John to explain why he was here and Sean to explain about his father and the shot. It was clearly a conspiracy!

She threw down her napkin, then banged her fist on the table, making the silverware dance a jig. She jumped to her feet. "Stop it!"

Both men gave her their polite attention.

She tossed her curls and gave Sean the back of her head. Then she spoke to John. "I've been missing for a week. How did you find me?"

"Father told me you were at Greystones."

"Ohmigod! How did he find out?"

"I informed him, of course," Sean said smoothly. "Where's the pleasure in wounding your enemy if you don't twist the knife, then rub salt in the wound?"

"Did they send you to fetch me back?"

Johnny turned to Sean. "Actually, they sent me to see how much money you'd accept for her return."

Sean laughed. "Tell them possession is nine-tenths of the law. That goes for the ship as well as your sister. I'm keeping them both."

"You don't mind making it difficult for me, do you?" John asked wryly.

"Not in the least. Adversity is a good character builder."

"Well, I suppose the Montague Line will have to manage with one less ship." John shrugged philosophically.

"Well, actually, it will be three ships less, this week. The slavers have vanished into thin air."

"Thank God for that," John said fervently.

"God had nothing to do with it, I assure you," Sean said pleasantly.

"Damn you both, you are doing it again!" Emerald cried.

Emerald's behavior shocked her brother. "Wherever did you learn such bad manners?"

"It's all right, I taught them to her. I like my women wild and willful so I can tame them."

She picked up her water glass and flung the contents in Sean O'Toole's mocking face. "I believe insanity runs in your family!" After pronouncing her judgment she regally swept from the dining room.

Emerald paced about her chamber, she flung the curtains across the dark window, she thumped the bed pillows in an effort to vent her frustration. She knew Sean had a domineering personality and though she hadn't understood all of their conversation, she gathered he had some sort of hold over Johnny and was using him like a pawn in a chess game.

Emerald knew she would get little out of Sean, so she had no intention of wasting her time in that direction. If she was to learn what was going on, she would have to pry it out of Johnny. When she heard a low knock on the door, she hoped it was her brother, but instead it was Mrs. McBride.

"I've brought the night rails and bed robe the earl ordered, ma'am."

"Why, thank you, Mrs. McBride." Emerald was startled. She hadn't known a thing about the intimate items he'd had specially made for her.

"Actually, the bed robe was my own idea. You'd freeze to death in the things he asked me to make." She explained in a low voice, "Men like silky things. Practical considerations fly out the window when it comes bedtime."

A blush dusted Emerald's cheekbones. "That was most thoughtful."

"Molly and I will be returning to Dublin tomorrow, now that most of your wardrobe is finished. When the other items the earl ordered are ready, we'll send them on to Greystones immediately."

Emerald had no idea what other garments had been ordered. Sean had a secretive side and took pleasure in surprising her. "I want to thank you, Mrs. McBride. You do such lovely work. I never had clothes that suited me before."

"Sure an' it's a rare pleasure to make garments for a lady as beautiful as you. I hope you'll use my services again. Good-bye."

Kate Kennedy came in and made herself busy, lighting the lamps and pulling down the bedclothes. Every now and then she sneaked a glance at a visibly furious Emerald.

"Are they still at table, Kate?"

"Faith, no, they've gone over to the gatehouse to hatch their plots. Likely be up half the night."

Emerald could not understand why her brother would spend the evening with a man who had shot at him. "Kate, is Shamus O'Toole...unstable?"

"Aye, his legs are almost useless."

"No, I mean up here." Emerald tapped her temple.

"Ye mean doolally? Faith, no. Mr. Burke is his legs, but his brain still thinks around corners." Kate thought she had her answer. No wonder the fur had been flying in the dining room, if Emerald had criticized Sean's father. "By the by, don't go wanderin' about outside tonight. There's three shipload of sailors anchored at the jetty, and ye know what crews are like after a keg or two."

"Thanks, Kate. I'm going to have a bath and go to bed." When she was alone, Emerald examined the pile of nightgowns. They were exquisite. She selected a white silk, embroidered with French knots, picked up the soft lamb's-wool robe, and took them with her to the bathing room.

When she returned an hour later, the mirrors in her chamber showed her how pretty she was tonight. She looked like a bride in the delicate white night rail. *"Get hold of yourself and stop dreaming,"* she bade her reflection. She wrapped herself in the lamb's-wool robe and slipped down the hall. She would await Johnny in his chamber. Emerald curled up in a big wing chair, prepared to wait all night if necessary. She was determined to learn everything her brother knew.

"Em, what in the world are you doing here in the dark?"

Johnny Montague set the candelabra on the mantel and lit the lamps.

Emerald had dozed fitfully while awaiting him, but she came wide awake immediately. "I'm in the dark because that is exactly where men like to keep their women! You *must* tell me what's going on."

"How much do you know?" John asked tentatively.

"I *know* nothing. I *suspect* Sean is using you as a pawn, forcing you to work against Father."

Johnny took hold of his sister's hands. "Oh, Em, he thinks he is forcing me, but never was there a more willing pawn since the dawn of time. Sean thinks this is his revenge, but it is mine!"

"What are you going to do?"

"We are going to ruin them. Don't press me for details, you are better off not knowing."

"I know why you and I hate Father, but I don't know what happened to make the O'Tooles hate the Montagues."

"Hasn't Sean told you anything?" Johnny asked incredulously.

"Sean keeps his mouth shut. The only time he opens it is to say something amusing or to woo me."

Johnny let go of her hands and took a turn about the richly appointed bedchamber. Then he took a deep breath and sank into a chair facing hers. "When Father learned Joseph O'Toole was heir to the Earldom of Kildare, he made plans to betroth you to him. Then he informed the authorities that Edward FitzGerald

240

was committing treason by arming the rebels. Father knew all the details because he was the one who supplied the guns. He decided to get rid of the earl so you would become a countess the moment you wed.

"When the English arrested their grandfather, Joseph and Sean were sent out of Ireland to London. But by the time they arrived, Father had learned that our mother and Joseph O'Toole were lovers. He went mad. All his murderous scheming had gone for naught, and he plotted his revenge.

"The very night the brothers arrived in London, Father took us all on a debauch to the Divan Club. The minute we got back to the ship a brawl broke out. It was all a plan for my father to rid himself of Joseph O'Toole. Jack Raymond helped him. Either one or both stabbed Joseph, and Father ordered the brothers be strung up by the thumbs. By dawn Joseph was dead and Sean delirious with fever. His thumbs turned black. I was there when they had to chop one off."

"They chopped one off?" she whispered with disbelief.

"Why the devil do you think he always wears gloves? Anyway, that wasn't the worst of it. No sooner did Sean regain consciousness than Father had him arrested for the murder of his own brother. It was a swift Admiralty trial with Father presiding and Jack Raymond the chief witness. I am ashamed to say I was paralyzed by fear of Father and never uttered a word in Sean's defense.

"He was sentenced to ten years aboard the hulks. It was a death sentence, of course. Men don't survive the living hell aboard the hulks for more than a few months. But Sean O'Toole survived. He lived on hatred for five whole years before he escaped."

As he talked, Emerald's face turned white. Her eyes closed against the tears that scalded her eyelids. A lump wedged in her throat, almost choking her.

"Are you all right, Em?"

She couldn't answer him.

"I'm surprised Sean can even look at me or stomach talking to me because I'm a Montague. How can he bear to touch you? He must love you very much, Emerald, to overlook the fact that you, too, are a Montague."

Emerald's hand went to her throat to try to ease the unbearable ache that threatened to suffocate her.

"He escaped only a couple of days before your wedding; far too late to stop it. So he simply came and took you. Laws don't mean much to Sean O'Toole, especially English laws."

"Why did you never—" Her voice cracked, her throat closed.

"Why did I never tell you? Because I knew you loved him. I wasn't blind or deaf. You once called him your Irish Prince. I couldn't break your heart, Em. After Mother left, your life was such a total misery, I couldn't add to your unhappiness."

She wanted to ask why he had let her marry

Jack Raymond, but it was unfair to blame Johnny. She had made the decision. Dear God, how she loathed her husband! She could see now that he had married her so he could become a Montague. The name was synonymous with evil. It was a curse. She'd have none of it. She was a FitzGerald, through and through.

Johnny poured a glass of Irish whisky from a decanter and brought it to her. Emerald shook her head. She knew she could not speak, let alone swallow. She lifted her hand to his cheek in a silent caress, then she pulled her robe more closely about her and went back to her room.

She walked quietly to the connecting door and leaned against it. The ache in her throat had expanded to encompass her heart. She glanced down and saw the light go out beneath the door. Emerald had never needed him as much as she did at this moment, yet she wanted to give, not take. She wanted to wrap her love about him so that nothing would ever hurt him again.

She saw her reflection in the mirror and knew she must compose herself. She moved to the washstand, poured water from the jug, and bathed her eyes. She sat on the edge of the bed and tried to breathe calmly. If she didn't get some air inside her, she would suffocate. After a few minutes she was able to take some shallow breaths, but she knew she could not get into bed.

The need to be with Sean overwhelmed

her. He was her love, her life. She must tell him, show him, what he meant to her. She picked up the lamp and turned the knob of the connecting door. It swung open silently as she stepped into his chamber, then moved with slow trepidation toward the bed.

As he saw the light approaching, Sean pulled himself up onto his elbows. "Emerald?"

With all her heart she wanted to say his name, but again it was impossible for her to speak. As she moved toward the bed, Sean saw that her hands trembled on the lamp and her eyes were blinded by tears. He sat up all the way and took the lamp from her hands. "What is it? What's wrong?" he demanded.

Her legs turned to water and she sank down on the bed.

He quickly concealed his left hand beneath the covers and reached for her with the other one. The defensive gesture undid her. The floodgates opened and she began to sob.

Sean's fingers splayed into her hair and he pressed her head to his chest. "Hush now, hush." His lips touched her brow gently. "Whatever it is, I'll make it better," he crooned. His words only made things worse. He cradled her against him for another minute, then bent his lips to her ear. "You're going to have to tell me, love."

Emerald lifted her head and swallowed hard. "Johnny told me what they did to you."

19

Sean's eyes flashed their terrible dark anger. "Damn him, he should never have told you!" he ground out.

"Sean, I love you so much, I can't bear it.... I can't bear it." She rocked back and forth, keening in the true Irish way.

He ground his teeth in frustration. "And if you cry, *I* cannot bear it!"

He lifted her chin and gazed at her. She looked so unbelievably young. In the white silk night rail she also looked innocent, pure, and untainted. But she wouldn't be for long, not if he had his vengeful way. "Don't shed tears over me, Emerald, I'm not worth it."

She smiled tremulously. "You have a dark side. Let me love you." She had a need to purge him of all the brutality he had suffered.

"It isn't merely a dark side, Emerald, it's black—beyond redemption. Go from me before it's too late for you."

For answer she reached beneath the covers and took his hand.

"No!" He jerked as if a red-hot iron had touched him.

"Sean, I love you. I love all of you. Your hand is part of you, please don't hide it from me."

"Here, then, damn you, look at the ugly thing!" He threw back the bedcovers to reveal the scarred stump of his thumb. His dark eyes watched her face intently for her reaction. He thought she did a creditable job of hiding her disgust. But it would be another matter if he tried to touch her. He never wanted to see her flinch from him.

His eyes widened as he saw her reach out to take his hand in hers. She drew it to her cheek in a caress, then she dropped a dozen tiny kisses upon the stub. Her eyes flooded and spilled over, dropping wetness on his scarred thumb.

Sean groaned as if making a decision against his better judgment. "Come. Come in to me." He pulled back the covers and Emerald slipped into the bed with him. He enfolded her in his arms and drew her trembling softness against his hard naked length. He cradled her gently in strong arms, stroking her hair and her back, while she sweetly clung to him.

Why didn't you run from me, Emerald?

Why did you make it so easy for me?

He cuddled her until she cried herself out. When her sobs subsided and she lay with her cheek pressed against his heart with his heat and strength seeping into her body, Emerald had never felt so safe and secure. Lying in the same bed together was like being in their own private, warm cocoon. This was what she wanted for the rest of her life.

She lifted her face so she could gaze up at him. His dark beauty was irresistible and she reached out a fingertip to trace the black eyebrow, the slanting cheekbone, and the dark stubble along the square jaw. It gave her such pleasure, she suddenly wanted to explore all of him.

His body was as yet unknown to her and she wanted to learn the feel of every hard, sculpted muscle. She wanted to look at him, to smell him, to taste him. She realized it might take her years to find out what was in his mind or even his heart, because he was not ready to share his inner self with anyone. But he was now willing to share his body with her, secrets and all. And for Emerald it was enough.

If she loved him without reserve, perhaps his inner wounds would heal so he would trust her enough to share his essence with her. His eyes were fathomless as she gazed up into them, but slowly his hands came up to cup her face, then his lips traced every feature from temple to chin. He was leading the way.

She duplicated his caresses, cupping his face, then setting her lips to cherish the planes and hollows of his dark beauty. Before she was done, he moved to her throat and shoulders, feathering kisses, nibbling her silky flesh, whispering love words. She followed his lead, running her lips down the powerful column of his throat, rubbing her cheek along his collarbone, caressing the sinews of his wide shoulders.

Sean's hands stroked down her body, taking the white silk with them. The feel of naked skin against bare flesh was so exciting, she wanted to scream. Yet his first caress was not on an intimate spot. Instead, he opened her hand and dropped a kiss inside her palm, then his lips traced the tiny blue veins at her wrist. He slid the tip of his tongue along her inner arm to her elbow, and she felt a thrill run up inside her armpit.

By exploring her so slowly and sensually he was arousing and heightening all her senses. Emerald wanted to do the same for Sean. She came up over him and lifted his arms above his head. Then she began her love play in the sensitive hollows, nuzzling, whispering, inhaling the heady male scent of him. She trailed kisses up his raised arms until her mouth could reach no higher, then she moved her body up on his, so that she could kiss his fingers and then his thumbs.

Her breasts brushed his face, filling his nostrils with her woman's scent. He closed his eyes, inhaling, savoring her awakening passion. Then without warning she took his injured thumb into her mouth and suckled softly, sensually, proving to him that even the scars on his body aroused her.

Sean, suddenly seized with a savage frenzy of lust, wanted to ravish her. He felt like a dark raptor, needing to seize his prey and devour it. He managed to crush down his need for depravity. There would be time for animal ferocity later. This first time Emerald must enjoy every moment.

To compensate for his rough elemental sexual cravings, he brought his hands to her waist and lifted her until his lips brushed against her mons, then his mouth took possession of her. Emerald cried out. When he thrust inside her with his hot tongue, it was as if she had been pierced by lightning!

In her wildest dreams she never could have imagined a man doing such a thing, yet she loved it so much, she opened wide to him, unfurling her petals like a flower in the hot sun. She writhed and arched with so much pleasure, Sean decided to draw it out, curling his tongue to flick her tiny bud between hot, wet thrusts. When at last he tasted her cream, his mouth became unquenchable and her cries could be heard in the highest tower of Castle Lies.

The bedclothes were long gone from their sexual exertions and they hungrily devoured each other with their eyes. "If only I could do that for you," Emerald gasped.

"What?" he asked huskily.

"Make love to you with my mouth."

"Little innocent," he murmured.

"What?" She reached out to touch his engorged sex. Sean almost came out of his skin. "Oh! It is so thick and hard, I had no idea it was so sensitive. Do you think my lips and tongue could give you pleasure?"

"Perhaps a little," he said wryly.

Her lips touched him lightly at first, uncertain of what to expect or what his reaction would be. Sean's response was so volatile, clearly showing her how much gratification he received from her ministrations, she became bolder. Wildly curious about the shape, color, texture, and taste of him, she lost her apprehension about his size. In fact, she was thrilled when she increased his length and thickness by teasing him until he became completely engorged.

"That's enough, Beauty," he gasped, threading his fingers into her hair and gently pulling her from him before he spilled. She was flushed with the knowledge of her erotic power over him, and Sean had never seen a woman more beautiful in her passion. He knew this was the moment he had been waiting for. Now in her pride and passion he would make her wholly, gloriously his.

He moved above her and opened her silken thighs wide. He positioned the throbbing head of his shaft against her tiny bud and slowly, firmly impaled her with one long thrust. Her sheath was so hot she scalded him, and he cried out in his passion. When he was sheathed to the hilt, he whispered all the things he would do to her, how it would make her feel and how exquisite it felt to be deep inside her at last.

Emerald was in a fever of need as she felt him fill her with his thick manroot. She wanted to yield all to his demanding body and wrapped her legs high about his back. When he started to thrust with savage strokes, the hot sliding friction aroused her to a frenzy. She loved the weight of his body on hers, adored the throbbing, pulsating fullness deep inside her, reveled in the exciting male scent of his skin, as he unleashed the fierce desire that had been riding him for so long.

She was half mad with passion, crying and biting his shoulders with sharp little teeth. She felt him take her higher and higher, as if climbing to the peak of a towering precipice.

She clung there for heart-stopping moments, then flung herself with him over the edge in an ecstasy of abandon. As he erupted into her, she cried out with the pure sensual pleasure his demanding body brought her.

Emerald held him there, not wanting him to withdraw from her. She stroked his back endlessly from shoulders to buttocks. She kissed him fiercely, in a fever to lavish him with adoration. He had made her feel luxuriant, equally sharing and enjoying the joining of their bodies, and it gave her such heady delight, she felt she could never have enough of him.

Then suddenly her fingertips felt the ridges on his back and she became aware of the scars that had been inflicted upon his body. Emerald was consumed by a raging fury. It mattered little to her that his dark beauty was marred, but when she imagined how powerless he had been and how much self-control he had needed to survive, it almost broke her heart. She wanted to kill her father, kill Jack Raymond, kill anyone at all who had given him pain.

As heat leapt between them, Sean sensed her anger. He rolled onto his back, taking her with him so that she lay cushioned on top of him. He knew of only one way to assuage her fury and set about rekindling her passion. He threaded his fingers into her hair and brought her lips down to his. He explored her mouth so intimately, she soon lost her ability to think clearly. His tongue thrust with such drugging strokes, while his hands made such possessive demands, that she gave herself up to his dominant insistence.

Before dawn, Sean made her replete. A delicious lassitude enveloped her, so that even her eyelashes felt too heavy to lift. She gathered her strength and stirred in his arms. "I must go back to my own room before the servants find me here."

His arm tightened around her like a steel band. "There will be no furtive sneaking about between bedchambers. I intend to carry you to bed every night and awaken you with kisses each morning. Like this." His lips brushed her brow, moved lightly over her temples, then gently kissed each eyelid. By the time his mouth covered hers, she was ready with an uninhibited welcome.

She was soft with surfeit, warm and pliant and generous enough to give him anything he desired, anytime. Sean knew this was the way he wanted her; this was the way he was going to keep her. He slipped from the bed and tucked the covers about her. "We are going riding across this county and the next, this morning."

When Emerald groaned, Sean laughed at her. "Not you, Beauty. I'll tell Johnny you rode all night." He leered at her.

"Sean!"

"Mmm, does that blush cover your lovely titties?" He pulled down the sheet and dropped a kiss upon each breast. Then he cupped them possessively as his playful look became intense. "I've wanted you since you were sixteen...you were well worth the wait, Beauty. Rest today so we can make the night explode."

At his words Emerald felt every naked inch of her skin shiver with gooseflesh, yet at the same time her insides were on fire. How could she wait until night?

Sean purposely chose two of the finest Thoroughbreds at Greystones for their long ride. The turf was luxuriously thick on the great plain, springing back into place as their horses' hooves thundered over it. Sean O'Toole knew Johnny Montague was in his element by the rapturous look upon his face and the endless questions he asked about Ireland's superb Thoroughbreds. He listened avidly as Sean told him the rich rolling meadows of Meath bred the finest horses and Kildare County was the center of Irish horse racing.

They spent the afternoon at Maynooth where Sean arranged for the transfer of his grandfather's books to his own library. While he was busy, Sean asked Nan FitzGerald to amuse their visitor. For a moment Johnny felt shy. In the five years since he had met Nan, she had changed from a pretty girl into a beautiful woman. But she hadn't changed on the inside. She was still the sweetest female he had ever encountered.

She put him at ease immediately, even though her own heart was dancing a jig at the sight of the aristocratic young Englishman. To entertain him, and to keep him from the other females of Maynooth, Nan took him up to the castle turrets.

"I'm flattered you remember me."

"Oh, Johnny, I could never forget you; I think of you so often."

"You're not married or spoken for?" he asked eagerly.

Nan quickly shook her head, hoping the news would spur him on, but Johnny flushed at his own boldness and fell silent. Nan decided she couldn't wait another five years to advance their relationship. Like many a young woman before her, she grasped her courage in both hands and plunged in. "Johnny, do you believe in love at first sight?"

"I do," he replied seriously. "That's exactly what happened between my sister Emerald and Sean."

"Is it true that he stole her and seduced her?" Nan asked breathlessly, momentarily diverted from her objective.

"It is, and I know it sounds a wicked thing for him to do, but my sister is so deeply in love, she absolutely glows."

"How romantic...now that I've seen you again, I realize I, too, am in love," Nan said in a rush. As she swayed toward him, Johnny's natural instincts took over. He clasped her hands and drew her close, then, tentatively, he brushed his lips against hers. They kissed, then clung, then kissed again, both carried beyond words by the intensity of their feelings.

When Sean cleared his throat behind them, they sprang apart guiltily. Pretending to be unaware of their newfound intimacy, Sean asked for the pleasure of Nan FitzGerald's company for the rest of the afternoon. They showed Johnny Maynooth's vast stables and pastureland as well as her numerous tenant horse farms for breeding stock. Sean watched his look of longing grow more covetous by the minute.

When Johnny sighed heavily and murmured, "How I wish I'd been born here," Sean knew he had accomplished his purpose. Parading horses as well as the captivating Nan before him was a subtle form of torture.

On the way back to Greystones as Johnny reflected on what he was leaving behind, Sean turned up the torment by reminding him of what lay ahead. "I'll take you and your crew back to London aboard the *Half Moon*. I know you're anxious to return home; will tomorrow be soon enough?"

"You're a cruel sod," Johnny accused wryly.

"Merciless," Sean agreed with mocking silver eyes.

Johnny decided it was a damn good thing Shamus O'Toole had fired the shot. The English crew was convinced he'd missed death by inches. The FitzGeralds had removed all firearms and ammunition from the *Swallow*, giving the English sailors the idea that they were prisoners. Johnny hadn't disabused them of the notion they could be murdered in their bunks at the whim of Sean O'Toole, partly because it was true and partly because it would serve his own purpose when the men were questioned by William Montague.

"In the next weeks, as the Montague Line becomes depleted of its ships, you must advise your father to buy more. I'll provide the financing, of course. Do you foresee any problems with such a plan?"

"I'm a piss-poor sailor, but on dry land my forte is the shipping business. The tedious paperwork is my sole domain. Father relies on me completely." John thought for a minute, then passed along a most useful piece of information. "When it comes to insuring cargoes, I play the odds. At any one time at least two out of ten carry no insurance. It saves a lot of money, so it's pretty standard procedure among the merchant lines."

Sean's look was bland. "I've recently become a shareholder of Lloyd's of London. *I* can tell *you* which Montague vessels are insured, or more to the point, which vessels are not insured."

"Do you leave anything to chance?"

"Very little, Johnny. I had five long years to lay my plans, and since Fate dropped a fortune into my hands when I inherited the earldom, I now have the means to carry out those plans."

Johnny Montague knew he shouldn't have been surprised. Why was it the English always underestimated the Irish? His thoughts flew to Emerald. He hoped she wouldn't make that mistake. For her own sake he hoped she was a match for Sean O'Toole.

Emerald couldn't stop singing. Through her eyes the world seemed different today. Everything and everyone were infinitely more beautiful. The sheen on the rosewood bedroom suite was dazzling, the sunshine on the windowpane turned it to pure gold. When Kate changed the bedsheets they seemed whiter and more crisp, her breakfast tasted like ambrosia, and even the water in the bathtub felt doubly delicious upon her skin.

She filled the house with flowers. Their scent and their colors enchanted her. Her heart was brimful of joy and she wanted everyone to share it with her. In the afternoon she decided to visit Sean's father in the gatehouse. Her feeling of outrage toward him had melted away, leaving only compassion in its wake.

She took an armful of blue and yellow lupines with her, thrusting them at an astonished Mr. Burke. She announced blithely, "It's Emerald FitzGerald, I've come to visit."

Paddy Burke knew by the twinkle in Shamus's eye that he was pleased to have female company.

As she chattered away, she tidied up the tower room, then perched on a stool beside Shamus and accepted his offer of a little French brandy. Her heart overflowed with pity for this man. Because of the Montagues his family had been torn asunder. His beloved wife, Kathleen, must have died of a broken heart when she learned both of her sons were lost to her.

Emerald skillfully guided the conversation so that Shamus could reminisce about the happy times. He was a man who loved to talk, especially if he had a beautiful and attentive audience.

When she departed, both men were sorry to see her leave. "Come back again; you brought the sunshine with you." Shamus beamed.

"I shall, I shall," she promised happily.

Emerald decided to dress for dinner. Of course, it wasn't dinner she dressed for, it was Sean FitzGerald O'Toole. She chose the peacock silk, then wound a wreath of cream rosebuds into her hair.

From her tall bedchamber windows she spotted the two riders while they were still a mile away. She imagined Sean was already scanning Greystones for a glimpse of her. She picked up her skirts and ran to meet him.

The moment he saw her, he was off the horse in a flash. He was every bit as eager as she for their reunion. He opened his arms so she could run into them. Then he picked her up and swung her around. He bit down on her earlobe and said low, "Stab me, is all this elegance just for me?"

She lifted her face to his and murmured, "Are you not the fastidious Earl of Kildare?"

"I am, madam." His swift, passionate kiss took her breath away. "You smell of roses and promises. I shouldn't even touch you until I get the stink of the stables off me."

She sniffed his male scent and rolled her eyes with appreciation. "Horse, mingled with the smell of leather, is an aphrodisiac to me."

"If I thought that was true, I'd forgo the bath and dinner and carry you straight to bed."

When Johnny emerged from the stables, he hung back to give them a private moment together.

Emerald pretended she had only just noticed him. "Oh, dear, I forgot we had company. I suppose we'll have to suffer through dinner after all. Never mind, I had Mary Malone prepare some of your favorite dishes."

Tonight in the dining room it was Johnny who felt left out of things. Though they politely included him in the conversation, Emerald and Sean had eyes only for each other. When dessert was served, Johnny saw that they were actually holding hands beneath the table. *If she can tame the savage beast that lurks inside Sean O'Toole, perhaps she is a match for him,* Johnny mused. Finally, he could bear the longing in their eyes no more and bade them good-night.

Sean set Emerald's feet to the thick-piled carpet, locked their chamber door, and stripped off his leather gloves.

"Don't stop there—let me see all of your secrets," she invited as her fingers began to unfasten the buttons on the bodice of her peacock silk.

"Don't undress. I want the pleasure of disrobing you."

She dropped her hands and watched him hungrily as he made short work of removing his garments. "Do you always get what you want?" she teased.

"With a little Irish charm and a bit of friendly persuasion." His body was all sinew and muscle; his swarthy skin stretched taut over the spare flesh. Jet-black hair curled on his chest, narrowed to a thin line across his flat belly, then curled in profusion over his groin. He was generously endowed, his manroot thick, his sac heavy.

As he walked toward her she saw he was already so hard, his cock jutted straight out from his body. She stood absolutely still while his hands went up beneath her silk skirts. His fingers played with her until her cleft was hot and sleek and creamy, then he braced his legs and lifted her onto his jutting, marble-hard cock.

Her hands clung to his shoulders, her nails digging into the firm flesh. By the time he had unfastened all the buttons of her bodice so that her breasts sprang free, she was panting with need. His tongue toyed with her nipples briefly, but it was enough to turn them into sharp little spears. He knew she needed no more foreplay.

Sean lifted off the silk gown and shift together, then he cupped her bottom and surged up inside her with a powerful thrust, a savage cry erupting from his throat.

The night exploded.

20

Sean enjoyed the aftermath of the storm almost as much as the tempest itself. He lay supine, while Emerald lay prone, full upon him, her head cushioned on his chest. This was how he liked to make her, soft with surfeit. His hands absently stroked her bottom, his lips brushed the top of her head. He felt bemused, beguiled, bewitched. He warned himself not to become too possessive. Their time together was not infinite. It was a means to an end. And it *would* end, he reminded himself.

He felt his sex stir between their bodies. His appetite for this woman was seemingly insatiable. Would he never have enough of her? "I'm taking your brother and his crew back to England tomorrow. Will you come with me? Will you trust me to smuggle you in and out of London? I'm good at it."

Her hand came up between their bodies to squeeze his shaft as it lengthened and swelled against her belly. "In and out, yes, you *are* good at that," she teased, trying to put off the decision. To Emerald, London was synonymous with Montagues, and she never wanted to see either again. Yet the alternative was unde-sirable. She did not want to be separated from this man, not even for a few nights. She raised her face to his. "Must you go?"

He kissed the corners of her mouth. "I'll keep you safe. Will you come?"

She knew she would follow him to the ends of the earth. The corners of her mouth turned up in a secret smile. "Persuade me."

Sean O'Toole's powers of persuasion were for-midable, and not only with women. Before the *Half Moon* docked in London, the Montague crew, to a man, was secretly in his pay.

Emerald bade her brother a tearful good-bye. "Johnny, I'm worried to death about you. How will you face Father? He will be far more livid over losing the *Swallow* than losing me."

Johnny kissed her brow. "He never really expected O'Toole to give you back, and as for the ship, he simply underestimated his enemy. It will be an expensive lesson. Don't worry about me, Emerald. I haven't looked after the Mon-tague finances without feathering my own nest."

Suddenly Emerald felt better about her brother's situation. He had come a long way from the boy who was terrorized by his father.

As it turned out, the timing of John's return proved most fortunate for him. King George had dismissed the Earl of Sandwich from his high post of first lord of the Admiralty because of the irrefutable charges leveled against him.

John Montague found his father at his wits' end.

"Thank God you're back. We're ruined! Thanks to the stupidity of my brother, the lucrative doors of the Admiralty are bolted against us. He's been thrown from office because he had too many enemies who worked for his downfall; and his downfall is ours! The entire Montague family is in disgrace."

"That is simply not true, Father. It is your brother who is in disgrace, not you. It is your brother who has been dismissed from high office by the king, not you. We will certainly feel the repercussions financially, but it is your brother whom society will censure, not you." John found that he enjoyed manipulating his father with half-truths.

Jack Raymond tried to placate his father-in-law. "My father is the Earl of Sandwich, with friends in high places. He'll land on his feet."

"The son of a bitch likely will! It will be me who suffers financial ruin. Get you from my sight. Any man who loses control over his wife doesn't deserve house room!"

"Father, sit down before you have a stroke," John ordered. "The loss of Admiralty business will give us more time and resources to invest in our own merchant vessels. You don't need your brother, Sandwich, or his great friend, the Duke of Bedford. The Montague Line will be your salvation. Shipping is a lucrative business. I think we should expand." John decided not to mention the loss of the *Swallow*, just yet. The old man would learn of it soon enough.

He masked the satisfaction he felt with a look of regret. "I'm afraid O'Toole refuses to return Emma. Still, look on the bright side; think of all the money that saves you."

Sean left Emerald in a suite at the Savoy Hotel while he went into the city to attend to banking and business matters. When he returned that evening, he had a surprise for her.

"But I hate London houses," she protested, "they are ugly and gloomy." Silently she added, *You won't like it either. It's like being shut up without air or light.*

He took her hands in his. "Trust me. Come and look at it." He dipped his head to steal a kiss. "Do you want me to persuade you?"

"Yes, please," she murmured, opening her mouth for his ravishing.

The elegant town house in Old Park Lane was the antithesis of the mausoleum where Emerald had grown up. It was a tall house whose front windows overlooked the Serpentine and Rotten Row, while the windows at the back gave an unhindered view of the spectacular flower gardens in Green Park. The rooms were freshly decorated in pale green and white with elegant French furnishings.

"I'm only leasing it, and it comes complete with servants," Sean explained.

Emerald needed no more persuading; she

fell in love with the house on sight, but looked askance at the very masculine male she adored. "Will you be comfortable here?"

"Are you insinuating I am nothing but a bogtrotter?"

She gave him a saucy glance. "Well, we could get a pig and a couple of hens, if it would make you happy."

He pulled her back against him and rubbed his arousal against her bum. "You know what makes me happy."

"Are you always in that condition?"

"And a damn good thing I am, since you're insatiable, my beauty."

"Aren't we lucky to have found each other?" she asked happily.

They moved in the next day and the earl gathered the servants to instruct them. His requirements were exacting. He freely admitted to being fanatic about personal linen, table linen, and bed linen. Hot water must be available at all times so they could bathe at any hour of the day or night, and the food was to be prepared by a master chef who would be arriving later in the day.

Over and above all was the single most important rule. His lady and her identity must be protected at all times. He had a great deal of business to attend to in the city, and while he was absent no one was to be admitted into the house without the earl's express permission.

Later in the day the earl himself brought back two visitors, one a wigmaker, the other a jeweler. "The styles in London have become preposterous. You will need a powdered wig adorned with ostrich feathers to attend even the theater."

"Oh, I know! I've been watching them parade about in the park. They are all powder, patches, and lace, and those are just the gentlemen!" she said, laughing.

While Emerald was fitted for her wigs, Sean viewed the pieces the jeweler had brought. He had no trouble selecting a necklace ablaze with diamonds. It would be spectacular with her crimson velvet, and when they were back in Ireland, where she could wear her own glorious dark hair, it would look even better. He pictured her in nothing but the diamonds and decided to wait until bedtime to give her his gift.

"We are invited to a great celebration the Duke of Newcastle is throwing tomorrow night."

Her eyes widened. "However do you know the duke?"

"I made a point of cultivating his friendship when I discovered we had enemies in common."

"You mean the Montagues?"

"In a roundabout fashion. Newcastle is so elated at the success of his sabotage campaign against Sandwich that he's throwing a victory ball to celebrate."

Emerald shuddered. "My uncle is a dreadful man. What happened?"

"The king dismissed him from the Admiralty," Sean said lightly.

Emerald was shocked. The Earls of Sandwich had ruled the Admiralty since the days of King Charles II. She looked at Sean with speculative eyes. How in the name of heaven had he maneuvered her uncle's downfall? She had no doubt it was his fine hand that had manipulated events. She understood his need for revenge. He had been scarred by the Montagues, both on the outside and the inside. His invisible scars could not heal until he had wreaked his vengeance.

"Won't they shoot a Montague on sight?" she asked in the same light tone he had used.

"You will be completely anonymous in your wig and mask," he promised.

It didn't take Emerald long to learn that Sean had lied. Two liveried footmen stood sentry at the entrance to the glittering ballroom, one to take the ladies' wraps, the other to announce the names of the guests. Sean handed her satin-lined cape to the footman and gave only his name.

"The Earl of Kildare."

Sean took her arm as they stepped into the ballroom. Every eye was focused upon them and a loud gasp could be heard, followed by a moment of silence. Emerald thought it was their clothes that had occasioned the gasps. In her red velvet with diamonds blazing at her throat she stood out vividly from the ladies in pastel satin and pearls, and Sean was the only man wearing black.

When their hostess, the Duchess of Newcastle, came forward to greet them, Emerald was quickly disabused of the notion.

"How very droll that Montague's niece is here to celebrate his downfall."

"How did you learn my identity, Your Grace?" Emerald asked woodenly.

The duchess cast Sean a provocative glance. "My dear, Kildare and I are very *intimate.*"

Emerald's eyes glittered beneath her mask. She was furious that Sean had deceived her into thinking her identity would be unknown. She was also jealous of his relationship with the Duchess of Newcastle, though she'd be damned if she'd let the woman know it. Suddenly she laughed and tapped him with her fan. "So it's true, you sly devil, you *are* attracted to older women."

The duchess went stiff. As Sean drew her hand to his lips for a perfunctory kiss, he was suffused with admiration for his delightful partner. She was a match for this promiscuous Englishwoman, and he was willing to wager she could hold her own against anyone present.

When Newcastle greeted them, Emerald threw Sean a challenging look and went off on the duke's arm. For the rest of the evening she received the lion's share of attention from the males present. It didn't matter to them whose niece or daughter she was, they appreciated her for her beauty and for the aura of sexuality she exuded.

To a man they envied her present lover. If she satisfied a dangerous devil like Kildare, she must be rewarding in bed. She was astounded to receive three offers of carte blanche, should she tire of her present lover. Emerald fended off amorous advances with an amused laugh, though she felt no such thing.

It dawned upon her that all London must know she had abandoned her newly wedded husband to become the Earl of Kildare's mistress. It also dawned upon her that Sean O'Toole was purposely flaunting her in the face of society. How naive she was. She knew he had stolen her to spite the Montagues, but that wasn't enough. He wanted the whole damn world to know what he had done!

Though the women's eyes followed him in open invitation, Emerald noticed that he did not flirt. He spent the evening discussing business affairs with men of power and influence. She almost wished it were otherwise. She could have contended with another woman. But how could she compete with this dark, driving need for vengeance?

She drank far too many glasses of champagne as she listened to the latest scandals. The so-called English *ton* fed upon itself, then, engorged with gossip, spewed forth filth to besmirch everyone. Only a few short hours in such vaunted company made her feel cynical and brittle.

Sean, engrossed in his conversation with Newcastle, was blissfully unaware of Emerald's mood.

"I believe it was the scandal of the slavers that did the trick. That, coupled with the proof you supplied of bribery and treason. It was suggested, strictly off the record, of course, that the government would be in your debt if you could do something about those embarrassing ships."

Sean's smile did not quite reach his eyes. "Your Grace, I have anticipated you."

At last Sean came to retrieve Emerald from her dancing partner and indicated that he was ready to leave. When they reached the ballroom doors, she turned to survey the crowded floor. Then very deliberately she removed the velvet mask and tossed it into the air. A group of men standing nearby eagerly scrambled for it.

With a grim look on his dark face and a firm hand at the small of her back, Sean pushed her through the doorway. His brow lowered and his jaw clenched as he retrieved her cloak and wrapped it firmly about her naked shoulders and half-exposed breasts. "What the hell was that all about?" he demanded as they emerged from the palatial house on Piccadilly. "You were acting like a little whore," he ground out.

"But, Sean, darling, that's exactly what I am," she said sweetly, "your whore. And you have made sure all London knows what I am."

"Get in the carriage." His tone warned her just how furious he was.

Emerald ignored the warning. "Would you like me on my hands and knees, my lord, so I can service you here in the carriage?"

He gripped her shoulders and shook her till her teeth rattled. "Stop it this instant. You are driving me to violence."

"I am aware of your violent nature, my lord. Perhaps I can match it! Come on, I'm licking my lips over you," she taunted.

He forced her down on the seat and crushed her mouth with his, mastering her. Only Emerald wouldn't be mastered, not without giving as good as she got. She bit down on his lip and raked the side of his face with her nails.

He flung away from her. "Little bitch!" he cursed.

As she had promised, she licked her lips over him and tasted his blood.

They entered the Mayfair house in silence. Emerald ran up two flights to their spacious bedchamber. She dismissed the maid who had waited up for her. Her anger at him did not cool, rather it grew hotter by the minute. She had thought the diamonds a gift of love; now she knew he wanted to flaunt her and the diamonds in the face of the English. Though the hour was late she decided the evening was not quite over; the fireworks hadn't yet started.

Sean lingered in the salon, trying to cool his temper with a snifter of French brandy. By the time he finished it, he felt in full control. He slowly mounted the stairs, and when he entered the bedchamber he was almost ready to forgive her.

She deliberately turned her back upon him.

He felt his control slip a notch.

She had removed the ostrich-feathered wig, but still wore her gown and her diamonds. Completely ignoring him, she unfastened the crimson velvet and stepped out of it. Naked, save for lace stockings and diamonds, she sat down at the dressing table and picked up her hairbrush.

Emerald knew his dark eyes were riveted upon her. She bent her head forward, allowing her hair to almost touch the carpet, brushed it vigorously, then tossed it back so that it fell in a smoky cloud about her shoulders. With hairbrush still in hand she padded over to the bed with feline grace to retrieve her night rail from beneath the pillow. It was a flame-colored diaphanous garment designed to give a man pleasure. She made no effort to put it on, but took it back to the dressing table with her and draped it across the stool. Then she made a display of admiring herself in the mirror. She tossed her curls and drew the brush through them one more time, then very deliberately she brushed the black curls between her legs.

"What the hell game is this you are playing?" he growled.

She dropped the hairbrush and with hands on naked hips walked provocatively toward him. "A harlot's game. Isn't that what you want? I was just admiring the diamonds one last time before I give them back."

"The diamonds are yours," he ground out.

"Oh, I don't think so. They are your property, just as I am. We are both for display purposes only."

"Stop this game now," he said with quiet authority. He knew if he didn't hang on to the last of his control, he would throw her to the floor and mount her. Lust now mingled with his anger, and lust was rapidly gaining the upper hand.

"When you gave me the diamonds last night in bed, I didn't realize the significance. I had no idea I was paying for them with sexual favors. Perhaps last night was only the down payment?" She knew she was deliberately goading him, as did Sean. She wanted to exercise her woman's power over him, to see if she could shatter his control into a million shards.

He reached out with powerful hands and jerked her against him. "If you want fireworks, I'll start with skyrockets."

She fought him like a spitting cat, enjoying every blazing moment. They were a perfect match, each driving the other to madness. In the end they both surrendered. Sean gave in because he was physically stronger and didn't want to hurt her. Emerald yielded because she didn't want to maul his pride. In the end it was his tenderness that melted her anger toward him. His loving affection for her was boundless and showed her just how much she meant to him.

Much later, as she lay cradled in his arms, they both whispered love words. "My honey love, I did want to show you off, but I swear it was your Irish beauty I wanted to flaunt in the face of so many raddled Englishwomen. You never have to wear the necklace in public again, but you must keep it. You have no money of your own and it will give you some financial security."

"My darling, you are all the security I'll ever need."

He pressed her to his heart. "Promise me you'll keep it?"

"I promise," she whispered. "Let's not accept any more social invitations. I heard enough gossip tonight to last me a lifetime. I don't give a damn that the Duke of Devonshire has impregnated his wife, Georgiana, and his mistress, Elizabeth Foster, at the same time. I want to go home."

"Only a few days longer, sweetheart. I have merchant ships docked here in London. I must speak with my captains before we leave. Tonight I'll show you London's pleasure gardens. Just the two of us. Have you ever been to Vauxhall or Ranelagh?"

"Of course not. I never did anything sinful or worldly."

"Until I stole you," he whispered.

She laughed seductively. "Now I sin on a regular basis." She slid a silken knee between his rock-hard thighs. "You taught me to be wild and wicked and to never say no!"

21

"He did what?" William Montague roared, turning purple in the face.

"He confiscated the *Swallow*. There was nothing I could do about it. We were virtual prisoners, outnumbered two to one by FitzGeralds. I was damn lucky to come away with my life, no thanks to you!"

"What do you mean?" Montague blustered.

"You knew Shamus O'Toole would shoot a Montague on sight; that's why the pair of you chose me for your scapegoat. You can consider yourself lucky he returned our crew."

"And what good is a crew without a ship? We still have a contract to supply and transport horses for the army, even though my cursed brother has fucked us with the Admiralty. But if there's any delay, we'll never get their business again and I'll lose face with Bedford, who's still able to pull some strings for us."

"I'll buy another ship today. If we want to make money we must expand, and we don't want to lose the crew."

"You can handle the paperwork, but Jack will decide which vessel we buy. You don't know a scow from a schooner."

"Your confidence in my ability overwhelms me, Father," John said dryly.

"I'd go myself if I wasn't a martyr to this goddamn gout!"

John knew it would be pointless to explain that the gout attacks were tied to his vicious temper, which he lost morning, noon, and night.

After they departed, Montague sat morosely at his desk. Why had life suddenly turned sour? he wondered. He shook his head. If the truth be told, the sweetness of life had been missing for years; ever since Amber left him. No one could comfort him as his wife had; nothing could ease the pain of his gout like her herbal concoctions. He had no idea what had become of her, but assumed she was living in Ireland, probably with the FitzGeralds at Maynooth. Perhaps he should forgive her and take her back.

As John Montague and Jack Raymond walked along the London docks, the latter was struck by the number of O'Toole vessels in port. "If I ever come face to face with that Irish son of a whore, I'll kill him with my bare hands."

John laughed. "Perhaps now is your chance. There's the *Half Moon,* he might be aboard."

Jack was stunned. "He sailed with you?"

"The Montagues don't intimidate him in any way. I believe he was guest of honor at New-castle's Victory Ball last night."

Jack Raymond ground his teeth in impotent rage. "Did he bring my wife with him?"

"Of course not," John lied. "He's nobody's fool." John nodded his head in the direction of the *Half Moon.* "Speak of the devil."

Raymond's head jerked up to see the figure

of O'Toole negligently leaning against the rail. Jack stared at the dark malevolent face with disbelief. He would never have recognized the hardened, dangerous man as Sean O'Toole. Despite the casual pose, O'Toole was so intimidating, Jack felt his bowels knot.

Why hadn't he rid the world of the Irish scum along with his brother? Perhaps it still wasn't too late. There was so much hatred and bad blood between them, he knew he'd never feel safe until O'Toole was dead. The thought that the Irishman had stolen his wife from under his nose was intolerable, but even worse was Jack Raymond's suspicion that Emerald had gone willingly. If and when he managed to get her back, he would make her pay for the rest of her life!

As Jack Raymond quickened his pace, John hid a smile of contempt. He knew Raymond was no match for O'Toole and would avoid a confrontation at any cost.

The two men spent the morning visiting the offices of the maritime brokers, the afternoon inspecting the vessels they offered for sale. Only two were seaworthy, despite claims to the contrary. One was an Irish schooner, the other a two-masted merchantman, newly arrived from Gibraltar and bearing that name.

The latter looked suspiciously familiar to John, even though she had a fresh coat of paint. When he saw it had had a recent lime washing to rid it of its stink, he knew it was one of the slavers they secretly owned—or had owned, until O'Toole relieved them of it.

Johnny's wicked juices began to bubble as he praised up the schooner, knowing Raymond was prejudiced against all things Irish.

"No," Jack said decisively, "the merchantman has a much deeper hold, and a blind man can see it won't need paint for a couple of years."

"I still prefer the schooner—it's a much faster vessel—but I suppose I must defer to your superior knowledge."

"You're here to do the paperwork," Jack reminded him.

"I'll get the *Gibraltar* transferred and registered to the Montague Line today. You get word to the captain and crew, if they're not all dead drunk by now." The minute Raymond left him, Johnny closed his eyes in prayer. *I ask only one thing—please let me be there when Father learns he's bought his own fucking ship!*

Sean O'Toole felt a prickling sensation at the back of his neck. It lingered on hours after Jack Raymond had slithered from his sight. It was not fear, it was more like a premonition or warning that something was in the wind. Confrontation wasn't Raymond's style, but O'Toole did not underestimate him for one minute. The hate and rancor that had been exchanged in one swift glance told him Jacko would try to retaliate.

It was midafternoon before he realized his unease centered on Emerald. He decided to

return to the house in Old Park Lane immediately, though he went by a circuitous route
so he couldn't be followed.

When Sean found her in the bath, he was
so relieved, he went weak. "Get dressed. I've
asked the maid to pack your things. We're
leaving."

"Sean! You promised to take me to Vauxhall."

He stared at her blankly and ran his fingers
through his hair.

Her hand stole to her throat. "You're frightening me, what's wrong?"

Realizing what he must look like, he forced
himself to relax. "Nothing is wrong. You
asked me to take you home last night. I'm only
trying to please you."

"Admit the truth! You completely forgot
about Vauxhall, didn't you?"

He laughed. "Ah, Beauty, seeing you in
your bath was so distracting, it wiped away all
thought of pleasure gardens." Now that he saw
she was here, safe and sound, he felt foolish
over his irrational apprehension. And so long
as he was with her, no harm could come to her.
He watched her swirl the sponge over the
high curve of her breasts where they swelled
from the water.

Emerald watched his eyes follow the sponge
and knew the effect she was having on him.
She lay back in the bath, then lifted the sponge
and squeezed. Water trickled over her shapely
shoulders. She dipped the sponge beneath
the surface, then lifted one leg so she could

trickle water down it. That did the trick. The corners of her mouth went up as she watched him remove his coat and unfasten his neck-cloth.

He slipped down beneath her, lifting her out of the tub and onto his lap as he sat on the stool next to the bath. He was unmindful of the water that dripped over him, soaking his remaining clothes. He kissed her ear. "I see no reason why we can't do both. I'll take you to Vauxhall, then we can go straight to the ship and leave on the midnight tide."

She wriggled her bottom about, to accommodate his growing erection. "I don't want to miss the fireworks," she said innocently.

He bit down on the earlobe he'd just kissed. "I'll give you bloody fireworks!"

"Promise?" she asked saucily, leaning back in his arms. His shaft hardened along the length of his soaked pants and it felt as though there were no material between them.

He reached out to cup her breasts in the palms of his hands and lifted them until they looked like melons.

They were so sensitive, she cried out.

He was immediately contrite. "Did I hurt you, love? I'm such a rough devil." He enfolded her in his arms.

She reached up to caress his cheek. "Of course you didn't hurt me. You could never hurt me."

When Jack Raymond returned to Bottolph's Wharf, where the Montague Line headquarters were located, he was surprised to find Captain Bowers and his first mate on the *Swallow* in William Montague's office. The old man had wasted no time in demanding an explanation of why they had allowed their crew to give up the *Swallow*.

The captain and first mate stood passively while Montague ranted, raved, and ordered the captain to mete out discipline to his gutless crew. It went without saying they'd receive no pay for the voyage to Ireland, but when Montague threatened no wages for a year, they were ready to revolt.

Jack wasn't displeased Montague had softened them up with his threats. Perhaps the fear of losing a year's wages would make them more susceptible to Jack's plan, for which they'd be well compensated should they agree to it. He made eye contact with William.

"Well?" the old man thundered.

"We've acquired another vessel. I'm sure Captain Bowers will read the riot act to his crew and they'll be more careful in the future."

"The scurvy bastards don't deserve another ship!" William roared, but it was just bluster. In wartime sailors were in demand, though most preferred to crew a merchant vessel over an Admiralty or Navy ship.

Jack Raymond gave them directions to the

Gibraltar, which was moored at Wapping, and praised the ship's fine points. He made sure William knew he had overruled John's choice of an Irish schooner.

William dismissed the men so he could ask Jack the price. "I'll go and see for myself if we've got our money's worth. I might as well dine at the Prospect of Whitby by the Wapping water stairs. Meet me there at eight."

Jack Raymond followed Captain Bowers and his first mate as they set out to round up their men. Most of the crew were at the Bucket of Blood, a hangout for merchantmen that Jack had never dared enter before. Jack spotted the two sailors sitting at a plank table with the bosun from the *Heron,* another Montague vessel that was in port.

Jack sat down at the table. "Let me pay for this round. I have a proposition that will put money in your pockets."

The men were all ears until he mentioned the *Half Moon.* "Where the hell would we get that much gunpowder?" asked a reluctant Bowers.

"Christ, I don't want to blow up London's docks. One small explosion in the hold will set the ship ablaze."

The first mate said skeptically, "Even if you supplied the gunpowder, it would be impossible to get it aboard. O'Toole has a day watch and a night watch."

Raymond pressed them. "Two quid apiece to demolish the *Half Moon.*"

They shook their heads.

Raymond upped the ante. "Five!"

With a great show of reluctance Captain Bowers turned him down. "Wouldn't attempt it at any price. O'Toole's too ruthless."

Jack stood up. "You gutless cowards! I can get a man murdered for ten quid. Any sailor on London's docks would take my arm up to the elbow for half that."

Jack Raymond stormed from the tavern in a temper and the bosun from the *Heron* soon followed.

When they were alone, Bowers grinned at his first mate. "If we tip off O'Toole, he'll double what Jacko offered."

Daniels, the bosun from the *Heron,* hurried after Jack Raymond before he could make a deal with someone else. Gunpowder was in plentiful supply since the war with France. The navy yards were stacked high with barrels of the stuff as well as other explosives. Reaching Jack, he tapped him on the shoulder. "I might be interested in yer proposition, mate. Pinchin' a barrel of gunpowder is child's play, but it takes balls to light the fuse. Obviously yer men from the *Swallow* 'ave none."

"How would you get it aboard?" Raymond inquired.

"There's ways an' there's ways," Daniels said cryptically.

"Such as?" Raymond pressed.

"I can walk aboard with the others if they take on cargo or supplies. Or I can blow a hole in the hull from the outside. I'm a bosun, hulls are my business. Failin' all else, I'll grease a palm."

"I'll give you five now; you'll get the rest tomorrow when the deed's done."

"I'll get it now, mate. Gunpowder is very tricky stuff—it can blow a man to smithereens so 'e can't even be identified."

Jack didn't argue the point. He counted out the money into the bosun's hand.

Daniels spit on the money and smiled. The bosun knew merchant vessels seldom sailed to Dublin without smuggling some contraband. All he likely needed to do was wait. Under cover of darkness all barrels and kegs looked much the same.

Sean and Emerald strolled hand in hand through the pleasure gardens of Vauxhall. The promenades beneath the trees, illuminated by colored Chinese lanterns, were designed to induce romantic nostalgia in its jaded London patrons. Paths laid out between flower beds, statues, and fountains led to various entertainments such as music, dancing, and sideshows.

They stopped to watch a Punch and Judy show and laughed at the classic battle of the sexes. Emerald added her voice to Judy's and called out, "Marriage is legalized slavery—an institution of bondage!" The other women in the crowd joined in, booing every time Punch opened his mouth.

Sean pulled her from the crowd, laughing. "You like to stir up trouble. I should have taken you to a prizefight."

"Ugh, I couldn't enjoy watching men bloody each other."

"It's not always men. At Figgs' in the Oxford Road they have lady sword fighters. They have to hold half a crown in each fist. If they drop the money, they lose."

"You're making it up," she accused.

"I'm not. Londoners are the strangest people on earth."

Emerald began to laugh. "You know, I believe you're right. Just look at these people. They're not here to see Vauxhall, they're here so Vauxhall can see them. They are parading around on show, like actors on a stage. They're not wearing clothes, they're wearing costumes. *Ridiculous* costumes! All the women look like strumpets and the men like buffoons."

He hugged her to his side. "That's because they are strumpets and buffoons."

When they came to the refreshment booths, Sean insisted she try everything. They sampled oysters, black peas, meat pasties, roast chestnuts, and plum cake and washed them down with ale and cider.

At dusk they found a secluded path that led to a private arbor, but after only two kisses their privacy was invaded by other amorous couples, so they strolled down to the river to watch the shower of fireworks. When they tired of the noisy crowds, a barge took them back downriver, where they disembarked at Tower Wharf. From there it was only a short walk to where the *Half Moon* was moored.

The docks were very poorly lighted, which was, of course, by design. More business was carried out under cover of dark than was ever done in broad daylight. To add to the sinister atmosphere, fog rolled off the Thames, shrouding the vessels moored at dockside and obliterating altogether the ships riding at anchor.

"Is it far?" Emerald asked anxiously, clinging tightly to his hand.

He slipped a strong, comforting arm about her, drawing her closer. "Don't be afraid. The *Half Moon* is moored next to the *Indiaman*." The prickling sensation was there again at the back of his neck. He put it down to Emerald's nervousness.

They were halfway up the gangplank before the man on deck watch saw them and lifted his lantern to discover who was boarding the ship.

"Good evening, sor, I'll inform Cap'n FitzGerald yer aboard. It won't be long before the tide turns." An eerie shout came from the fog and an answer floated down from the yardarm.

"Tell the captain once I get my lady settled, I'll join him at the wheel. An extra pair of eyes wouldn't go amiss on a night like this," Sean called.

"Aye, aye, sor."

The companionway was dim belowdecks.

Wisps of fog turned the light from the ship's lanterns a sulphurous yellow.

Inside the main cabin the bosun from the *Heron* sat waiting in the dark. He'd simply walked aboard with the barrel of gunpowder on his shoulder while kegs of illegal French brandy were being loaded in the hold. When he heard footsteps approaching, he held his breath and raised the brass-barreled boarding pistol chest high.

Sean turned the knob on the cabin door. As it swung open the hair on the nape of his neck stood on end like raised hackles. One hand swept Emerald behind him while the other drew a small, deadly pistol from his belt. Sean's heart was in his mouth, for though his pistol was loaded and primed, there was no powder in the touch hole for safety reasons. Before he could tilt the gun and tap the powder, the intruder struck a flint and set it to a hurricane lamp.

"It's a bloody good thing ye didn't shoot or ye'd have blown us straight to hell," said a mocking Irish voice.

"Is it Danny—Danny FitzGerald?" Sean hadn't seen him in over five years. "What the devil are you doing?"

Danny tapped the barrel of gunpowder sitting on the map table. "I'm here to blow up the *Half Moon,* an' a bloody easy task it would have bin. Yer security is nonexistent. Ye have enemies out there—I know, I work for 'um."

"My father told me he had FitzGeralds aboard every Montague vessel."

He nodded. "I'm bosun on the *Heron*. I go by the name of Daniels. I report regularly to the Murphy brothers."

"My thanks, Danny, for your loyalty to the O'Tooles."

Danny shrugged. "Shamus pays me well."

"My captain and crew will feel the rough edge of my tongue over this business."

"What can ye expect from bloody FitzGeralds?" he asked with a straight face.

Emerald was trying to piece together what had happened. "Did my father pay you to blow up Sean's ship?"

"Yer husband."

"Jack? Oh, my God! Sean, he wants to kill you." She began trembling.

He winked at her. "I wonder why?"

"It's because of me," she whispered, not sharing his amusement. Her eyes flooded with tears.

"Well, it will take a better man than Jack Raymond, my beauty." He sat her down and poured her a stiff drink. "Sip slowly on this. I'll be back shortly."

They heard the anchor chain being raised through the hawsehole. "Tide's turning," Danny said, heading for the door.

"Aren't you forgetting something?" Emerald cried.

"Sorry," Danny said, hauling the barrel of gunpowder to his shoulder. As he and Sean headed up the companionway he said, "I had to take his money before somebody else did. Most Montague crewmen would take a bribe."

"They certainly took my money," Sean said with irony.

"If the Montagues tried once, they may try again, closer to home."

"Forewarned is forearmed, Danny," Sean said, lifting the gunpowder from his shoulder. "Mr. FitzGerald!" he roared, striding down the deck toward his captain.

David FitzGerald's hands froze on the ship's wheel.

22

As often happens, the night fog was a harbinger of heat. The next day, as the *Half Moon* passed the Isle of Wight, the sun shone brilliantly and the English Channel experienced only a light westerly breeze.

Sean rigged a canopy so Emerald could spend the days up on deck watching the crew unfurl the sails and untangle the lines. She stared spellbound as the men, Sean included, climbed the rigging with the agility of monkeys.

The *Half Moon* took on fresh supplies and water when it reached Cornwall, where Sean took Emerald ashore to explore Land's End. As they stood on the cliffs he slipped his arm about her and pointed across the glistening water.

"This is said to be the entrance to a fertile land, which was swallowed by the sea in the eleventh century. It reached all the way to the Scilly Isles, twenty-eight miles in yonder direction. From where we are standing, some people claim to have had visions of a lost city."

"Oh, yes, the legendary land of Lyonesse! My mother told me all about it when I was little. The domes and towers and battlements of the drowned land sometimes appear far out to sea."

"Do you believe in myths and legends, Emerald?"

"Yes, yes!" she said passionately. "Don't you?"

He gazed out to sea, his eyes reflecting silver in the clear light. He shook his head. "I used to, once upon a time. Hang on to your childhood beliefs and memories, Emerald. Don't let them slip away as mine did."

His reflective, melancholy mood lasted all through the next day as he pointed out landmarks along the coast of Wales, recounting their haunting legends. Then he showed her how to predict the weather by observing the brooding mountains. "If their heads are shrouded in mist, run for cover; but if you can see clear to the highest peaks, it will be sultry, as it has been the last couple of days."

Sean pointed out the different seabirds and taught her their names. Soon she could tell razorbills and petrels from gulls and gannets. On the third day she joined him at the wheel while he relieved David FitzGerald by navigating the *Half Moon* from St. George's Channel into the Irish Sea.

At his urging she took the wheel, feeling most daring, yet knowing his powerful arms were ready to correct any mistakes she might make. "Guess where we are heading," he murmured into her ear as his hands covered hers.

She looked up at him over her shoulder and saw the teasing light in his eyes. Realizing his introspective mood had vanished, her heart quickened with excitement. "Give me a hint."

He smiled down at her. "I'd better take the wheel now; the Menai Strait is a bit narrow."

"Anglesey!" she breathed joyously.

"Your memories of the island are happy ones. I want to make more memories today. Unforgettable ones. Memories to cherish. I want you and me to be able to look back on the next few hours as the happiest of our lives."

They left the crew swimming in the warm turquoise waters and, hand in hand, sought out their crystal cave. They undressed in silence, each knowing that the most sacred rituals should be performed naked. All their senses and thoughts were attuned to each other.

In wonder they explored the glittering labyrinth whose walls were encrusted with diamondlike crystals. To them this high-vaulted cavern would always be a place of enchantment; its pool made magic by a myriad of dancing rainbows. In awe they touched its jeweled walls, then dipped their toes into the gin-clear water.

Sean watched Emerald flaunt her beauty before him in the iridescent light and shadow. His silver eyes told her just how lovely he found her.

Emerald, watching Sean's dark, powerful beauty, allowed herself to become intoxicated by his nearness. He had taught her how to feel, how to appreciate the beauty of colors and sounds and to live to the full in the present moment, separating it from past and future.

When he took her hand and they slipped into the pool together, they were transported to a magic realm. Emerald felt her skin tighten, her blood tingle with excitement, her body stir with arousal, and her heart overflow with love. Being here together was perfectly sublime...sublimely perfect.

Their mood became playful as they swam and splashed. She climbed upon his back, her arms clinging to his neck, as he dived deep, playing dolphin to her undine. Underwater, as they played and kissed, they felt the world recede, leaving them alone in their intimate paradise. Since neither had any fear of water, their play was both intemperate and incautious, plumbing the depths of joy and freedom until at last she threw herself with quivering abandon into his arms.

Sean lifted her onto the ledge and levered himself up beside her. As he enfolded her in his arms she felt such a heady bond of trust and love, she whispered, "Only you can hold me close and make me feel free."

By mutual consent, but without the need for words, they left their clothes where they lay and emerged from the crystal cave into the hot sun. The coral sand beckoned and neither wanted to resist its pagan temptation. Emerald lay down and stretched her limbs blissfully, letting the heat from the sand beneath her seep into her body.

She closed her eyes and knew it would be impossible to feel happier than she did at this moment. Sean FitzGerald O'Toole was her entire world. She could not imagine not knowing him, not watching the lithe way he moved, not hearing his deep voice murmur her name. Without him she had been lost; with him she felt complete. Surely a love this strong would last throughout eternity.

As Emerald lay on the sugary sand in the sunlight, a delicious sense of anticipation spiraled about her, dancing on the soft sea breeze that ruffled her dark curls. She felt a sense of joy that went beyond happiness, for she knew that soon, soon he would love her.

She kept her eyes closed until she felt a flutter, like a butterfly wing, touch the corner of her mouth. She smiled a secret smile and slowly lifted her lashes. He knelt before her, watching her intently, his dark pewter eyes brimming with laughter. Holding his gaze, she came to her knees slowly and knelt before him.

They needed no words, yet the longing to touch was like a hunger in the blood. At the same moment each reached out to the other to trace with their fingertips...a cheek, a throat, a shoulder. Emerald's hand brushed his heart and felt it thud beneath her fingers. He was the perfect male. He was her Irish Prince.

He bent to capture her lips with his, and when he was a heartbeat away, Emerald began to whisper his name with heart-scalding hunger. "Sean, Sean."

He set his mouth against her throat so that she would not stop saying his name. "Your skin feels like hot silk. I love to touch you and taste you when you are heated by the sun." He ran his fingertips along the valley between her breasts, down to her navel, then dipped them between her legs to touch her woman's center. He lifted his fingertips to her mouth. "Taste," he insisted.

She licked once, tasting herself, then watched with slumberous eyes as he sucked her honey-eyed essence from his fingertips. The things he did to her never failed to make her feel wild and wicked.

Sean laid her back on the sun-drenched sand and spread her hair about her heart-shaped face in a dark halo. His eyes were stained black with passion. He felt so possessive of her, it bordered on obsession. He told himself that it was because their time together would be fleeting. It compelled him to enjoy her to the full while he had her.

If only—he clenched his fists and stopped the thought before he could complete it. He forced himself to stop thinking. He could see and hear and smell and taste and touch. It would have to be enough. He must not complicate matters with his dark thoughts. She might not conceive for months, a year mayhap; he did not have to give her up yet.

He had taught her to live in the moment, to savor the here and now. They were together this minute. That was all that mattered. He would make them experience a thousand days and nights in one shining, unforgettable hour. Desire was running rampant through his blood, but he banked the fires so he could concentrate on Emerald's pleasure.

He had not counted on her scalding passion. Her legs slithered high about his back, then she arched so high, she impaled herself upon his thick, pulsing shaft. He had taught her to take what she wanted without pause and it gave him deep satisfaction that she demanded everything he was capable of giving her.

He knew what she loved best so he plunged and withdrew, over and over, deeper each time, until she gasped and writhed and clung. Each time he withdrew, her body mourned the loss as the high peak of sensation receded. But immediately he rebuilt it, so that each time she peaked higher.

Never had either of them been so hot as they made love upon the burning sand with the blistering sun beating down on their bare flesh. Both were burning on the outside, afire on the inside, their blood like a river of flame, running from one to the other until both were completely out of control in their raging need.

The brilliant gold behind Emerald's eyelids flashed into flaming orange, turned to bloodred, then deepened to purple. She hung on the precipice of the volcano for long, exquisite minutes, then, when she could bear the intense pleasure no longer, they erupted together, both shuddering uncontrollably as he flooded into her.

They lay in each other's arms for a full hour, kissing and whispering love words as if they were in a world apart. When Emerald closed her eyes to drowse, he studied her face intently, so he could remember forever what she looked like on this special day. They wanted it to last forever and stayed until the sun began to sink into the sea.

When they finally meandered back to the ship, the crew surprised them with a mouthwatering feast supplied by the ocean. They had built a fire of driftwood on the beach to cook the fish, shrimp, and lobster they had found in such abundance among the rocks. The sun, the sand, and the sea, combined with the broiled shellfish, ensured that their day ended on a perfect note.

The *Half Moon* didn't reach Greystones until full dark that night. Sean and Emerald climbed the path that took them up to the big house slowly, their arms about each other's waists, her head leaning on him, not quite reaching his shoulder. Neither of them wanted the day to end, but the sun and the sea air, their play and their passion, had exhausted the last ounce of Emerald's energy.

Sean carried her upstairs and undressed her, while Emerald could do no more than yawn her head off. He slipped into bed beside her and curved his long body against her back with one possessive arm firmly about her. As she drifted into sleep a smile curved her mouth; without a doubt Emerald knew she had never felt better.

Emerald couldn't recall feeling worse in her entire life! She hung over the edge of the big bed, vomiting into the chamber pot. Kate Kennedy, hearing Emerald's distress, hurried into the master bedchamber. The scene before her gave her pause.

"Yer breeding," she announced in her direct way.

Emerald lifted a pale, woebegone face. "That's what I've been thinking." No sooner had she uttered the sentence than she was swept with another great wave of nausea. She groaned, lowered her head once again, and voided what remained of her stomach contents into the china pot.

When her sickness subsided, Kate changed the sheets and helped Emerald bathe. Though Kate's tongue was sometimes sharp, her actions were usually kindness itself. In truth, she enjoyed having Emerald at Greystones. When Kathleen died, the heart and soul of

Greystones seemed to have perished with her. Emerald had brought the big stone house back to life.

As Emerald nibbled on some dry toast and sipped a little watered wine, her heart soared. She was secretly elated at the thought of a child. The only reason she had allowed her father to coerce her into marriage, was so that she could have children. Knowing that it was Sean O'Toole who had planted the seed of a child made her heart dizzy with happiness.

The only thing that worried her was Sean's reaction. He was an unpredictable man and a domineering one, who was only happy when he could control people and events. If a baby was not in his scheme of things, perhaps he would be angered at the news.

The dry toast and watered wine made her symptoms miraculously vanish. Emerald chose one of her prettiest gowns, took great pains with her hair, then went down to Greystones's library to sort through the books that had been brought over from Maynooth. The leather-bound volumes gave her a great deal of pleasure. She found that opening a book was like opening a window on the world. Perhaps in the afternoon when she visited Shamus she would take a book and read to him.

"So this is where you're hiding."

She looked up in surprise as Sean came into the library; she hadn't even heard him approach. "You look very beautiful in yellow. The sun has turned your skin to gold and I believe those are authentic Irish freckles across the bridge of your nose."

Emerald was dying to share her news with him, but didn't quite know how to broach the delicate subject. "You were up early this morning."

"You were sound asleep; I couldn't bear the thought of disturbing you."

"When I awoke, I was quite ill. Kate thinks I'm breeding," she blurted.

"Utter nonsense!" Sean declared. "Too much lobster would be my guess." He drew close with a worried frown and cupped her cheek. "Perhaps you have a touch of sunstroke."

"Well, whatever it was, I'm feeling much better now."

"Good. I want you to take it easy today. Our strenuous exertions yesterday were enough to undo both of us." He winked. "I'm delighted to see that you also enjoy less physical activities such as reading."

He wanted to see her blush and she obliged him. "I could stay in this library a year and still be entertained. There's simply everything here: mythology, fairy tales, legends, adventures, history, geography. Do you think your father would enjoy some of these?"

"I'm sure he would, especially if you accompanied the books. I believe he has developed quite an infatuation. Looking at a beautiful woman is much more interesting than looking through a spyglass all day."

After Sean left, she pondered on his words

and reaction. He was so totally convinced there was another explanation for her sickness, that she, too, was persuaded. When her nausea returned the next morning, however, and persisted with regularity every other morning for a week, Emerald began to reconsider.

The strange thing was that Sean arose early each morning before she awoke and, as a result, never witnessed her morning sickness. Every time Kate Kennedy alluded to Emerald's condition, Sean refused to even entertain the possibility that she could be with child.

When Kate hinted about Sean's reluctance to face the facts, Emerald grew fearful. Of course Sean would be displeased if she were pregnant! He would have no doubt the child was his—how could it be otherwise? But in the eyes of the law, the child would legally be considered Jack Raymond's. He was her husband still, after all. Emerald could only imagine how fiercely territorial Sean would feel about his own child and how intolerable it would be to have another man publically acknowledged as the father.

Perhaps it wasn't that at all. Maybe Sean didn't even like children. Could it be that the news would displease him because he didn't want to share Emerald? She would just have to give him time to get used to the idea.

Emerald smiled a secret smile. He could deny it all he wanted, but she knew without a shadow of a doubt that she and Sean FitzGerald O'Toole were making a baby together.

She decided to say nothing further. She would give him extra attention and make sure he knew that she loved him to distraction and that he was, and would always be, the keeper of her heart. In a few months, when her breasts ripened and her belly swelled with the fruit of their lovemaking, Sean wouldn't be able to deny the evidence of his own eyes.

Emerald sighed with contentment. She vowed to become a perfect mother. It felt so right, how could anything spoil this miracle their love had created?

23

When the *Silver Star*, an O'Toole merchant ship, arrived at Greystones, her captain, Liam FitzGerald, brought numerous messages for the earl and also a letter for Emerald. Liam delivered them all to Sean; it was his decision whether his woman was allowed correspondence.

Sean weighed the letter in his hand, immediately recognizing Johnny Montague's handwriting. His shrewd mind told him exactly why Emerald's brother had sent her a letter. He found her coming from the garden, her arms filled with blazing chrysanthemums. "Hello, my beauty. What prompts your undying passion for flowers?"

"I never had a garden before. Our house in London was surrounded by gray pavement. Flowers only grew in parks, and when I was small I was severely chastised for picking them."

"Well, if it makes you happy, you may pick every bloom that Greystones grows. Have you seen the meadow behind the stables? It's purple with Michaelmas daisies."

"Actually, these flowers make me sad," she said softly.

"Ah, Beauty, you become more Irish every day. You have flowers nodding on every windowsill, you pick the lovely things for your heart's replenishment. You display loving hands when you pluck them; you fill up your senses when you smell their fragrance, yet now you tell me they make you sad."

"It's because they are autumn flowers. Our summer was so short. Next thing you know, all the leaves will be falling and winter will be upon us."

To banish her melancholy he gathered her in his arms, flowers and all, and lifted her high. "Our summer was hot and sweet; never regret it, never forget it, Emerald. The memories we made will last forever." His eyes darkened with desire. "I can no longer walk through wet grass without becoming aroused. You make every season bloom for me."

As he lowered her feet to the ground, their bodies touched and Emerald knew she wanted to stay in his arms forever. He reached into his shirt. "Here is a letter for you."

She gazed at it with pleasure. It was addressed to Emerald FitzGerald, rather than Montague, which immediately told her it was from Johnny. She didn't open the letter until she had put all her russet blooms in water and carried them to the library. Then she sat down in a great leather wing chair by the window and broke the sealing wax. A second letter fell onto her lap addressed to Nan FitzGerald at Maynooth.

Dearest Emerald:

Please be an angel and deliver this letter to Nan. I've never felt this way about any other girl and know in my heart that I never shall. I have agonized over whether I should see her again. It has been such a moral dilemma for me. How could I ask a FitzGerald to think kindly of a Montague after our parents' disastrous relationship? But the truth is, I could not help myself.

Late last month, I went to Summerhill, a breeding farm in Meath, to select and pay for horses to fill an army contract. When I realized Maynooth was less than twenty miles away, I rode to see Nan. I've never acted so impulsively before. It's torture being so far away from her, and God knows when I'll get to Ireland again.

I envy you and Sean so much. I would sell my soul for one-hundredth part of the happiness you have found together.

Your loving brother,
Johnny

Emerald's eyes lifted from the parchment as Sean joined her. He sat down at the library desk to read his own letters. Johnny Montague had written to him as well, but he would warrant it enclosed no love letters to pass on.

Sean's hidden amusement turned to satisfaction as he studied the information John sent him. The *Heron* and the *Gibraltar* were to pick up a total of five hundred horses at week's end from the port of Drogheda. Montague had bought them outright and would double his money when he delivered them to the army. John assured him the ships were not insured, and it went without saying that neither were the animals. The cost of insuring live cargo was exorbitant because there were always heavy losses.

Sean perused the rest of his messages before his eyes lifted to Emerald. "I have to visit Maynooth tomorrow; will you come?"

How had he known she was about to broach the subject of a visit to Maynooth? She was certain he hadn't opened her letter; she doubted he had supernatural powers, yet somehow he had discerned her need. "What made you ask?" she challenged.

He grinned at her. "A shrewd guess. I know who wrote your letter." He held up his own. "His writing is familiar to me. Early last month I threw Johnny and Nan FitzGerald together. The inevitable happened; I believe your brother is smitten."

"Let me finish for you," Emerald said. "You concluded a brother wouldn't bother writing to his sister unless he had an ulterior motive, and when you saw me biting my lip, wondering how I was going to deliver the love letter, you offered to take me to Maynooth!"

Sean pulled her up into his arms. "When I see you bite your lip, it gives me very wicked ideas."

"Stop this minute. How am I to face the FitzGerald females?"

He took her hands, spread them wide, and looked down at her. "You are a match for any woman breathing, not only in beauty, but in wit, intelligence, and confidence. Don't pretend you haven't the courage to face the FitzGeralds."

She cast him a saucy look from beneath her lashes. "I'll not only face them, I'll outface them. I, too, am a FitzGerald!"

He cupped her face. "The fairest of them all."

She stood on tiptoe to lift her mouth to his. He indulged his need for half a dozen lingering kisses before he gave her back her words. "Stop this minute; I've pressing business."

"Indeed, sir, I can feel the evidence of it." She slipped her hand between their bodies to stroke that part of him that was suddenly demanding attention.

Sean's hands inched her skirts up her legs until he could caress bare thighs. "I'm glad you are spending time in the library, it can be most educational."

She traced his top lip with the tip of her

tongue. "Only with the proper tutor, and the right tools."

"That's true, you definitely need a desk." He lifted her so that her bare bottom sat on its polished surface. He opened her knees wide and stepped between them.

"I have a thirst for knowledge," she assured him, lifting her arms about his neck and threading her fingers into his black curls.

Sean opened his breeches and groaned as his swollen flesh sprang free of its tight constraints. "I'm a demanding teacher; I shan't spare the rod," he warned.

She arched against him teasingly, then withdrew. "Let the lesson begin."

The moment she arched her body, his hands slipped beneath her bottom cheeks to hold her imprisoned for his thrusts. He was delighted that she was uninhibited enough to let him take her here in the library where passion had stolen upon them. Obviously he had the power to make her forget about servants, and the fact that it was the middle of the day.

They were so hot for each other that within seconds Sean, too, was oblivious of their surroundings. Their passion built with such incredible speed, Emerald's cries of ecstasy filled his mouth. When his climax came, it was so hard, she screamed as his white-hot seed spurted into her. Her thirsty sheath closed on him tightly, draining him to the last creamy drop.

When she could think and speak again, she murmured, "Did I pass, sir?"

"Cum laude," he replied huskily, then added, "I must see to my other pressing business, but there will be homework tonight."

Emerald chose a few books to take up to the watchtower, then on impulse also took one of the vases of chrysanthemums.

Shamus brightened the moment he saw her. "Yer more beautiful every time I see you; my lad must be doin' something right."

She blushed, wondering if Mr. Burke had learned from Kate that she was probably with child.

"My Kathleen bloomed with radiance when she was carrying, and you're the same."

"So, you do know my secret," she said softly.

"What secret? Anyone with eyes in his head can see you ripening like a luscious fruit."

"Anyone but Sean," she said wistfully.

"What does he know; isn't it his first?" He leaned toward her as if imparting something confidential. "Men are not comfortable with the endless talk of childbearing. Ye need the women of yer family to confide in."

"I have no family."

"Don't be daft. Yer a FitzGerald; there's more women in yer clan than bees in a hive."

"And I've felt their sting...the FitzGerald females hate me."

"That's all ancient history; you were their rival then. Yer a rival no longer, not when yer carryin' his child. When they learn of it, the ranks of the sisterhood will close about ye to serve and protect, to coddle an' commiserate, to bully an' bless, to advise an' admire. Bless my soul, child, has no one ever taught ye these things? Do I have to play mother to ye?"

Emerald suddenly burst into tears.

"What the hell have I done now?" he asked Paddy Burke.

Mr. Burke cleared his throat. "I think it was the bit about her mother."

"I'm sorry," Emerald whispered, wiping her tears away with her fingers. "I vowed to hate her forever for abandoning me, but I don't. I miss her so much."

Shamus and Paddy exchanged a significant look. They all knew her mother lived only thirty miles away in Wicklow. It was wrong to keep them apart, especially now Emerald was having a child. Shamus decided to speak to Sean about it. "Come, dry yer eyes. I'm expectin' a visit from the crew of the *Silver Star*. Us O'Tooles have a reputation for puttin' a smile on a woman's face."

Emerald laughed then. She was willing to bet Shamus had been as big a devil as Sean in his day.

"That's better, Beauty." He winked and held up one of the books she had brought him. "We'll delve under the covers another day when we can be certain we won't be interrupted."

There was a commotion below as half a dozen sailors came laughing up the gatehouse stairs. As Emerald arose to leave, Mr. Burke followed her. "I've been meaning to have a word about Himself. He can no longer get from the bed to the chair without help. I'm almost afraid to leave him unattended."

"I'll speak to Sean. Shamus must come back to Greystones."

"He's too stubborn fer that. The young maids Kate sends up from the house are no match for him; he terrorizes them. He gets lots of company when one of the ships arrive, but in between, he's too much alone. Since you've bin here, I see how much he enjoys female company. I believe he would benefit from family visits."

"Do you mean the FitzGerald women?" Emerald asked thoughtfully.

"I do. He wouldn't be able to order a FitzGerald about, the way he does a servant."

"Sean and I are to visit Maynooth tomorrow. I'll speak to him about your suggestion, but I want you to tell him what you have told me. You have far more influence with him than I will ever have, Mr. Burke."

For the ride to Maynooth, Emerald was mounted on a placid sorrel mare who trotted along at her own slow speed, making Lucifer restless. "Devil take it, but that's a slow old jade you're riding." He grinned down at her. "I'd like to put something exciting between your legs." His grin widened. "I adore the way you blush."

" 'Tis a wonder I've any blushes left, between you and your father."

Sean's face sobered. "Paddy Burke thinks he'd benefit from the company of a FitzGerald female."

"So do I," she said emphatically. "He's lonely, and he likes women—"

"Beautiful women," Sean amended.

"All FitzGerald women are beautiful."

"Not by any stretch of the imagination," Sean disagreed, then deliberately made an offhand remark while carefully watching her reaction. "The only two real beauties were my mother and yours."

Emerald closed her eyes at the memories he had conjured. When she opened them, he saw they were liquid with unshed tears. *So, my father and Mr. Burke were right as usual,* he thought silently. He made a mental calculation, then decided, *As soon as this horse business is taken care of, I'll go to Wicklow and have a good long talk with Amber FitzGerald.*

Even though Emerald was resplendent in a cream velvet riding habit, her braided hair fashioned into a regal coronet, her full breasts luscious beyond comparison, the FitzGerald women welcomed her with genuine delight. This was her first time at Maynooth, and their warm hospitality made her feel that she was one of them. Of course, Sean was now Earl of Kildare and Maynooth his. He lived openly with her at Greystones, clearly showing that

Emerald was his chosen lady. And Sean's choice was their choice; it could be no other way.

She was surrounded by aunts and tried to keep their names straight as Sean introduced them in their pecking order. Emerald gave up after Maggie, Meggie, and Meagan all spoke in unison. Next came a group of younger women, all wanting to be fast friends. She saw the wicked glint in Sean's eye as he began the introductions. "You remember Bridget? She entertained thoughts of becoming a nun once upon a time. Of course, that was before she became the mother of four."

Emerald was astounded. The young fat woman bore no resemblance to the naked nymph who had cavorted in the cabin of the *Sulphur* five years earlier. Emerald realized that even though most of the cousins were now married, they and their families all dwelled at Maynooth. There was no end to the menagerie and never would be, by the look of how many offspring they had produced in the last five years!

A group of FitzGerald youths clustered about Sean, most hoping he would deem them old enough to crew his merchant ships. The FitzGerald females had married Murphys, Wogans, and O'Byrnes, yet still their sons and daughters were known as the FitzGeralds of Kildare.

"I shall leave you in the bosom of your family," Sean told Emerald with a straight face. "I have to make the rounds of Maynooth's tenant farms, so don't expect me until dinner tonight."

Maggie immediately took charge. "You'll be staying the night. Upstairs with ye', Fiona, an' plenish the master suite."

Emerald made eye contact with a tall, slim young woman who immediately flushed rosy as an Irish dawn. "I'm sorry, but I didn't catch your name."

"I'm Nan," she said softly.

Emerald liked her at once. She had a sweet face and a gentle voice. She didn't have that cheeky look about her that marked a number of the female FitzGeralds. "Will you give me the grand tour?" Emerald requested.

"With pleasure," Nan murmured, blushing again.

"Not before you sit yourself down an' refresh yourself with a glass of wine, or do you prefer ale?" Maggie inquired.

"Ale indeed! She shall have my rose cordial," Tiara decreed, sweeping the others aside. "Nan, you may do the honors." Tiara leaned close to impart a confidence. "She has gentle hands—clean, too, which is more than can be said for others in my court."

As Emerald sipped the delicious cordial, which most certainly contained something stronger than roses, she realized that the pecking order was set aside whenever Tiara spoke. She tucked the knowledge away for further consideration. Tiara fair beamed upon her when Emerald held out her glass for a refill. "You are a lady with a delicate palate. There are so few of us who are both well bred and discerning." Someone made a rude noise. "You see?" Tiara said serenely.

When Emerald had finished her drink, Nan took her upstairs to the master suite, where Fiona was remaking the wide bed with a fresh drift of snowy sheets. Apparently they were aware of Sean's exacting standards.

"I'll send Michael up to lay the fire," Fiona offered.

"Thank you. There's no hurry, we won't need to light it until we retire."

When she and Nan were at last alone, Emerald gave her the letter. "My brother, Johnny, asked me to give you this; it arrived just yesterday."

Nan seemed completely tongue-tied.

"I know that he rode from Meath to be with you last month, though I doubt Sean knows of the tryst."

Nan let out her breath with relief. "Oh, I'm so glad I can confide in you. May I call you Emerald?"

"Of course. I'm just as glad I can confide in you. Johnny and I are very close. Our father is a vile man. He was particularly savage with Johnny when he was a boy. He took pleasure in punishing him. Our mother protected us from his rages, but after she abandoned us, we only had each other."

"Your mother is my aunt Amber. I never knew her. She married your father and went to England before I was born."

"From what I've heard she married him to

get away from Maynooth and Ireland, then ironically she wished every day she was back here. I don't think she ever loved him, though she pretended to. Nan, I'm asking you never to do that to Johnny. Please don't pretend you love him so that he will take you away from here."

"Oh, Emerald, please don't think that. Johnny doesn't want to take me away; he wants to come and live here."

"Could you be happy and content here?"

"I could be happy anywhere with Johnny."

That's exactly how I feel about Sean, Emerald thought. "Read your letter." To give Nan privacy Emerald went into the adjoining bathing room to wash her hands and face.

She had thought the rooms sumptuous at Greystones, but this spacious bathroom took her breath away. The walls and ceiling were mirrored, the floor tiled with pale pink marble. The high, square tub and the steps leading up to it were also pink marble, as was the matching water closet.

"This is heavenly," she called out, "like being in the heart of a rose."

Nan came to the doorway, tucking her precious letter inside her bodice. "Would you rather take a bath than tour Maynooth? I can come back later."

"Good Lord, no! I'm not going to waste this decadent room on a bath by myself. I shall wait until Sean is free to join me."

When Nan's cheeks burned hotly, Emerald guessed she had been newly introduced to the secret intimacies of male and female.

314

Phrases from her brother's letter flashed into her head. *I could not help myself.... I've never acted so impulsively before.* Emerald closed her eyes and inwardly groaned, *Oh, Lord, Johnny, what have you done?*

24

The vast dining hall at Maynooth had been designed in ancient times to accommodate the family and its men-at-arms. From the head table on the dais Emerald looked across the room, imagining what it must have been like in centuries past. It did not take a great leap of imagination. The FitzGeralds employed no servants, since there were so many hands to share the work, but all members of the family had their own duties. The food was served by the younger ones aged ten to twelve, looking for all the world like page boys of yore, except that now some of them were girls.

For the most part the tables seemed to be segregated by sex; the men sitting together, while the women sat with their younger children. One table was filled by elderly ladies whose ages must range between seventy and eighty years, and Emerald concluded these must be the sisters of Sean's grandfather.

Great steaming haunches of beef and lamb were carried in on carving boards, followed by heaping platters of vegetables, loaves of bread, bowls of gravy, dishes of pudding, trays of fruit, and whole cheeses. It was suddenly brought home to Emerald just how much food was consumed each and every day by the FitzGerald clan.

"Where does all the food come from?" she asked Sean.

"Maynooth is self-sustaining," he explained. "We have thousands of acres. As well as horses, we breed cattle, sheep, and pigs. Potato, turnip, and cabbage plants stretch for miles, though cabbage is never served when I am in residence," he emphasized.

For the first time Emerald saw him in the role of earl, seated at the head of the table on the dais, master of all he surveyed. As usual, Sean was dressed in black, relieved only by immaculate linen at throat and wrist. These days he wore a black leather glove on only his left hand. He never removed it outside of their bedchamber. With them at the head table were his mother's sisters and their first cousins, who comprised the hierarchy of Maynooth.

"Ladies, I am in need of your advice and your help." He had their complete attention. "As you know, Shamus lives in the gatehouse watchtower. The use of his legs is much diminished. Paddy Burke is invaluable to me in running the shipping business, but at the moment he is reduced to nursemaid. Can you help solve my dilemma?"

The ladies all spoke at once. The discussion

was both lengthy and heated, bordering upon argument. Emerald felt alarm until she glanced uncertainly at Sean and saw him lower an eyelid in a deliberate wink. As she listened to them catalog Shamus O'Toole's faults, she feared none of them would offer her services. Therefore it came as a complete surprise when every last one volunteered, then argued about who should take precedence. It was an impasse, with each of the three elder sisters—Maggie, Meggie, and Meagan—presenting valid reasons why she should be the one.

When Sean raised his all-powerful hand, they deferred to him immediately. "I propose you take it in turns, say a month at a time."

They agreed to adopt his suggestion. "But who shall be first?" Maggie demanded.

"Give me credit for some intelligence. I wouldn't step into that trap if it were baited with gold. The choice is yours, ladies."

"In that case I shall be first. I take it we shall leave for Greystones in the morning?"

Emerald was almost afraid to look at Sean, for it was Aunt Tiara, his grandfather's sister, who had spoken. There was not even a murmur of dissent, because she was slightly mad they let her have her way. When no one overruled Tiara, Emerald summoned enough courage to glance at the Earl of Kildare. He was smiling broadly, and for once it reached all the way to his pewter eyes.

When they retired to the master suite, Emerald gave vent to her amusement. She rolled

317

on the bed with laughter, gasping for breath. "Ohmigod, whatever will your father say?"

"A great deal, liberally sprinkled with blue oaths and filthy curses," Sean replied with amusement.

"We are laughing now, but it won't be funny when we have to face him."

He came to the bed and stood looking down at her. "You're not afraid of him?" he asked quizzically.

"Of course I am," she admitted.

"But he has the softest heart in the world, especially where women are concerned. My mother had him wrapped about her little finger. Any man foolish enough to let that happen is vulnerable to all women."

His words clearly implied that he would never be so foolish. Emerald chose to ignore the warning. In her newfound confidence she not only believed she had Sean wrapped about her little finger, she believed she could make him jump through hoops.

There was a light tap on their door. Sean frowned, then moved to answer it. "Hello, my lovely, we were just talking of you."

"Then you weren't wasting your time," Tiara announced blithely. "I've brought Emerald a bedgown." She handed him a diaphanous wisp of magenta. "Purple will kindle her passion."

"I will kindle her passion."

She looked him up and down. "Yes, I believe you will. A man who is cocksure is irresistible. Good night, my darlings, I wish you joy of each other." Once again, they were left alone.

"And what does your maiden aunt know of cocks?"

He grinned. "Just because she never married doesn't make her inexperienced. Sexuality is probably the wellspring of her creativity. Take a look at this." He spread the sheer night rail across the bed.

" 'Tis indacent!" she said in a thick brogue.

"Speaking of indacent, have you seen the bathing room?"

"Oh, yes, I thought dinner would never end." She peeled off his black leather glove, then rolled over on the bed and presented her back to him. "Unfasten me."

The moment his hands touched her, he turned rigid. It would be nothing short of a miracle if they made it as far as the pink marble steps.

Sean lay awake long after Emerald had drifted off to sleep. His body curved about her protectively, one hand cupping her breast. A month ago it had fit his palm perfectly, now it was much fuller. Her body had subtly changed so that it was softer, more curvaceous; even her skin glowed like polished ivory. He finally acknowledged that she had quickened with child, and as he had feared, his need to cherish her doubled.

It had taken such a short time to accomplish the deed; he was filled with regret that he had impregnated her so quickly. Yet he had counted on the inevitable outcome when he lured her from her family, so regrets were as useless as an aging whore. Though giving her up would be like mutilating himself, he knew he would pay the price. The oath of revenge he had pledged while on the hulks paled beside the sacred vow he had sworn at his mother's grave.

His mind firmly cast aside regrets. He need not give her up for months yet. He must not even think about the future; he must live for today. When a woman carried her first child it should be the happiest time of her life, and he silently vowed to make it so. He would lavish attention upon her, he decided. Then he mocked himself. She was at her loveliest; how selfless of him to pledge his complete devotion!

The next thing Sean knew, it was morning and Emerald was softly moaning. He scooped her up and carried her to the bathroom water closet, where she was indelicately sick. He knelt behind her, his hands firmly holding in her stomach muscles as she retched. When her spasms subsided, he sat her on the pink marble steps and tenderly bathed her face.

"I'm sorry," she whispered.

"Never apologize to me again, Emerald." *I am the one who should beg your forgiveness.*

He carried her back to bed. "Stay put until you are feeling less fragile." He dressed quickly. "I'll bring Tiara, she is a wizard with herbs and potions. I'm sure it's unnecessary for you to suffer like this."

In no time Sean was back with Princess Tiara. "Just as I suspected!" she declared.

"What can I do to help?" Sean asked.

"Have you not done enough?" She pointed to the door. "Since you are the author of her misery, you may leave us. She cannot go to the dining hall and face gammon ham in her delicate condition. But of course, that won't stop you," she accused.

Emerald's eyes glittered with amusement as they met Sean's. "I'm feeling better already."

When they were alone, Tiara gave her a brilliant smile. "Ah, little one, I have so much to teach you. Lesson number one: Guilt is a formidable weapon. It allows you to rule all save those without conscience. Now, then, I have many remedies for morning sickness. There is chamomile, mint, barley water?"

"You decide."

Tiara was delighted. "How brave you are!"

"Not really," Emerald murmured confidentially. "I've guessed your secret. You only pretend to be doolally."

The older woman looked alarmed. "Mary and Joseph, promise me you won't tell the FitzGeralds. Sean knows, of course, he's always been a shrewd devil, but the rest of them think me quite mad."

When she returned, she not only brought an antidote for Emerald's queasiness, she brought her a flagon of almond and rose oil. "This works magic. You must rub it on your belly, breasts, and thighs every day so you will have no ugly stretch marks."

"Ugly stretch marks? God help me, but I'm ignorant," Emerald admitted.

"Then it's a grand thing I'm coming to Greystones. Are you feeling up to riding?"

"Oh, yes, the nausea has vanished. Will you ride, Tiara?"

"Of course I shall ride. I'm not quite ready for the knacker's yard. And by the way, my name is really Tara. The family changed it when I took to wearing the tiara. Their pathetic idea of wit, I suppose."

When Sean returned from breakfast, he was relieved to find Emerald completely recovered. As he helped her fasten her cream riding dress, a frown creased his brow. "Darling, how would you like to invite one of the younger FitzGeralds for a visit? My business is going to take me away for some days at a time, and I'd be happier if you had someone to keep you company."

"I like Nan best of all," she said tentatively, watching his reaction. She knew he had deliberately used Nan as bait to tempt her brother.

"Nan would be perfect," he agreed.

Emerald wondered just how perfect she would seem if he knew Johnny had already stolen the bait right off his hook. "Can she ride?"

"Darling, she's a FitzGerald of Kildare, she rides like the wind."

"Good. She can keep pace with you and Lucifer while I plod along with Tara."

He raised his eyebrows. "Tara, is it? You're a shrewd little baggage."

"I had a good teacher," she said, casting him a provocative glance. "While she's at Greystones she's going to abdicate her throne and teach me how to act like a princess."

"You, my beauty, need no lessons; you are quite haughty enough."

Emerald tossed her curls. "You wouldn't want me any other way."

It seemed the leaves had changed from green to blazing autumn colors overnight, and on their ride from Maynooth to Greystones the sun showed them off to perfection. When they arrived, Tara inspected the gardens, then laid claim to the stillroom as her own private domain.

Emerald put Nan in the bedchamber that Johnny had occupied, then, thinking to please Tara, offered her the room done in lavender.

"I'm sick to death of this color. Don't you have something in a nice calming green? I'm entering a new phase where I need to get back to nature," she announced theatrically.

"Of course," Emerald said, leading the way into another wing of Greystones. She put her in the green room next to Kate's, wondering what the no-nonsense housekeeper would make of Princess Tara.

In the morning when Emerald opened her eyes, the bed was heaped high with the last roses of summer and Sean stood gazing down at the enchanting picture he had just created. He handed her a lovely fluted wineglass filled with chamomile, mint, and rosewater, which she sipped gratefully. Tara's concoction was miraculous. Emerald sighed with relief and then happiness.

"What a lovely way to awaken. You must have plucked every rose at Greystones."

"Orders from Tara. She intends to distill them, so I thought I'd surround you with their beauty before she swoops down and carries them off. She also insists we are in for some very stormy weather."

"Perhaps she means when you tell Shamus she's here."

"You have such a delicate touch, I thought I'd let you do that."

"You devil! This situation amuses you, doesn't it?"

"Highly," he freely admitted. "I have complete faith in your witchery."

The very next hour brought such a blustery wind with a decided nip in it, that Emerald thought perhaps it was Tara who performed witchery. Leaving Nan in the library to reread and dream over Johnny's letter, Emerald decided to beard the lion in his den. She knew that Shamus had withdrawn from the big house after Kathleen's death, because he couldn't bear to live there without her. Emerald also realized he avoided the FitzGerald women because of misplaced pride regarding his disabled legs. She and Tara, wrapped in warm shawls, braved the wind and ran across the lawns to the gatehouse that stood at the end of the driveway. As they climbed to the tower,

Sean and Mr. Burke descended the stairs in an unseemly hurry.

"Cowards!" Emerald flung after them, then the two women covered their mouths so the laughter that threatened to bubble out did not reach the ears of Shamus O'Toole.

He sat by his favorite window with a warm plaid shawl tucked about his knees, his spyglass in hand. The smile of welcome on his still-handsome face faded the moment he laid eyes on Tara FitzGerald.

"What's this?" he demanded, wary as a wolf who always ranged alone.

"You remember your wife's aunt Tara, don't you, Shamus? She has graciously offered to stay for a month to keep us company and to help look after us. She is an absolute wizard with herbs and potions and thinks she can concoct something that will help your legs feel better."

"Wizard? Don't ye mean witch? I need no bloody nursemaid!" he shouted.

Emerald sank down upon her knees before him and took his hand. "Darling Shamus, I know you don't. It is Mr. Burke who needs help, but he is far too proud to ask for it."

"She's doolally," he mouthed frantically.

"I heard that, Shamus O'Toole," Tara declared, pulling a chair up to his and sitting herself beside him. "Did you know it was you who drove me to it?" she asked enigmatically.

Emerald watched his face as curiosity warred with rejection. Perhaps it was loneliness that allowed curiosity to win. Both of them listened raptly as Tara told her tale.

"When you first came to Maynooth to woo Kathleen, you were the handsomest young devil us FitzGerald females had ever clapped eyes on. There were a dozen of us about the same age at that time and you fair set all our hearts aflutter.

"Kathleen snubbed you. She was the eldest daughter of an earl and too overproud to allow a merchant sailor to woo her. Back then my predominant sin was not pride, it was vanity. I decided I wanted you, and with my great beauty I saw no earthly reason why I couldn't lure you from your infatuation with my cousin Kathleen. No matter how many times I threw myself across your path, you pretended to be oblivious and doubled your efforts to win Kathleen.

"To save my pride I told myself you preferred her to me because she was the eldest daughter of an earl, and you were only doing what was expedient. I was so madly in love with you, it broke my heart. I couldn't eat, I couldn't sleep, I couldn't even think coherently. I went completely out of my senses.

"I received so much sympathy and attention from the family that I began to enjoy it. I also realized it gave me power. So when I came to my senses I wisely kept it to myself and didn't let on. I also learned an invaluable lesson. The more Kathleen scorned you, the more determined you were to have her. The more proud and haughty she acted, the more you loved her. You were so masculine and domineering that Kathleen finally yielded to you. When she did that, I realized she had wanted you from the start and that was her clever way of making certain sure she got you."

Shamus had such a bemused look on his face that Emerald knew Tara had drawn his sting. He patted Emerald's hand. "I'll put up with her for Paddy's sake. A month isn't a life sentence."

"Are there blue iris in the garden?" Tara inquired.

"Yes, but the flowers are all finished now."

"It's the root I need; it warms and comforts the joints like nothing else."

"Ye'll have me walking in no time; it's the only bloody way I'll get away from ye," Shamus said testily, but Emerald knew he had capitulated.

"Would you show me where the blue iris grows, little one?"

"Yes, they're in the walled garden." As they left the gatehouse, Emerald said softly, "I was touched by your story."

"Ah, that was the idea. It flattered him outrageously to think we were all attracted to him. Then I used guilt to gain his sympathy, and finally I told him what he longed to hear, namely that Kathleen wanted him from the start. What a load of claptrap!"

Emerald was shocked at Tara's duplicity, yet as she thought over the tale she decided there was more than a grain of truth in it.

The wind continued to strengthen during the rest of the day and howled all night. Emerald slept only fitfully and the moment Sean quit the bed in the gray light of dawn, she opened her eyes. She watched with disbelief as he folded clean linen and shirts into a small trunk. "Where are you going?"

"I told you I had to go away for a few days. I'm only going up the coast."

Her worst fears were realized. "Surely you're not sailing in this?"

"It's only a squall, love, you needn't worry."

Emerald flung back the covers and padded over to the window. What she saw filled her with dire apprehension. The sea was roiling with anger. " 'Tis a gale!"

He came to the window, standing behind her with his hands resting on her shoulders. "It looks worse than it really is. Autumn always brings squalls."

She turned furiously, ready to fight if it would keep him safely home beside her, but his face was filled with such eager anticipation, her words died on her lips. For one reckless moment she thought of using guilt to keep him from leaving. Perhaps all she need do was pretend to be unwell. She could feel that his excitement was barely held in check. He was clearly bent on this adventure. She shuddered, afraid to pit herself against whatever it was that lured him.

"You're cold." He gathered her up and carried her back to bed. He tucked her in firmly. "Your condition is making you fanciful. I'm a sailor, I relish high seas." He lifted her chin until his eyes met hers. "Emerald, nothing can happen to me. After all, I have made a pact with the devil!"

25

The *Sulphur*, hidden in the mouth of the River Boyne where it emptied into the Irish Sea, waited, patient as a predator for its prey. Sean O'Toole had aboard his usual crew of FitzGeralds, as well as the Murphy brothers, along with a dozen of Maynooth's best horse handlers.

Sean slipped ashore under cover of dark and learned that the horses from Meath had already arrived at Drogheda. Montague's ships were overdue because of the unexpected early storm, but shortly after dawn the *Heron* sailed into harbor and dropped anchor to await the more cumbersome *Gibraltar*.

Sean waited for four hours, and still the *Gibraltar* hadn't come. They watched as the captain of the *Heron* gave his crew orders to start loading the livestock though the other ship was still missing. Just as the last animals were being led aboard in the late afternoon, the

Gibraltar lumbered into view. By now the sea had calmed down, so Captain Jones of the *Heron* sent a message to Captain Bowers of the *Gibraltar* informing him that he had already loaded his cargo and was weighing anchor immediately.

O'Toole knew exactly when dusk would fall. The *Heron* was safely out of sight of Drogheda, sailing down the coastline, when the *Sulphur* took on sail and rapidly closed the distance between the two ships. With the brawny Murphy brothers at his back, Sean O'Toole boarded the *Heron,* quietly brandishing a pair of brass-barreled pistols.

One look at the devil and his disciples was enough to prevent the captain from bellowing for help. Then his bosun, Daniels, emerged from belowdecks with his own brace of pistols. The captain knew defeat when it stared him in the face. His crew were dog tired, half of them nursing bites and kicks from their vicious cargo.

"If you know how to follow orders, this could turn out to be your lucky day," O'Toole said quietly. "If you had one wish, Captain Jones, it would be to rid yourself of these bloody horses. I am about to grant that wish."

Sean O'Toole took over the ship's wheel and sailed the *Heron* into the tiny port of Rush. The *Sulphur* stayed on the *Heron*'s stern, her carriage cannons threatening to blow Montague's ship out of the water.

Jones and his crew stood by in disbelief at how quickly and smoothly over two hundred animals were unloaded. Sean dispatched half of the handlers to Maynooth with the herd before he laid his proposition before Jones and his weary sailors.

"As you are probably aware, gentlemen, Fortune is a fickle jade. Once she stops smiling upon you, disaster usually follows. Fortune has turned her face from the Montagues. The losses the Montague Line has sustained, coupled with those that are yet to befall, will put them out of business within a few short months. But your fate need not hinge on theirs. Until now you have been overworked and underpaid. That is about to change.

"The *Heron* now belongs to me. I am sending her to Charleston to bring back a cargo of cotton. You are welcome to sign on for the voyage." He knew sailors had restless souls and were always eager for a change. When he laid out the pay scale, any reluctance the crew felt was quickly overcome. "You are free to enjoy the hospitality of Rush for a few days while the *Heron* is transformed into the *Dolphin* and she is victualed for the voyage to America."

Leaving the Murphy brothers in charge, Sean reboarded the *Sulphur,* taking Danny FitzGerald with him. They prowled back up the coast, knowing the *Gibraltar* would not start loading the rest of the horses until full daylight the next day. Again Sean O'Toole waited until the ship was headed down the Irish coast before he and Danny FitzGerald boarded her.

The crew of the *Gibraltar* already was in O'Toole's pay, though they had done nothing yet to earn it. They assumed O'Toole was adding the *Gibraltar* to his own line, as he had the *Swallow*. Sticking to the principle of divide and conquer, he sailed past Rush and made port at Malahide, where he unloaded the horses and sent them on their way to Maynooth. Only then did he inform Captain Bowers and his crew of the fate of the *Gibraltar*.

"She's a stinking old bitch who is going to a watery grave. Mr. Daniels will return to London and report that the *Gibraltar* ran aground on Lambay Island in the gale and that the damage to her hull, unfortunately, could not be repaired. Montague will have to send a vessel to take you off the island. He will no doubt send someone to investigate the disaster.

"There will be lots of physical evidence to support your claim. The three horses you somehow managed to kill while loading can remain in the hold. They'll wash up on the island with the timbers of the *Gibraltar*. I presume Captain Bowers would prefer to be reported missing than be held to blame for this loss?"

"You presume correctly, Lord Kildare."

"Then I think I can arrange a voyage to America for you, Bowers. Tim Murphy will be the captain, but I believe you'll settle for first mate?"

"That sounds most expedient, my lord."

"Are there any women on this island?" one of the crew asked Danny FitzGerald.

"Christ Almighty, a fortnight's holiday isn't enough, ye want jam on it too?"

At Greystones the priest who looked after the spiritual needs of those who resided there was a FitzGerald, familiarly known as Father Fitz. The entire staff attended Mass every day, then afterward, the elderly priest climbed the gatehouse watchtower to give Shamus communion. The only two people in all of Greystones who never went to the chapel were Sean and Emerald.

When Tara and Nan took it for granted that she would join them for Mass, Emerald decided that it was high time she did go to church. Of course she prayed about her baby every day, but suddenly she knew she would feel better if she did her praying in church and made friends with Father Fitz.

The small chapel was magnificent on the inside. The autumn sun streamed through the stained-glass windows onto the polished oak pews padded with red velvet. The altar cloth was a thing of beauty, heavily embroidered in gold thread, complementing the jewel-encrusted chalices and solid-gold candlesticks that sat upon it.

In contrast, Father Fitz wore a plain black cassock; the only thing colorful about him, his red shiny face wreathed in smiles. He served communion to everyone except Emerald. When he came to her, he fixed her with piercing blue eyes and said, "A word in private."

Disconcerted, Emerald nodded obediently, anticipating what the priest might say to her. The smell of incense, mingled with candle wax, was not unpleasant; it brought back memories of the times she and her mother had secretly attended church when her father was away.

One by one the staff slipped into the confessional booth, each emerging after only a minute or two. Nan waited until last. When she came out she looked quite happy. "I feel comforted," she whispered to Emerald. "Father Fitz is so understanding. Shall I wait for you?"

"No, go and have your breakfast. This is my first time, it may take a while."

The chapel was now completely empty, and Emerald was uncertain about what to do. Should she go into the confessional booth or wait for Father Fitz to come to her? She closed her eyes and said a prayer for Sean. She had been racked with worry for his safety ever since he had sailed off in the gale. The crashing sea and lashing wind had made it impossible for her to sleep since he left. She opened her eyes as an Irish voice intoned, "Emerald Montague." He was standing directly in front of her.

Though she hated to be called by that name, she did not contradict him. "Yes, Father. I know I should have come before this," she said contritely, "but—but at least I'm here now."

"Why are you here, Emerald Montague?" he demanded, his red face no longer wreathed in smiles.

"I—I have so many prayers, and I would like your blessing. I came to pray for Sean's safety and to pray for my—" Something in Father Fitz's face prevented her from uttering the word *baby*.

"Sean O'Toole has not set foot in God's House since he returned to Ireland. His soul is blackened with sin, yet he makes no confession, shows no contrition," he accused.

Compassion and understanding for the man she loved rose up in her. "You surely must know he was imprisoned for five years in unspeakable conditions. The sins were committed *against* him, not *by* him."

"He is guilty of committing deadly sins and breaking God's commandments every day of his life. Hate, wrath, pride, lust, consume him! His god has become vengeance, and in order to achieve it he will do anything—lie, steal, kill, or commit adultery. You would do well to use your influence to turn him back to God so he may cleanse his soul and receive absolution."

"I will try, Father," she said in a tight voice, thankful that she had not mentioned the child.

His eyes burned into her. "Are you ready to go and sin no more?"

"Go?" she echoed, terrified of his meaning.

"You must return to your husband, Emerald Montague. You are an adulteress!"

Her flaming cheeks blanched as the blood drained from her face and she turned icy cold.

"Are you ready to confess your sins and ask God's pardon?"

"I—I confess that I love Sean O'Toole, and if that is wrong, I ask God's pardon."

"Do not mock God, woman! Unless you are ready to end your adulterous relationship and return to your husband, you can neither ask forgiveness nor receive absolution."

"I—I am not Catholic," she said distractedly.

"Adultery is a venal sin in any religion, in any country!"

He turned from her then, and Emerald felt anger well up inside her and boil over. "You are guilty of both wrath and pride, to say nothing of self-righteousness, and if that is not considered one of your stupid sins, it ought to be!" she cried.

She hurried out of the church and back to Greystones. Avoiding everyone, she went straight up to the bedchamber she shared with Sean. She stared at the wide bed, feeling riven with guilt. The priest had called her an adulteress, and how could she deny it? In his eyes she was committing a deadly sin. What about God's eyes? she wondered wretchedly. She rationalized that it would be a greater sin to sleep in Jack Raymond's bed without love than to sleep in Sean O'Toole's. Emerald walked to the window, staring out to sea with haunted eyes. "Come home...come home.... I need you."

Sean O'Toole felt a great deal of satisfaction over all he had accomplished. Maynooth was richer by five hundred horses, paid for by William Montague, and his enemy's merchant shipping line was now reduced to four vessels.

As Sean had planned, he sailed down the Irish coast to the seaport where Emerald's mother lived. As the *Sulphur* dropped anchor in the Bay of Wicklow, he wondered if he was doing the right thing. He had known of Amber FitzGerald Montague's whereabouts as soon as he returned to Ireland. Mr. Burke told Sean all about her arrival the day before they buried his grandfather, and how Shamus had provided the money she used to set herself up in business.

Sean had hated her for years because she was a Montague and for the part she had played in Joseph's destruction, but he had begun to realize that Emerald loved her mother deeply and longed to be reunited with her. He decided to see the woman for himself; talk to her, question her. Only then would he make the decision about inviting her to Greystones. After what Montague did to her, she must hate the man almost as much as Sean did himself. Perhaps she would make a better ally than enemy. Perhaps he could use her, too.

Sean left his crew aboard and disembarked his ship. He walked past the boardinghouses and grog shops that lined the docks and made his way to the more affluent end of town. He went up the steps of an elegant stone house at the end of a long street and lifted the heavy brass door knocker. He was shown into a business office by a maid in a starched cap and asked to wait.

Amber FitzGerald entered her office briskly, then her footsteps faltered as she came face to face with the gentleman who was waiting to see her. She was shrewdly knowledgeable about men, usually able to size them up in a glance, but this one was different. He had the most arresting face she had ever seen, as well as the proudest carriage, and darkest eyes.

It was impossible to tell his age. Though not advanced in years, there was nothing youthful about him. Dressed dramatically in black, he was, she saw immediately, a figure of authority. He looked like a man who would break the rules if it suited his own purpose; he looked dangerous.

Amber knew she had never laid eyes on him before and yet there was a vaguely familiar quality about him, as if she should have been able to guess his identity immediately.

Sean O'Toole found it difficult to believe that the ravishing young woman before him could be old enough to be Emerald's mother. He looked more closely and saw the fine lines about her eyes and mouth. They did not diminish her attractiveness; rather they added to her allure, hinting at worldly experience.

Her gray silk gown was tastefully elegant and understated, yet it was a clever foil for her blazing hair. He watched her mouth curve into an easy smile, expressing complete confidence that she could handle any man breathing. Joseph's words stole to him from the past: *If you could see her, you'd understand.* And now he did understand. Perfectly. She was feminine down to her fingertips; exactly like Emerald, except for her coloring.

"I am Sean O'Toole."

Amber's eyes widened. How could this possibly be the young Irish Prince her little girl had fallen in love with? He had a stark male beauty an older woman of vast experience might appreciate, but how could such satanic looks appeal to a child? Looking at him brought all Joseph's essence rushing back to her, making her gasp at the bittersweet memories.

"Please...sit down." Her hand indicated an elegant gilt chair. She poured him Irish whisky and a small glass of dry sherry for herself, then she sat in the chair opposite his, rather than placing the barrier of her desk between them.

"I know what he did to me, and I have learned what he did to Joseph, but I can only imagine what he did to you."

"No"—he slowly shook his head—"I don't believe you can, Amber."

As he spoke, she watched his face, his eyes,

and felt some measure of his pain. She realized he was greatly altered both on the inside and on the outside. "You survived."

Again, he slowly shook his head. "Not wholly. Much of me died." Why was he telling her these things? Perhaps because she was a man's woman, easy to talk to, and she, too, had suffered and survived, but not wholly. "The part of me that survived lives for revenge."

"I understand that concept. It almost consumed me, until I learned to set it aside until the moment of reckoning arrives. All things come at their appointed time."

Sean sipped his whisky, rolling it about his tongue, savoring it. "That is a platitude that has helped you survive. I am too impatient to await the sands of time. The first thing that died in me was my faith in God. I replaced it with faith in myself."

"Perhaps it is simply pride. When we are forced to do degrading things, the heart swells with hatred and pride."

"I have no heart, no conscience, no fear, no love, no pity, no shame."

"If most of your emotions are dead, will you be capable of enjoying your revenge when you take it?"

"Passionately; I am quite capable of hatred. I am well along the road of revenge. These days I simply think of it as justice."

Amber smiled. "We are so alike." She knew he was here for a purpose and since he had only one purpose in life, he meant to use her. Well, let him try. She had learned to turn the tables on men. Now it was *she* who used *them.*

"What do you know of your children?"

Amber's heart lurched, then stopped for a moment. Dear God, how vulnerable she became at the mere mention of them. "I know nothing, save the fact that they are children no longer." She could not conceal the longing in her eyes; she hungered for news of them.

"Your daughter is wed to Jack Raymond."

Amber shot to her feet, her hand clutching her breast. "That whoreson married my precious Emerald to his brother's bastard? I'll kill him!"

"At the present time she lives with me at Castle Lies."

Relief washed over her. Emerald had loved Sean O'Toole since she was a child. Amber's relief was short-lived. Had he not just told her he could not love? Had he not referred to Greystones as "Castle Lies"? Sean O'Toole had an agenda; he would use anything and anyone to accomplish it. He held her daughter in the palm of his hand. What about her son? She looked at Sean's hands encased in black leather, and she shuddered.

"What of Johnny?"

"He is far shrewder than his father ever dreamed. We are allies, just as William and Shamus once were."

"No good ever came from a FitzGerald-Montague alliance," she said bluntly.

"I do not seek *good.* I have the means to ruin Montague financially and to utterly destroy his reputation, but I shan't be satisfied until I have heaped humiliation upon Montague and Raymond in the eyes of the world." His eyes glittered dangerously. "I have such a weapon in my hands." He veiled the hatred in his eyes and turned to the reason that had brought him. "Amber, will you come to Greystones, for a visit with Emerald?"

She paced to the desk and back, wondering if Emerald would ever forgive her. It didn't matter. She would sell her soul for a chance to be with her daughter again. *Damn you, Sean O'Toole, you knew when you came here what my answer would be.*

Amber opened her mouth, then shut it again and paced to the desk one more time. She turned to face him. "I will come if you give me your word about something."

"Your secret is safe with me, *madam*. I will not tell Emerald that you own a brothel."

26

The raging sea calmed, the wind dropped, and the autumn sun reappeared. Though Emerald did not believe that God had answered her prayers, nevertheless she offered up thanks as she sipped Tara's potion that banished her morning sickness.

When she was dressed she went along to

Nan's bedchamber, thinking a ride in the sunshine would do them good. Perhaps Nan could teach her to be a better horsewoman. When she opened the door, she was dismayed to find Nan with her fair head hanging over the edge of the bed, vomiting into the chamber pot.

"Oh, dear, no," Emerald murmured softly.

Nan raised startled eyes. "I must have eaten something that upset my stomach."

"Nan," Emerald said softly, "there's no need to pretend with me. You are likely having a baby. I know all about morning sickness; I, too, am with child."

"God in heaven, what am I to do?"

"The first thing is to stop your nausea. I'll get Tara."

"No, you must not!" Nan cried with alarm.

"She knows about me and the shock didn't kill her."

"Oh, Emerald, it's not the same," Nan moaned.

"I'll get you some of my chamomile and rose. I'll be right back."

When Nan's retching finally ceased, Emerald bathed her face and hands.

"I don't want Tara to know. She'll tell my mother and I shall bring terrible shame down upon her."

"Which one is your mother?" Emerald asked, feeling embarrassed that she couldn't keep the FitzGeralds straight.

"Maggie is my mother."

"Oh, dear," Emerald said, knowing immediately that chastity was exceedingly high on that good woman's list.

"I'm so sorry that you, too, are in trouble, Emerald. But no one would dare challenge the earl, or breathe one word of criticism about you."

"Ha! You should have heard the things Father Fitz said to me yesterday, and he doesn't even know I've conceived. In his eyes and in God's, I'm an adulteress! Neither you nor Johnny is married, so it's not nearly the sin I've committed."

"Is Sean happy about it?"

Emerald reflected a minute before she answered. "I'm not sure. One thing is certain, he isn't delirious. He refused to believe it until last week at Maynooth."

"Men are funny," Nan murmured. "Johnny won't believe me either; we only did it once. He'll be that angry with me."

"Damn it all, Nan, it's you who should be angry at Johnny, not the other way about! Nan, the FitzGeralds will find out sooner or later. A pregnancy isn't something you can hide for too many months."

"Can I stay here?"

"Of course you may, but Sean will find out."

"Ohmigod, he'll be furious with me!"

Emerald silently agreed with her.

"Please don't tell him?" Nan pleaded.

"I won't tell him."

"And don't tell Johnny?"

"Nan, I won't, but you should tell him.

344

He should marry you—and sooner rather than later."

"Oh, wouldn't that be wonderful?"

"The FitzGeralds may not agree. They hate the English in general and the Montagues in particular."

Nan rocked herself back and forth, trying to find a way out of her terrible predicament. "If the earl approved, they'd capitulate. Emerald, you must start working on him the minute he gets back. Don't mention the baby, but suggest that your brother should marry a FitzGerald. A few hints at the right time wouldn't go amiss and might make him amenable to the idea."

Emerald rolled her eyes. God Almighty, the girl hadn't the faintest notion of Sean's immalleable personality. "Do you feel better? I'll get Tara to mix up some more of her magic elixir, without letting on to her that she's making it for two." Emerald realized they wouldn't be riding this morning. "I want you to stay in bed and rest. I'll take a book up to Shamus and read to him. He enjoys it so much, and it will keep Tara away from you."

When Emerald arrived in the watchtower, Tara had just given Shamus a limb rub with the ointment she had mixed from the root of iris. His spyglass lay forgotten on the windowsill and he looked more relaxed and contented than Emerald had ever seen him.

"I've come to read to you. I hope this is more to your liking than the last book I brought."

"What is it, Beauty?" he asked eagerly.

345

"It's Marco Polo's *Travels.*"

"Ah, just the ticket to fuel my wanderlust." He winked.

Emerald settled herself beside him and, becoming as engrossed as her audience, didn't stop reading for almost two hours. Finally she closed the book. "My throat is dry as a bone."

"Tara, pour us all a dram. What's yer poison, my beauty?"

Tara poured Shamus whisky, but for herself and Emerald she served a liqueur that tasted of pears.

"This is delicious. Did you make it, Tara?"

"Of course I made it. I spend hours in the stillroom communing with nature."

As she sipped her drink, Emerald said reflectively, "I didn't realize Nan was Maggie's daughter."

Shamus chuckled. "Maggie, now, there's a straitlaced woman for you. Wouldn't approve of your brewing intoxicants from pears."

"Nor of your whisky imbibing," agreed Tara. "She's the next one to spend a month at Greystones."

The chuckle left Shamus's voice. "Why is it women enjoy depriving men of their pleasure?"

Emerald stood up and squeezed his hand. "Not all women, Shamus." She picked up his spyglass and lifted it to her eye. "Some of us understand what pleasure is all about." Suddenly, she gasped as if she had seen something she couldn't believe. She put the glass to her other eye to make sure. "He's home! Sean's home!" She dropped the glass into Shamus's lap, lifted her skirts in both hands, and began to run.

"By the Virgin, I'll bet my son understands what pleasure is all about!"

Emerald ran down the tower steps, then beneath the arch of the gatehouse and across the lawns that led to the short causeway above Greystones's harbor. Breathless, she paused to watch the *Sulphur* dock at the stone jetty; it was truly a beautiful sight. Her eyes traveled the deck, skimming over the dark heads until she saw him at the wheel. There was no mistaking the tall figure, garbed in black. The moment she saw him she began to wave frantically. When he raised a black-gloved hand, she began to hurry down the long descent to the jetty.

Emerald could hardly contain her excitement as she waited impatiently for him to disembark. She was so glad she had donned the soft peach wool gown this morning, for she knew how flattering it was. As he came striding toward her, she cried out his name with joy, "Sean...Sean," and then she was enclosed in powerful arms, lifting her face for his kiss.

"Oh, I missed you.... I love you.... I missed you so much," she cried between kisses.

Sean lifted her high and swung her about. "I'll have to go away more often, if this is the homecoming that awaits me."

She grabbed two fistfuls of black curls in mock fury. "I'll chain you to the bed, you roving devil!" The minute she said it, she could have cut out her tongue. How could she have reminded him that for years he'd slept in chains? "Oh, God, I'm sorry!" Wildly, she covered his face with kisses to take the sting from her thoughtless words.

Sean cupped her face and laughed down into her eyes. "Never pick and choose your words with me, Emerald. I hope you know you can say anything to me." He grinned. "If it's too outrageous, I'll simply take you over my knee and tan your arse."

"You wouldn't dare be fierce with me in my condition," she challenged saucily.

He looked down at her, shaking his head. "You're still so slim; I expected you to look like a little pudding by now." Again he lifted her feet from the ground.

"You devil, put me down this instant."

"I brought you a present," he said low.

She slipped her hand inside his black leather jack to discover where he had hidden it. He bit her ear and whispered, "Lower." She gasped as her eyes glanced down at the bulge between their bodies. "Cocksure devil!"

"I'm only teasing. It's another sort of present." He stepped to one side so that her view of the ship would be unimpeded.

Emerald tore her laughing gaze from his to scan the ship. Her eyes came to rest on the elegant figure of a woman with amber-colored hair who stood at the rail watching them. Emerald's hand went to her throat. She stared unmoving, as if she were seeing a ghost, then she began to tremble like a leaf. She felt rooted to the ground. After all this time, she feared her imagination was playing a trick on her. "Mother?" she whispered, then her feet began to move toward the ship.

The moment Amber saw her daughter move toward her, no matter how tentatively, she stepped onto the gangplank.

Emerald's step quickened until they stood facing each other. Her green eyes searched her mother's, then flooded with unshed tears. Both were momentarily unable to speak, but they enfolded each other in loving arms as they fought back tears of happiness. When Emerald looked at Sean, the tears spilled over. "However did you find her?"

"I live in Wicklow," Amber said quickly, pointing south to the purple mountains.

Emerald dashed the tears from her eyes as her heart swelled with emotion. She was reunited with the two people she loved most in the world. She had a million unanswered questions, but at this moment she was content to just look at them.

Sean waved the two women up to the house. "Don't worry about your luggage. The pair of you have years of catching up to do."

When they reached the lawns, Amber stopped to take in the splendor of the palatial Georgian mansion.

"Welcome to Greystones." Emerald led the way to the magnificent receiving room, where Amber sat down on the cushioned window seat overlooking the walled garden, exactly where Emerald had sat the first time she entered this room.

"I came to Greystones once, but only to the gatehouse." Amber paused, trying not to let old wounds overwhelm her. They were suddenly tongue-tied, not wanting to indulge in useless small talk, yet not sure where to begin. "You have turned into a beautiful, vibrant young woman. I was so afraid your father would crush your personality and destroy your very essence."

"But he did!" Emerald cried. "From the moment you deserted us, he made my life as intolerable as he'd always made Johnny's."

"Oh, my darling, I didn't desert you, how could you ever think it? He almost beat me to death. He vowed I'd never see you again. He left me dying, locked in my room without food or water."

Emerald was horrified. She remembered as if it were yesterday. "He told me you'd run off with your lover, but I couldn't believe you would go without us. I came up to your chamber...the door was locked; you didn't answer. Oh, Mother, I'm so sorry Johnny and I left you there."

"There was absolutely nothing you could do. Montague is evil incarnate and when the madness is upon him—no power on earth can overcome it."

"I didn't think I could hate him any worse than I did, but now I know that he savagely beat you, my hatred has doubled. But, Mother, you are wrong. There is a power stronger than his. Sean O'Toole possesses that power. He intends to destroy him."

Suddenly, Amber was more afraid for her daughter than she had ever been. Emerald was caught between two terrible forces, and only pain and suffering could result. The last thing she wanted to do was frighten her daughter. She must go slowly when warning her against Sean. Emerald was obviously head-over-heels in love with the man and would immediately jump to his defense.

"He told me you were married to Jack Raymond. How could such a thing happen?"

Emerald sighed heavily. "It's such a long story; endless, it seemed to me. After you left us—I mean, after we returned to England—Father wouldn't allow me to go to school. Instead he employed a horrible woman as my governess to obliterate every last trace of Irish in me. I was forbidden to utter your name, and my own was changed from Emerald to plain Emma. And they succeeded in turning me into plain Emma. They changed everything about me: my hair, my clothes, my speech, my behavior, my personality. When they finished, I was a little English mouse, cowering in my hole at Portman Square."

Emerald shuddered, remembering that dark house. "It was like a prison. Nay, I lie, it was like a tomb, where I felt buried alive. I had no suitors, nor any slightest hope of any, save my bastard cousin Jack. When he asked me to marry him, I reluctantly agreed. I thought it would get me out from under Father's cruel dominance. I thought it would be my escape from that ugly brick monstrosity. I was never more wrong in my life. My uncle's by-blow wanted only to become a Montague and live in the Montague mausoleum. I was caught in a trap of my own making."

Her daughter's suffering was so much harder to bear than her own. "Oh, my darling, you repeated my tragic mistake when I married your father to escape the Maynooth menagerie."

They saw each other through new eyes, not as mother and daughter, but as two women with all the same needs and emotions and passions.

"Sean O'Toole rescued me."

My God, no wonder she thinks him her Prince. She was a classic damsel in distress; he her knight in shining armor. How can I open her eyes to the fact that he will use her vulnerability to play out his revenge? Amber knew the task before her was monumental. O'Toole was not only dangerously attractive—witty, charming, virile, and powerful—but he was also domineering, manipulative, and a ruthless seducer. In short he was a man, and therefore a woman's natural-born enemy. How could she make Emerald face these facts, before life ruthlessly taught her its lesson? *I cannot gain her confidence immediately. But I will do everything I can to help her if she needs me.*

As they were talking, the Greystones servants, one after another, found excuses to walk past the elegant receiving room, until Kate Kennedy descended upon them and sent them packing.

Emerald couldn't very well ignore the woman who had done so much to make her feel at home here at Greystones.

"Kate, come in. Come and meet my mother."

In no way loath to satisfy her curiosity, Kate came forward to meet the young woman she'd persistently heard stories about over the years.

"My mother, Amber FitzGerald...Kate Kennedy, Greystones's housekeeper. As well as being extremely good at what she does, Kate has been both kind and fair to me. She doesn't resent my presence here, not any longer."

The two women sized each other up.

So this is the FitzGerald hussy who caught herself an English aristocrat and lived to bitterly regret it. No wonder Joseph lost his head over her, then paid for it with his life. She has a rare beauty and no mistake, which Emerald has inherited, but Emerald has a sweetness about her this woman never possessed.

Amber was thinking, *She's shrewd as well as capable and she certainly has no love for me, but that doesn't matter. It is good for my daughter to have such a one in charge here.* "I'm extremely pleased to meet you, Mrs. Kennedy. Greystones must be a heavy responsibility."

"Your daughter has brought sunshine and laughter back to this house after we despaired of ever having either again."

Emerald flushed with pleasure. "Kate, you are too kind."

"You have brought joy to Sean and Shamus. I won't go so far as to say you have replaced

Kathleen, that would be an impossibility, but you have filled a great void at Greystones."

"Kate, would you find Nan FitzGerald? I'd like her to meet my mother."

"She's hiding in her chamber. It'd take a crowbar to pry her out of it."

"Oh, well, never mind; you'll meet her at dinner. And Tara's here, do you remember her?"

Kate cut in with a sniff. "And who could ever forget her? The place is overrun with FitzGeralds. I'll plenish the lavender chamber for your mother." Kate nodded her head in lieu of a curtsy before she departed.

"I remember Aunt Tara with great affection, even though Kate Kennedy seems to have none for her."

"Well, they think she's doolally because she pretends to be a Celtic princess. But she's not mad at all; she's most wise."

"She was the one who taught me all about herbs and their medicinal properties."

"She's only been here a week, but she's completely taken over the stillroom." Emerald wished they could get back to the personal conversation they had been sharing when they were interrupted. She wanted to learn all about her mother's life, but hesitated to put questions to her, hoping instead she would volunteer the information. When Amber was not forthcoming, Emerald decided she would ask Sean when they were alone tonight.

"Come upstairs and make yourself comfortable. You simply have no idea how happy your visit has made me. If only Johnny were here!"

"Does he visit you?" Amber asked hopefully.

"He and Sean have business together. He's been here once and he has written to me. I'm hoping he will become a regular visitor."

Amber's eyebrows elevated. "Either he has learned to stand up to his father or he has learned to be devious, as I did."

"I think he learned to do a bit of both in order to survive. Apparently, Father gave up trying to make a sailor of him; he presently runs Father's shipping business."

"Ah," Amber said, nodding wisely, "now I see why Sean O'Toole is cultivating him."

Emerald flushed. She wanted to deny that Sean was merely using him, but she could not. "Johnny loves Ireland. He's crazy about Maynooth."

"That's understandable, he always had a passion for horses. He probably belongs there."

"We'll ride over one day. You must be dying to see all the FitzGeralds again."

"You go too fast, darling. Maynooth belongs to the Earl of Kildare. Perhaps he doesn't want me there."

Emerald tossed her curls and smiled her secret smile. "The earl wants what I want. I have him eating out of my hand."

"Never mistake him for a gelding, Emerald. He is a stallion and I doubt you'll ever tame him," Amber warned.

"I don't wish to tame him, Mother, I want him exactly as he is."

Be careful what you wish for, Emerald. A wish
that is granted can turn into your worst nightmare.

27

"I cannot come down to dinner; I can't face her," Nan said miserably.

"You're being ridiculous! My mother is kind and gentle. When she finds out that you love Johnny, she will adore you. No one will guess your secret, Nan, unless you arouse suspicion by hiding."

When the two young women finally arrived in the dining room, Tara and Amber were having a lively conversation about the beneficial properties of spices. Sean, too, was awaiting them. He was a charming host, making the proper introductions, then seating them one by one. He put Amber on his right, Tara and Nan on his left, then sat Emerald opposite him, so that he could feast his eyes upon her.

With four Irish females in one room, three of whom enjoyed being the center of attention, the conversation was animated and filled with laughter. Even Nan contributed occasionally, though she blushed scarlet each time Amber's warm eyes rested upon her.

Sean amused his guests without monopolizing the conversation, giving each lady his undivided attention when he spoke to her. Emerald found it difficult to tear her eyes from him. The snowy linen at his throat contrasted sharply with his swarthy skin, black hair, and pewter eyes. Excitement was mounting inside her until all she could think of was the moment they would close their bedchamber door and be free to express how much they had missed each other.

Before the meal was over, Amber realized just how deeply in love her daughter was with the earl. She also knew that Sean O'Toole was by no means indifferent. Those dark eyes told her that in addition to a raging desire for Emerald, he felt possessive of her. And yet Amber could not rid herself of the suspicion that, rather than stealing her because he could not live without her, he had likely taken her for revenge against the Montagues.

Sean O'Toole had told her plainly that he would not be satisfied until he had heaped humiliation on his enemies in the eyes of the world and that he had the weapon in his hands. *Could that weapon be Emerald?*

Amber's gaze was drawn again and again to the dark, magnetic man at the head of the table. His revenge was nowhere near complete. *Justice,* he had called it. She wondered uneasily exactly what and whom his justice encompassed. Amber knew she must have a serious talk with Emerald. Not tonight, of course; Sean and Emerald's longing for each other was so palpable, it saturated the very air.

Sean secretly watched Emerald, but as the

meal progressed, he watched her openly. He knew he had done the right thing by reuniting her with her mother. Emerald was vibrant tonight, she glowed with happiness, and it brought him a measure of deep satisfaction that he was partly responsible for the joy she felt.

He had been good for her; there was no comparison between this ravishing woman who spoke and laughed with passion and the pale pathetic girl he had spirited away from London. He admitted that Emerald had been good for him too. She was generous in her love for him, holding nothing back, and he knew she had helped to heal his more superficial wounds. They had been equally good for each other; he could never have regrets for their time together. It was as close to perfect as anything could ever be in this life.

Amber spoke to him. He gave her his immediate attention. "Forgive me, I was distracted." Their eyes met, clearly revealing their thoughts to each other.

"If you will excuse me, Tara has promised to show me the stillroom."

Tara spoke too. "This could take hours, so we will bid you good-night."

Even Nan murmured, "I need a book from the library."

Sean grinned unabashedly at Emerald. "The FitzGerald females are conspiring so that we can be alone."

"Are we that transparent?" Amber smiled.

"Are *we?*" Sean laughed.

As they ascended the stairs Sean slipped his arm about Emerald. "You look well. How is your morning sickness, sweetheart?"

"It is much improved," she assured him, basking in his tender concern.

Emerald went straight to the window and threw back the curtains that Kate must have drawn. "Darling, thank you, thank you, thank you for bringing my mother. You have made me blissful; my happiness is now complete! Oh, I feel so alive tonight, like the sea!"

He lifted her in his arms for the sheer pleasure of holding her. "I thought you were afraid of the sea," he teased.

"Only when you're out there—but it's as if you conquered it and you are come back to me and I'll never fear it again!" She twined her arms about his neck. "When you are with me, I fear nothing and no one in the world."

He bent his head to taste her. "It has little to do with me, and everything to do with the confident woman you have become." He kissed her ear, then traced the tip of his tongue down her throat, setting her all ashiver. "Let me light the fire before I undress you. I don't want you to catch cold."

"It's so lovely to be surrounded by your tender concern for me. I'm the luckiest woman alive. Did you miss me?"

"I more than missed you, I craved you, my blood hungered for you, and now that we're here alone, I want to intoxicate you with my passion." He took the pillows from the bed and tossed them before the fire he had just lit, anticipating another fire he was about to kindle. He lifted a glass flacon from beside the bed. "Is this some love potion Tara has brewed you?"

Emerald lifted her skirts, warming her legs at the fire and allowing him a tantalizing glimpse of creamy thighs and a riot of tiny black curls. "No, it's rose and almond oil to prevent stretch marks and keep my skin beautiful for you."

"Then it is indeed a love potion. I am about to anoint you, but let me warn you, beloved, my hands will steal your reason. When I am done, I will own you body and soul."

As he stalked toward her she threw him a provocative look from beneath her lashes. Didn't he know he already owned every particle of her being? He removed the soft wool gown, followed by her undergarments, then gently pushed her back to lie naked among the pillows. His eyes, dark with passion, roamed over her at their leisure, caressing, adoring, worshiping her flesh; his piercing gaze promising to bring her total and absolute pleasure.

He poured the perfumed oil into his palm and warmed it at the fire. Its fragrance stole to her, then enveloped her senses as his hands made initial contact with her body. He began at her throat, then drew his palms downward to caress her heart. Next, he cupped her shoulders, then glided down her arms, holding back from anointing her breasts until she was breathless with anticipation. When his firm hands did cover her breasts, spiraling in circles, she began to tingle and throb with pleasure.

"Mmm, that feels absolutely heavenly." She stretched her arms above her head, bringing the tips of her hardening breasts close to his mouth as he bent over her. His tongue shot out to flick her rosebud nipples and she cried out at the delicious sensation it evoked.

Sean's hands moved over her rib cage, then onto her soft belly, rubbing, circling, massaging, until she began to arch her mons in arousal. With oil-slick fingertips he traced the delicate folds beneath the silky black tendrils, outlining her cleft with featherlike strokes. Then his possessive fingers pressed her open so he could slide one inside.

Slowly, he advanced and withdrew the long finger until she made a love sound that told him she wanted more. Then he thrust two fingers into her silken sheath. She was so burning hot inside, it felt as if he had thrust his fingers into the flames of the fire! As he brought her to climax, his dark eyes watched each flicker of excited enjoyment, every shudder of sensual release.

Sean poured more oil and began again at her toes. He gave her a foot massage, then drew his hands up her legs in long, firm strokes. By the time he reached her silken thighs, Emerald was tossing and writhing once more as the delicious sensations of arousal rippled up inside her. As the firelight turned her body to molten gold, he watched her as long as he could, then, all his resistance gone, he dipped his dark head to tease her, to please her.

His tongue delved and danced, licking, tasting, swirling, plunging, until her moans turned to sharp cries. She lay wantonly sprawled before him, eyes closed, limp from his lavish loving, yet every inch of her skin so sensitized, she knew the moment he touched her again she would be instantly riven with need.

When she lifted sultry eyelids, she saw that he had finally removed his clothes. As he knelt before her, naked, she reached out avid fingers to encircle his engorged manhood. "You've loved me twice, why don't you take your own pleasure?" she whispered.

"You've pleasured me twice," he murmured. "Watching your enchantment, knowing I alone can do this to you, wildly excites me." He turned her over then and began his ministrations all over again. The powerful strokes down the entire length of her back made her skin feel sinuously smooth. His lips traced tiny kisses down her spine. "You are like warm satin. I've had a recurring erotic dream about you for years, Beauty. Your back is the only thing that is exposed to me. I know it is you by your glorious cloud of hair. I vow you have the most exciting back on earth."

Sean's hands took total possession of her derriere. His fingers slipped into the cleft between her bottom cheeks, working their devilish magic. When she arched her bum, he slipped a possessive finger inside her and circled the tip about her woman's center.

Emerald clutched the pillows with her fists. "Sean, I need more," she gasped.

"I know you do. I am going to give you more." He straddled her back, curving his long, lithe body over hers. With loving hands he raised her bottom and entered her from behind.

Emerald had never experienced such a thing, never dreamed that such a position was possible, yet as he began to move with wild, rhythmic gyrations, she realized that this was the elemental way a stallion covered a mare. The sensations inside her were different, far more intense and overtly carnal as each thrust played over her hard little bud with hot sliding friction, before impaling her with each drugging stroke.

She felt him throbbing, then she became aware of both their heartbeats inside her body. She wondered blissfully how it could last this long, then she knew how wise he was in the way of her body. He had brought her to orgasm twice, before he had buried his manroot hard inside her, knowing she would be quick to arousal but slow to climax.

He held her breasts in his hands, cherishing them as if they were made of precious porcelain, yet demonstrating that at this moment, her whole body belonged to him. When Sean felt her third spasm shudder through her and grip his cock, he allowed himself to spend, flooding into her with liquid fire. The scream that had been building in

Emerald's throat was drowned by Sean's harsh cry of release.

Amber knew there was someone she must see at Greystones and something she must say that was long overdue. Though Shamus would probably be reluctant to see her, Amber had to thank him for the generous financial aid that had literally saved her life.

She sought out Paddy Burke, also needing to thank him for the part he had played in her survival. Amber was vastly relieved when Paddy greeted her warmly. They left the big kitchen arm in arm, quite aware of the resentful looks cast their way by Mary Malone and Kate Kennedy.

When Mr. Burke took Amber up to the gatehouse tower, Tara greeted them, then left discreetly with Paddy.

Amber was shocked when she saw Shamus. The last time she had been here he was a handsome, vital man at the peak of his strength and energy. Now he was a mere shell of his former self. "Shamus." She said it like an endearment.

He studied her for long minutes, his emotions warring inside him. Amber FitzGerald was a beautiful woman. She possessed a fatal attraction that Joseph had not resisted, yet he could not lay the blame at her door for all that had happened. Amber was a victim of Montague, just as was his own precious family. He lifted his hand toward a chair, inviting her to sit.

"I've come to thank you for the money you provided. You have a generous nature, Shamus."

He pierced her with his gaze. "That night I still had Kathleen, I still had my sons; I was not blackened by hatred."

Amber resisted the guilty urge to lower her lashes. "I cannot ask you to forgive me for the part I played; I cannot forgive myself. All I can do is offer to repay you."

"There is only one way you could ever repay me. Lure Montague to Greystones."

"Shamus, I want William Montague dead... plain and simple; that's the only revenge that will satisfy me. But I have no influence with the man. He hates me as much as I hate him."

"Ah, my dear, I doubt that very much. Losing you is probably the one great regret of his miserable life. Yer a FitzGerald woman; none can compare to ye! I know, I was lucky enough to be married to one. Amber, you have a fatal allure."

This time she did lower her lashes. Her allure had indeed been fatal to Joseph and she was still drowning with guilt, but there was no way on earth she would ever put herself in a position where William Montague's evil could reach out to touch her. She smiled sadly at Shamus and said something to placate him. "If the opportunity ever presents itself, I shall repay you, Shamus."

For Emerald and Amber the days melted away too quickly. Though they spent all their waking hours in each other's company, they were seldom alone.

Sean took them for a day's outing to Maynooth, where Amber was warmly received by her cousins and aunts. The FitzGeralds reminisced for hours, outlaughing and outtalking one another until Amber could almost imagine she had never left.

In the late afternoon Sean took them to one of his tenant horse farms to choose a new mount for Emerald. She was drawn to a milky steed with a flowing mane, and when both Nan and Sean agreed with her choice, she declared she would name him Bucephalus. Sean teased her. "You've been reading that encyclopedia again, English."

It delighted Emerald that their first encounter was still fresh in his memory. "Nay, it's from reading *Alexander the Great* to your father."

Sean urged Amber to select a horse for herself and offered to transport it to Wicklow when he sailed her home.

Amber graciously refused. She did not wish to be obligated to this powerful man.

Sean read her thoughts and grinned disarmingly. "In actual fact," he said for her ears alone, "Montague paid for these horses. I simply relieved him of their transport and upkeep."

Amber laughed at his frankness. "In that case I shall accept your offer. It would be churlish to do otherwise."

The following day Amber knew their time together was rapidly running out. Midmorning she took Emerald aside. "I have asked Sean to take me back to Wicklow tomorrow."

"Oh, no!" Emerald cried. "I'm sorry, I know you have a business to run, but our time has galloped away. It seems as if you've only just arrived."

"Darling, it won't be like before; we'll see each other again."

"I don't even know what sort of business you have."

Amber caught her breath. "It's a...catering business. I employ women who cater parties, affairs."

"Is there a demand for such a thing?" Emerald asked curiously.

"A great demand," Amber answered truthfully. "Darling, I need to talk with you privately. Where can we go?"

Emerald searched her face. Obviously her mother did not want anyone inside Greystones to overhear them. "We can take the dogs for a walk."

"That would be good. Wrap up well, I feel the nip of winter in the air."

When Emerald came back down she was wearing her green velvet cloak with luxurious red fox trim about the hood. Amber felt a lump in her throat. "That cannot be the one I made for you."

"No, I left England with only the dress on my back. A very ugly dress, I might add. Sean had this made for me, copied from the one I wore to Ireland the day of his birthday celebration. He remembers everything."

They found the dogs in the stable. "The greyhound belonged to Joseph, though they had little time together."

Amber bent down to put her arms about it. " 'Tis all so heart-scalding."

Sean's wolfhound greeted Emerald by standing on his hind legs and plopping his great forepaws on her shoulders. "Oh, darling, be careful of the baby!" Amber cried.

"You know?" Emerald asked in amazement.

"I suspected. Not at first, but you have such a glow that I began to really look at you. I hoped against hope that my fears were unfounded."

"I was afraid to tell you."

"Is it your husband's or is it Sean's?"

"It's Sean's, of course!"

"Then it's a bastard," Amber said softly.

"Don't say that! Sean and I love each other."

"Let's walk," Amber said, needing to gather her thoughts. The dogs took off across the meadow, heading to the woods on the far side. Slowly they followed. "I know you are in love with Sean O'Toole. I would have to be deaf and blind not to realize it. But does he love you?"

"Of course he loves me," Emerald avowed.

"Think carefully. Has he ever told you he

loves you? Has he ever told you he cannot live without you? Has he ever spoken of marriage? Has he ever said he wants you to be the mother of his children?"

"I have a husband, how can he? You sound as disapproving as Father Fitz. He called me an adulteress and told me to go home to Jack Raymond. Is that what you want?"

"God in heaven, no. I just wish you hadn't thrown yourself so readily into his enemy's arms." They came to a low stone wall and sat down upon it.

"They made me believe that you were a wanton, tainted by depraved Irish blood. I couldn't bear it when Jack touched me. The things he did to me made me feel sick. I wanted to escape, but I was trapped."

Amber knew only too well how her daughter had felt. She had been trapped for eighteen long years with William Montague.

"And then my miracle happened. Sean brought me to Ireland and I knew I had always loved him. You are quite right in thinking I threw myself into his arms. He didn't try to force me in any way. By the time he did make love to me, I was craving for him. Once Sean O'Toole loved me, I was ashamed of the thoughts I'd had about you. If you are wanton, then I must be the wickedest creature to ever give myself to a man. He may never *say* that he loves me, but he shows me in every possible way that he does.

"He is never ever fierce or harsh with me. He never hurts me. He has loving hands when he touches me. We did have a fight once, when he took me to England and I accused him of flaunting me as his mistress. And it was true, he used me to revenge himself against the Montagues, but we both gave in and begged forgiveness of each other. After the things they did to him, I completely understand his need for revenge."

"But, darling, there may be no room in his heart for anything but his need for revenge."

"Mother, he has taught me to live for today, because it's all we really have. If it ended tomorrow, I wouldn't regret one fleeting moment of our time together. And I don't regret this child. It is part of him and part of me, per-haps the best part."

Amber had a difficult time keeping the tears from her eyes. "Just as you are the best part of me, Emerald. Just promise me that if he ever hurts you, if your dream turns into a nightmare, you will come to me."

Emerald wrapped loving arms about her mother. "Who else could I ever turn to?"

28

When William Montague received the news that he had lost two ships in an Irish gale, he cursed heaven and hell and everyplace in between. When he learned that the uninsured horses he had already paid for were lost at sea, he went berserk. Life at Portman Square, always unhappy for Johnny, now became intolerable; the old man's temper was making life hell. Now that John could afford to live elsewhere, he moved out and took a flat in Soho.

When John arrived at the offices of the Montague Line, his father was still raving on about Ireland and how everything connected with the accursed place had always been disastrous for a Montague, but at least John was thankful the old swine was no longer blaming him.

"Nobody loves horses more than I do, but we lost the entire crew of the *Gibraltar*. You don't seem to give a tinker's damn about them!"

"I don't! Too bloody bad the crew of the *Heron* didn't drown as well; they're nothing but lowlife incompetent drunken scum."

"You should be thankful they didn't drown, if only for the reason their families won't be screaming for compensation."

"Eh? Not a penny piece, you hear me? If any families come whining about Captain Bowers or his crew, tell them to see Jack. He'll soon set them straight!" William Montague sat down heavily and rested his throbbing foot on the brass spittoon. "Both ships were adequately insured, I take it?"

"Of course," Johnny lied smoothly. "But you know how long Lloyd's takes to settle these claims. We need more ships immediately, we can't wait for the insurance money. I have a source who will give us a marine loan at a low rate of interest. I'll make all the arrangements, but you'll have to scout the ships you want. You recall what happened when you let Jack choose the vessels."

John watched with satisfaction as his father's face took on a dangerous purple hue, as it did every time he reminded him that he had bought a ship they already owned.

"This time I'll trust you to buy the ships."

"Father, I can't do everything. I have to sail to Lambay Island to pick up the stranded crew and see if the *Gibraltar* is worth salvaging. If she's begun to break up, I'll have to make out a report for the insurance claim."

William's jowls sank to his chest. Christ, money and ships were disappearing faster than they could ever recoup them. They were hanging on by a thread. How different things were from the good old days when he and Shamus O'Toole raked in so much profit, they didn't know where to spend it all. If only he could turn back the clock.

John Montague took full advantage of his quick trip to the Irish coast. Rather than sailing directly to Lambay, he first went to Greystones.

As soon as Emerald realized the ship that had just arrived was the *Seagull* with her brother aboard, she threw open Greystones's massive front doors to welcome him. Emerald was bursting with the news about her mother and couldn't wait to tell him.

"You look radiantly happy," he said, giving her a warm kiss of greeting.

"Come in. I have something wonderful to tell you! Mother was here! Sean found her living in Wicklow and brought her for a visit. You've just missed her: Sean has taken her home."

"In Wicklow? But that's just down the coast. My God, I can't believe it! Is she all right?"

"She is wonderful, hasn't changed at all; she's as lovely as ever. Johnny, she didn't desert us. Father almost beat her to death for what she did with Joseph O'Toole and tossed her out so she could never see us again."

"I suspected that's what happened, and I was glad she was free of him. I always hoped she was living happily in Ireland. Wicklow's not far off, we'll be able to see each other from now on."

"She'd just love to see you, Johnny. Why don't you sail down to Wicklow?"

"Oh, I shall, but *damn,* I can't go today, Em. I shouldn't even be here. Perhaps I can see her next week. Did you take my letter to Nan?" he asked anxiously.

"I did," she said evenly, wanting to tell him of Nan's plight, but remembering that she had promised not to.

"Will it be all right if I borrow a horse? I want to ride to Maynooth to see her."

"That won't be necessary, she's staying here with me."

"Oh, God, that's marvelous news. Where is she?"

"She's upstairs in the same room you used when you were here. Speaking of marvelous news, I believe Nan has some for you, but you'll have to coax it from her."

He was gone in a flash and remained upstairs for the next two hours. At lunchtime Emerald decided to go upstairs herself, rather than have Kate round them up. Through the closed bedchamber door she heard Nan crying and Johnny trying to soothe her. She knocked lightly and waited to be invited in.

Johnny was pale; his eyes sought out his sister's for support. "I want us to get married. I want her to come home with me."

Emerald recoiled. "You can't take her to Portman Square."

"I've moved into a flat of my own. I want us to be married."

"Johnny, I agree you and Nan should be married, but don't take her to England. An Irish girl wouldn't be happy away from her family, especially a FitzGerald."

Johnny sighed heavily, knowing Emerald spoke the truth. He ran a distracted hand through his brown hair. "Then we'll have to be married and live apart, at least for the present. There is no way I am leaving Nan with an English bastard in her belly."

Emerald closed her eyes at the harshness in his voice. This was the second time in as many days she had been reminded that the child she was bearing would be a bastard. She pushed her own problem away to concentrate on Nan's. "Do you think Father Fitz would marry you?"

"Oh, I'm sure he would!" Nan's face lit up with renewed hope.

"Do you mind being married by a Catholic priest, Johnny?"

"Of course not. Let's go to the chapel right now and talk to him."

"Thank God Sean isn't here," Emerald murmured. "Nan, I think we should take Tara with us. Father Fitz is a bigoted, opinionated authoritarian. We need someone from the family who can overrule him if he turns obstinate."

Father Fitz, a beatific look on his round face, joined Nan and John in holy wedlock, then he blessed them. Emerald was astounded at the kindly way he looked at and spoke to Nan, while turning a stony countenance in her direction. Emerald knew that if she asked Father Fitz to keep this from Sean, his wrath would descend upon her, so when she kissed Nan she whispered a suggestion in her ear.

"Please don't tell the earl, Father. We'll find the right words ourselves when the time is right."

"What you have done today, my child, pleases God. I am not in the business of informing on my flock."

Instead of returning to the house, Nan and John went down to the stables, where they could be private to say their farewells and pledge their love and devotion to each other. The Greystones stables were quite large, so hand in hand they made their way to the back and slipped into an empty stall. Johnny sat down in the fresh straw and gently pulled his bride down beside him.

"I love you so much, Nan. I'm sorry that I let this happen to you. I don't know how I could have been so damn careless and thoughtless."

"John, it's my fault. I didn't realize it could happen after just one time. I don't want you to think I did it to trap you into marrying me."

"Nan, sweetheart, don't blame yourself. I'm the one who should have known better. But I'm not the least bit sorry. Because this happened, we are married a lot sooner than we would have been otherwise. My only regret is that we have to be apart. But Emerald is right about your staying safely in Ireland. My father and I have unfinished business that I must protect you from. I don't know when I can see you again, but I'll write to you and if you need me, get a message to Soho. Don't sign your name; there is only one lady who will be writing to me."

She lifted her mouth for his kiss. "Love me, Johnny, it may have to last us for months."

Before John went back aboard to continue his voyage, he left a brief note for Sean. "He'll know

I was here within five minutes of dropping anchor. Explain that I only came to give him a report."

"He has an uncanny way of discerning everything that goes on," Emerald said doubtfully.

The worried look came back over Johnny's face.

"Don't you worry about Nan. The FitzGerald women are like a sisterhood when it comes to childbearing. They close ranks and will look after her and protect her at all costs, and so will I."

Johnny's eyes widened in comprehension. "My God, I must have been blind! What the hell will you do?"

She smiled. "I will have Sean's baby, of course. Johnny, I couldn't be happier or safer than here at Greystones. Just look after yourself, Johnny."

Johnny enfolded Nan in his arms for a tender good-bye. He hated to leave his bride, but knew he had little choice. He kissed her for the tenth time and murmured, "Try not to worry about anything, Nan. I promise to write and always remember that I love you!"

Nan was on cloud nine. Even though she was wistful that Johnny had sailed away so quickly, she was vastly relieved that she was no longer in trouble. "Emerald, I can't believe I'm married! I needed him and he came. Isn't he just the loveliest man in the entire world?"

Emerald's strained face softened. "Well, we love him, so perhaps we're prejudiced.

But I am very proud of the way he faced up to his responsibility; he's a good man who doesn't give his love and trust carelessly. I'm so thankful Sean didn't arrive home in the middle of the ceremony."

"Oh, Emerald, I'm such a coward; I don't want to face him. Would you mind if I went home? I can't wait to tell my mother, and the cousins will be grass-green with envy."

"Of course I don't mind. Would you like me to come with you?"

"No, no, I'll ask one of the grooms to come with me. If you're not here when Sean returns, he'll come to Maynooth for you."

"Does he intimidate you so much?"

Nan shivered. "He's the Earl of Kildare."

Within an hour of Nan's precipitous departure the *Sulphur* slipped into Greystones's own harbor. Emerald spent that hour making herself beautiful for Sean's return. As she changed her gown for one that had arrived recently from Mrs. McBride in Dublin, a disconcerting thought struck her. The new garments both accommodated and camouflaged her ripening figure, yet at the time Sean had ordered them, even she herself hadn't been aware of the child. There was only one possible explanation. Sean had anticipated her pregnancy.

As she brushed her hair and threaded a jade-green ribbon through it to match her gown, she admitted that the man she loved was an enigma. He shared many things with her, but never his inner thoughts. He kept them locked inside and he hadn't yet given her the key.

Suddenly he was home and all her introspection vanished like a magician's rabbit. Whenever Sean was with her, he lavished all his attention upon her. She knew she was spoiled and felt guilty about wanting more of him.

As he bathed and changed his linen, Emerald joined him. Simply watching him and listening to his deep voice gave her untold pleasure. "Sean, I can never thank you enough for bringing Mother to Greystones, and would you believe it? Not an hour after you both left, Johnny arrived. I do wish she could have seen him; it would have made her so happy."

"Well, you had her all to yourself. He'll see her another time. I've been half expecting him."

"He left you a letter...a report, he called it."

When he took the letter from her, Sean noticed a strained look of anxiety on her face. He opened the note and scanned its contents. "The news is good, but I don't know why he didn't wait for my return. Still, he's only gone over to Lambay Island. I'll sail over and talk with him."

His dark eyes examined her face. "You look tired. Are you feeling all right, sweeting?" Without waiting for her reply, he scooped her up in his arms and carried her to the bed. He laid her down tenderly, then stretched out beside her and gathered her close, smoothing dark tendrils from her brow.

"I don't need to leave just yet. I'll stay with you to make sure you rest. Would you like me to rub your back?"

Emerald buried her face in the hollow of his throat. "No," she whispered, "I just want to lie quietly with you and feel your love surround me."

Sean stayed with her until she drifted off to sleep. He smiled down at her. After the excitement of her visit with Amber and then with John, a little quiet time would do her good. He lifted a curl from the pillow and rubbed the silky texture between his fingers. The tender smile reached all the way to his eyes; at this moment he knew Emerald was happy.

When Johnny saw the sails of the *Sulphur* approaching Lambay so soon after his own arrival, he stiffened with wariness. Had O'Toole learned about him and Nan so quickly, and was Sean here to beat his brains out? Johnny's resolve hardened; to hell with it, there was nothing he could do about the marriage short of making Nan a widow. For that matter, Sean O'Toole's behavior didn't bear close scrutiny. It had been morally wrong to impregnate Emerald when he couldn't marry her.

When Sean dropped anchor and came ashore he was happy to see the skeleton of the old slaver was beyond resurrection. Danny

FitzGerald had done his work well. Sean greeted Johnny and turned his eyes toward the ship that belonged to the Montague Line. It was one of only four that remained, according to his calculations. Since the crew from the wreck had already boarded the *Seagull*, O'Toole joined them. Over his shoulder he asked Johnny, "How many crew did you bring?"

"Only three. I was mate and also worked the lines, though I hate the damn job."

Sean clapped him on the back and grinned. "You're a mite pale, but you're holding up well. Summon the *Seagull*'s crew; since they've sailed to Castle Lies, we can't let them go back to Montague carrying tales, can we? From your note I take it the Montague Line is ready to secure a hefty marine loan?"

"Father thinks it will be temporary until the insurance pays our losses."

"You're a shrewd devil; I admire that in a man. It will help you survive in this corrupt world. I'll be in London shortly. Your loan will be coming from a company called Barclay and Bedford. Doesn't the name have a solid English ring to it? All I need to secure the loan is the deed on the Montague house in Portman Square."

John stared at him with renewed admiration. When Sean vowed to ruin Montague, he meant it quite literally. When O'Toole was done with his father and Jack, they wouldn't even have a roof over their heads. It was a bloody good thing his father was expecting insurance money from Lloyd's or he'd never get him to temporarily sign the deed on Portman Square. O'Toole's next directive emphasized that he was still not done with Wily Willie.

"Why don't you suggest the Montague Line concentrate on illegal French brandy? The profits far outweigh the risks and the demand will become unquenchable as Christmas approaches."

As the *Sulphur* and the *Seagull* sailed away from Lambay in opposite directions, John was thankful there were more hands aboard to set the sails. The encounter with Sean O'Toole had been particularly unsettling and his stomach threatened to void its contents with every successive wave.

O'Toole's vengeance was relentless. John could not forget the night he had awakened to find Sean's knife between his legs. When he learned that Nan was with child, would he and his knife be back?

At the wheel of the *Sulphur* Sean O'Toole's thoughts did dwell on Johnny Montague for a while, but those thoughts were filled with a grudging respect. Sean knew without John's cooperation, his task would be prodigious indeed. One thing was evident, Johnny Montague was no longer gutless.

The hour was late when Sean arrived back at Greystones. He trod softly as he ascended the stairs and slipped silently into the master bedchamber. Nevertheless Emerald sat up in bed and lit the lamp on the bedside table.

"I'm sorry, love, I didn't want to disturb you."

Mischievous green eyes tempted him from beneath black lashes. "How different we are, for I certainly want to disturb you, my lord. It's one of life's more titillating pleasures."

Sean removed his leather jack and stripped off his linen shirt. "An evening's rest seems to have restored your vitality." He stepped toward the bathroom.

"And my appetite. Don't wash; I want to smell you and taste you."

Her husky words stopped him in his tracks. His compulsion to be immaculately spotless melted away for the first time since he had left the hulks.

29

As autumn turned into winter, Emerald was most thankful that Ireland did not experience freezing ice and snow. There were many days that were damp and raw, and of course the hours of daylight were considerably shortened, but this made the evenings longer.

Most nights Emerald and Sean retired upstairs early, shutting out the world, needing no one but themselves. Sometimes they even dined in their bedchamber and afterward they would play chess, read together companionably, or make love.

Her pregnancy was evident now, but like many small women, she carried it well and did not look clumsy. Her plumpness merely added to her femininity. Sean became more tenderly solicitous and protective as the weeks slipped by, often carrying her, regularly massaging her back and thighs, making her feel totally cherished.

Until now Sean O'Toole had effectively held at bay all thoughts of returning Emerald to her family; it was something he would do in the future. But the future had an implacable way of becoming the present.

Sean had visited his mother's grave every single day since returning to Ireland after his long imprisonment. He never missed taking fresh flowers and kneeling beneath the willow tree in the walled garden. Of a sudden he began to avoid Kathleen's grave, as he fought an inner battle. During the long nights he held Emerald for hours, needing to feel she was there as he restlessly drifted in and out of sleep.

Steeling himself for what he knew he must do was more than difficult, it was one of the hardest things he'd ever faced. He mentally counted, for what seemed the thousandth time, how far along she was. It had been May when she told him of the baby and it was now late November.

By Sean's calculation she would have the child in February; perhaps early in February. However, he had first made love to her in April, and if she'd conceived immediately it might even arrive in January. The sea voyage could be a risk to her health if he put it off much longer. His tortured thoughts chased each other in circles. One thing was certain: He wanted her with him for Christmas, and he made a firm decision they would spend it together at Greystones. He stubbornly refused to think beyond the festive holiday.

Once his decision was made, Sean put aside all his misgivings, all dark thoughts, by sheer dint of will. As a result his mood lightened considerably and he was able to join in the plans Emerald and the staff were organizing to make this Christmas a joyous occasion.

The big house was gaily decorated with holly, ivy, mistletoe, and evergreen boughs. Tara was once again at Greystones. Maggie, Meggie, and Meagan each came for a month, then Tara insisted it was again her turn. She spent hours in the stillroom making scented candles and bowls of potpourri, as well as distilling liqueurs from pears, quince, and apricots.

All during December, whenever an O'Toole vessel arrived, the FitzGerald crews were invited in to share the festive food Mary Malone prepared from morning till night. Mr. Burke brought ale and whisky up from the cellars and Greystones rang with laughter and music.

Even Shamus allowed Sean or Paddy Burke to bring him down from his watchtower to join the merrymaking. He teased Emerald unmercifully about being a Christmas pudding and she joined in the banter, giving as good as she got.

In Ireland Christmas Eve was a holy night and at Greystones after the evening meal, everyone went along to church for a carol service and a celebration of midnight Mass. Everyone, that is, except Emerald and Sean. Together they snuffed the candles on the tall fir tree, then Sean lifted her high against his heart and carried her upstairs.

"Do you miss going to church?" she asked softly.

He gave a short bark of laughter. "No. Religion is for the ignorant."

"I went one day when Nan was here. Father Fitz refused me communion."

He set her feet to the carpet and stared down at her. "Did you really feel the need to go?"

"I wanted to pray for the baby and for your safety when you sailed out in the storm."

"You were being fanciful. There is no personal God to watch over us and keep us from harm, Emerald. Adversity taught me to rely on myself, and I have tried to pass that lesson along to you."

"The priest is angry with you because you have not set foot in church since you returned to Ireland."

"What did Father Fitz say to you?"

Emerald hesitated, not wanting to repeat the accusations he had flung. Sean cupped her shoulders with compelling hands. "Tell me."

"He said your soul is blackened with sin, yet you show no contrition."

Sean laughed, his voice sounding harsh. "He spoke the truth. What else did the old incense-swinger have to say?"

She did not repeat any of the deadly sins the priest cataloged, nor that he said Sean's god had become vengeance. She was afraid that Sean would freely admit it was all true. Emerald decided to close the subject. She went up on tiptoe and placed her lips against his. "He told me to use my influence on you."

"You do that every day and every night." His voice turned from harsh to husky.

"Ah yes, I have a vast influence on you, right down to your reading material."

Sean grinned at her and picked up two books from the night-table. One was *The Inferno* by Dante; the other was *The Prince* by Niccolò Machiavelli. Sean resolutely put the books down and picked up the one Emerald was reading. It was *The Decameron*. "Mmm, Boccaccio. Why don't you use your influence by reading to me?"

He threw the bed pillows down on the rug before the fire and began to disrobe. Emerald undressed and slipped a soft wool robe over her nakedness, not bothering with a night rail. Then she picked up her book and sank down before the inviting fire. Naked, Sean lay down beside her, propping his chin on one powerful fist as his dark gaze licked over her.

Emerald began to read, but her eyes kept straying from the page, drawn to the magnificent male body stretched out beside her. Firelight flickered over his taut belly, long, lean flanks, hard-muscled chest, and wide shoulders.

She returned to the book and read a few more paragraphs. Boccaccio was both sophisticated and candid about the love-laden essentials of romantic mastery. From the corner of her eye she saw Sean's phallus, which lay along his thigh, awaken and stretch. The head came out of its cowl and Emerald abandoned the book, watching with fascinated delight as he lengthened and thickened.

The desire to touch him and taste him flared in her. Her hands ached to weigh his heavy, hot sac, her fingers wanted to encircle the thick shaft, and her lips longed to kiss the smooth, velvety head that the flames turned to carmine. His eyes had the look of a predatory male animal, which emphasized his tempting masculinity. He knew what she wanted to do.

"Come," he invited.

She saw his pulse beating in his throat, then her eyes traveled down his lithe, hard body to watch the pulse throb in the head of his long shaft. She knelt before him and cupped his whole sex in loving hands. Then she brushed her lips across the velvet, sweetly kissing, then gently blowing on him until he began to quiver.

"Go on your knees for me."

He drew in a swift breath and raised himself so that he was on a level with her beautiful mouth. She began gently, delicately, with the tip of her tongue, touching the tiny opening, then swirling in ever widening circles until she licked the entire engorged head. Holding his testes in one hand, the root of his shaft with the other, she opened her mouth and took him inside the hot, dark cave. She alternately sucked and tongued him, making love sounds that were so erotic, he felt he must explode or die.

Sean tried to hold on to his control to make the exquisite pleasure last all night, but Emerald was so sensually provocative, his control shattered into a million shards. She tasted the first drops of his pearly climax before he arched backward in the throes of release, sending his white-hot seed spurting up across his belly. Emerald opened her robe and pressed her breasts against his hard body until they were slick with his musky male essence.

Sean reached down between her legs to give her release and was amazed to feel her orgasm into his hand the moment he touched her. "My little beauty, you give so generously." They lay before the fire wanting to stay in each other's arms forever. Finally, she stirred from her drowsy dreaming.

"I have a gift for you, too, but first, let me bathe you."

"If you like," she murmured, touching his cheek.

"I like," he said, scooping her up and carrying her to the bathing room.

The warm bath water was delicious. He

held her in his lap and soaped her lavishly, marveling at the satin texture of her smooth skin. "I adore the feel of you against me. You have the most tempting back in the world."

Emerald smiled. "My front is a little less tempting these days."

His hands slid over her luscious ripe breasts. "Not true, my beauty. I can't wait to dry you and rub your satin skin with the rose oil."

"I can't wait either," she admitted.

Sean wrapped her in a towel and carried her back to the fire. With infinite patience and tenderness he dried her with the soft towel, then warmed the oil for her massage. When he was done, Emerald reached a languorous hand to caress his cheek. "That was the loveliest present I ever had."

He chuckled deep in his throat. "That's not your present." He got up and went to the drawer of his night table, then came back to kneel before her. "This is," he said, placing a velvet box in her hands.

She lifted the lid slowly, then gasped at the magnificent jewels within. "Emeralds!" she breathed with reverence. The flames made the gems glow with green fire.

"Happy Christmas, sweetheart."

Her green eyes were liquid with unshed tears. "You shouldn't have."

"I should. No one deserves them more. Emerald, you have given me so much."

"I hope I can give you a son." As she put on the earrings and bracelet she did not see the shuttered look come into his eyes. He moved behind her to fasten the necklace about her throat. His voice roughened. "Get some rest, tomorrow will be a full day."

On Christmas morning they dragged in the yule log, then it was time to give the staff their gifts. The tenant farmers and their families dropped in one after another, all bearing gifts and receiving the customary O'Toole largesse, which was a generous tradition. Midday, the *Silver Star* docked at the jetty and her crew was invited to Greystones's Christmas dinner; a feast beyond compare, where the family were joined by the staff.

Captain Liam FitzGerald brought the best Christmas present Sean O'Toole could have wished for. The newly appointed head of the British Admiralty, acting on tips from the FitzGerald captains, had intercepted two vessels belonging to the Montague Line smuggling in illegal French brandy. Because England and France were at war, the Admiralty seized the ships and were about to levy a crippling fine as well.

The captain also had brought a letter from Johnny Montague confirming the information. Sean tucked it into his shirt and went off to look for Paddy and Shamus, wanting to share the news with them immediately. It took him an hour to locate Mr. Burke, whose face looked haggard. Sean recalled he had been in high humor at dinner, sharing toasts and proposing one of his own.

"What's amiss?" Sean asked the steward.

"It's Shamus. I can't find him; he's gone missing."

"Strange...he can't have gone far," Sean assured him, thinking of the condition of his father's legs. "Maybe one of the lads took him back to the watchtower."

They went together, searching the gatehouse and the tower, but found no trace of Shamus. "Christ, ye don't think he fell down the cellar steps?" Paddy asked with alarm.

"Come on. You check the cellars; I'll go upstairs."

Sean searched methodically through every room at Greystones, without success. Then, from an upstairs window overlooking the walled garden, he saw something that knotted his gut. His father's body lay prone on the ground.

Sean bolted down the stairs, then through the elegant receiving room's French doors that led to the walled garden. Judas, how long had Shamus been lying on the cold earth? Sean's steps slowed as he neared his father; the disquieting sounds he was making were terrible to hear.

Shamus lay beside Kathleen's grave, sobbing uncontrollably. Sean went down on his knees to him, reaching out strong hands to comfort him, but Shamus was inconsolable as he grieved for his beloved wife. Sean intended to carry him away, but the aging man was adamant. "No! I want to be here. I've failed her! I vowed to make Montague suffer for what he did to her sons. That broke her heart and she died from it."

"Father, you are upset because it is Christmas; you miss her more than usual at this time of year."

"Shut yer mouth! Don't you understand I miss her every day, every hour? She was the heart and soul of Greystones, the center of my life. They punished me through her. They used my woman to make me suffer; she was my only vulnerability."

As Sean knelt beside his mother's grave, guilt's savage fangs sank into his throat, almost choking him. He knew exactly what his father was talking about. When he first saw his mother's grave, Sean was so outraged at what their enemy had done, he swore a sacred oath on his knees that he would pay them back in kind. The Montagues would suffer through the woman at the center of their lives. Daughter to one and bride to the other, Emerald was the perfect vessel for his vengeance.

He took Shamus in strong arms and held him close in a powerful embrace. "I pledge you we won't fail Kathleen FitzGerald O'Toole, Father."

Shamus's heart-scalding sobs eventually wore him out. Sean picked him up and carried him to his bed in the watchtower. Paddy Burke put heated stones to his feet and Sean called Tara to administer a powerful sleeping draft that she distilled from whisky and the ground-up seed of the white poppy.

Christmas night Emerald tumbled into bed, exhausted but happy. Sean, Paddy, and Tara conspired to remain silent about Shamus to keep her from unnecessary worry, and Emerald fell asleep immediately.

Sean lay beside her, hands behind his head, slowly coming to terms with the fact that one period of his life was coming to a close. He had drawn it out as long as he dared. Now he must act decisively. He would not allow himself the indulgence of introspection or self-pity; both were pointless as well as pathetic.

Mentally, he had already withdrawn from the woman beside him, rationalizing that she no longer needed him. She was not the passive, shy girl who had left England. Since coming to Ireland, he had taught her to be a woman who could hold her own against anyone. Though he had almost beggared her father, he had given Emerald a fortune in jewels to make her financially independent, and if she no longer wished to reside with the Montagues, she could remove herself to the town house in Old Park Lane.

When Emerald awoke, Sean was already bathed and dressed. He did not come to sit on the bed to talk with her, but strode to the window that overlooked the sea. Johnny's letter told Sean exactly where William Montague and Jack Raymond would be on the last night of their ill-fated year, and he knew he must use it to his advantage.

"I have business in England."

"You're not leaving today?" she asked mutinously.

"No, you may have a couple of days to prepare for the voyage."

Emerald's face brightened. "Good—if you were thinking of leaving me behind because of my delicate condition, I was ready to fight you tooth and nail!"

Sean slanted a black eyebrow, humor coming to his rescue. "Delicate? You have the teeth and claws of a wildcat."

Emerald was about to remark that he had the scars to prove it, but she could never tease him about scars, he had too many, both visible and invisible. She was mildly surprised that he was willing to take her with him on another voyage to England. She had fully expected him to put his foot down and order her to stay safely at home.

Still, there were far more doctors and midwives in London than lived near Greystones. The O'Tooles' doctor lived in Dublin, but she'd never seen him because Shamus refused his services. Emerald smiled to herself, fully understanding his attitude. She herself had ignored Kate and Tara's advice to see the doctor and have him examine her. Emerald reasoned that she and Sean would be back long before their baby made an appearance. She just hoped she wouldn't suffer from mal de mer on the voyage. She waved her hand like a queen. "Order me a calm sea."

"Don't forget to ask Tara for a good supply of her oils and the stuff that settles your stomach, just in case." He made a mental note to ask Tara for some of the sedative she had used on Shamus. He had an idea that he would need it. His plan would be far kinder than exposing Emerald to a confrontational scene.

"Do you think I'll be there long enough to see Johnny?"

"I'm sure of it," he said smoothly, leaving her to pack. "I'll send Kate up."

Two days later, as Sean helped her aboard the *Sulphur,* he was shocked to see how much she had expanded in the few short days since Christmas Eve. As her warm cape fell back, he wondered how her rounded belly could have doubled in size so quickly.

"Emerald, are you feeling well?"

"Perfectly well, thank you, my lord, in spite of the fact that Kate isn't speaking to me."

"Come to think of it, she snubbed me completely at breakfast this morning. What maggot is eating her brain?"

"She's scandalized that I'm off to England in my flagrant condition. She believes I should conceal myself in my chamber where no one can see me. She thinks me an immodest baggage, and of course she's right!" Emerald laughed. "But, bless her, her heart's in the right place. She offered to come with me, and you know that stepping on English soil to Kate would be tantamount to walking through Dante's Gate of Hell."

"You didn't bring much luggage," Sean remarked, opening the cabin door to reveal the small trunk standing beside his own. He pictured her wardrobe filled with the clothes he had bought her.

"Well, I don't imagine I'll be attending any gala receptions with His Majesty or masquerade balls at Carlton House," she said lightly. Emerald didn't want him to see how short of breath she was or how clumsy her movements had recently become. "Go up on deck where you belong, while I get settled in. You know I can look after myself!"

30

William Montague was at his wits' end. The shipping line, his only means of income these days, was almost finished. Since Christmas he had even avoided the offices on Bottolph's Wharf, and instead roamed about the house in Portman Square, drinking himself into oblivion. To meet household expenses he would be forced to sell off the furniture, piece by piece. All London would know he was a pauper.

Jack was the only one who would tolerate his company. Johnny's visits were few and far between, and even the servants made themselves scarce.

"It's like swallowing bitter aloes! To think the *Admiralty* has seized our ships—the sodding *Admiralty*! Your father and I ran the British Admiralty—we *were* the *Admiralty*!"

Jack poured William another drink and one for himself. It was the last of the brandy and Jack knew no more would be forthcoming, because it could only be purchased cash on the barrel.

William raised red-rimmed eyes to his son-in-law. "Do you know how much it galled me to go hat in hand to my brother?"

Not as much as it humiliated me. I'm his bastard, for Christ's sake, Jack answered silently. *When I married your fucking daughter and finally became a Montague, I thought my days of humiliation were over.*

"I just don't understand how bad luck has dogged us, over and over. It doesn't make sense that all these losses are coincidence. I didn't think there was any connection between the disappearance of the slavers and the ships we lost in that gale, but I'm suddenly suspicious. One of your father's enemies, mayhap that son of a bitch Newcastle, informed on us!"

His hand gripped the glass so viciously, it shattered. A shard sliced into his thumb, and dark red blood bubbled up from the wound. William stared down at the thumb in fascinated horror. It stirred an unpleasant memory, long

398

suppressed. *O'Toole.* He did not speak the name aloud. It would be too much like invoking the devil.

"I wouldn't trust my father's *friends,* let alone his enemies. They are dissolute to a man. Who is supposed to be at this New Year's auction he's arranged?" Jack Raymond did not relish returning to the Pall Mall mansion where he had grown up as one of the many bastards of the Earl of Sandwich.

"Quite an eclectic gathering, I understand: poets, politicians, earls. George Selwyn will be there, as well as Bute and March. Naturally the Prince of Wales and his cronies won't be able to resist. But I hope my brother gives me credit for some brains. I won't sell my collection to Prinny; his finances are shakier than ours, if that's possible. I'm counting on Francis Dashwood. He will pay any price for erotic drawings or sketches."

"I've heard some wild stories about Medmenham," Jack prompted, becoming aroused at just the thought of the lewd acts reputed to take place within the chalk caverns.

"An unusual place, to be sure. The gardens are filled with obscene statuary and phallic symbols. Even the pathways divide like female legs to give entry into bushy vaginas!"

" 'Tis whispered they celebrate the Black Mass," Jack suggested.

"Well, it's a common enough practice to dress as monks and lay *nuns* on the altar. Who among us hasn't indulged that fantasy? But

Dashwood carries it further. He's a fanatic about defiling Christianity and has an addiction to anything blasphemous. That's why I think the bidding will be high for my caricatures of the twelve Apostles. They are so brutal." William chuckled.

"Personally, I prefer the pornographic pictures drawn by Rowlandson. Sadism and sodomy don't do much for me unless women are depicted."

"You are right, there is something compellingly arousing about females engaged in unnatural coitus." William's mouth hung loose at the thought. He knew he'd consumed too much drink to make it to the Divan Club, and in any case that was only putting money in his brother's pocket. His heavy sigh came out as a loud belch. He'd have to make do with one of the scullery maids again.

Sean O'Toole charted the voyage carefully so that they would arrive in London on New Year's Eve. The seas cooperated until the last night, when the English Channel was lashed with a vicious storm that threw bolts of lightning, followed by hailstones large enough to tear the shrouds to ribbons.

Needed both above- and belowdecks, O'Toole spent the night alternating between the two women who needed all his attention: Emerald and the *Sulphur*. No one aboard had slept, least of all Emerald, who cried that she should never have come. The storm had abated somewhat by morning, but the seas still roiled, and twice Sean had to order her belowdecks for her own safety.

Tears streamed down her face. "If I'm going to die, I want to be with you!"

Sean's temper was at the breaking point. He swept her into his arms and carried her below. "No one is going to die. Stop being ridiculous, Emerald!"

When she clung to him, needing his strength, needing his assurance, needing his comfort, it almost unmanned him. He swept back the covers on the berth and put her to bed fully clothed. "You need sleep; I want you to rest."

"I can't sleep!"

"You must; we'll be docking safely in London in just a few hours. Trust me." The minute he uttered those two words, he wanted to bite off his tongue. He went to the locker and took out the bottle Tara had given him. He half filled a wineglass and lifted it to her lips. "Drink this, it will soothe you."

"What is it?"

"One of Tara's infallible remedies." He watched her sip the poppy-laden whisky obediently, trustingly. She shuddered halfway through, but resolutely lifted the wineglass to drain it. Sean sat down on the edge of the berth and took her hand. He watched her fear subside, saw her eyelids begin to droop as he stroked his thumb across the backs of her fingers and patiently waited for Morpheus to claim her.

When she finally slept, he tucked her arms

beneath the blanket, then stood gazing down at her. As if his ship were jealous of the attention he was giving to his other woman, she lurched and groaned, then began to list. Sean cursed beneath his breath, but before he tore himself away from Emerald, he pressed a gentle kiss upon each closed eyelid.

Seven hours later Emerald still slept heavily. She had been oblivious when Sean had lifted her from the bunk, wrapped her in her velvet cloak, and carried her to the hired hansom cab.

As the carriage made its way along the Strand, then turned toward Piccadilly, snowflakes drifted past the yellow gas lamps. Sean did not feel the cold night air; he was devoid of any feeling at all. He had said his good-byes and was simply going through the motions of delivering her safely. His dark thoughts were already focused on the social gathering taking place at the Earl of Sandwich's marble monstrosity in Pall Mall.

When the carriage stopped, O'Toole sat there a full minute before he took the final step. Then, with hooded eyes, he opened the door and lifted the sleeping woman into his arms.

Belton, the heavyset majordomo in Portman Square, wore a permanently sour expression after having worked for the Montagues for a decade, but when he saw the dark, threatening face of the man at the front door holding William's daughter in his arms, his expression became alarmed. He stepped aside as the satanic figure swept into the house and carried the sleeping girl, large with child, into the grand reception room.

Sean laid down his burden on the overstuffed couch as if it were precious, then, without a backward glance, strode from the house. Belton followed him to the front door, summoning enough courage to demand, "What's going on?"

Sean O'Toole returned with Emerald's trunk, set it inside the front door, then issued his warning. "Take absolute care of this woman, Belton." He reached into his breast pocket and handed him a letter addressed to William Montague and Jack Raymond. It spelled out in no uncertain terms that if anything happened to Emerald, he would kill them and see them in hell.

As O'Toole disappeared into the swirling snow, Belton muttered sarcastically, "Happy New Year," knowing it would be anything but.

The lights blazing from the windows of the mansion lit up Pall Mall. The Earl of Kildare, in formal black, encountered no difficulties gaining entrance. The salon filled with men enabled him to blend into the crowd. The smoke-filled room rang with coarse laughter and the loud voices of men who had been liberally plied with claret. Pornographic books, pictures, and sketches were prominently displayed along one wall in anticipation of the auction.

The earl planted his feet beside a marble pillar and allowed his gaze to travel the length of the salon, observing in a detached way just how many prominent men were in attendance. He did not feel contempt or even distaste for the profligates crowded about the graphic works of art; he felt only indifference.

As the Prince of Wales sailed past him, His Highness condescended an aloof nod, murmuring, "Kildare," before turning back to his friend Churchill, who drawled, "I warrant the brothers Montague have enough filthy pictures between them to paper Carlton House."

Sean O'Toole's eyes slid impassively over John Montague, Earl of Sandwich, as they scanned the crowd for the two men who fueled his savage need for vengeance. When he finally located William Montague, he was in conversation with John Wilkes. To O'Toole the irony was unbelievable. Did Montague not recognize one of the enemies responsible for his downfall? O'Toole felt no surprise that Wilkes was here for the auction. Though he was a pious political reformer, he was also a coarse sensualist and pornographer addicted to practical jokes.

The Earl of Kildare knew he could not have selected a more perfect audience for his announcement. The Montagues would be devoured by these vicious sadists; their humiliation totally devastating.

The raptor inside him watched and waited for the right moment to strike. As Jack Raymond joined William and His Royal Highness, they became the focal point of attention. Kildare stepped forward and raised his glass.

"I believe a toast is in order. Your daughter is about to produce your first grandchild." He gestured toward Raymond. "I knew he was incapable, so I did the job for him. Never underestimate the Irish."

The hush that fell encompassed the entire room. Kildare held up his hand, exposing his mutilated thumb. "Don't bother to thank me, gentlemen, the pleasure was all mine."

As he walked out the crowd parted, then closed in behind him, jubilant to have witnessed such a shocking and ruinous revelation. Public disgrace and shame provided a succulent dish to feast upon.

Emerald, caught in a nightmare from which she could not awaken, struggled to free herself from its bonds. But like the tentacles of a clinging octopus, the bad dream held her fast, imprisoning her so completely, it was impossible to break free.

She dreamed that she was back at Portman Square and no matter how she tried, she could not awaken. She struggled to her feet, extremely disoriented, yet slowly realizing, against her will, that she was not dreaming. She denied the reality of what was all about her. *This cannot be happening to me!*

Her thoughts in total disarray, her hand went to her head in an effort to clear away the cobwebs. With a trembling hand she brushed her disheveled hair back from her damp brow and stared about her in horrified disbelief. The last thing she remembered was the storm. *How did I get here? Where is Sean?*

She had insisted on sailing to England with him, never dreaming in a million years she would end up back in Portman Square. The child inside her felt as if it did a somersault and suddenly Emerald knew she was going to be sick. Somehow she made her way to the staircase and, with the help of the banister, began to climb, hoping she could hold down her gorge until she reached the bathroom water closet.

Emerald retched violently, clutching her belly, fearing it would turn itself inside out. Gradually the nausea lessened, but the sick feeling in her heart increased with every breath she took. Emerald heard someone approaching. She struggled to her feet and turned, thinking it was one of the maids come to help her. She stared into the aghast face of Jack Raymond and watched it contort with fury and loathing.

"You filthy bitch! O'Toole said he'd return you when you had an Irish bastard in your belly! Have you no shame, you faithless whore?"

White faced, Emerald shielded her distended belly with her arms as if she could protect her baby from his hatred. Jack was lying; Sean could never have done such a brutal thing.

"Get out! I won't take you back! I won't have that dirty swine's leavings."

Emerald refused to be cornered like a rat. She gathered her pride about her, pulled her back as straight as she could, and raised her chin. "You will never have that opportunity, Jack Raymond. The Earl of Kildare is a magnificent lover. It is laughable to think I would allow you to ever touch my person again." In spite of her advanced pregnancy, or perhaps because of it, she found the inner strength to sweep regally from the room.

"He won't foist his Irish bastard on the Montagues; I'll destroy it first!"

At the top of the staircase Emerald turned with alarm, realizing he had followed her and sensing his evil intent. As if time and motion slowed, she saw his arms rise up to push her down the stairs. Emerald reached out to grasp hold of the banister in a desperate attempt to save herself from falling.

She felt the hard impact of his cruel hands against her back, felt herself going down. She lunged against the handrail, grabbed, and held on for dear life. Her foot slipped off the step, her leg twisted beneath her, and Emerald heard the bone snap as it broke. She screamed in agony, but beyond her own scream, she heard her father's voice roar, "What in Christ's name is going on here?"

Through a red haze of pain she saw the hated figure of William Montague standing at the foot of the stairs. Behind him stood the corpulent Belton, agog at the scene he had just witnessed. He tried to dismiss two housemaids who also had seen and heard everything, but fear seemed to have rooted their feet to the floor of the vestibule.

"Get a doctor," Montague ordered. He looked at Emerald with disgust, but his duty as her father was clear.

Belton dispatched one maid for the doctor and ordered the other to prepare a bed for the patient.

"Not in my suite," Jack hissed. "This woman is no longer my wife."

"Put her in the servants' quarters," William ordered.

They made up the bed in Irma Bludget's old room, but when Jack moved toward Emerald, she spat venom. "Don't touch me, you murdering swine!"

In the end it was the cook, Mrs. Thomas, who carried her to the bed, undressed her, and found one of her old nightgowns. The pain in Emerald's leg felt like a searing red-hot poker, but her overriding concern was for her baby, not her leg. Mrs. Thomas questioned Emerald about her pain and checked for blood. When she found none, both were fervently thankful.

William Montague was livid. If he had been carrying a pistol when O'Toole strolled in and made his shattering announcement, the Irish swine would now be dead, and no court in England would convict him! Even worse than the humiliation over his daughter, however, was the instant realization that O'Toole was the one who had ruined him financially. When those black eyes bored into him and he heard the mocking words *Never underestimate the*

Irish, William knew all their losses were the culmination of O'Toole's compulsive revenge. Well, the fucking O'Tooles weren't the only ones who could wreak vengeance, as they'd learn to their everlasting sorrow.

The arrival of the doctor interrupted Montague's plotting. He was momentarily dismayed that the stupid maid had brought his own personal physician. Any doctor would have done to set a broken leg; preferably one not privy to his family's affairs. But then William realized Dr. Sloane could be an ally.

"There's been some sort of accident?" Sloane asked, looking from William to Jack. "By the looks of things you could both use a sedative."

William, looking askance at the maid, said, "Come into the library, Doctor. You, too, Jack. This concerns you, even though you think to wash your hands of the matter."

William firmly closed the library door before he spoke. "My daughter has broken her leg, which will need splinting, but that isn't what concerns us. She is large with child and by the looks of things very near her time." William glanced at Jack. "It is not her husband's baby. We want you to dispose of it."

Dr. Sloane's eyebrows bristled with outrage. Montague loved power for its own sake, but if he thought he was in charge here, he had another think coming. "*Dispose?* I shall give you the benefit of the doubt and assume you are not suggesting a criminal act. If you mean find someone who will take the child off your hands, however, that can be arranged. For a price."

Goddamn money! In the end everything boils down to pounds, shillings, and pence. William's temper was rising by the minute. The O'Tooles had a bloody reckoning coming.

"I'll see the patient," Sloane said gravely.

William led the doctor to the servants' quarters, where Mrs. Thomas, still panting from her exertions, was doing her best to make Emerald comfortable.

The young woman on the bed cringed when she recognized the family doctor. She recalled his brusque manner and rough hands from the few times he had tended her as a child.

Sloane did nothing to conceal his disdain as he stared at Emerald's belly. Finally, he took shin splints from his voluminous bag and began to straighten the leg. Though Emerald tried to remain stoically silent, the pain was too agonizing and she cried out.

"What?" Sloane demanded.

"It hurts," she whispered through bloodless lips.

"Of course it hurts; it's broken," he said brusquely. He gave the leg short shrift, dismissed the cook, then focused his attention on the protrusion that threatened to burst the seams of the nightgown. After a few pokes and probes he placed both hands on the mound that continually changed shape. His bushy brows drew together in a frown.

"What's wrong?" Emerald demanded, her

eyes apprehensively watching the expressions that crossed the doctor's face.

Sloane put a rubber cup device against her swollen belly and bent his head to listen. After a full minute he straightened and in a voice that clearly condemned her for committing a double sin, he said, "There is more than one child here. You are having twins."

31

Montague was pacing in the front receiving room while Jack slumped in a chair.

"Is she in labor?" William demanded, as if he could not wait to get the humiliating business behind them.

"No, I would say another week; perhaps more, perhaps less."

Montague made a rude noise that conveyed his estimation of the doctor's learned opinion. "Just be here for the birth, so you can remove the little Irish bastard from Portman Square!"

"I've just examined her," Sloane informed him, not without a trace of malice. "There will be two little Irish bastards."

The minute Sloane departed, William vented his temper on Jack Raymond. "You are useless as tits on a boar, sitting there with your stupid head in your hands. Don't you realize it's been O'Toole systematically destroying us all along?"

William's words penetrated Jack's drink-sodden brain. He sat stunned as realization dawned.

"Mayhap O'Toole is right; you have no balls!"

Jack came to his feet, stung into taking the offensive. "You old swine! It is *your* daughter who has played the whore, just as it was *your* wife who played the whore before her! It was *you* who betrayed the old earl, *you* who betrayed your partner, *you* who plotted Joseph O'Toole's murder, *you* who sent Sean O'Toole to the hulks with a mutilated hand. Well, I've had enough of the Montagues for one bloody night!" Jack flung from the room, then the house, slamming the front door after him.

William, now in an uncontrollable rage, rushed to the library and rifled through the desk drawers for his gun case. To hellfire with everybody. His son-in-law had turned out as useless as his son. He would have to take care of O'Toole himself. His ship had to be moored in the Thames, and sooner or later O'Toole would have to return to it.

Emerald was in shock. As she lay in Irma Bludget's bed, she paid little heed to the angry male voices echoing from another part of the house. The pain in her leg was so piercing and pervasive, it began to radiate into the rest of her body. And yet she clung to the pain, refusing to separate from it, for if she did, she feared the greater pain in her heart would kill her.

Sean had done this thing. He had done it for revenge. And what devastated Emerald the most was the knowledge that she still loved him. She realized that when one truly loved, it was forever. How ineffably sad that Sean's heart was so filled with hatred, there was no room for love; not for her, not for his babies.

Her hands stroked her abdomen. The instant she learned there were two, her love had doubled. Her greatest concern was not for herself, it was for her children. "Everything will be well," she whispered to them. "We won't stay in this house long. We'll go to my mother. Johnny will help us."

Emerald turned her face to the wall. The tears she had been fighting spilled over. She had never seen a woman give birth. It had not daunted her when she thought she belonged to Sean O'Toole. How would she get through it alone?

Johnny Montague sat in the dimly lit office at Bottolph's Wharf, a great wave of relief washing through him. The brief visit from Sean O'Toole had lifted a heavy burden from his shoulders. Sean had been cool and detached; all business. John went over their conversation in his mind to assure himself that he had heard correctly.

"Johnny, I want to thank you for all your help.

I could have done it without you, but never this quickly, never this thoroughly. I no longer require your aid. It is over and done. I have accomplished all I set out to do."

"They will be forced to sell the two new ships to pay the Admiralty fines."

"Johnny, you don't think Barclay and Bedford actually paid for those ships?"

"So he owes for the ships as well as the fines," Johnny said slowly.

"And I am in possession of the deed on Portman Square," Sean said with brisk finality.

It took a minute for John to digest it all. "How is Emerald?"

"She was well when I left her." Sean didn't elaborate.

Johnny wanted to tell him about Nan FitzGerald, but there seemed to be a gulf between them tonight. Because he no longer needed John's help, O'Toole seemed to have withdrawn, and clearly he was disinclined to linger.

"I'll bid you farewell; I'm sailing back tonight."

Johnny's gaze swept slowly around the office. How he hated it all, the paperwork, the bills of lading, the manifests, the tide tables, the shipping routes, the cargoes and crews. He hated the very sound and smell of ships, but as he sat there, his spirits began to lift. If O'Toole no longer needed him, he was finished with the filthy business.

He was free! Free to go to Ireland; free to go to his wife; free to be with Nan when she had their child. Suddenly he wanted to drink a toast. He opened a filing cabinet and found a bottle of Irish whisky. "How apt," he said aloud. "Here's to a brand-new year, a brand-new beginning."

No sooner did Johnny lift the glass to his lips than his father heaved himself through the door. The wild look in William's eye and the pistol in his hand filled John Montague with dread. "Father, what in the name of God are you doing here?"

"I came to kill him, but he's gone!"

Johnny immediately knew he meant Sean O'Toole.

"He came to the auction...he's ruined us!"

Johnny steered him toward a leather chair, but William refused to relinquish the gun until John bribed him with a glass of whisky.

"He's planted his filthy Irish seed in Emerald!"

Christ, Sean must have flung his virility in their faces at the auction, for everyone to hear, thought John. *No wonder O'Toole was in such a hurry to leave.* He carefully tapped the powder from the pistol's flash pan before refilling the old man's glass.

"I'll get him, Johnny. He's the one behind all our losses!"

Dispassionately, John wondered why it had taken him so long to figure it out, and how long it would be before he suspected O'Toole must have had inside help.

Suddenly, Montague burst into tears. He rocked back and forth, sobbing piteously. His son stared at him with hard eyes. Surely his father didn't expect sympathy from him? Moribund with self-pity and maudlin from the Irish whisky, William moaned, "I miss your mother; I miss Amber."

Johnny felt his fists clench into balls. Until now he had been coldly indifferent to his father's words. But at the mention of his mother's name, a wedge of deep-seated anger rose in his throat, almost choking him. His beautiful young mother had lived a life of hell under Montague's domineering thumb. Then he had tossed her out like a piece of Irish offal, but not before he'd vented his vicious temper on her. John Montague saw his opportunity to twist the knife in his father's wound.

"Strange no one ever told you; it's common enough knowledge. Shamus O'Toole is her protector."

William jerked as the low blow found its mark.

"Never mind, Father, she only married you for your money. Now it's Shamus who squanders his gold on her."

As William's drink-sodden brain absorbed the lie, utter defeat engulfed him. Johnny led him to the leather couch and covered him with his overcoat. When William stopped his drunken rambling and fell asleep, John realized the great debt of gratitude he owed Sean O'Toole. The man before him had been his enemy all his life. Now, thanks to O'Toole,

416

William Montague was so reduced that Johnny no longer feared him or hated him. He was truly free.

During the next week John Montague set about putting his affairs in order. At the shipping office he went through every document to make sure that he did not leave an incriminating paper trail. At his flat in Soho he terminated the lease and packed his bags. Then he bought a coach ticket to Liverpool. A four-hour run across the Irish Sea was infinitely preferable to a four-day voyage from London to Dublin.

Though John did not know what lay ahead, he reasoned it could never be as bad as what lay behind him. He was eager to open the door to the future and close the one on his past. He hadn't seen Nan for months and the ache inside him grew with each passing hour. He looked about the room with a feeling akin to relief, knowing it would be the last night he would spend here.

John's relief was short-lived. When he heard the knock on the door and opened it to find Mrs. Thomas, the cook from Portman Square, he suspected she had come about his father. The old swine had lived at the top of his voice for years, courting apoplexy.

"Good evening, Mrs. Thomas. If my father has sent you for me, I'm afraid you've wasted your time."

"No, sir, it's Mistress Emma."

"Emerald?" John asked, at a complete loss.

"She sent me to fetch you," Mrs. Thomas whispered, almost afraid to give him the message.

"Where is she?"

"At Portman Square, sir."

"Portman Square? What in the name of God is she doing there?" he demanded.

"She's...poorly. She's bin there near a week. Please, sir, don't let on it were me who fetched you."

John grabbed his cloak. "Let's go."

"They put her in the servants' quarters. Dr. Sloane set her leg."

"She has a broken leg? How did that happen?" Every time the woman opened her mouth, she alarmed him more.

"I daren't say, sir, but her husband has a very nasty way with him."

They took a cab to Portman Square. When they arrived at the massive redbrick house, Mrs. Thomas slipped around the back to the servants' entrance. John Montague, who had thought he would never have to step over this threshold again, straightened his shoulders and rapped sharply on the front door. Belton looked almost glad to see him.

"Is it true? Is my sister here?" John demanded.

When the servant led the way to Irma Bludget's old room, John's blood began to boil. When he saw Emerald lying white faced in the bed, her belly distended beyond belief, he almost wept. He took her hand. "Em, my God, Em, what have they done to you?"

She squeezed his hand gratefully. "Johnny, I'm having twins."

His eyes widened in disbelief. "O'Toole abandoned you! The vengeful son of a bitch wasn't satisfied just using me to get at them, he had to use you too! I'll kill him! So help me God, I'll kill him!"

"No, Johnny, no more revenge, please, I beg you."

"I had no idea you were here. I was on my way to Ireland." He ran a distracted hand through his hair. "You can't stay here. But you're too far along to go back with me."

She winced as she pulled the cover aside to show him her leg wrapped in splints. "Much as I hate it, I'll have to stay here for a while. At least until after my babies are born. Dr. Sloane has been twice. He's going to deliver my twins. The minute I go into labor, Mrs. Thomas has promised to bring him."

"Mrs. Thomas hinted it was Jack Raymond who broke your leg."

"He tried to push me down the stairs so I'd miscarry. It was Father who saved me from him and sent for the doctor."

Suddenly, all the hatred and fear that had left John Montague came flooding back. Not for himself, but for his beloved sister who was so helpless and vulnerable.

"John, when I've had the babies and I'm well enough to travel, I want you to take me to Mother in Wicklow. She made me promise to let her know if I needed help."

Inside him John Montague felt his fury

build. He was on his way to Ireland, all right, but his destination wasn't Wicklow, it was Castle Lies. Somehow he'd make the Irish son of a bitch do the honorable thing for Emerald. O'Toole had rendered the Montagues penniless, while he enjoyed the wealth and title of Earl of Kildare. John vowed to make him pay in more ways than one.

Torn almost in half, John didn't want to leave her at the mercy of a vicious, jealous husband like Jack Raymond, but he feared he could do little good here. He would be useless at the impending birth. John felt a compulsion to act quickly. He feared Emerald's time was running out. For once he would act decisively.

He kissed his sister. "I love you. Try to rest and gather your strength." He then went in search of Belton.

"Is Raymond here?" he demanded, hardly able to hold his fury in check. He needed a physical outlet for his anger and Raymond was the perfect target.

"No, sir. We've seen very little of him this week."

John ground his teeth in frustration. "And my father?"

"I'm expecting him; he usually has a late dinner at home."

John went to the kitchen and pressed twenty pounds into Mrs. Thomas's hands. "This is all the money I have with me. If Emerald needs anything, get it for her. If for any reason Dr. Sloane can't be reached, get another doctor, or a midwife. Don't let my father know you have this money, or he'll have it off you."

When John opened the front door, he couldn't believe his luck. Jack Raymond was coming up the front steps. For the first time in his life Johnny experienced bloodlust. It was a heady feeling. As Raymond reached the top step, John's fist shot out, hitting him full in the face with a sickening thud. Raymond catapulted backward down the five steps, landing in a crumpled heap with one leg sprawled across the bottom step.

Without compunction John Montague raised a booted foot and stomped down on the limb until he heard it crack. Then he bent down and grabbed Jack by his bloodied neckcloth. "I won't break your leg next time, I'll break your balls. Now, don't you ever touch Emerald again!"

The man who had taught Johnny Montague to issue such brutal threats spent the day alone. At Greystones none had dared approach him, since his return from England. The entire staff, from the lowest stableboy to Paddy Burke, wanted to know why Emerald hadn't come home, but the dark, forbidding face of the earl caused them to leave their questions unasked.

Sean O'Toole drew apart, distancing himself behind a grim wall of silence. He was either mute or taciturn to any who dared approach him. They, too, finally distanced themselves, having no choice but to respect his need for privacy and seclusion.

Astride Lucifer, he swept through the hills with unseeing eyes. Icy rain, turning to sleet, cut into his face, yet still he rode on relentlessly. He was oblivious to everything save his own dark thoughts. He had left her behind, yet Emerald was still with him. His every waking thought was obsessed by her, and the few times he'd found sleep, his dreams were saturated with his need for her. He was fast in a snare of his own making. He had stolen her and molded her into his ideal mate.

Trust me! He'd said it over and over to her. And not only had she given him her trust, she had given him her love. Contempt for himself rose up within him until he could taste it on his tongue. His self-respect was mutilated; mauled by his own ugly, maimed hand. Yet even his hand wasn't as unpalatable as his soul. It felt corrupt.

Suddenly he cursed himself aloud, then laughed at the fool he was fast becoming. What little self-respect he had left would be destroyed if he did not stop wallowing in self-pity and introspection that was utterly useless. O'Toole knew he was what he was; he must come to terms with himself. *Easier said than done. I rewarded her love with lies and betrayal.* Then his dark thoughts once again came full circle. He was incapable of love; Emerald was better off without him.

Finally, soaked to the skin, chilled to the bone, he headed back to Castle Lies. The harsh weather matched his mood and he cared nothing for its ravages. In the end it was pity for his horse that drove him homeward.

As he gave Lucifer a thorough rubdown, the stablemen kept their distance. He entered Greystones by the back door, then headed through the vast kitchen. The servants scattered before him so that the rooms and hallways echoed with emptiness. So it was with surprise that he entered the dining room and found Shamus sitting before the blazing fire, waiting to confront him.

"The mountain has come to Mohammed."

Sean's face remained closed, his eyes hooded.

"Why have you shunned me?" Shamus asked.

"I am not fit company," he replied bluntly.

"Where is she?" Shamus demanded.

Sean raised hooded eyelids and looked directly at his father. "She is back in the bosom of her family with an Irish bastard in her belly."

"Why? Why?" Shamus thundered, wondering if he had ever really known the man who stood before him.

Sean stared at his father. Surely his reason was obvious. The concept was simple enough for a child to grasp. "They used your woman to make you suffer. I paid them back in kind."

"Never say ye committed this dreadful deed fer me?"

"Not for you, for her! Kathleen FitzGerald

O'Toole was the heart and the soul of us; she was the center of our lives. I swore a sacred oath at her grave I would avenge her through the woman at the center of *their* lives!"

Shamus snatched up the iron poker as if he would smite his son. "Such an evil act defiles her memory! Your mother was everything that was fine, everything that was gentle. Kathleen is weeping in heaven that you have done this in her name. I want my grand-child—her grandchild—even if you don't." Shamus flung down the poker. "Paddy! Get me out of here."

Sean stood naked before the fire in his chamber, leaning his forehead against the massive oak mantelpiece. The flames danced merrily, mocking his black mood. He had consumed half a decanter of whisky but, to his great disgust, remained coldly sober.

"Kate!" he bellowed, then realized she would not attend him. He hadn't set eyes on her since the night he'd returned alone from England to find the cradle in the master bed-chamber. The words they'd exchanged that night were so cutting, they had both bled. As penance for the cradle he ordered Kate to remove everything that belonged to Emerald, and tight lipped she had done his bidding beneath his relentless pewter gaze.

Sean O'Toole's insides gnawed at him. He needed to touch something that was hers. It wasn't just an ephemeral fancy, the need was as real as the breath of life. He searched frantically for the key that would unlock the adjoining door between their bedchambers. In his haste he searched the same drawer three times before his hand closed over it. He moved swiftly across the room, then fumbled with the lock, cursing it soundly before it would cooperate.

As he opened the tall chiffonnier, her fragrant smell filled his senses. Even in the dim light he knew the drawer held her exquisite nightgowns. Almost reverently he reached out to lift a handful of the silken garments to his cheek, but his fingers came into contact with something hard and cold.

Sean's gut knotted sickeningly. His brain cried out in denial of what his touch told him. He savagely yanked the drawer from the chest and carried it into his own chamber. There among the silk and lace lay her diamonds and her emeralds, given to her to assuage his guilt at betraying her. A cold hand slid icy fingers about his heart and began to squeeze. He had left her without a penny to fend for herself and her unborn child.

32

When John Montague disembarked the mail boat in Dublin in the late afternoon, he went straight to the Brazen Head, where he hired a mount and a packhorse for his luggage. The interminable, cold, soaking rain did nothing to dampen his temper. By the time he arrived at Greystones his blood was up and he was ready for the fight of his life.

Though the hour was advanced, he saw with satisfaction that lights were still lit at both house and stables. He dismounted in the courtyard and, taking the bridles of both horses, led them inside out of the rain. There was no mistaking the tall, dark figure of O'Toole, who had just entered the stables through the back door.

Without even wiping the rain from his eyes, John Montague dropped the reins and launched himself at the startled man before him. It was momentum rather than the resounding punch to the jaw that dropped O'Toole to the stable floor. They rolled together as John tried to land another facer and Sean did his best to avoid his angry fists.

O'Toole had no desire to be brutal to Johnny Montague. The lad was no match for someone who had cut his teeth brawling with the FitzGeralds and Murphys. Sean chose not to beat his assailant into submission. Instead, he rolled to one side, gained his feet, and grabbed a pitchfork. Then he backed Johnny, cursing and spitting invective, into an empty stall.

"You son of a bitch! I used to respect you!"

"I used to respect myself." O'Toole's voice was low, mocking.

"I can understand your driving need for revenge. I can even understand your using Emerald to humiliate them, but you'll not bloody well abandon her with no means of support. Everything has a price. I've come to collect it."

"Emerald didn't send you." He said it in a flat, disappointed voice. "She has too much pride."

"I wonder who taught her that?" Johnny hissed.

"She wouldn't accept money from me; she'd fling it in my face."

"Man, her plight is desperate! She's in no position to pick and choose."

Sean's fingers slackened on the pitchfork. "What the hell do you mean? Talk to me, Johnny."

"Put that bloody thing down."

Sean threw the fork into a pile of straw. "Come up to the house, you're soaked." He unfastened John's bags from the packhorse and summoned a young groom to tend the horses.

As Johnny stripped off his clothes before the fire in the bedchamber, Sean showed him

427

the jewels. "These belong to Emerald, believe it or not. Until tonight I thought she had them with her." Sean's mind winged back to the argument they'd had over the diamonds. He clearly remembered making her promise to keep them. *You have no money of your own; the necklace will give you some financial security,* he had warned her. But her reply also came back to him. *My darling, you are all the security I will ever need.*

Johnny looked him in the eye. "If she had known you were taking her back to Portman Square, she would have taken the bloody things fast enough! You didn't tell her, did you?"

Sean almost replied "It was kinder," but he caught his words back. It had not been kinder, it had simply been easier. He had done what was expedient. "When I found the jewels tonight, I went down to the stables and dispatched a groom to Maynooth recalling the *Sulphur*'s crew. We'll sail in the morning."

Johnny heaved a sigh of relief. It didn't matter if he'd persuaded O'Toole, or if Sean had decided on his own. All that mattered was that he was returning. But Johnny wasn't finished with him, not by a long chalk. He had Sean O'Toole on the defensive and it felt good.

"In your relentless quest for vengeance, did you never pause to think what *they* might do to Emerald?"

"She's more than a match for the bloody Montagues!"

"Is she? Think back; were you a match for

them that night they had you at their mercy? Was your brother Joseph?"

Sean snatched up the empty whisky decanter and smashed it into the hearth. "Emerald is his daughter! Surely she's precious to him."

"Precious?" Johnny laughed. "Obviously she never told you of life with Father. She was blamed, punished, and controlled every waking hour until he broke her spirit. She married Jack Raymond in desperation, looking for an escape from Father and her Portman Square prison, but instead she found herself serving a life sentence with two jailers."

Sean felt his blood run cold. Emerald had never once complained of mistreatment, yet nevertheless he had known. Emerald had been stripped of every freedom just as surely as he had. And it was obvious to him. That was why he had taken such great joy in restoring those freedoms. Watching her come alive and return to the vibrant, passionate female she had been when they first met gave him the greatest pleasure he'd ever known.

Suddenly, he went icy. Johnny wouldn't be here unless something had happened to her. He didn't want to ask the question because he didn't want to hear the answer. He faced his growing fear; fear he'd thought he was incapable of feeling.

"What did they do to her?"

"Jack tried to push her down the stairs so she would miscarry. She saved herself, but she has a broken leg."

Sean's fear was now full blown.

"When my father's doctor came to set it, he discovered she is carrying twins."

Sean's fear immediately doubled. He turned a look of furious incredulity upon Johnny. "And you left her in such a plight?"

"No, you son of a bitch, *you did*!"

When Dr. Sloane was again summoned to Portman Square, he did not expect to be called upon to set another broken leg.

"It's an epidemic," he said dryly to William Montague, who paced about the bedchamber calling down curses on every member of his family.

Jack Raymond alternately howled with pain and swore a blue streak at the servants who were running about obeying orders. When Sloane suggested he should conduct himself with Emerald's dignity as a patient, Jack turned his wrath on the doctor.

"I'm going to sedate him," Sloane told William.

"Is that necessary?" William shouted. "I need him lucid. We have serious problems to discuss—business matters—"

"They'll have to wait," Sloane snapped. "You'll have plenty of time to talk. He isn't going anywhere for a few weeks."

Emerald, who had been receiving little enough attention before, got considerably less, now that Jack had to be nursed. She had very little appetite, which was fortunate, since Mrs. Thomas had little time to cook. For company, during her days of solitude, Emerald had only her own thoughts.

Fear of the unknown was terrifying, so doggedly she focused on today, telling herself that tomorrow did not have to be faced until it arrived. She told herself calmly that she had two choices: Either she allowed panic to snatch away her reason, her very sanity, or she coped with her situation the best way she could.

Women down through the ages had given birth. She told herself that even if she had a dozen attendants at her beck and call, *she* was still the one who would have to suffer the pain. No one else could do it for her. She also reassured herself that she had enjoyed good health throughout her pregnancy. Her morning sickness had been nothing more than an inconvenience, easily remedied. She knew she was strong physically, mentally, and emotionally and was convinced that after her babies were delivered, she would rapidly regain her strength and vitality. Since her leg no longer throbbed with heavy pain, she reasoned that it was healing as it should.

As well as talking to herself, she spent a great deal of time praying. She asked for help, she prayed for strength, and she begged for forgiveness. But most of all she talked to her unborn babies. She reassured them constantly that all would be well, she soothed them with memories of her happy times in Ireland, and she whispered to them of their father, Sean FitzGerald O'Toole, Earl of Kildare.

Sean O'Toole paced back and forth across the chamber like a caged animal. The frustration of awaiting his crew was killing him. "As soon as they arrive, we'll sail; no matter the hour." To keep his hands busy he began to pack a bag.

"*You* will sail," Johnny corrected quietly. "I can't go back; I've burned my bridges. By now Father will know my part in all of this. Before I left I attacked Jack Raymond and deliberately smashed his leg."

"I would have enjoyed doing that," Sean said savagely.

"You'll have enough to do. Your duty is to Emerald...mine is to Nan."

"Nan FitzGerald?" Sean's dark eyes challenged him.

"Nan is my wife. She's having my child. I've neglected her long enough."

"Your wife?" Sean's eyes glittered in outrage. "When the hell did all this happen?"

"You were so bent on vengeance, you didn't see what was going on under your nose. We were married here at Greystones by Father Fitz."

"How dare you scheme behind my back? Am I the only one in ignorance here?" O'Toole crossed the room in two strides, grabbing Johnny by the throat.

John ground out, "I couldn't leave her with a bastard in her belly. And I love her."

432

John's words carried more impact than his fists could have. Sean's shoulders slumped and he loosened his vicious grip. Both men turned at a knock on the chamber door. It was Mr. Burke.

"Rory FitzGerald and the crew are here."

"Thank God!" It was the first time in over five years His name had passed Sean O'Toole's lips. "Tell them we're sailing tonight."

Paddy Burke cleared his throat. "Kate and I are ready to come with you. We knew you would go back for her."

Sean stared at him in amazement. He hadn't laid eyes on them in a week, yet they were aware of his every move, his every thought. Their loyalty and support overwhelmed him. Then he had a most humbling thought. They weren't doing this for him, they were doing it for Emerald.

When Emerald's labor finally began, just before dawn, nothing on earth had prepared her for the pain. Mrs. Thomas assured her she would fetch Dr. Sloane, but she returned without him, explaining to Emerald that a first labor was always protracted and that he would be along in due course.

Due course stretched into twelve long hours, during which Emerald cried, prayed, cursed, screamed, and lost consciousness; then, revived by a pain that threatened to tear her in half, began the cycle all over again.

Before she was done Emerald had cursed

father, husband, mother, Sean O'Toole, and God. Then she cursed herself. Mrs. Thomas stood vigil, talking with her, soothing her, and reassuring her, in spite of the fact that she herself felt overwhelmed by the double birth.

At five o'clock Dr. Sloane came by as if he were dropping in for tea. When he saw Emerald thrashing about the bed, he ordered Mrs. Thomas to tie her leg down so the patient would not do herself or her doctor an injury.

In rapid succession Emerald went rigid with a hard labor pain that proved unendurable, then she screamed and lost consciousness as Dr. Sloane delivered a tiny female child. He spared one glance for the pale infant, which barely showed signs of life, before he passed it to Mrs. Thomas without instruction.

That good woman had hot water and plenty of clean cloths at the ready, so she cleansed the tiny infant, murmuring over and over, "Poor wee mite." The baby girl had no strength to protest, all she could do was struggle for gasps of shallow breath.

Dr. Sloane washed his hands and dried them. "I'll go up and see my other patient," he announced.

"You can't leave her, Doctor, she's unconscious!" protested a scandalized Mrs. Thomas.

"It could be hours before she is ready to deliver the next one. She'll regain consciousness fast enough when hard labor begins again."

William Montague was in a vile temper by the time he arrived at Portman Square. He had spent the last few days at the shipping office, trying to salvage something, anything, of the decimated Montague Line. All that was left was one ship, the *Seagull,* and the only cargo he had been able to arrange was a shipload of coal from Newcastle.

Then, this afternoon, he had received a visit from a solicitor representing the Liverpool Shipping Company. The bank draft they had received from Barclay & Bedford for two ships purchased by Montague was nothing but a worthless piece of paper. The solicitor informed William the ships already en route would be reclaimed the moment they arrived in London, and told him in no uncertain terms that the Liverpool Shipping Company would be pressing charges and suing for damages.

Montague, already livid with his son, John, for having inflicted a broken leg on Jack Raymond, began to suspect he had inflicted far worse damage. The young swine had disappeared into thin air, and by the looks of things John had had good reason to take a powder. To be betrayed by an enemy was only to be expected, but to be betrayed by your own flesh and blood was an abomination against nature. These last few months had aged him ten years; he felt old, and bitter and very ill used.

Belton informed William that the doctor was upstairs.

"I don't smell anything good from the kitchen," William said ominously.

"No, sir, Mrs. Thomas has been with Miss Emma all afternoon. Her time has arrived."

William felt distinctly peevish. This last week the shipping office had been his only refuge from the bedlam of Portman Square, but after today he would avoid it too. A man's home was supposed to be his castle, but his had been taken over by unwelcome invalids who brought him nothing but trouble, humiliation, and unpaid bills.

William glanced impatiently up the stairs, then checked his pocket watch. Muttering obscenities beneath his breath, he climbed the stairs and made his way to the wing Jack Raymond occupied. He heard the complaining and moaning all the way down the hall. He stepped across the threshold and cursed, "You bloodsucking leech! Living here in the lap of luxury and not lifting a hand to prevent the treachery all about me!" He looked at Sloane and snapped, "Christ, give him a sedative, man, and a strong one. I can't stand all this weeping, wailing, and gnashing of teeth!"

Suddenly the three men heard a woman's screams.

Jack hissed, "Let her suffer."

Dr. Sloane said, "I must go down to her."

Jack flung, "She's only having a baby, for God's sake. I'm in agony, Doctor!"

"We all have our cross to bear," Sloane sympathized, rolling his eyes at William.

The two men descended the stairs together. "How long will this take?" asked William, sorry he had come home.

"It shouldn't be too much longer. I delivered one before you arrived. I'll be as quick as I can with the other. You're not the only one who wants dinner, Montague."

The girl on the bed was in hard labor. She was drenched in perspiration and clearly exhausted from her day-long ordeal. Her eyes were glazed and she was as pasty as the soiled sheet on which she lay panting.

Sloane slapped her sharply across the face. "Come on, woman, you have a job to do."

Emerald's eyes slitted open, then they widened at the heavy pain that took hold of her. She opened her mouth to scream, but nothing came out. *Let me die, let me die,* she prayed.

"Push, woman, push!" ordered Sloane, and somehow she did as he bade her. Pain like nothing she'd ever felt before was followed by a gushing, rushing feeling as if she were turning inside out. A loud indignant wail filled the room and Sloane muttered, "Well, this one is lusty enough."

"Oh, it's a boy, God be praised," said Mrs. Thomas, hastily taking the blood-covered child from Dr. Sloane.

As he washed his hands, he glanced at the female Mrs. Thomas had bundled up and laid at the foot of the bed. Unfortunately, it was still breathing. Sloane closed his bag and stepped from the room. Montague was just outside the door on his way back from the empty kitchen.

"You will be relieved to know the distasteful business is all over and done, Montague."

"Did you find a place for the brats?"

"Yes. Fortunately only one will survive. I'll be around to sign the death certificate in the morning, and take the other one off your hands."

"Very good, Sloane. I'll walk out with you. There will be no dinner for me here tonight."

Inside the room Mrs. Thomas looked at Emerald to see if she had heard the shocking things the men had said, but the exhausted girl seemed unaware of her surroundings. The cook had always known William Montague was a nasty old swine, but now she realized he was cold blooded as a reptile. And Dr. Sloane was no better, the callous old pig. She wished now she had brought a midwife for Emerald. It might not have helped the baby girl, if the poor wee mite wasn't strong enough to survive, but the mother needed attention.

The male child Mrs. Thomas cleansed and wrapped was screaming so lustily, she didn't take time to bathe Emerald. Instead she pulled aside her nightgown and tucked the baby against one bare breast. The child suckled instantly and noisily in a little frenzy to be fed. Emerald seemed only semiconscious. To Mrs. Thomas the young woman looked deathly ill.

The cook stretched and put a plump hand

to her aching back. She had been on her feet since before dawn and felt ready to drop. She pulled a chair up to the bed and sat her weary bones in it. She cast a troubled look at the tiny bundle at the bottom of the bed, then her eyes traveled to its mother.

It was all so overwhelming for Mrs. Thomas. She knew something should be done, but she didn't know what. She watched Emerald's eyes close and prayed she was sleeping. She decided there was nothing anyone could do; it was all in God's hands.

33

When he was not at the wheel of the *Sulphur*, Sean O'Toole paced the deck. By the time they arrived at the London Docks, he had walked most of the way to England. He knew he was racing with time, hoping against hope that he would arrive before Emerald went into labor. He wanted to get her out of the Portman Square mausoleum and take her to the lovely house in Old Park Lane where they had spent such happy hours. Even more, he wanted to be there for the birth of his children. He knew he must somehow make up for what he had done to her. In every man's life there was a turning point, a defining moment, and this was his.

It was two o'clock in the morning before the *Sulphur* dropped anchor. Three o'clock before the big black carriage conveyed its three occupants to the Montague house in Portman Square. Sean sprang to the pavement, strode up the steps, and crashed his clenched fist against the door.

Belton, who had fallen asleep in the vestibule waiting for William, jumped up so quickly, he knocked over the brass umbrella stand. Biting back a foul oath, he opened the door and discovered to his dismay that it was not the master, but Montague's enemy, who loomed over him. What was more, the man showed every intention of sweeping into the house as he had done before.

"You cannot come in here; it's the middle of the night!"

O'Toole curbed the violence that surged barely below the surface. "Step aside," he said quietly. "I own the deed on this accursed house; it is mine."

Belton, rendered speechless, staggered back a step, allowing not only O'Toole room to enter, but also the man and woman who accompanied him.

"Take me to her immediately." The order, given so quietly, carried a deadly threat.

"This way, my lord." Belton's face flushed because the daughter of the house was in the servants' quarters.

When Sean stepped into the small chamber, his heart sank to the pit of his stomach. He was too late for the birthing, and by the look of things he was almost too late for anything. His entrance awoke a sleeping servant, but the girl tied to the bed with a drowsing child at her breast did not even rouse. The burned-down candles provided scant light.

"Light the lamps," Sean bade the servant, as he went down on his knees beside the bed and took Emerald's limp hand into his own. The lamplight flared, revealing exactly what he had feared. Emerald was ill. Her pallor was like death. He smoothed the damp hair from her brow and felt her fever burn his fingers.

He was outraged that his beloved lay on soiled sheets. Behind him he heard Paddy Burke exclaim, "Holy Mother of God!" Murder rose up in Sean. He knew a need to kill her father and her husband for the acts they had committed and for their gross neglect. With an effort he let the violence fall away from him. He must not spare even a thought for anyone save Emerald and their newborn babies.

He heard Kate Kennedy draw in a ragged breath. "We need a priest. This wee soul has drawn its last breath."

Her words galvanized him to action. He snatched the tiny bundle from Kate and looked down into a little blue face. Swiftly, he bent his head to the scrap of humanity and gave it his own breath. "We need no priest. There'll be no dead to shrive this night!"

When the infant began to struggle for its own pitifully shallow breaths, Sean handed it back to Kate. He unbound the strips of cloth that tied Emerald's leg to the bed and said urgently,

"We've got to get them out of here." The baby boy, slumbering beside his mother, opened his mouth and began to scream. Sean plucked him from his warm cocoon and thrust him at Paddy Burke.

"Clear a path for me," he ordered, then lifted Emerald into invincible arms. Carrying her downstairs and through the front door, Sean felt as though he had retrieved something utterly precious that had been lost. No. That he had almost thrown away. He set her inside the carriage as gently as he could.

Emerald opened her eyes, then closed them again, murmuring, "No more."

The words scalded Sean's heart. He knew she was in no condition to be jostled about, but it was not her leg that worried him; he feared for her very life. He knew Emerald was paying for the sin he had committed, and he wanted to curse heaven for the injustice of it.

Mr. Burke handed the child he carried to Kate, then climbed up with the driver. Sean crouched on the carriage floor, holding Emerald as still as he could. The ride from Portman Square was brief, taking only minutes, but to Sean, in his race against time, it felt like hours.

Their arrival at Old Park Lane turned the household into a hive of activity. The entire staff was summoned and given specific duties. One was dispatched for a doctor, fires were lit in every chamber, water was heated and beds prepared.

Sean laid his precious burden on the snowy

linen. He murmured huskily, "It will be all right, love. Trust me!" As his eyes swept over Emerald and their babies, his priorities were jolted into line. He turned anguished eyes upon Kate and Paddy. "Tend them for me." It tore at his heart to relinquish Emerald's care to others, but he had no choice, his efforts were needed elsewhere. "I need whisky," he told Mr. Burke.

Sean carried the silent little bundle before the sitting-room fire and carefully unwrapped it. Sean's icy heart melted when he saw the tiny female. When Paddy brought the bottle of Irish whisky, Sean poured some into his palm, warmed it at the fire, and began to rub it directly on the baby's skin.

He began at the tiny chest, then turned the baby over and massaged its little back. With gentle fingers he rubbed his daughter's arms and legs, then massaged her tiny buttocks. Beginning again at the baby's rib cage, his hands stimulated the infant's circulation.

After an hour the ominous blue tinge began to disappear. After two hours the little female's skin turned a frightening red. Sean cursed himself for a clumsy fool. He had been overzealous in his efforts. He tucked the baby in the crook of his arm and went to the kitchen. "Have we any milk?" he asked the chef's assistant.

"A milkmaid delivers fresh milk every day, my lord."

"I need a cloth sterilized; linen would be best."

The kitchen maid set a pan of water to boil

and produced a linen serviette. As the cloth boiled she said, "With two babies, my lord, you need the services of a wet nurse."

"Why didn't I think of that—can you get one for us?" he asked eagerly.

She smiled, happy he was open to her advice. "The agency that places butlers and house servants provides such a service. English ladies do not suckle their own babies, my lord."

Sean carried a cup of milk and the linen napkin back to the sitting-room fire. He poured a bit of the smoky whisky into the milk, then dipped in a corner of the linen cloth. Holding open the baby's mouth with his fingers, he began to feed his daughter one drop at a time.

Suddenly, she began to choke and Sean momentarily froze, horrified at what he had done. He turned her over and smacked her narrow little back. All at once a lump of mucus dislodged from the infant's throat. The moment Sean cleared it from the baby's mouth, she took in a great gulp of air and let out a thin, pathetic little wail.

"Good girl, Daddy's girl. Come on, it's time for breakfast."

Paddy Burke came to the sitting-room door. "God in heaven, that's an encouraging noise. Now, if I could only shut this lad up."

"There's milk in the kitchen, and in the morning we're getting a wet nurse. Did that bloody doctor come yet?"

"He'll be along at daylight. Physicians to the wealthy set their own rules."

Sean's intense gaze held Paddy's. "How is she?"

"Kate says she's lost a lot of blood. Our lass is weak and exhausted, but at least she's clean." Paddy did not tell him Emerald was still feverish and becoming delirious.

It was not until Sean had painstakingly fed his daughter a quarter cup of milk, drop by drop, that it dawned on him the other twin was a male child. So, he had one of each! At least for tonight he did.

All of his ridiculous convictions did an about-face. As he looked down at the tiny scrap in the crook of his arm, he knew there was a God, a supreme being who held dominion over heaven and earth. He shook his head at his own arrogant folly. When you held your own baby in your hands and its life hung by a thread, you acknowledged God's existence fast enough. Not only did he begin to pray, he did so fervently, beseechingly, opening his heart to God's love.

What a self-righteous swine he had been to insist there was no room for love in his heart. At this moment his heart overflowed and love poured from him. He loved this woman and these children beyond reason, with all his mind, all his heart, and all his soul. He had more love than they would ever be able to use in one lifetime. His love was eternal, it would go on forever.

When his tiny daughter slept, he wrapped her snugly. He did not delude himself about the baby's chances. She was too small and too frail. She would need constant care, love, and attention; even then her chance for survival would be a slim one. His own mother had been a twin; her baby brother had not survived.

Sean carried the sleeping infant to the bedchamber and laid her on the wide bed. He placed his hand on Kate's shoulder. "I want you to get some rest. I'll take over here."

Kate immediately protested.

"Kate, I mean it. You'll be no use to her if you're dropping on your feet."

"I'll put my legs up for a couple of hours," Kate consented. "Now here's a pile of clean linen for the bed and I have one of the maids tearing up flannel sheets for baby nappies."

"Thank you, Kate."

"Oh, and I asked yer fancy chef to make some barley water. There's nothing like barley water for an invalid. Would you believe it, he didn't have a clue. Devil fly away wi' the man! I'll just go and make sure he's doing it properly."

Sean looked down at Emerald with alarm. Her face was no longer pale, it was flushed a dull red. Her eyelids were heavy and swollen closed. She murmured continually, incomprehensibly, as her head moved restlessly on the pillow. He touched the back of his fingers to her cheek, confirming that she was still hot with fever. Though Kate had bathed her, Emerald was no cooler. He decided to do it again.

He fetched a bowl of tepid water and a sponge to her bedside. As he worked, he talked to her. "Kate probably struggled to get you into this pristine nightgown, but off it comes, my beauty. You'll be much cooler, and only I know you prefer to be quite naked in bed. There, now, that's better." He grimaced at the soiled bandages on her leg. If the doctor didn't arrive by the time he'd bathed her, he would remove the bandages himself.

He sponged her face and throat over and over with infinite patience until they seemed to cool down. Then he sponged her shoulders and her arms. He noticed that when he kept up a running conversation, Emerald quieted. As he bathed her breasts he saw how motherhood had enhanced their natural beauty. They were enlarged, firm and smooth as satin, her nipples rosy and moist.

"You are a rare beauty, Emerald my love; a true Irish beauty! I'm going to take you back home as soon as you're strong enough to travel. You've done a magnificent job, Irish. You once told me you'd give me a son, but you outdid yourself! Not only did you give me a boy, but a wee lass too."

He tenderly sponged her tummy, still swollen and distended from the birth. "Not a stretch mark in sight, thanks to Tara's magic potion." He bathed her unbound, sound limb, gently blotting her dry with a linen towel. When he touched her now, it seemed to him that she was somewhat cooler.

He eyed the soiled bandages and made a decision. "I'll try not to hurt you, love, I'll try not to hurt you ever again." On sea voyages he'd set broken bones, so he wasn't a complete novice. He unwrapped the leg and examined it closely from top to bottom. With his fingers he probed her unswollen thigh. When she did not flinch, he decided her thighbone had suffered no injury and the splints were unnecessary.

The lower part of her leg told another tale. It was swollen and puffy from knee to ankle. Obviously, it was the tibia bone she had fractured, and Sean hoped and prayed it was a clean break. Slowly, gently, he bathed and patted dry the limb. He then tore a linen sheet into strips. Making sure it wasn't too tight, he bound the leg firmly, swathing it in layers of linen until it was secure and immobile. As the swelling went down, the bandage could be tightened.

Paddy Burke let the doctor in and brought him to the bedchamber where the patient lay. Dr. Brookfield introduced himself, examined the leg in a cursory fashion, and concluded it had been tended quite adequately. "Either a bone heals, or it does not." He could see the Earl of Kildare would not be put off with half-truths. "If she stays off the leg for six weeks, it should heal."

"She's feverish, Doctor. What can I do to break it?"

Brookfield took Emerald's pulse and felt the temperature of her skin. "Childbed fever is very common. Generally, those who receive good nursing care and are kept clean, stand the best chance of recovery. Those who are neglected die. But sometimes just the opposite occurs."

Sean had to curb the desire to take the doctor by the throat to choke off his banal platitudes. Obviously he had no intention of doing anything, he was simply there to state his opinion. He continued, telling Sean what he already knew.

"The birth was complicated because it involved twins. She most likely hemorrhaged. If she does not recover—"

Sean cut him off. "She will recover, Brookfield. Tell me what to do to speed that recovery."

"You could try to get some liquids into her and I'll leave you a sedative. Since I'm here, I may as well take a look at the infants."

Suddenly, Sean didn't want him passing his pompous opinion on his babies. "They will be fine, Doctor. How much do I owe you?"

Brookfield glanced at the pitifully small bundle on the wide bed. "It doesn't look fine to me. Kildare, you are an intelligent man; one who can face facts, I'm sure. With twins, one usually thrives, one fails. Infant mortality is high, even for normal, healthy children. Prepare yourself for the inevitable; this baby will not survive. Sometimes death is a blessing in disguise."

"Get out," Sean said tersely. He closed his eyes. *Christ, can I not get through one night without committing violence?* he thought.

"Paddy!" he bellowed. Mr. Burke came in immediately, and set his sleeping bundle down on the bed. "See the doctor out, while he's still in one piece," Sean said quietly.

Sean prayed that Brookfield's words had not penetrated through Emerald's torpor. There was nothing wrong with her hearing; she had responded to his own voice. He set about reassuring her in a confident tone he was far from feeling. "Our babies are right here with us. They've been fed and now they are having a nap. I'm going to get you a drink; your lips are very dry."

He would begin with cool water. If she kept that down, he would try her with barley water. He brought a cup of each to the bedside and wondered how to go about the business so that she would not choke on the liquids. He eased the pillow from beneath her head, then sat behind her, against the bed head. Gently as possible, he raised her shoulders until she lay half reclined against his chest.

Emerald's head rolled against his shoulder, then nestled there as if she had discovered a comfy spot. Sean raised the cup to her lips and urged her to drink. "Just a tiny sip, now. That's right, that's good! You are really thirsty and no one gave you a drink. Have a rest now, catch your breath."

He switched to the barley water, and again raised the cup to her lips. With infinite patience and encouragement he managed to get half a cup of liquid into her. When she could swallow no more, he set the cup aside and simply held her. He did not think she was much cooler, but she was far less restless.

Sean wanted Emerald to know that he was there with her. He wanted her to know that he had come back for her. He needed her to realize it was he and no other who held her against his heart. Gently taking her hand, he curved her fingers around the place where his thumb was missing. By touching his maimed hand she would know it was Sean O'Toole and no other.

Perhaps his body could draw off some of her heat; perhaps his body could infuse her with some of his strength. He set his mind to it, knowing all the while that it was a coping device, yet telling himself fiercely that if love could heal her, he would surround her with it, saturate her with it. He didn't know if it was imagination or wishful thinking, but he thought he felt Emerald's fingers tighten their hold on his hand.

Sean sat holding her for hours. Darkness turned into dawn, then dawn turned into clear morning light. He watched his son awaken and start to cry. Sean's mouth curved as he watched the little imp become furious in his demand for food and attention.

Kate appeared and picked him up. "We have a wet nurse at last. This child is the living, breathing image of you. God help us all!"

"Perhaps we should get a wet nurse for each of them." He did not try to hide his fear that Emerald might not recover. "What do you think, Kate?"

"Emerald's milk will come in today. She will

suffer terrible discomfort if she doesn't suckle one of them. Perhaps she'll be well enough by tonight."

Kate's words encouraged him and spurred him on. Today he would double his efforts to get liquids into her, and he would bathe her every hour. If it was humanly possible to break her fever, Sean O'Toole was determined to do it.

The efforts of the entire household were concentrated on one thing and one thing only: making sure that this mother and her babies survived. Mr. Burke went out and returned with a cradle that rocked. Two servants were sent on a shopping expedition to buy baby clothes, blankets, nappies, bottles, and teats. Kate sat with Emerald while Sean bathed, changed his clothes, and wolfed down some food. Then he returned to hold her, talk to her, sponge her down, and coax her to drink.

Daylight faded into twilight, then gradually full darkness descended. Sean sat quietly propped against the head of the bed, enfolding Emerald in his arms. His gut was knotted with fear because she still hadn't roused. Gradually, he became aware of a growing dampness between their bodies. Suddenly, his hopes began to soar. He felt her brow, then moved his hand down her cheek to her throat. Emerald was soaking wet; her fever had broken!

34

This time after Sean bathed her, he helped her into a nightgown, then lifted her from the bed so that fresh sheets could be put on it. He talked to Emerald softly, telling her where she was, explaining that Kate and Paddy were here to help take care of her.

"Don't try to talk, love; it will only tire you. All you have to do is get well; we will do all the rest."

Though she didn't answer him, Sean knew Emerald understood what he was saying. He smiled often to reassure her, but inside he was pure panic. He knew the best reassurance that all was well would be for her to see her babies. But if she saw her daughter, she would become frantic with worry. Though Emerald's fever had broken, she was far from well and Sean suspected her recovery would be slow and tenuous at best.

He sat on the side of the bed and took hold of her hand. "Did you know you had a little boy and a little girl?" His heart turned over as her mouth curved in a half smile, for even this small effort seemed to tax her strength. "I'm going to bring them, one at a time, so you can see the miracles for yourself." He winked at her. "Don't go away, I'll be right back."

Sean went along to the bedchamber that had been transformed into a nursery and conferred with Kate Kennedy, who came up with a novel suggestion. "To keep her from fretting herself to death, you could show her the same child twice."

Sean frowned. How easy it would be. The illusion would be so much kinder than reality at the moment, yet Sean knew he must never deceive her again, no matter the temptation.

"No, Kate." He turned to Alice, the young wet nurse who was such a Godsend in their predicament. "Is my daughter able to suckle, Alice?"

"Not very well, sir. She hardly has the strength. She takes a couple of sucks, then drifts away in sleep."

"Keep her awake; don't let her sleep until she's been fed properly. Kate, help her keep awake, tickle her feet or something."

Sean found Mr. Burke in the sitting room. "Paddy, you're going to wear out the carpets, walking his nibs about."

Paddy grinned. "Takes me back to when you were born. Many's the time Shamus walked you all night long."

"Give him to me; I'm taking him to his mother."

When Emerald saw her son, her lovely green eyes shone with unshed tears of joy.

"He's a beauty all right, but he's got a rare temper. When he cries, he makes enough racket to raise the rent."

Emerald smiled through her tears.

"Your milk has come in, love, would you like to feed him?"

When she nodded, he tucked the baby beside her and opened her nightgown. The little mouth needed no guidance to his mother's engorged nipple. As she watched her son, Emerald's face lit with radiance, and Sean truly felt blessed that he was privy to such an intimate moment.

After a while Sean lifted the baby to the other side. "What shall we call the young devil?"

Emerald lifted her gaze from her son and looked into pewter eyes. "Joseph," she whispered.

The lump that rose in Sean's throat made it impossible for him to reply for a moment. She was still the most generous woman in the world. What the hell had he ever done to deserve her? When Joseph started to drift into slumber, Sean plucked him from his cocoon and held him upright against one broad shoulder while he rubbed the little back as Kate had shown him.

"Do you think you can stay awake long enough to greet your daughter?" In truth, he wished Emerald had fallen asleep, so her discovery could be postponed one more day. "Then at the risk of being repetitive, don't go away, I'll be right back."

When Sean left the room with his son, Emerald closed her eyes in distress. From the time she went into labor she had been aware of almost everything. She overheard the conversation between her father and Dr. Sloane, whereby she learned the fate of her newborn babies. When she realized one was dying and the other also was to be taken away from her, Emerald gave up. Giving birth to the twins had used up every drop of strength she possessed and more. Then all hope had been snuffed. She withdrew inside herself and waited for death.

What happened next was like a dream. The Angel of Death swooped down and carried her off. It was only later that she realized it was no dream, and the apparition that descended upon Portman Square was Sean O'Toole in the guise of an avenging angel. His will was so strong, he refused to let her die. Somehow, he had even forced death to take a step back from her baby daughter. But Emerald had little hope. She had heard two doctors say the baby girl was too small and frail to survive.

Sean was putting up a brave front for her sake. Emerald was overwhelmingly grateful for all he had done. He had struggled tirelessly from dark to dark, infusing them with his own strength, refusing to entertain even the possibility of failure. She closed her eyes and prayed for strength to face what lay before her.

When Sean stepped into the bedchamber, he carried the tiny bundle so possessively, her heart turned over. "She's very small, Emerald, I don't want you to be alarmed. The nurse has already fed her and she has just fallen asleep." He placed the baby against her heart, but he did not let go of the child.

Suddenly, Emerald knew she could not take away his hope. As she looked down her face softened with love and she fought back the tears that threatened to drown her in sorrow. "We'll call her Kathleen," she whispered.

The moment touched him so deeply, Sean wanted to weep. Then he clearly saw she was holding back her own tears for his sake. He slipped to his knees to bring himself closer. When their eyes met, all pretense between them fled.

"Emerald, I swear to you on my knees, if there is any way I can save our daughter, I shall. Kathleen is a perfect name. Perhaps my mother has been chosen to be her guardian angel." He touched the slumbering child beside her mother, then left them alone for a few private minutes.

When he returned he carried in the big wooden cradle on rockers and set it beside the bed. Then he brought in a sleeping Joseph and laid him inside. Sean turned the lamps down low and lay down on the wide bed beside Emerald. One protective hand curved around the tiny baby that lay between them. So long as they lay touching, they were a part of each other. Joined together through the dark hours of the night, they might not be separated.

During the next fortnight Sean never left their side. Joseph started to thrive. With both his mother and Alice feeding him, he began to grow.

Baby Kathleen did not grow. Her appetite

was minuscule, sometimes nonexistent. Often her breathing was labored and her pink color would turn waxy. Whenever this happened, night or day, Sean patiently massaged her until her circulation was restored. She seldom had enough energy to cry, but when she did, the sound was quite pitiful. Sean and Emerald made a pact that one or the other would hold her at all times. Both were convinced of the magic power of touch.

Emerald herself gained a little more strength, but Sean knew it would be a long, slow road back to perfect health. When she looked unwell, he exuded tenderness. He didn't leave the house in Old Park Lane until the third week. February brought early-spring sunshine flooding through the windows, bathing every cheerful room in golden light. Everyone in the house seemed to brighten. So far things were going as well as could be expected, and an air of optimism crept upon them that things would improve.

When Sean returned he brought an armful of daffodils and scattered them across the foot of the bed. He smiled at the lovely picture she made, propped against the pillows, cuddling her baby daughter.

"I know you have an inordinate love of flowers and accept them from me willingly—unlike jewels," he added softly. He sat down on the bed. "There's something else I want you to accept." He took the baby and handed Emerald a long envelope.

She opened it and found the deed to Old Park

Lane. She lifted her eyes from the crackling document. "You bought it?"

He nodded. "I know how much you love this house. I bought it in your name, not mine. I should have done it long ago."

"Thank you. It is such a lovely, thoughtful gesture."

"I love you, Emerald."

"Don't say that," she said quietly.

So, you haven't forgiven me after all, he thought. He understood completely. He hadn't expected her to; yet, Sean realized now, he had been harboring a glimmer of hope. He smiled at her to show his understanding. He hadn't given her enough time. He would give her all the time she needed, and in the meanwhile he would show her by his actions, by his dedication and devotion, that he loved her with all his heart.

All four of them slept together in the bedchamber and Emerald had no objection to this arrangement, rather he could tell she took great comfort from it. She allowed him to bathe and feed her, until she became strong enough to feed herself, so it was obvious to Sean that she had no objection to his touch. He thanked God for small mercies, noting wryly she only rejected his verbal declaration of love.

He chose his words carefully. "I don't want to push you before you're ready, but I want you to think about going home to Greystones." He was relieved when she seemed quite eager.

"If you think it's safe for Kathleen to travel, I'm ready anytime, Sean."

He took Emerald's hand and squeezed it. "I won't lie to you ever again.... Sweetheart, I can't guarantee she'll make it."

"I know that," she said softly.

"I'll carry her all the way to Ireland."

Her mouth curved. "And what about Joseph?"

"Hell, he's big enough to sail the ship!"

It felt wonderful to see her laugh. He did not know the main reason she was eager to go home was to put distance between him and the Montagues. Each day she wondered when he would take up his vendetta again. He had done a superb job of controlling his anger and hatred, but she knew it could not last. She and their babies were his first priority right now, but she feared it wouldn't last long, and knew his retribution would be terrible.

The next time Sean gave Emerald a sponge bath, he voiced a concern. "Having to stay in bed is not strengthening. I don't want your muscles to deteriorate. I think you will benefit from a good massage every day. You have another three weeks to go before you can even attempt to walk."

"I was beginning to worry that even with all the bed rest, I don't feel much stronger."

"Muscles that are never used begin to atrophy. We won't let that happen. I'll give you some bed exercises."

"Oh, my, I warrant you are most inventive at bed exercise," she teased.

"Ah, if your thoughts are drifting in that direction, it is a most encouraging sign."

Emerald abandoned herself to his ministrations. After he bathed her, his hands slicked on perfumed oil, stroking and massaging every muscle of her body. Her eyes half closed in bliss. "It feels soooo good," she murmured, stretching like a feline being stroked. She watched him from beneath heavy lids, thinking him sinfully attractive.

Her gaze slid down his body to see if he was aroused by what he was doing. The corners of her mouth lifted with secret satisfaction. "Encouraging signs are everywhere," she murmured wickedly.

With a perfectly straight face he replied, "This is most uplifting work."

"Good. They do say anticipation is the best part and denial is good for the soul." Keeping her face as serious as his, she asked, "Is it very hard?"

"Irish, you have no idea."

Emerald reached out and cupped him with her hand.

"You are cockteasing," Sean said lightly.

"Just testing. Muscles that are never used begin to atrophy." She gave him an inviting glance. "How about a little oral stimulation?"

Sean removed his hands from her thigh, pushed her back against the pillows, and looked deeply into her teasing green eyes.

"You are thoroughly enjoying this wicked game at my expense. By *oral stimulation* I suspect you mean kissing, even though you want me to think otherwise."

She gave him a little slap. "Stop reading my mind, you devil."

"When you've done your exercises, I'll give you kisses, and not before."

Their playful banter came to an end as they both concentrated on helping her regain her strength.

Kate came in with a baby on each arm. "Here we are, all bathed and ready for a cuddle."

Sean winked at her. "I'm game if you are, Kate."

"Beware," Emerald said, laughing, "he's feeling very frisky."

"Ha! Must be something in the spring air. Paddy Burke's sap seems to be rising, an' all."

They both stared at her in disbelief, but the minute she departed, they both dissolved into helpless laughter.

"It really is time we went home. Those two have been thrown too much together."

During their last night at the house in Old Park Lane, Sean departed the bed to carefully lay Kathleen in the cradle beside her sleeping twin.

"What are you doing?" Emerald whispered.

"I want to hold you for a while; you can have

her back in an hour." He slipped into the bed and moved over until they were almost touching. Then he propped himself on his elbow and gazed down at her. Earlier he had washed her hair, and the pleasure it had given him lingered on.

"Your hair is prettier than ever. It's silky soft and curlier than it ever was." His fingers lifted a tress, then rubbed it against his cheek.

"It has something to do with having babies."

His hand moved to her breast. His fingertips traced a delicate pattern over their crests, then moved into the deep valley. "You are so luscious and ripe."

The corners of her mouth lifted. "Like forbidden fruit."

"Forbidden indeed. It feels like forever since we made love. I know you are not yet strong enough to indulge me entirely, but perhaps you are ready for a little dalliance?"

"What choice do I have? I'm your captive. I can't exactly run away from you," she teased. "At least not yet."

"Shall we play captor-captive?" he asked huskily, as the head of his shaft brushed against her thigh.

"That might be rewarding, at least until my leg is healed."

He touched his mouth to her lips, needing to taste her, yet enjoying their verbal foreplay. "And then?"

"Then I shall give you a run for your money," she vowed. "I'll run so bloody fast, you won't know what hit you."

"I'll just come panting after you, hot and heavy."

"Hot and heavy?" She slid her hand between his legs, cupping his sac. "That describes you perfectly. Mmm, you are very tempting, but I'll still run."

"Not tonight you won't, little captive, not tonight." His mouth took complete possession of her and showed her exactly what a captor did when he caught his prey. And Emerald, his willing captive, found inventive ways to satisfy all his desires.

For once, Sean fell asleep before she did. Being confined to bed had given her long hours to review the past and contemplate the future. In hindsight she recalled the subtle warnings he had given her. He had taught her to live in the present and never consider the future, because he knew they would be apart. Before he first made love to her he had warned: *I'm black, beyond redemption. Go from me before it's too late for you.* He had also insisted she keep the jewels. *You have no money of your own; the diamonds will give you financial security.*

As Emerald lay quietly in the darkness, contemplating her plans, she let her gaze drift over his dark face. Fair was only fair— she had warned him clearly that she would run from him.

When the *Sulphur* sailed into Greystones's harbor, Sean was amused to see that Shamus was flying the ancient green-and-gold flag of Ireland from the watchtower turrets.

Kate gathered all the household servants together and asked which of them would like to be trained as nursemaids to the twins. When eight eager young women volunteered for the position, Kate selected two who were clean, hardworking, and had come from large families.

Ellen and Jane, both young, eager, and biddable, were put into training immediately, learning how to do the babies' laundry and how to sterilize and fill bottles. Kate told them sternly that when they had mastered these elementary chores, they would graduate to rocking the twins to sleep and even bathing them.

As soon as word reached Maynooth that Emerald and her twins were home, half the FitzGerald clan descended upon Greystones. Maggie, who was already in residence, helping Tara in Mr. Burke's absence, refused to let her daughter, Nan, return to Maynooth in her advanced state of pregnancy. It turned out to be a wise decision. Late in the afternoon Nan went into labor and gave her husband a son. Johnny was beside himself, carrying the child about for all to admire.

With three babies at Greystones there was never a dull moment. Even Shamus gave up his watchtower and moved back into the lovely Georgian mansion, so that he could be part of the family again and share in all the happiness.

The two new fathers sat sharing a quiet

drink after the household had retired. "John, I only just arrived in time. When I got there, my little girl was at death's door and Emerald was gravely ill. Thanks, it took courage to come and bully me into returning for them."

"You would have gone back for her without my urging," Johnny insisted.

"Yes, but it might have taken me a while. If you hadn't spurred me to action, I would never have been in time."

"Emerald looks marvelous, compared to the last time I saw her."

"Yes, she's gaining strength every day. Another week and we'll have her walking again."

"Kathleen is so tiny, do you think she's out of danger?"

"I don't know, Johnny, I hope so. She'll never be robust. We'll just have to coddle her; wrap her in cotton wool and never let our guard down."

"Being a good father is quite a responsibility. I've been thinking…if one of the tenant horse farms belonging to Maynooth becomes available, I'd like to rent it from you and try my hand at breeding horses."

"I had a bigger job in mind. How about taking over the management of Maynooth for me? The stables, paddocks, and pastureland are vast. Some of the FitzGerald lads are good grooms and stable-hands, but none has a head for business. In the old days my grandfather bred the finest racehorses in Kildare. I think you are the man to restore the Maynooth stables to their former glory."

John Montague couldn't believe what Sean was offering him. "Where's the catch?" he asked slowly.

"I owe you, John. You did everything I ever asked of you, and I asked some rotten things. When I financially ruined your father, it left you penniless. When you threw in your lot with me, I vowed you'd never be sorry." Sean handed him an envelope. "This is the deed to Portman Square. It's yours, not mine. You've earned it." Sean's mouth quirked with irony. "Another reward I had in mind was Nan FitzGerald."

"I couldn't help myself," Johnny explained.

"On the contrary, you bloody well helped yourself handsomely!" And the two men laughed.

Before Sean went upstairs, he knew there was something he had to do that could wait no longer. He wrapped himself in his black cloak and slipped along to the chapel. He did not beg forgiveness for anything he had done. He would never have called the tune if he had not been willing to pay the piper. But he did give thanks to God for his children. He promised to guard them with his life and asked humbly, for Emerald's sake, that Kathleen be allowed to live.

35

Every afternoon for a week Sean carried Emerald out onto the stone terrace so she could bask in the spring sunshine. The twins lay in an old-fashioned perambulator just outside the glass French doors, where Kate and the two young nursemaids could hear them if they so much as whimpered.

Nan, already up and about, brought her new son outside to join them. Nan had so much milk, she sometimes fed Emerald's son, as well as her own.

"Nan, I'm so grateful to you."

"Rubbish, my breasts get so full, they ache."

"No, no, I'm talking about Johnny. I've never seen him so happy. He's like a whole new man these days, and it's all due to you."

"He loves all the FitzGeralds and they love him. He actually seems to enjoy being part of the menagerie."

"He always needed a family to love, and now he has one."

"Sean, too, is a changed man. I never dreamed he'd be such a devoted father," Nan said. "The other night he was rocking both of them to sleep; one on each arm."

"He's the kind of man who puts a high value on something, only when he's in danger of losing it," Emerald said lightly.

"He loves you very much, Emerald."

"Yes, I know that." *But sometimes love isn't enough,* thought Emerald.

Just as the afternoon shadows were starting to lengthen, Sean reappeared on the terrace.

"Did you dispatch the message to my mother?"

"I did, my love. I invited her to spend a month, if she can stand to be called 'Grandma.' "

"I've got to be walking properly by the time she gets here."

"Well, this is the day you've been waiting for. Are you sure you feel up to it?" As he lifted her from the chaise, his lips tenderly brushed her brow.

"I've never been more sure."

"I'll miss carrying you about," he murmured.

"Oh, I'll still let you carry me, at least for a little while."

Sean carried her upstairs, knowing she would prefer privacy the first time she attempted to walk. His heart was in his mouth, his apprehension for her dangerously bordering on fear. He had been a stranger to fear for so long, yet these days fear for his wife and children never seemed to leave him.

He set her on the bed, lifted her skirts up to her hips, then removed the heavy bandage from her leg.

"Ooh, that feels sooo good," she breathed.

Sean skimmed his hands up both legs and over her thighs. "Mmm, you are absolutely right," he teased.

Emerald smiled, knowing he was using humor to cover his apprehension. She moved to the edge of the bed and set her feet to the carpet, then she looked down, comparing one leg with the other. It was a shade paler and slightly thinner than her other limb, but she hoped it would return to normal with exercise.

Sean held out his hand, but Emerald shook her head. "I must learn not to lean on you."

If her words hurt him, he did not show it.

Slowly, Emerald stood up so that her legs supported her full weight. She stood still for a full minute, waiting for the pain to start. When it did not, she felt bold enough to take a step. Suddenly, both legs felt very strange, as if they would buckle beneath her. Her knees dipped, she saw Sean brace himself to catch her, but then miraculously she straightened them and took three faltering steps. She grabbed the back of a chair to catch her breath.

"Does it hurt?" he demanded.

She shook her head in wonder.

"Try it again," he encouraged, allowing his hopes to rise.

Emerald turned to face him, then slowly put one foot in front of the other until she reached him.

Allowing his hopes to soar, he picked her up and swung her around. "You did it!" He kissed her soundly.

"Oh, isn't it marvelous? I want to exercise it every day. I want my legs to be stronger than they ever were. Will you take me riding tomorrow?"

"Easy does it, Emerald," he cautioned.

"Oh, I don't want to take it easy. I want to ride and swim and do so many things! How long? How long do you think before it's completely strong?"

The radiance on her face gave him untold pleasure. "With daily exercise and a nightly massage it shouldn't take longer than a month."

"I'll do it in less!" she vowed. "I want you to teach me to dance a jig on a keg of ale."

"That's a bit ambitious, Irish." He laughed.

"No, I want to do everything!" She moved against him temptingly, allowing her voice to become husky. "I want my legs to be very strong so I can do something extra special with them."

He pulled her against him, imagining her long legs wrapped high about his back. "Tell me what you want to do."

"Sean O'Toole, I want to kick your arse all the way to Dublin for the cruel thing you did."

Sean laughed so hard, he rolled onto the bed and took her with him. "Hallelujah! I despaired of your ever being contentious and willful again. I love your passion and your anger. How long do you intend to go on punishing me?"

"For the rest of your life, of course." Though her words were said lightly, he saw the spark of green fire in her eyes and suddenly his apprehension was back. He had become so vulnerable where Emerald was concerned, she had the means to mortally wound him if she really should seek revenge.

471

She reached down to scratch her leg. "Oh, God, suddenly it's so itchy, I could tear it to ribbons."

"I prescribe a bath," he said, kissing her nose.

"A bath; what divine bliss! I haven't enjoyed a bath in almost two months."

"There's something else you haven't enjoyed in almost two months."

Emerald threaded her fingers into his thick dark hair and traced his top lip with the tip of her tongue. "Then why don't I let you start with the bath and we'll see where it leads?"

As he lifted her in his arms he suspected she was holding part of herself back from him. He decided she was giving him a taste of his own medicine and knew he would have to be very persuasive if he wanted everything. And Sean O'Toole did indeed want everything!

At the house in Portman Square, Jack Raymond also was learning to walk again, but he was not quite as lucky as his wife. His leg bone had sustained a far worse break than Emerald's and he had received no tender, loving care.

During the weeks he lay abed, Jack formed a hatred for William Montague that grew daily until it matched what he felt for William's offspring. He cursed the day he had ever been born into the Montague cesspool.

William, however, treated Jack as a friend and confidant, totally unaware of the hatred that festered beneath the surface. When he saw

Jack limping, he brought him his favorite walking stick, the one he used when his gout plagued him.

"Here, lad, use this until your limp goes away."

Jack wanted to break it over the old swine's head. Did he not realize the limp would never go away?

"I'm glad you're back on your feet. Now we can get down to serious business."

The only business I'm interested in is murder: you and your fucking son; my faithless wife and her fucking lover!

"We are reduced to one lousy ship. I've had it on a coal run, earning a few stinking pounds. But I've had a bellyful of humiliation. It's time we struck back!"

"I'm listening," Jack ground out.

"The O'Tooles have everything that once belonged to me. They stole my ships, my daughter, and my beautiful wife. They even turned my own son against me, until now he's one of them!"

So, the yellow coward has run off to Ireland, Jack realized.

"I say we go and take back what's ours!" William shouted.

Are you mad, old man? I don't want anything back, I want everything destroyed! "What's your plan?" Jack asked, wondering if he could turn it to his own advantage.

"Well, we only have one ship, but we have two extra crews sitting idle. They haven't earned a penny since the Admiralty seized our vessels. With that many men, we could mount a raid and take back our ships. We could sail to Anglesey and use the island as our base. Castle Lies is only a few hours run from there. We'll be able to keep a watch on their activities; pick and choose when the cursed O'Tooles are most vulnerable."

"These sailors are cutthroats. We'll have to show them the color of our money."

"You round them up; I'll get the money." William was determined to finance this venture even if he had to strip the rooms bare.

Amber arrived in her own coach. The pair of high-stepping carriage horses were perfectly matched, and her driver's livery elegant enough for a duchess. The coach was piled high with presents for her three grandchildren, for Emerald, and for her son's wife, Nan.

When Johnny walked proudly into the room carrying his son, Amber kissed them both and suddenly began to cry. "Don't cry, Mother, this is a happy occasion."

"It's been so long," she whispered helplessly.

Johnny handed the baby to Nan and took his mother in his arms.

"I know you'll make the best father who ever lived," Amber said, laughing through her tears.

"Not a bit of it," Sean O'Toole said, elbowing Johnny aside to show Amber his own son. "I'm the best father, just ask me."

Amber's tears vanished completely as she

looked at the pair before her. The baby had jet-black hair and big round pewter eyes. "He's the spitting image of you."

"God help the poor little devil," chimed in Shamus from his chair beside the fire. "This calls for a celebration. Paddy! Fetch some of the good stuff from the cellars."

"Yer havin' no drink without food," Tara said firmly. "I'll help Mary Malone rustle up some dacent refreshments."

"I liked ye better when ye were doolally," Shamus declared. The teasing had started and no one was spared.

Sean said, "Ah, at last, here comes the beauty of the family."

Johnny teased, "Emerald thinks you mean her."

Amber winked. "She always was a vain little witch."

"I take after my mother." Emerald laughed.

"My daughter's beauty really puts her mother's in the shade," Sean explained to Amber.

Emerald knelt beside her mother to show her Kathleen. The little female with the rosebud mouth had tiny spirals of curls about her heart-shaped face, and eyes like green emeralds.

"Why, she's the spitting image of you," Amber declared, then laughed when she realized she had repeated herself.

"We've been so worried about her, but I think she's finally started to pick up," Emerald explained.

"Let me have her. I think she will do just fine. You were always undersize; no bigger than a farthing."

"But she made up for it with cheek," Johnny teased.

The celebration lasted until dark. Greystones hadn't rung with so much laughter in years. There was a tussle among Kate, Tara, Maggie, and Amber over who would bathe the babies.

"My God, there's no pecking order around here. I say the grandmother should be in charge," Amber declared.

"Well, now, since I'm the grandmother, I agree with ye," Maggie said with triumph.

"Yer all flown with wine," Tara accused.

"Well, it's your bloody wine," Kate said, laying the blame where she thought it belonged.

"You're not even a FitzGerald," Maggie accused.

"One Kennedy outranks three FitzGeralds any day of the week!" Kate declared, the light of battle in her eyes.

Suddenly, they all dissolved into laughter and trooped upstairs en masse. The young nursemaids, Ellen and Jane, despaired of ever actually getting to hold the babies.

"I'm going to tuck you into your bed," Sean said, scooping Emerald into his arms. "You're still no bigger than a farthing."

"But I make up for it with cheek," she said, pulling his hair.

Sean knew she'd enjoyed herself today, but he also knew she was tired and needed her rest if she was going to keep up with the others. After he had tucked her in, he went downstairs, where he knew Amber would seek him out, once the household had retired.

Sean poured them both a small snifter of French brandy.

"Not another toast?" Amber asked lightly.

"In a way. I salute you, Amber; you sold the business."

She did not ask how he knew. Sean O'Toole had an uncanny knack for knowing most things. "I could hardly be a respectable grandmother if I still owned a brothel, so I did the honorable thing."

"If that's a barb, I'm the first to admit I deserve it."

"I don't know what you mean," Amber said truthfully.

"Didn't Emerald tell you of the dishonorable thing I did?" he asked in disbelief. "I think that's what I love about her the most...her generosity." He walked to the fire, warming the brandy in his hands, then slowly told Amber the whole story from beginning to end. "After all that, she was generous enough to call the twins Joseph and Kathleen."

"But she hasn't forgiven you, has she?"

He shook his head. "No. I don't expect to be forgiven. What I did was unforgivable."

"It wasn't totally unexpected, though. I warned her against you. I told her you would use her for revenge."

"What did she say?"

"She said she understood your need for revenge. She said that you had taught her to live for today and that if it ended tomorrow, she wouldn't regret one fleeting moment of your time together."

"She said those words because she trusted me. I betrayed that trust." He could not hide the pain in his dark eyes. "I suspect Emerald is going to leave me."

"And what will you do?"

"Bring her back, of course. I'll never let her go!"

As if spurred on by a devil that rode him relentlessly, the following day Sean gifted Emerald with her own ship.

"Come and see, I've had the crew of the *Sulphur* painting for days."

The entire household made its way to the jetty to see that the *Swallow* had been fitted out with new sails and renamed *Emerald Isle*. As if throwing down a challenge, Sean told Emerald, "I'm giving you your own crew so you can be the captain of your fate."

"Is this for pleasure sailing, or to start my own merchant business?"

"Emerald, it is for anything you want. It's merely my way of showing you that whatever is mine is yours."

She wondered if he was ready to share his inner self with her. Sean had always kept a part of himself completely private. Now she found herself doing the same. Once she had given him everything—her heart, her love, her trust. Now, she kept her inner self from him. It was as if, deep inside, the core of her heart had frozen and refused to melt.

Emerald smiled brightly. "Tomorrow we shall have a sailing party. Who will come?"

"Not I"—Johnny laughed—"from now on I intend to keep both feet planted on terra firma."

"Then it shall be ladies only," she declared. "We needn't go far. Why don't we sail to Dublin Bay and back?"

Amber, Nan, Tara, Maggie, and Kate agreed immediately. "Now that's settled, what shall we do today?" Amber questioned.

"Johnny and I would like to have the baby baptized while you're here," Nan said shyly. "We've decided to call him Edward, after my grandfather."

"What a lovely idea," Amber declared. "I don't believe being a grandmother precludes being a godmother, do you?"

When the party started its climb back up to the house, Emerald lingered, gazing out across Greystones's bay, where half a dozen ships rode at anchor. Sean closed the gap between them.

"I'm sorry we haven't taken the twins to be baptized. Does it upset you?"

"A little," she admitted. Neither of them wanted the children christened Montague, but since it was impossible to baptize them O'Toole, they did nothing.

"I have an idea. Let's get them baptized

FitzGerald, since it's a family name for both of us. You know what Shamus says: *Always do what's expedient and ye'll never go far wrong.*"

"Father Fitz would refuse." Her face flushed, recalling the things he'd said to her.

Sean's face hardened. "Fitz will do my bidding, Emerald, never doubt it."

Later in the day as the household gathered in the chapel for the ceremony, Emerald realized that Sean must have had a private word with Father Fitz to lay down the law. *His* law. Not by look or word did the priest hesitate to administer the sacrament of baptism for all three babies.

As Johnny and Sean stood proudly holding their sons, Emerald's heart was heavy over the thing she planned to do. It was wrong to deprive a father of his son. She looked down at the tiny girl in her own arms and knew she could never bear to part with her. Shamus's words about expediency went through her head and she realized that was exactly what she had done. She had let Sean O'Toole rescue them and care for them until they were strong. Now she was going to leave him.

Emerald knew she would be eternally grateful to him for what he had done. She also knew she would love him forever. But he had put vengeance before her and his own flesh and blood, and would do so again anytime the opportunity presented itself. As she handed her child to Father Fitz and heard him intone, "I name this child Kathleen FitzGerald," she knew she was doing the right thing.

The following day Emerald and Amber stood at the prow of her ship. Both were so alike, believing this the most exhilarating place to be when sailing. The other ladies preferred a more sheltered spot where the wind could not dishevel their coiffures, but these two loved the feel of the wind whipping their hair about their faces.

As the small ship swept around Dublin Bay, Emerald and Amber found the courage to broach what was foremost in their minds. "Sean told me what he did to you."

Emerald was surprised, then angered. How dare he tell Amber his side first? "Damn him to hellfire!"

"Darling, he offered no defense."

"That's because it's against his nature to be on the defensive. He always takes the offense! Well, he has offended me and I am leaving him."

"When you were in mortal danger, you sent for him and he came."

"No, I did not! I sent Johnny to you. I had no intention of ever returning to Castle Lies after Sean abandoned me in England. We agreed that if Sean ever hurt me, I would come to you. When you leave, I'm coming with you."

"It is an exercise in futility, Emerald. He will come after you."

"Mother, the Earl of Kildare may be all

powerful, but whether I stay or leave is my choice, *my free choice*, not his. It can be no other way."

A cross the bay, while the two women were deeply engrossed in their discussion, stood a shadowy figure, transfixed by the sight of them together. William Montague could hardly believe his eyes, as he stood rooted to the deck of the *Seagull*. There, in the middle of Dublin Bay, was his beautiful wife aboard his own favorite ship, the *Swallow*. He licked lips gone suddenly dry. Soon, he vowed, he would reclaim both, even if he had to destroy Castle Lies and everyone in it.

36

W henever one of the Murphy brothers made home port at Greystones, it was believed the other brother would show up within a day. The FitzGeralds joked that the Murphy brothers had magnets up their arses. And so, when Pat Murphy, who now captained the *Brimstone,* arrived, Sean O'Toole expected that Tim Murphy wouldn't be far behind.

Sure enough, the following day the *Heron,* which had been renamed the *Dolphin,* sailed into home port. Sean and Paddy spent most of the day with the Murphy brothers, inspecting their cargoes, going over the ships' manifests and bills of lading that accompanied the goods they were importing from Spain and Morocco.

When the work was completed, Tim Murphy took Sean aside for a private word. "Bowers sez he spotted a Montague vessel just as we were leavin' Dublin this mornin'. I didn't see it meself, but Bowers swears to it."

A frown settled between Sean's black eyebrows the minute he heard the disturbing news. "Come up to the kitchen, Tim. We'll have a word with Shamus."

Since she was planning to depart the following day, Amber had packed her trunks and Johnny was carrying them downstairs. A grim-faced Sean swept into the house and called Johnny away from his task. When Mr. Burke carried Shamus to the kitchen, at a signal from Sean, Emerald was alerted that something was in the wind.

"God, I hate it when they do this," Emerald bristled.

Amber tried to soothe her ruffled feathers. "They're just talking business. Sean doesn't mean to be secretive."

"You don't know him very well. Whenever there is trouble, they close ranks to keep the females in ignorance."

"Emerald, you're jumping to conclusions."

"Am I? One look at Sean's face told me all I need to know. Calling in Johnny just confirms it. He's back to seeking vengeance! It's like a craving in his blood; he's addicted to it! He lives for it! Within the hour he'll set sail for God knows where and fob me off with a lie."

"I think you have an overactive imagination."

Minutes later Sean O'Toole strolled into the front parlor and said casually, "Emerald, I'm taking the *Sulphur* on a run. Don't wait up for me, love, my business may take a while."

Emerald looked him straight in the eye. "Where are you going?"

"To the customs in Dublin. There's some sort of paperwork I have to fill out for the imports."

"That shouldn't take long," she said stubbornly.

"Well, I have other business," he said vaguely.

"Can't it wait? This is Mother's last day and Johnny and Nan are leaving for Maynooth tomorrow. I would like us to spend the day together."

"Tim Murphy wants me to look at a ship. Johnny's coming too; they won't be leaving for a couple of days." His face had the closed look upon it Emerald had seen so many times before. *If you go out that door, I won't be here when you return.* She made one last appeal. She closed the distance between them and lifted her face in supplication. "Sean, please don't go?"

He slipped his arms about her and dipped his head so that he could look into her eyes. "Sweetheart, you're being fanciful. I'll try to be back in time for dinner tonight, if it will stop you from worrying." He kissed her swiftly and departed without a backward glance.

Johnny came in from the kitchen. "Where's Nan?"

"She's upstairs with the baby. What lie will you use to fob her off?" she demanded.

"Emerald, stay out of men's affairs," Johnny warned.

Emerald's shoulders slumped as her anger left her and was replaced by an infinite sadness. Finally, she looked at her mother. "I'll go and pack; we're leaving today."

Emerald spoke with Ellen and Jane. "I am taking the twins to Wicklow to stay with my mother for a while. I would like to take both of you with me. Will you come?"

When both young nursemaids nodded eagerly, Emerald felt a little guilty that she was deceiving them, but promised herself she would let the girls return if they became unhappy. "Thank you both. I couldn't make this trip without you. Go and pack your things, we are leaving today."

As the pile of luggage by the front entrance started to grow, Kate approached Emerald. "It looks like you are planning to leave."

"Yes, I'm leaving with Mother."

"Yer never taking the babies?" Kate asked, scandalized.

"Ellen and Jane are coming along; we'll manage just fine, Kate. I want to thank you for all you have done. I shall miss you terribly."

Kate sniffed back tears. "How long will you be gone?"

Emerald did not want to hurt her. "I have no firm plans," she said softly.

"Mmph, they look firm enough to me," Kate said, stalking from the room.

"I've upset her," Emerald murmured.

"Darling, Kate isn't the one you have to worry about."

"I've left him a note," Emerald said low.

"Ah, well, that should certainly appease him," Amber said with mock relief.

It took a considerable amount of time to pack everything, and this time Emerald did not hesitate to take her jewels or the lease on the London town house.

When Amber's carriage pulled out of Greystones, the luggage was piled so high, it looked in danger of toppling off. Inside the coach Ellen and Jane each held a drowsing infant. Emerald had left their feeding until the very last moment, hoping they would sleep for most of the journey to Wicklow.

The *Sulphur*, with Rory FitzGerald at the wheel, sailed from Greystones's natural bay. Johnny and Bowers, the ex-Montague captain, stood at the ship's prow scanning both the shoreline and the horizon for the *Seagull*. Sean O'Toole was high in the rigging with his telescope to his eye.

They swept Dublin Bay twice, identifying every ship they passed, but saw no sign of a Montague vessel of any sort. The *Sulphur* then sailed around the Eye of Ireland that sheltered Dublin Bay from the open sea. When they did not sight their prey, they scoured the coastline in both directions, from Bray all the way to Lambay Island.

Satisfied that no Montague ship lurked within thirty miles of Greystones, Sean gave the order to head home. He came down the rigging and had a private word with Johnny. "What do you think?"

"Bowers must have been mistaken," Johnny declared.

Sean slowly shook his head. "I have a gut feeling."

"The last time I saw Father he was pathetic. He was crying like a broken man, and I made sure Jack Raymond couldn't even walk. I don't think we have much to worry about."

"I'm glad you've lost your fear of them, Johnny, but so long as there is breath left in their evil carcasses, they could pose a threat."

"Well, if they were here, they are gone now."

Gone where? Sean asked himself. "Anglesey," he said aloud. "Tomorrow we'll take a run over to Anglesey, just to be certain sure." As the *Sulphur* headed back to Greystones, Sean could not dispel the uneasy feeling that something was wrong.

The premonition did not leave him even as he climbed from the jetty up to the house. Greystones was strangely quiet; not one servant was in evidence. Suddenly a baby's cry broke the eerie silence, but the grim look did not leave O'Toole's face. He knew the baby was neither his son nor his daughter; he could tell their cries from those of a hundred other infants.

Sean burst into the master bedchamber with curses already dropping from his lips. He did not need to throw open the wardrobe doors to know that Emerald had packed everything and gone. He knew exactly what she had done. The minute his back was turned, she had left with Amber. Emerald had done what was expedient!

His eye fell on the envelope that she had left on his pillow. He snatched it up and thrust it inside his leather jack. He'd be damned if he'd read it! He wasn't interested in any of her reasons for doing what she had done. He focused all his energy on one thing only. He would return Emerald and the twins to Greystones this night!

Sean O'Toole stalked a direct path to the stables and saddled Lucifer. He did not stop to consult with anyone; he needed no one else's help or advice to bring his wayward woman to heel. He had no idea how long ago the carriage left Greystones. It made no difference to him; no matter how many miles it had traveled, he would overtake it and return it.

The first ten miles he looked neither right nor left, but straight ahead. Then Sean glanced at the sky, gauging how much light was left before evening turned into night. He realized there was only about an hour left before darkness fell. The city of Dublin lay before him, and its busy streets forced him to slow his reckless pace.

Suddenly, he spotted Amber's carriage plodding along in a line of coaches, wagons, and pony carts that had just reached the center of the ancient capital. He spurred Lucifer onto the bridge that spanned the River Liffey and caught up with the carriage just as it reached the other side.

"Stop this coach!" he ordered.

The driver took one look at the dark and dangerous face of the Earl of Kildare and drew rein immediately.

Emerald, already exasperated with the slow-moving traffic of Dublin, again glanced out the window to see what this new delay was all about. When her eyes fell on the black horse with its black-clad rider, she wanted to scream with frustration. He had caught up with her before she had even left Dublin!

Anger came to her defense. With bright red flags flying in her cheeks, she flew from the carriage to confront him.

Sean's eyes flashed their terrible dark anger. "Get back inside the carriage, madam, I shall deal with you at home."

Emerald tossed her head in defiance, even though she knew she had never seen him as furious as he was at this moment. "I am going to Wicklow. Don't try to persuade me otherwise, you are wasting your time!"

"*Persuade* you?" His deep voice warned her he had no intention of doing anything so civilized. "The only persuading I'll do will be with the flat of my hand," he said quietly.

He had never once been harsh or fierce

with her in all the time she had known him. Never once had he touched her in anger. Perhaps that's why Emerald still chose to defy him. "Must you make a scene in the midst of all this traffic?" she demanded.

"Obviously, I must," he said, dismounting and advancing upon her. He loomed above her, his eyes glittering a dangerous silver.

"I am going to Wicklow!"

"*Greystones,*" he said implacably.

People began to climb from their carriages to watch the row that threatened to explode into violence at any moment. Sean's powerful hands cupped her shoulders; there was no gentleness in the touch.

"Get into the carriage this instant, madam."

"Make me!" she flung.

Without the slightest hesitation he raised one iron-hard thigh, bent her over it, lifted her skirts, and gave her three resounding slaps across her arse. As the crowd applauded, Sean opened the carriage door, lifted her by the waist, and plunked her down on her stinging bottom. He tied Lucifer to the back of the carriage, then strode forward. "Move over," he ordered the driver.

Her dignity in tatters, Emerald ignored the shocked young nursemaids and stared at her mother through tear-filled eyes.

"Darling, I told you this was an exercise in futility."

★   ★   ★

When they arrived back at Greystones the nursemaids carried in the twins, and Emerald followed behind. Kate, Tara, Nan, Johnny, Mr. Burke, and Shamus were all in the front room as if they had been awaiting their return. Amber rolled her eyes at Kate and Tara as if to warn them of the impending storm.

When Emerald heard Sean's unmistakable step behind her, she whirled on him, ready to take up the battle where they had left it. Sean held up an all-powerful hand that warned her she had better remain silent.

"I shall give you one hour to attend to the children."

With her stubborn little chin in the air Emerald swept from the room into the grand entrance hall, placed her hand on the banister, and climbed the stairs, her back as stiff as a ramrod.

Sean followed her to the foot of the stairs. "One hour, on this very spot."

Emerald tossed her head and did not dignify his words with a reply.

She washed the telltale sign of tears from her face, then fed her babies. It was all she had time for in one hour. Emerald made up her mind to ignore his ultimatum. Then she realized that if she did not go downstairs, he would immediately take the offensive to make sure she obeyed him. Waiting for him to seek her out would put her on the defensive, so she changed her mind.

Emerald turned her babies over to their young nursemaids. "I would be most grateful if you would put the children to bed tonight." She brushed her hair until it crackled, then she straightened her back and marched down the staircase to confront the man who was spoiling for a battle royal.

When her foot hit the bottom step, she opened her mouth to fire a broadside. As his hand closed about her forearm, he cut off her verbal attack. "Not one word, madam."

He strode to the front door, taking her with him. An ominous silence descended as he marched her down the driveway in the direction of the gatehouse. He did not loosen his grip from her arm until they had reached the tower steps.

Emerald had nowhere to go but up. Her anger was now tinged with apprehension. Whatever it was he planned to do to her, he wanted no witnesses. When he let go of her, Emerald dug her fists into her hips.

"Do you enjoy playing the bully?" she demanded.

"You are clearly in need of a firm hand. You are out of control."

"I felt your firm hand—in the middle of Dublin—with everyone gaping at me!" she shouted.

"It put a stop to your defiance," he growled.

"Temporarily!" She was angry as fire, her temper flaming and crackling in reckless passion.

"Explain yourself. How dare you try to take my children away?" he thundered.

"I left you a note."

He pulled the envelope from inside his shirt and thrust it beneath her nose.

"You didn't even read it!" she accused.

"And never shall! If you have something to say, be woman enough to say it to my face."

"How *dare* you be angry with me? You are the one who is in the wrong. You deserve everything you get!"

"I am the one who saved your life. I am the one who spoiled you rotten. You repay me by taking away my children and then pretend outrage when that angers me."

Emerald flew at him, pummeling her fists against his chest. Her hair tumbled about her shoulders like a cloud of dark smoke. "You self-righteous swine. My outrage is no pretense; it is very real, as you will learn the minute I leave again."

He grabbed her hands and held them immobile. "You mean as soon as my back is turned?"

"Yes!" she hissed defiantly.

"I shall never allow you to leave!" he shouted.

"How will you stop me?" Her eyes blazed green fire. She was panting from her fury.

"I'll lock you in this tower and throw away the bloody key, if I have to!"

"Why don't you beat me again?" she flared.

"Beat you?" he said incredulously. "You deserve a damn good beating, but I've never laid a hand on you in anger...yet! I've been anticipating your reckless behavior, Emerald; give me credit for a little intelligence. I am aware that you have been keeping a part of yourself from me, and knew it was just a matter of time before you ran off altogether."

"You have always kept your inner self from me, along with your thoughts. Now you know what it feels like."

"When I tried to tell you that I love you, you wouldn't listen," he accused.

Her anger cooled to impatience. "For God's sake, I know you love me; I've always known you love me."

"I gave you jewels, a house, a ship," he said in a quieter tone.

"This isn't about jewels or houses or ships," she cried.

"Then tell me that you don't love me," Sean challenged.

"Of course I love you; I've always loved you beyond reason. This isn't about love!"

"Then what in the name of God is it about?" he demanded.

"It's about trust," she said softly.

Dear God in heaven, what could he say? She had suddenly swept away every defense.

"Sean, you taught me to live for today, but you don't do that; you live for yesterday. You live for vengeance. I trusted you completely and you betrayed me for revenge."

The pain in his eyes told her he could not deny it. "So you want to leave me. Whether you realize it or not, Emerald, you, too, want revenge. You won't be happy until you've taken your pound of flesh. You want to take the children and never see me again."

Emerald stared at him in horror, her eyes flooding with tears. Dear God, that wasn't what she wanted at all! She wanted him to sweep her into his arms and swear his undying love for her. She wanted him to vow that he would do anything to keep her. She wanted a pledge that she and their babies would come first from now on. He lusted for revenge when she wanted him to lust only for her. She wanted to come first, last, and always. She wanted a bond of trust that would never be broken again, no matter what.

As his eyes searched her lovely, heart-shaped face, he knew he had loved her from the beginning. Even while he was denying it and closing his heart to it, love for Emerald had found its way inside, blithely disregarding his protestations. He had never dared to acknowledge love's existence, because he believed he could not keep her.

Sean touched her tear-stained face with poignant tenderness. "My love for you and our children is absolute and unconditional. I will agree to anything you want."

You say it, but do you mean it? She had to be sure. Though she hated what she was doing, she tested him. "What if—what if I let you keep your son?"

She watched the anger return to his dark eyes.

"Emerald, are you mad? Surely you know any son of mine could fend for himself if necessary, it is my little daughter who needs my strength. But I would never separate them in a million years. I want both or none."

Sean had passed the first test with flying colors, but would he pass the rest?

"What if—what if I let you have both?"

His black brows drew together in rage at her suggestion. "Without you? The answer is no! I want all or nothing. I would never consider separating the twins from their mother."

Emerald smiled tremulously. She never wanted to doubt him again. She wanted him to remove the threatening cloud of revenge from her horizon. She wanted someone she could count on.

"Sean, your need for revenge was so great, I became expendable. If people cannot let go of the hatred of their enemies, they risk sowing the seeds of hatred among themselves. I know you lost your brother and your beloved mother, but revenge isn't the answer. To deal with loss you must celebrate life. It isn't enough to survive; you must thrive. To thrive, we must love."

"Damn it, woman, I love you more than life!"

"If that is true, you will trust me enough to share your inner self. And I will trust you to give up your revenge." Emerald held out her hand in supplication.

As Sean looked at her face tender with love, it finally came to him that in the end it wasn't revenge that mattered, it was the depth of his commitment, the sum total of his devotion to her and their children. Slowly, he reached out his hand until the tips of their fingers almost touched. "Come. Trust me."

37

Emerald had heard him say it many times before, but she'd had no idea until this moment how she'd been longing for him to say it again. She placed her hand in his and thrilled as his fingers closed possessively over hers.

He enfolded her in strong arms so that they stood quietly together, her head beneath his chin, her cheek pressed against his chest, listening to his heartbeats. Sean's hand reached up to stroke her hair. "I love you, Emerald."

As he spoke, she could both hear and feel his heart and knew he spoke the truth. She took his hand and placed it over her own heart. "I love you, Sean."

As he held her, he envisioned a circle of love surrounding them, and as he stood within the circle, he felt all his anger, all his grief, all his hatred, slowly drain away. Then like a vessel refilling, he felt a deep and abiding love. But, miraculously, he also felt at peace, and with it came a new sense of self-worth that had nothing to do with title or wealth.

Suddenly, he was happy, joyously happy. He swept her into his arms and carried her to the bed. As he undressed her, he paid homage to her beauty, telling her all that was in his heart. In the bed he lifted her so she lay full upon him, then with his lips touching hers so that he could kiss her a thousand times and more, he told her how happy she made him.

"I am the luckiest man in the universe. You are the most generous woman alive. When you give, you give all. I'm not surprised you had twins. Giving me one child wasn't enough for you; you gave me a son and a daughter at the same time. I want you to teach me your generosity. Let me give you something. Ask for anything you like," he urged.

"Well, there is something," Emerald said softly. "The first time you seduced me with an ulterior motive in mind. This time I'd like you to woo me and win me in the traditional way."

Sean groaned. "You little minx, I'm a heartbeat away from being inside you, where I long to be, and you suddenly want me to initiate a formal courtship."

"Indulge me," she whispered against his lips.

The *Seagull* weighed anchor and glided away from the jetty on Anglesey. It was two hours past midnight and they would arrive at Greystones's harbor a little after four in the morning, just before dawn; an hour when Castle Lies and all its inhabitants would be held fast in the arms of Morpheus.

Of the dozen sailors aboard the *Seagull* only three had any loyalty to the O'Tooles, the others had loyalty to none, not even each other.

William's plan was to recover his own ships, the *Heron* and the *Swallow*, and to confiscate an O'Toole vessel that he could use for bargaining purposes. In the dark recesses of his brain he imagined the O'Tooles would exchange his wife, Amber, in return for their ship.

Jack, on the other hand, wanted to destroy and sink every vessel that lay at anchor in Greystones's harbor. With the *Seagull*'s carriage cannons that shot four-pounders, it would be like shooting fish in a barrel. Most of the crew sided with Jack's plan because it was without risk. They had the element of surprise on their side; they could destroy everything in the bay before the O'Tooles could retaliate.

When William Montague and Jack Raymond issued the crew conflicting orders, dissension broke out.

"Go in closer, why the hell are you hanging back?" William bellowed at the first mate.

"No! Stay back! We can hit every ship afloat from this position," Jack countermanded.

As the gunners ran to man the cannons, Montague roared, "What in Christ's name are you doing? No cannon fire—you'll sink my ships!"

As arguments broke out among the crew, Jack shoved William aside. "Out of the way, you old fool. You've been running things too long; now it's my turn!"

William, purple in the face, lunged at Jack, lusting to get his beefy hands about the young bastard's throat. Using his walking stick as a defensive weapon, Jack struck Montague across his gouty leg. As the old man staggered back in pain, he realized he had lost control of the whole operation.

Seized by fury akin to madness, William made his way to the arms chest and snatched up a brown Bess musket. He loaded it with shot and powder, climbed to the deck, then advanced upon Jack Raymond with the musket aimed straight at his head.

"No fucking by-blow is going to control my ship!" Montague roared. "Relay my orders or draw your last breath."

Jack had no illusions about his father-in-law; William Montague was the most cold-blooded man he had ever known. Treachery was his way of life. Jack gave the order to take the *Seagull* alongside the *Heron*. When they were close enough, Jack relayed William's orders for three crewmen to board her. The first three over the side were the sailors in O'Toole's pay.

As the *Seagull* glided toward Montague's favorite ship, the *Swallow,* which was moored at the jetty, Jack Raymond knew this would be his last chance to escape William's insanity. The minute he relayed Montague's order to board, Jack attempted to join the three crewmen who went over the side.

William squeezed the trigger of the brown Bess musket without hesitation. The lead balls tore into the flesh of Jack Raymond's back, dropping him to the deck, a scream of agony bursting from his throat.

★   ★   ★

Sean O'Toole came awake in a flash, his instincts telling him the sharp crack that had awakened him was a musket shot. For one split second Sean was disoriented, then, realizing he was in the watchtower, he sprang to the high window that overlooked the causeway and the harbor. It was still dark outside; he could see nothing but the riding lights of the ships anchored in Greystones's bay.

As Sean began to throw on his clothes, Emerald sat up in the bed and groped to light a lamp.

"Don't illuminate us, love!"

"What's happening?"

Sean hesitated, fearful of alarming her.

"Tell me! You swore you would include me!"

Quickly, he sat on the edge of the bed and took her hands. "Yesterday, I got news your father's ship was seen in Dublin Harbor. That's where we were. We went looking for it, but found no sign. I think this is a predawn attack."

"Ohmigod, the babies!"

"I don't believe they could get to the house without alerting us. They are probably targeting the ships."

Emerald began to throw on her clothes. "I must go to the children."

"I'll go—you'll be much safer here."

"No, Sean, I have to go to the house, I can't stay here in ignorance."

Sean crushed down the urge to rush down to the jetty. He must not let her think he put his ships before her, because he did not. "Come, then, I'll take you to the house. We'll go together to make sure the twins and the others are safe."

Emerald clung to his hand as they descended the watchtower steps. "It's starting all over again."

The hopelessness in her voice smote him to the heart. As they stepped from the gate-house, the first hint of dawn lightening the sky, he squeezed her hand. "No, Emerald, I swear to you I will try my utmost to prevent more violence."

When they entered the big house, they found everyone rushing about half dressed. Sean and Emerald ran upstairs to see for themselves that their babies were unharmed. Kate and Amber met them on the hall landing.

Kate demanded, "Was that Shamus shooting off one of his guns, frightening the very life out of us?"

"No. Father doesn't have his guns, they're still up in the watchtower."

A grim-faced John emerged from a bed-chamber. "Goddamn it, you were right! There is no such thing as a harmless enemy!"

Sean took hold of Emerald's shoulders. "I want you to promise me you'll keep all the women inside where it's safe." He bent swiftly and pressed a kiss to her lips. "Trust me, Emerald." Then he was gone, taking Johnny with him.

Amber saw her daughter's face blanch with fear. "It's your father, isn't it?"

"And my husband. The *Swallow* was sighted in Dublin yesterday."

"Don't worry, darling, Sean O'Toole will annihilate them!"

"Oh, God, I feel so guilty. I've sent him out there to face his enemies with his hands tied behind his back!"

"Whatever do you mean?"

"I told him I'd leave if he didn't give up his need for revenge and hatred. He promised me he would. He swore it to me! Mother, what if he won't retaliate because of what I demanded? They'll kill him!"

"O'Toole has enough good sense to know the difference between vengeance and self-defense."

When the babies started to wail, Kate picked up Joseph, and Emerald lifted baby Kathleen into her arms. "I'll feed her first," she told Kate.

"I'll give his nibs a bottle to keep him quiet. You take your time," Kate urged, knowing Emerald wouldn't worry as much if she was occupied.

Emerald kissed her baby's brow and sat down in the rocking chair. As her tiny daughter suckled, she knew that without Sean's love and devotion this baby would have died. Tears hung on Emerald's lashes as she smoothed the curly tendrils from the baby's temples. Both this child and she had almost lost their lives. Now that they were starting to thrive, how ironic it would be if Sean should be the one to die. Emerald closed her eyes and began to pray.

Downstairs, someone was cursing and raving at the top of his lungs. "That's Shamus," Amber said, "I'd better go down to him before he has another stroke."

Aboard the *Dolphin,* which had once been the *Heron,* a naked Tim Murphy stood listening to the sailors who had just boarded his ship. "If my sodding night-watch had been doin' his job, youse three would be corpses," he said grimly.

"Montague wants us to retake this ship, but his son-in-law wants to blow every vessel outta the water! The bloody cannons trained on you were almost fired; all of us could have been in purgatory!"

Tim Murphy strode to the quarterdeck bellowing orders. In the faint dawn light he could just make out the *Seagull* gliding toward the *Swallow,* which was moored at Greystones's jetty. Murphy ordered the anchor weighed and ordered the gunners to their stations. "I'll blow the English swine straight to hell," he vowed.

Sean, along with Paddy Burke and Johnny, arrived at Greystones's jetty in time to see and smell the pitch torches being lit. Rory FitzGerald, who captained the *Sulphur,* was ready to take her out into the harbor to challenge the enemy.

"Signal Murphy to hold his fire!" Sean bellowed up to Rory.

Though frustrated, Rory FitzGerald obeyed O'Toole's order.

Paddy Burke watched Sean pull off his boots and realized he was going into the water. "Hold it, Sean. Rory Fitz might obey yer orders, but Murphy has a hell of a temper. Don't be reckless enough to swim out to the *Seagull*. If Montague doesn't shoot you, Murphy could blow you to smithereens. Murphy knows if you strike first, you will strike last; you taught him!"

"Paddy, I promised Emerald I'd put a stop to it, without violence if possible."

"The lass doesn't understand that the only defense against the treacherous is treachery."

"I have to try, Paddy," Sean said, slipping into the cold, black water.

As he swam toward the *Seagull,* the ship began to move away from him, farther out into the harbor. He now realized they had only moved in close to the *Swallow* so that ship could be boarded. Montague's ship was now headed for the *Half Moon,* which had no one aboard. Her captain, David FitzGerald, and crew were all on leave at Maynooth.

Sean cursed silently. If Montague succeeded in putting a crew aboard, they could either destroy her or sail off with her before he could stop them. Every instinct told him he should have boarded the *Sulphur* and destroyed the Montague vessel with the Montagues aboard; yet, deep in his heart, he was glad he had chosen the honorable course.

Sean swam on doggedly. He knew that if he had not had all those years diving and dredging the Thames in winter, he would never have been able to swim this far in the cold sea.

At last his hands came in contact with the *Seagull*'s stern. The back of the ship was one of the few places with decorative touches. Sean took hold of the molding and braced his feet against the hull. Slowly, painfully, he hauled himself a few inches at a time up past the lazaret, the storage space where supplies were kept, then the aft cabin, until his fingers finally touched the deck.

Sean knew he would come aboard directly behind the wheel and whoever was navigating would have his back to him. Morning had now dawned, and though it wasn't yet full light, he would not be under cover of darkness as he climbed over the ship's rail to the deck. He rested a few minutes to catch his breath, then cautiously lifted his head just high enough to look across the deck. He was not prepared for the sight that met his eyes.

William Montague stood facing him with a musket trained upon the man at the wheel. Another man lay facedown on the deck in a pool of blood. He was not yet dead, because O'Toole could hear his labored gurgling and rasping. Sean knew it was impossible to gain the deck without Montague seeing him, and he knew as soon as William saw him, he would shoot.

All Sean could do was rely on the element of surprise. He gathered his muscles and leapt over the rail. As if in slow motion he saw Montague's eyes widen, then saw him take aim. Suddenly, a cannonball exploded across the deck and smashed into the mainmast, which came crashing down, sending a deadly torrent of wooden splinters in every direction. Before the debris had finished falling, another exploded into the ship's bowels, tearing a gaping hole in the *Seagull*'s side.

"My ship! My beautiful ship!" Montague cried. Her crew jumped into the sea immediately, before she went down.

Sean tore the musket from William's hands and watched in horror as he fell to the deck on his knees and groveled for his life. "I'm not going to kill you; I wouldn't dirty my hands," he spat with contempt.

Sean knew the *Seagull* was sinking and he also knew Montague would drown unless he saved him. But there was another man still alive; he doubted he could save both of them. O'Toole went down on one knee and rolled the wounded man over onto his back. He recoiled as he saw the face of Jack Raymond. Sean realized if he left him where he lay, Raymond would go down with the ship and Emerald would be a widow!

When Jack opened his mouth to plead for help, Sean decided that in spite of everything, he would aid him if he could. The *Seagull* was listing badly now. Sean stood up to look for a piece of wood big enough to use as a raft. With an enormous sense of relief he saw his own ship, the *Sulphur*, pulling alongside. Suddenly, FitzGeralds were swarming over the sinking ship. They grabbed William Montague and took him across to the *Sulphur*.

"Rory! Give me a hand," Sean ordered. Sean lifted Jack's shoulders, while Rory took his legs. But as they lifted him, blood bubbled and frothed from Raymond's mouth. His lungs had hemorrhaged.

"Sean, he's dead, let's get the hell off this sinking coffin!"

She will never believe I didn't kill him! Sean thought wildly as he leapt across to his own ship. He saw Johnny standing observing his father, and walked across the deck to them. Montague was blubbering and rambling about his ships, his wife, his treacherous son-in-law.

"See what I mean about him being pathetic?" Johnny asked. "What will you do to him?"

"I won't take matters into my own hands. I'll turn him over to the authorities and hope justice finally prevails. I'm sure he'll deny killing Jack Raymond, but perhaps we can recover the corpse and find witnesses. Let's get those men out of the water and put the whole crew under lock and key until we get the truth."

Shamus O'Toole was enraged, and now he had an audience, he cursed bitterly. "The English son of a whore is destroying our ships out there, while I sit here useless, without bloody legs to stand on! Amber, do you know how long I sat in yon watchtower waiting for Montague to set foot on my land? And the bloody day he arrives, I'm sitting on my arse in Greystones! Amber, you've got to help me get to my tower!"

"Shamus, you can't walk and I can't lift you. All the men have gone down to the harbor; there is no one up here who can carry you."

"Go and fetch Paddy Burke. He'll take me to my tower!"

"Shamus, Mr. Burke went with Sean and Johnny. Believe me, if it were possible, I'd find a way to get you up there. I want the evil swine dead more than you do!"

"Amber, lass," Shamus pleaded, "I own four guns, yet not one of 'um here to my hand. I'll never live down the shame! I swore a sacred oath to shoot him the minute his shadow fell on my bailiwick!"

"Shamus, you won't need a gun. They can't possibly get as far as the house."

"We don't know that! Wily Willie wouldn't attack without a great show of force. I heard two explosions. We don't know how many of ours have been killed! After the ships the next target will be Greystones. Be a good lass and run up and fetch me a gun, Amber."

Though her demeanor was calm enough, inside Amber was racked with apprehension. What if Montague and his men did storm Greystones? She knew she would feel better herself, if she had a gun in her hand. "All right, Shamus, I'll go, but if anyone asks for me, don't tell them I've left the house. Where will I find these guns?"

"I always have 'um loaded and propped against the wall by the big window. Ye can't miss 'um."

Amber slipped out a side door. The air smelled of pitch and gunpowder, but there had been no explosions for quite some time. She could hear men's voices from out on the water, but for the most part things seemed to have quieted down. She fervently hoped all danger was past.

Amber picked up her skirts and ran down the driveway to the gatehouse, then climbed the steps that led up to the tower. She spotted the guns immediately. They were exactly where Shamus had left them, close by the window. She wondered if she should take all four, or just one for Shamus and one for herself. She glanced from the window and froze.

From this high place she had an unimpeded view of the harbor and the causeway that led to Greystones. At least a dozen men were heading for the house, and their leader appeared to be William Montague!

She stared in horror as her stomach knotted with fear and loathing. And then she saw clearly that Montague was not leading the men. He shambled along in front because he had been captured. Her fear suddenly receded, leaving ample room for hatred to take its place.

Amber picked up a gun, rested the sight against the windowpane, held her breath, and took careful aim. When she pulled the trigger, the gun kicked into her shoulder painfully as it fired. *That's another bruise I can chalk up to you, William, but it will be the last.* The glass was gone from the window and she could hear the men shouting as they gathered about the heap lying on the ground.

Sean detached himself from the others and sprinted toward the gatehouse. As he mounted the steps two at a time, he was shouting orders to Shamus to cease shooting. O'Toole's tall dark shadow fell across the doorway, then stopped dead. His pewter eyes took in the elegant woman in the gray silk gown with amber-colored hair. They stared at each other without speaking for long minutes, then the corners of Amber's mouth lifted slightly in satisfaction.

"Always do what's expedient and you'll never go far wrong."

38

When Emerald heard a shot ring out so close to the house, she began to tremble. She handed her daughter to the nursemaid. "I must know what has happened."

Kate crossed herself. "Don't go out there, child. You promised Sean the women would stay inside where it's safe."

"Kate, I cannot remain here one moment longer in complete ignorance. Sean is my whole life; if he is hurt, I must go to him."

Emerald ran downstairs and flung open the front doors of Greystones, then ran across the wide lawns in the direction of the sea. She immediately saw the group of men on the causeway, gathered about someone lying on the ground.

Don't let it be Sean, don't let it be Sean!

When she recognized Johnny, her heart almost stopped. Then, as she reached her brother's side, she saw the man on the ground was her father. He had been shot in the chest and lay dead at their feet.

"Where's Sean?" she whispered through bloodless lips.

Johnny looked at her blankly for a second. "He's in the watchtower."

Emerald picked up her skirts and ran across to the gatehouse. Her mother had been wrong. This was not self-defense, it was revenge! As she reached the foot of the steps, Sean was about to descend. She stared up at him, her emotions in total chaos. Relief that he was unharmed warred with the knowledge that he had just committed a supreme act of violence.

"Why did you have to shoot him down like a mad dog?" she cried.

"Because he *was* a mad dog," Amber said, stepping from the tower room, still holding the gun.

"Mother!" Emerald ran up the steps, concern and compassion sweeping away all other emotions.

Sean took the gun from Amber's hands and Emerald led her back into the tower room.

"Shamus sent me for his gun. He swore a sacred oath to kill him if he ever set foot on this land. I had the gun in my hands when I saw Montague, and I knew I had to do it."

Johnny came through the door, his eyes widening in comprehension as he realized it wasn't Shamus who had done the shooting. He immediately went to his mother and gathered her into his arms. "It's over; he'll never harm any of us again."

Johnny's eyes sought Sean's. "What will happen to her?"

"Nothing. Castle Lies keeps its secrets to itself."

"Thank you," Emerald cried, throwing her arms about Sean and burying her face against his chest. "You're soaking wet!"

"The reckless fool swam out to Father's ship, knowing any second he could be blown to bits!"

"You did that for my sake, to try to prevent more violence." Emerald was openly crying now because Sean had kept his word to her at great risk to his own life.

"When I reached the *Seagull* your father had already shot Jack Raymond. You are a widow, Emerald."

"I—I can't believe it." She looked at her mother and they realized they had become widows on the same day. The relief was overwhelming.

By the time the FitzGeralds recovered Jack Raymond's body from the sea, Paddy Burke had two stout coffins built.

Amber and Johnny decided to take the bodies to England for burial and while they were there, they would put up for sale the Portman Square house they had always hated.

On the morning they sailed, Johnny kissed Nan and his son good-bye, while Amber warned Sean, "Don't you dare have the wedding without me."

Sean laughed. "Emerald wants to be courted, but don't be away too long; I'm not a patient man!"

On a glorious day at the end of May, when every hawthorn tree was crowded with bee-filled blossoms, Greystones was celebrating. Not only was there a wedding today in the lovely chapel, but once that ceremony was solemnized, the twins were going to be baptized with their father's name.

Emerald sat before her mirror in her own bed-chamber, brushing her dark hair into a cloud of smoke, then pinning on the wreath of cream-colored rosebuds. She smiled softly at her reflection as she thought about Sean's courtship.

He had pursued her relentlessly, flattered her outrageously, and wooed her shamelessly.

He continually showered her with attention, paying homage to her beauty, and praising her virtues, so that when he proposed marriage her answer would be yes. At the same time he was merciless in tempting her to allow him intimacies.

He cornered her in every chamber, stealing kisses, teasing, touching, whispering, laughing. He made it almost impossible for her to say no, but somehow she managed to keep him, if not at arm's length, at least the few crucial inches from his goal!

Finally, Father Fitz told them it was scandalous to delay holy matrimony any longer when their union had already produced two children. Emerald relented and told the priest he could post the banns.

Sean groaned, "That means three successive Sundays. I can't hold out any longer; you've tortured me enough!"

She glanced at him from beneath her lashes. "Irish, I haven't even begun."

In the final week of abstinence, her dreams became positively indecent, making her curious about her lover's dreams. She blushed whenever he looked at her and became aroused every time she saw him or heard his deep voice. They spent every day together, then every evening, only parting at their bedchamber doors.

Sean took her riding, sailing, swimming, and to the theater in Dublin. Wherever they were, he could not keep his hands from her and every conversation had a smoldering sense of foreplay. His was no gentle wooing, but a bold and blatant seduction!

In the mirror Emerald saw the door behind her open as Amber joined her. "Darling, everyone has gone to the chapel; it's time."

"Mother, you look lovely in lavender. Are you ready to give me away?"

"Sean O'Toole has had your heart since you were sixteen, I believe."

"He has."

As Emerald walked down the aisle on Amber's arm, the chapel overflowed with FitzGeralds. She felt Irish down to her bones, wearing a cream linen gown embellished with old Irish lace. Her face softened with love as her eyes fell on her babies in the arms of their nursemaids. Then Emerald only had eyes for Sean as he waited by the altar.

Though he had returned to the fun-loving young man he had been when she met him, his youthful appearance was gone forever. The high cheekbones, dark pewter eyes, and the planes of his face gave him a stark look that was pure Celt. When she reached his side he flashed her a smile that was cocksure and arrogant. *My Irish Prince; how I love him.*

The scent of candle wax mingled with incense and the fragrant roses in her hair. Father Fitz's face was beatific as an archangel's as he said the holy words, mixing Latin and Gaelic outrageously.

Kate Kennedy looked up at the tall figure

516

of Mr. Burke looming beside her. "I've often considered a permanent relationship. Have you ever thought about it, Paddy?"

"That I have, Kate, but who would have us?" he asked, winking. Then he became serious. "Do you think you might consider *me*?"

She gave him a saucy look from head to toe, then tossed her head. "I might, if I was courted properly."

Kate wasn't the only female feeling mischievous today. When Father Fitz asked Emerald if she promised to love, honor, and obey Sean, she replied sweetly and clearly, "I do," then, lowering her voice so that only her bridegroom could hear, added, "upon occasion."

Sean bent a severe look upon her, but his eyes told her of his passion and his delight. Her humor matched his own; what more could a man ask? He slipped on her wedding ring with loving hands, then bestowed the most chaste kiss of his life.

"I now pronounce you man and wife, and may God have mercy upon you," Father Fitz added fervently, before launching into the sacrament of baptism.

The bride and groom emerged from the chapel into the brilliant sunshine and led the way back to Greystones, where long tables had been set up outside for the feasting.

"The babies were smiling, did you see, Sean?"

He looked down at her and cupped the curve of her cheek with his long fingers. "They weren't smiling, they were laughing at their father for being so besotted with their mother!"

During the entire day there wasn't a stain in the sky as the celebrants fêted the newlyweds. They feasted, drank, sang, danced, laughed, shouted, and argued the day away, enjoying life as only the Irish could.

When the afternoon shadows lengthened into evening, Sean looked for an opportunity to spirit away his bride, but the merrymakers wouldn't let them leave until Sean promised to dance his famous jig on top of a keg of ale.

Emerald called for two kegs to be set up, side by side. Then she lifted her skirts and matched him step for step. The applause was like thunder. Sean jumped to the ground, held out his arms, and Emerald tumbled into them, gasping and laughing. The applause turned to shouts of encouragement as Sean threw her over his shoulder and began to run. He didn't stop until they were inside Greystones's master bedchamber with the door firmly bolted against all comers.

He lifted her from his shoulder and let her body slide down his. "How is your leg?" he asked with tender concern.

"My leg is absolutely perfect," she murmured, lifting her face for his kiss.

He touched his lips to hers. "I'll be the judge of that," he murmured, sliding up her skirt so that he could slip a seeking hand beneath the creamy folds.

"Oh, ouch, it hurts dreadfully!"

He slid his hand to her bottom cheek and gave it a pinch. "You little tease, that's the wrong leg."

"Me? Tease? Never!" she vowed.

Sean slipped his other hand beneath her skirt. "You've been cockteasing me for the last two months."

She touched her lips to his. "And loving every delicious moment."

"Let's get you out of this wedding gown; I've never seen a countess naked."

"What about that Lady Newcastle?"

"She was a duchess, and she kept on her corsets," he teased.

"You devil, Sean O'Toole!"

He kissed her then, slowly, possessively, deeply, leaving her in no doubt that she was the only woman he wanted, now or ever. "We have memories to make," he murmured as he helped her from the gown.

Emerald was proud of her body. Her breasts were luscious, her belly flat once more, her skin pearlescent in the lamplight. She wanted to flaunt her beauty before him in all its splendor. She moved away from him and slowly walked nude across the bedchamber. His pewter eyes never left her.

Emerald felt her skin tighten; her blood, already hot, suddenly blazed into a firestorm. She came back to him as he removed the last of his clothes, unable to resist his hard nakedness one moment longer.

He lifted her against him, burying his face

in the soft loveliness of her scented skin. As he carried her to their bed, she knew she could never escape the power of this man. She melted against him with desire, knowing their bodies would soon be coupled in love, legs entwined, as he plunged inside her.

He eased her back against the snowy drift of sheets, spread her cloud of smoky dark hair across the pillows, then touched his mouth to every inch of her silken skin. "My heart forever, Beauty," he vowed, then his desire, long simmering, exploded in white-hot demand. He loved her in every way possible for a man to love a woman.

As Emerald lay replete, sprawled against his heart, he whispered, "Did you see the words inside your ring?"

She slipped it off her finger and held it to the lamplight so she could read the two words. *Trust me.*

"I love you, Sean O'Toole," she whispered.

"Love is a journey from the first blush of physical attraction to a marriage of souls."

Her fingertips drifted over his face, throat, chest, then she curled her fingers into his so that their hands and their hearts were joined.

In that moment Sean realized that he had had to let go of the past before he could embrace the future, just as Emerald had told him. How could one small female possess so much wisdom? He simply adored her. From this moment on, he would hold nothing back.

Emerald drew in her breath as she felt him quicken once more against her thigh. With his mouth against her ear, he whispered, "Do you remember when you were sixteen and you slapped me?"

"I do," she murmured languorously.

"I promised you that someday I'd do something to you to earn that slap."

Emerald slid her hand between their bodies. As her fingers closed about him, she gasped at the size of his arousal, but refusing to let him have the last word, she sighed, "I've waited forever; ready when you are, milord!"

AUTHOR'S NOTE

I chose the island of Anglesey, Wales, as the place where my lovers first meet because of its extremely mild oceanic climate. Warm spring sunshine bathes Anglesey so early in the year that flocks of newborn lambs are taken there so they will thrive.

An occasional dolphin has been known to follow the Gulf Stream into the Menai Strait, and caves of glittering anglesite crystal look as if their walls are encrusted with diamonds.

The fact that Anglesey is directly across from Dublin was pure lucky chance for my story. However, the sailing time between these two places would have been longer in the eighteenth century than I have suggested. I took such license for the benefit of telling a love story.